12-29-1   506   ③

"ONE OF THE BEST AD'...

*The call for a Holy War ha...
and a bloodthirsty despot who still firmly hol...
reins of power in an enslaved land is aiming his
devastating chemical weapons arsenal at the heart of
his most hated enemy. Meanwhile, in the threatened
nation, the way is being prepared for the inevitable
response: nuclear retaliation.*

FIREBREAK is a riveting and chillingly possible novel of
courage, strategy, aerial skill and political gamesmanship in
a volatile world on the brink of catastrophe. With a nuclear
clock ticking dangerously close to the zero hour, a U.S.
President, weakened politically and militarily, places the fate
of the world in the hands of an able squadron of F-15 Eagle
Fighter pilots—and, specifically, Matt Pontowski, a cocky
young ace with a blood connection to the White House,
whose explosive passions could prove more liability than
asset. But desperate times call for bold actions—and one
remarkable gamble that will either avert Armageddon…or
hasten its coming.

"On a par with Tom Clancy."
Denver Post

"A Big Book…Herman delves into power politics in
Washington, the Mossad in Israel, the Israeli Air Force and
the United States Air Force…The flying sequences are great."
The New York Times Book Review

"Richard Herman is a 'top gun' of a writer."
Dale Brown

(more praise for the novels of Richard Herman on the following pages)

THE WARBIRDS

"A GRIPPING STORY...
From the first scramble to the last victory roll,
The Warbirds soars into the wild blue yonder."

Pittsburgh Press

"SUPERB...Herman's characters are richly and vividly
drawn...It will keep you reading long into the night
and wishing there were more."

Richmond Times-Dispatch

"A MILITARY THRILLER THAT STANDS OUT
FROM THE PACK...Unusually well written...
truly hair-raising...thoroughly believable."

Kirkus Reviews

"HERMAN WRITES A GOOD ONE...
There's no slowing down, the dialogue never lags or wavers
and the novel's men and women come across
as real people facing true-to-life problems."

Chattanooga Free Press

"ONE OF THE MOST HONEST NOVELS
OF THE AIR FORCE IN A VERY LONG TIME...
A tip of the wings to Richard Herman."

W.E.B. Griffin

FORCE OF EAGLES

"HERMAN EARNS A SNAPPY SALUTE
FOR A RIVETING ADVENTURE NOVEL."
Rocky Mountain News

"A SKILLED STORYTELLER...Richard Herman knows how to
describe the pressure and unpredictability of battle, on the
ground and in the air,..He has a sure command
of what it takes to hold the reader."
Sacramento Bee

"*FORCE OF EAGLES* IS A MUST...The pace is fast
and believable, riveting the reader.
Herman brings realism into his tale."
San Antonio Express-News

"THE GROUND COMBAT AND AERIAL SCENES
ARE AS INTENSE AS A 200-COMBAT MISSION AUTHOR
CAN MAKE THEM."
Oklahoma City Oklahoman

"WILD...[THIS] BOOK FLIES...[His] expertise as a pilot
pays a bonus in excitement. Even better is Herman's
understanding of the military politics that pit uninformed
bureaucrats against uniformed warriors."
St. Louis Post-Dispatch

Avon Books are available at special quantity discounts for bulk purchases for sales promotions, premiums, fund raising or educational use. Special books, or book excerpts, can also be created to fit specific needs.

For details write or telephone the office of the Director of Special Markets, Avon Books, Inc., Dept. FP, 1350 Avenue of the Americas, New York, New York 10019, 1-800-238-0658.

RICHARD HERMAN

FIREBREAK

AVON BOOKS ◆ NEW YORK

AVON BOOKS, INC.
1350 Avenue of the Americas
New York, New York 10019

First Avon Books Printing: September 1992
First Avon Books International Printing: August 1992

AVON TRADEMARK REG. U.S. PAT. OFF. AND IN OTHER COUNTRIES, MARCA
REGISTRADA, HECHO EN U.S.A.

Printed in the U.S.A.

WCD 10

For my mother,
Mildred Leona,
who taught me to meet life
head-on and still dream.

Acknowledgments

This novel is a work of fiction that I tried to root in reality. In it, I branched far beyond my own area of expertise and owe much to those who shared their time, knowledge, and experiences. I am indebted to Mr. Randy Jayne and the crew at McDonnell Aircraft Company who introduced me to the complexities of one cosmic jet—the F-15E. To John York, Gary Jennings, Mike Boss, Bill Kittle, Gary McDonald, and Dave Vitale, many thanks.

On the operational side, I must thank Colonel Dave "Bull" Baker, Lieutenant Colonel Skip Bennett, Major Keith Turnbull, and Captain Steve Farrow, all of the 405th Tactical Training Wing, Luke Air Force Base, Arizona, for showing me how the F-15E really works.

I had no idea what tanks were all about until I met the First Battalion, 149th Armor, of the California National Guard. To Master Sergeant Doug Krelle, Staff Sergeant Lee Harner, and Sergeants First Class David Hooper and Kerry Harris, I can only say thanks and I hope I got it right.

A word about the F-15. The battle damage an F-15 can take and still fly, and which I depicted in Chapter Twenty-seven, is based on a true incident. During my last tour in the Air Force, I logged quite a few hours in the pit of the Eagle, but only in an air-to-air role. I was impressed. But what the E model of the F-15 can do in a ground attack and interdiction role defies the imagination, and that is what I wanted to capture. The jet does have its faults; but then, all aircraft do.

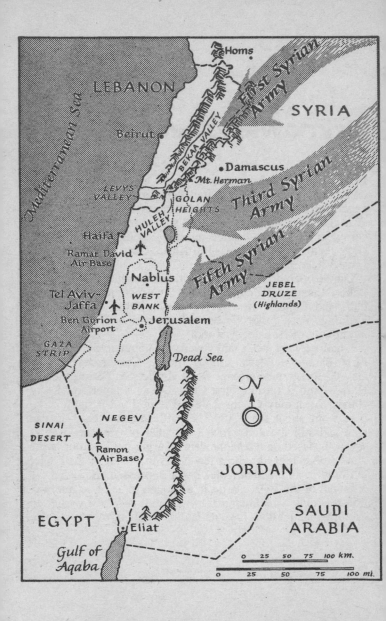

FIREBREAK

PROLOGUE

The five ships rode easy in the gentle swells of the South Atlantic, a welcome break after the pounding they had taken for three days. Avi Tamir stuck his head out of the main control room on the command ship and sampled the weather change for himself. Since he was a rotten sailor, he could still feel an occasional twinge of seasickness in the lower regions of his stomach. Satisfied that the storm had blown through on its race to the east and that his stomach would improve, he stepped onto the main deck and pulled the hood of his duffel coat over his head. Slowly, and then with increasing confidence, the heavyset man lumbered toward the outside ladder leading to the bridge.

Tamir mumbled in Hebrew as he climbed the steps to the bridge, wondering what in the hell he was doing halfway between the southern tip of Africa and Antarctica. He knew exactly why he was there, but he needed to jolt himself back to reality and the task at hand. He paused on the port wing of the bridge, swept the horizon with his binoculars, and pinpointed two of the South African cutters on patrol. There was a third somewhere over the horizon maintaining station with its two sister craft and his ship, all in a giant circle around an old freighter.

Harm Van Dagens was on the bridge and stepped outside, joining Tamir. "They must have taken a beating last night," Van Dagens said, marking the two cutters with a wave of his right hand. "I fell out of my bunk." The big Afrikaner snorted. "Forty foot waves . . . sixty mile an hour winds . . . too much for an old crock like me. Come on inside. It's warmer and there's coffee."

The two men stepped through the hatch onto the bridge. As promised, it was much warmer and a steward handed them each a mug of coffee. Tamir had worked with Van Dagens for three years and had come to like the gruff old man during that time. If this test was successful, Tamir calculated, he just might be home in Israel in time for Yom Kippur and would probably never see Van Dagens again. He would miss the crusty old South African scientist.

"Time to work," Van Dagens said and stepped up to the radar scope in front of the helmsman while Tamir put on a headset and ran a checklist. Van Dagens studied the scope, ensuring the five ships were alone. He became all business. "Status of the freighter?"

"Taking on water and listing seven degrees," the first officer told them. "They had a bad night and lost one of their pumps. They were lucky the old scow didn't sink."

Van Dagens continued to look at the scope. "It would not be good if ground zero sank before the 'package' arrived. Weather?"

"Perfect," Tamir told him, flipping through reports on a clipboard. "Visibility thirty nautical miles plus, winds steady out of the west at sixteen knots, the ceiling is unlimited. The tail end of the storm left a scattered cloud deck at twelve thousand feet in the southeastern quadrant. It will blow out."

"Stations?" Van Dagens asked, looking at Tamir from under his bushy eyebrows.

Tamir spoke into his boom mike and waited for a reply. "All stations are in the green and transmitting. Recorders are on." The seventy-four South African and Israeli scientists and technicians scattered over the command ship and the three smaller cutters that ringed the old freighter in the center of the giant circle continued to run their checklists. They were a well-rehearsed team and, one by one, they checked in as they completed their assigned tasks. Finally, Tamir glanced up at the ship's clock on the bulkhead, noted the time, and spoke into his mike: "We've got a go. Evacuate ground zero, send the launch message, button up. Resume countdown on takeoff."

Six hundred miles to the north at an airfield near Port Elizabeth, South Africa, two unmarked Israeli F-4 Phantoms taxied out of a heavily guarded bunker and lined up on the runway. The two aircraft maintained radio silence as the first ran up its engines. A green light blinked from the tower and it roared down the runway. Twenty seconds later the second

Phantom started its takeoff roll. The first Phantom turned to the south, arcing out to sea and allowing the second F-4 to out it off and join up as they climbed out.

A Bantu construction worker noted the time and that both aircraft were configured with three fuel tanks; one on the centerline and one under each wing. He also photographed the first Phantom, which carried a silver-gray dart on its left inboard wing pylon. He judged it to be a 500-pound bomb, approximately ten feet long. Actually, it weighed 765 pounds, was fourteen inches in diameter, and twelve feet long. He did not risk taking a photo of the other aircraft, which carried eight air-to-air missiles. He later reported the second Phantom as an armed escort.

It had been a standard Washington, D.C., dinner party, and now the last of the guests were standing at the door, waiting for their drivers to bring their cars down the elegant Georgetown street. Senator Matthew Zachary Pontowski stood just inside the door with his wife, bidding the speaker of the House a good night.

"Zack, think about it," the speaker said. "We can make it happen if we start now." He gave the senator and his wife an encouraging smile and walked down the steps, disappearing through the open door of the Lincoln that was waiting for him.

Zack Pontowski stood for a moment and watched the car drive away. The Secret Service agent who had been detailed to guard the entrance that night watched him, thinking how much the sixty-year-old man looked like a senator: exactly six feet tall, lanky with slightly hunched shoulders, a full head of gray hair deliberately left long, and a hawklike nose. The senator sniffed the balmy night air as if he was sensing a change in the weather, nodded at the agent, and closed the door.

"Two-thirty in the morning," the senator's wife said. "Most unusual for the speaker to stay so late but it does make for a successful evening." He followed his wife down the hall while her practiced eye surveyed the final cleanup by the catering crew. She was satisfied with their performance and that the house would be ready for whatever the day would bring. "Emil does these things well," she allowed. "We'll use him again.'' She looked around for a moment before calling, ''Melissa?''

A tall woman in her early thirties came out of the kitchen. She was drying her hands on a towel and a dark wisp of hair had fallen over her left eye. Her simple black cocktail dress revealed her shapely legs and accentuated a trim figure that had never known the stress of childbearing. ''We're almost finished, Mrs. Pontowski. Another five minutes.'' Melissa Courtney-Smith was one of the senator's more efficient and long-suffering aides.

''Thank you, Melissa. You helped make the dinner a huge success and I know you gave up your evening.''

The woman smiled and pushed the errant strand of hair back into place. ''I'm glad it all turned out well. Besides, I enjoy it. I'll make sure you're all locked up when I leave.''

''Did Matt bother you tonight?'' the senator asked. ''I saw him hanging around.''

Melissa stifled a frown. ''No, not really. I found him lurking around the back stairs dress all in black with his cassette recorder. I chased him off to bed.''

The older woman paused on the stairs and sighed. ''What's he up to now? That boy's always into something.''

''Probably James Bonding it,'' the senator explained. ''He's been reading spy novels lately. I'll talk to him in the morning.'' He followed his wife up the stairs.

''Senator,'' Melissa called after them, ''I think he's discovered girls.'' She didn't mention the pat Matt had given her well-shaped behind when he scampered up the stairs or the clip she had given his right ear in return.

''A bit early for a twelve-year-old,'' the senator mumbled. ''Now I *will* talk to him in the morning.''

His wife gave him a rueful grin. ''Just like his father and grandfather.''

''I'm a bit past it, at my age.''

''Miss Courtney-Smith obviously doesn't think so. But for your sake''—she smiled at him—''I hope you are.'' It was the way their lovemaking always started.

''And if I'm not?''

''Then you better bring it to bed or I'll do some nipping and tucking where it counts.''

He put his arm around her waist and gave her a playful squeeze. ''If I remember right, it's more like gnashing and gnawing." They walked down the hall together. "Matt's light is still on," he said. "I'll check on him." He watched his wife go into their bedroom before he nudged his grandson's door open.

"Grandpop?" a voice from the top bunk called.

Pontowski walked over, ruffled the boy's sandy brown hair, climbed into the bottom bunk, and stretched his frame out. "Matt, you been bugging our home with your tape recorder?"

"Ah, I was just messin' around, Grandpop. Tryin' to see what it could pick up."

"You record anything?"

"Naw, too far away. I need a remote mike. But I could hear real good and learned some super stuff. I'd make a good spy."

"You going to be a spy now?" Pontowski asked.

"Naw, I'm going to the Air Force Academy and be a fighter pilot just like my dad was."

The senator caught his breath at Matt's latest announcement and he could hear the same enthusiasm in the boy's voice as in his father's. The old hurt welled up inside of him and he thought about how much he loved Matt.

"Well, you got lots of time to think about that. About this spy business, what did you learn tonight?"

Matt hung his head over the edge of the bunk and looked down at his grandfather. The impish grin was in place and his hair hung down. He was bursting to tell his secret.

"You're going to need braces," Pontowski told him.

"Aah, Grandpop, don't change the subject. I know why they want you to run for governor and not for the Senate next time."

"Matt, we've got to keep that a secret between you and me," Pontowski cautioned him.

"Okay," the boy agreed, pulling back into the bed. Silence. Slowly, the senator rolled off the bunk and walked to the door. He paused, remembering the night in 1957 when Matt's father had told them he wanted to go to the brand-new Air Force Academy and fly jet fighters. With a single-minded purpose that surprised the senator and his wife, the teenager had pursued that goal and graduated with the class of 1964—the class that would lead the air war in Vietnam.

The senator turned off the light when Matt said, " 'Night, Grandpop."

"Sleep tight, Matt."

Then: "Grandpop, are you really going to be President of the United States?"

The waiting, the grinding delays, the years of frustration and failure were almost over. Avi Tamir had left the bridge of the command ship and taken his position in the control room. He kept glancing at the master clock above his head as if it were the force driving him. In a very real sense it was, for Tamir had been racing it since 1967 when he first started on this project; ever since that evening in Tel Aviv.

Like most of his countrymen, on the twenty-fourth of June, 1967, Tamir was still basking in the glow of Israel's victory in the Six-Day War that had been over for two weeks. He found life exceptionally sweet and, with a little luck, he would break free tomorrow and join his wife who was in her eighth month of pregnancy. But there was much to do, so much captured equipment to collect before it was lost or damaged. The Israelis had reaped windfalls of Soviet technology from the war and it was up to Tamir to see that it was examined and exploited.

Tamir was suffering from a twinge of guilt for not participating in the war. He had tried to join his reserve unit during the mobilization, but his reputation as one of Israel's finest scientists had preceded him and orders were waiting that sent him right back to his office. Afraid that he had not done his part, he now drove himself, and his staff, ruthlessly.

He had worked through the Sabbath in his office on that Saturday so he could break free for two days to see his wife. He was a bit annoyed by the phone call late in the evening summoning him to another meeting, but since the call came from a secretary to the minister of defense, he could not ignore it. Five minutes later, a car picked him up and he was surprised to see his former boss, Ahrele Yariv, the head of military intelligence, sitting in the backseat. Yariv motioned for Tamir to join him but didn't say much as they drove through Tel Aviv. Tamir was certain of their destination when the driver turned down the street where Levi Eshkol, the prime minister of Israel, lived.

They found the prime minister in his living room, relaxing

in slippers. Tamir was taken aback by the two other men with Eshkol—Meir Amit, the head of Mossad, and Moshe Dayan, the minister of defense. Even though Israel is a small, egalitarian country given to informal ways, Tamir knew this was an important meeting and that he was in the middle of something big. Eshkol did not come right to the point but instead started talking about bomb-disposal techniques and the men who engaged in that line of work. He pointed out that the situation of Israel was much like that—for their first mistake would be their last one. And sooner or later, Israel would make a mistake. He wanted to talk about insurance for just such a time, he didn't want to be like a bomb-disposal man.

Tamir said nothing as he followed the conversation, his mind racing. He knew what was coming. Finally, Eshkol had leaned forward, his elbows resting on his knees, hands clasped together in front of him, and looked directly at Tamir. "We are now producing weapons-grade plutonium at our Dimona reactor. We want you to build us a nuclear bomb."

"Six minutes," Van Dagens announced to the control room. He was in radio contact with the delivery aircraft and spoke into the microphone attached to his headset. "We have an arm light." The control room was eerily silent and the men could barely hear the ship's engines as they maintained their station exactly twenty nautical miles due north of the old freighter.

Tamir noted the fast-moving blip on the radar scope in front of him and scanned the banks of the monitoring equipment lining the bulkheads of the large room. But his eyes always came back to the master clock above his head. The radar blip was exactly forty miles from its release point. Five minutes to go. In the back of the room, a radar controller was talking to the crew of the F-4, tracking them and ensuring that they were on course and would pickle at the exact spot that would allow the parachute-retarded weapon to descend directly over the freighter. The radar controller confirmed the F-4 was on course and on time.

Tamir took a deep breath. "Send the release code," he said, his voice matter-of-fact. Again, Van Dagens spoke into his microphone. Both F-4 crew members acknowledged the call, agreeing they had a valid release message. In the front cockpit, the pilot rotated a wafer switch to the BOMB AIR position. In the rear cockpit, the weapon systems officer toggled the Nuclear Stores Consent switch to the RELEASE position.

"We have a green release light," Van Dagens said. Now they had to wait. At five seconds to go, the radar tracking equipment on board the ship activated a warning tone that was transmitted on the radio. When the tone stopped, the aircrew in the F-4 would know that the radar showed them at the release point and their system should have dropped the bomb.

The tone stopped.

Tamir watched the blip on the radar scope turn sharply to the right and reverse course. He glanced at one of the screens linked to a TV camera with a telephoto lens that was tracking the descending parachute. Again, he looked at the clock. Then he stood up and stared at the screen that was slaved to the TV camera aboard the old freighter. He could clearly see the parachute.

The screens flared into incandescent brightness as filters automatically snapped into place, protecting the lenses and circuitry. The picture from the freighter went blank—the camera was destroyed. Another TV camera aboard the command ship recorded the explosion as the fireball grew to over a half mile across. At two seconds into the explosion, the top of the fireball began to rise. At three seconds, a neck appeared under the fireball and narrowed into a twisted, left-handed screw—the stem. On top, the fireball mushroomed into a canopy cloud of bright, spectral blue as the air superheated from the fireball condensed in the cooler layers of the upper atmosphere. It was not the gigantic, thick-stemmed mushroom of a thermonuclear bomb but of a less powerful atomic bomb. Still, the pillar of steam would rise more than twelve miles above the earth.

"The shock wave," Van Dagens said, pointing to another screen. The men could see a shimmering wall of air rushing at them. But they were far enough away that the wave was little more than a sharp gust of wind when it passed over the ship.

"My God," Tamir whispered. The Israeli scientist felt what no camera can record—fear, terror, and shock. The old freighter had disappeared and Avi Tamir was awestruck by the forces he had unleashed. "I had no idea. . . ."

The equipment hummed as the web of telemetrically linked ships and sensor buoys that had been positioned in the ever expanding circles around ground zero transmitted data to the commanding ship. For Tamir, the numbers the readouts reported had reality and meaning. "The fireball touched the surface," he said. "We were wrong about the size." Again, he glanced at the fresh numbers pouring in. How grossly had he miscalculated? How much else had he underestimated?

"More fallout then," Van Dagens grunted, all business. "We must take that into account. What force do you calculate for the weapon?"

Tamir looked at the instruments around him. "We'll have to retrieve the data and . . ." He was still shaken by what he had just seen.

Van Dagens walked up behind him and clapped him on the shoulder. "It's okay. The important thing is that we now have a fully operational bomb." It was September 2, 1979.

Shoshana sighed and gazed into the mirror, willing the image in front of her to change. Nothing happened and the round chubby face with the same pair of big brown eyes stared back at her. She shook her head. The twelve-year-old face in the mirror shook and its long black hair flopped back and forth. It was her. In disgust, she fumbled through the wreckage of her aunt's dressing table and found a pair of scissors. Without pausing, she grabbed her hair and started hacking, throwing the long ringlets that had reached to her waist into a pile on the floor.

"Shoshe," her grandmother called, pronouncing her name "Show-she." "Hurry. Your uncle has gone to get the car." Shoshana could hear her grandmother complaining to her aunt while she finished the job. "That child, always daydreaming in front of a mirror."

"It's allowed," her aunt replied, not really arguing. Shoshana liked her aunt and wished she could live with her instead of her grandmother. Everything about her aunt was stylish— her clothes, her figure, this modern apartment in Jerusalem— everything. Unfortunately, her aunt and uncle's apartment was too small for another person and, Shoshana decided to be honest with herself, she did like her grandmother's spacious and airy flat on the hillside in Haifa. She dropped the scissors and walked into the living room.

Both of the women gasped when they saw the girl. Her grandmother kept whispering, "Shoshe, Shoshe," as tears ran down her cheeks.

Her aunt took charge. "Mother, it will be all right. She is twelve years old and it is time her hair was cut. Go tell Doron we'll be fifteen minutes late. Wait with him." With that, she hustled Shoshana back into the bedroom and set her down. "Well, Miss Shoshana Tamir, it's time to see the new you." She deftly cut the girl's hair even shorter, turning it into a stylish bob.

"Aunt Lillian, will I ever be thin and pretty like you?" Shoshana asked. Tears were rolling down her cheeks now as she watched her aunt work, sorry she had been so rash.

"Shush, girl. You've got a lot of growing to do yet. You'll never be thin, but you'll be pretty. Oh, you will be pretty." Fifteen minutes later, Shoshana and her aunt piled into the car, all giggles about the girl's "new look."

Doron, Shoshana's uncle, smiled, reassuring her, and pulled out into traffic. Within minutes, they were past the university where he taught history. The mood in the car turned somber as they neared their destination, Yad Vashem, the museum dedicated to victims of the Holocaust. Doron held Shoshana's hand as they walked from the parking lot and entered the Avenue of the Righteous, the treelined walk leading to the museum. "Those are carob trees," he explained. "Each one has a plaque with the name of a gentile that helped our people during the Holocaust. Many of them were killed by the Nazis."

Shoshana gave her uncle's hand a squeeze. "I know. We studied this in school and I remember from the last time I was here." She was trying to act grown up and responsible now. They joined the line of people filing into the museum, into the first hall where photographs chronicled the twelve horrible years from Hitler's rise to power to the final cataclysmic days of 1945.

"One of the ironies of history," Doron explained to the girl, "is that Franklin Delano Roosevelt was President of the United States when Hitler ruled Germany. One history will remember as a great man and the other as an evil genius. It's as though they were fated to oppose each other. Both came to power in 1933 and both died in 1945.''

But it was the art museum that drew Shoshana and she sought out the sketch of the hollowed-eyed children that had been smuggled out of Theresienstadt, the Czech ghetto the Nazis had created as a showplace concentration camp. For a few minutes, she stood transfixed before she let her uncle lead her away. "Why did they have to die?" she asked him.

"Because many people, good people, did not believe such a thing could happen. No one stopped Hitler when they could. Then it was too late." It was the best answer he could give a twelve-year-old. The reality was so complicated that even he was unsure of the full truth.

They joined another line in the courtyard and entered the Hall of Remembrance, the heavy, brooding crypt of basalt and concrete that was a memorial to the six million victims of the Holocaust. And then they were finished, back in the parking lot.

"Well," her uncle said. "We have plenty of time to get you two to the station to catch the train to Haifa."

Shoshana didn't answer and only crawled into the backseat where she fell into a deep silence. The three adults marked it up to be one of the moods of a girl entering adolescence. They were surprised when she asked, "That's what my father does, isn't it?"

"What's that?" her grandmother replied.

"He makes sure that it won't happen again." There was pride in her voice.

"We don't know exactly what he does," Doron said. "But yes, he makes sure that won't happen again. That's why he's gone so much."

"I know I won't ever be pretty," Shoshana announced. "But—"

"Oh, Shoshe," her grandmother interrupted.

"That's what I'm going to do . . . make sure it won't happen again."

"Damn," the pilot grumbled to himself. "Never seen a reading that high." He checked the gauge again, confirming that the atmospheric sample he was collecting at seventy thousand feet contained a most disturbing amount of radiation. He duly noted the time and position on his knee pad and checked his flight plan. Time to go home. He tweaked the autopilot and banked the U-2 into a graceful turn back to the north, heading for his recovery base in Australia.

The pilot retracted the probes and started a gentle descent, still over two hundred miles out. He scanned the horizon in front of him, looking for a cloud to fly through. He wanted to do a little impromptu decontamination while airborne, but he would still call for a decon procedure after he landed. He groaned. That meant at least another twenty minutes before he could crawl out of the cramped cockpit. Well, he decided, the spooks were right about this one; that bright flash a satellite had recorded the day before was a nuclear test. Who in the hell was testing nukes in the South Atlantic? he wondered. The intelligence briefing he had received prior to take-off hadn't covered that.

"So much of this is little more than inspired guessing," Tamir said, still not satisfied with his latest analysis. He threw the results of the latest computer run onto the neat piles of printouts in front of him and walked over to a porthole. The sea was still calm twenty-four hours after the test but he could see fresh clouds piling up on the western horizon. Another storm was coming through and it was time they returned to port.

"No more than twenty kilotons at the most," Van Dagens said. "The force of the detonation exceeded our expectations by a factor of one point three."

"It was bigger than that, Harm," Tamir said, turning away from the porthole. "At least twenty-two kilotons, maybe twenty-three."

"So we learn," Van Dagens snorted.

"What have we created?" Tamir asked, not really expecting a reply.

"Only what is necessary if we are to keep our peoples safe," Van Dagens told him. He had agonized over the same question himself and reached his own answer.

"I want to believe that you're right and this is a firebreak we need."

"A firebreak?" Van Dagens puzzled. He had never thought of their work in terms of a firebreak before.

Tamir's brown eyes sought out the framed photograph of Shoshana, his twelve-year-old daughter, that stood in the corner of his desk. "An man-made barrier that contains a fire and keeps it from spreading and becoming much bigger, maybe uncontrollable." He paused, thinking. "This is a firebreak the Arabs won't cross."

1

Gad Habish joined the crowd hurrying to work and pushed into the building with them. There was nothing to distinguish Habish from those around him: five feet eight inches tall, thinning brown hair, brown eyes, slightly overweight, a family man concerned about his kids and paying the bills. He was just another faceless bureaucrat entering another government building in the heart of Tel Aviv. Since he was only going to the second floor, he took the stairs, turned right down the corridor, and walked briskly to the end office. Once inside, the secretary sent him through another door with a smile of recognition. But that door did not lead to an office but to a steep stairwell that descended into the basement.

The stairs, the sequence of heavy doors at the bottom, and rigidly controlled access into the basement were the first signs that Gad Habish was not just another paper-pushing bureaucrat. Habish worked for Israel's Central Institute for Intelligence and Special Missions, the organization known to the world simply as Mossad.

One of the secretaries was waiting for him. She nodded to the office in the rear and arched an eyebrow. The Mossad's chief wanted to see him. Habish retrieved a thin file from a safe and ambled into the back office. The skinny, wizened gnome working at the desk did not look up and Habish sat down, waiting for his turn. The casual ways of the office were misleading, for there were strict protocols in dealing with the irascible, stubborn chief. Habish sat quietly until he was recognized.

"Are you making progress on our problem?" the chief demanded. He was staring at an expense account through the thick glasses perched on his prominent, red-veined nose. From the flush of the gnome's face and the reddening of his ears, Habish judged that some agent had spent too much money on an operation. Around Mossad, the chief was nick-named Ganef, the Yiddish word for "thief," for the way he stole from his agents when he disallowed their expenses and made them pay out of their own pockets.

"Some. I think this is the key." Habish handed the man a thin folder from his file. "She's finished her first six months of training and has been given a field-training assignment with a citrus export firm."

"Why is she the key?" the Ganef asked.

Habish handed over another folder. "Because this young Iraqi male, Is'al Nassir Mana, purchases magazines filled with nude photos of her type." The silence on the other side of the desk warned Habish to be quiet as the old man scanned the folder. Habish had never heard of Mana until the previous week when the woman running the Baghdad station for Mossad had traveled to India for a routine debrief. One of the operatives she controlled in Baghdad had stumbled onto Is'al Mana and passed his name to her. She had checked on Mana and discovered that the young man possessed three qualities Mossad might find useful. He was from a wealthy and influential family, had a degree in chemical engineering, and was responsible for developing a new chemical plant outside Kirkuk. A tornado of violence and destruction had swept through Kirkuk in the aftermath of the Kuwait war and now the Iraqi government was hiding the plant's construction amid the rebuilding going on around it. It was all carefully documented in his case folder and included in the new operations file that Habish had opened.

"He could be a target," Habish explained. "He has a fixation on European women with big tits and, ah, rather classical figures."

"So?" The Ganef stared coldly at his most experienced operations man.

"He's going on a working vacation to Marbella on the Costa del Sol in Spain. He's negotiating for petrochemical equipment the Iraqis claim they need for reconstruction. Some of it is very interesting because it could be used to make things other than insecticides. The tab is being picked up by the German chemical company WisserChemFabrik, which makes that type of machinery. Whoever gets the contract will make a very lucrative profit."

The Ganef studied the space above Habish's head. "It's

amazing," he said, "how quickly it's back to business as normal for our Western European allies. They have learned nothing."

Habish agreed with his chief. Europe had easily reverted to its old habits of selling war-making machinery and techniques to Iraq once the threat to the Middle East oil had been removed and Kuwait liberated. "Well," he ventured, his voice tinged with sarcasm, "the Iraqis did promise to never, never do it again." The Ganef was not amused. "But," Habish continued, "this does give us a window for an agent to make contact. We have to move fast."

"Why her?" The chief was now interested.

"Besides her obvious physical qualifications, she speaks English with a slight Canadian accent. Her mother was Canadian. We can build a cover around that. Also, her psychological evaluation indicates she is capable of carrying out her assignment properly." Habish was observing one of the more rigid protocols in the office—the Ganef had to be convinced that the right agents were assigned to a special mission. "True believers" who merely hated Arabs were unacceptable to the old man. He wanted agents who were trained to exploit, betray, seduce, and if need be, kill their target and still harbor a deep-seated aversion to what they were doing. It was his personal formula for what made a successful agent.

"She also happens to be Avi Tamir's daughter," the Ganef said. "It would be difficult if she fell into the wrong hands."

"I don't plan on sending her inside at this time," Habish said. "But if she were detained by, shall we say, the correct people, that might open up some interesting opportunities for new channels."

"Your 'opportunities' are often too rushed, too dangerous."

"They do work if properly developed," Habish replied.

"Pursue it for now," the Ganef told him. "I want to see a proposed budget." Habish gathered up the file, rose, and left the office. He had just been made the case officer for a new operation.

The Director Lights on the bottom of the KC-10 indicated the F-15E was in position to hook up for an in-flight refueling. But the visual cues the pilot used to maintain station told him they had to taxi forward and climb a few feet. Close, but not perfect. The boom operator had the boom in trail and extended ten feet—they were ready for contact.

"Mike, you want this one?" the pilot, First Lieutenant Matt Pontowski, asked.

"Rog, I got it."

Matt could feel his weapon systems office, Captain Mike Haney, take control of the stick. He almost chuckled at his backseater's eagerness to fly the jet. The lieutenant liked flying with the older captain in his pit for Mike was one of the few backseaters that shared his penchant for bending rules. The Air Force was very careful about the men they selected to fly the super Eagle and known screw-offs were not allowed to even stand close. Both men knew that letting the wizzo, the unofficial name for weapon systems officer, fly the bird during an air-to-air refueling did more than just "bend" the regulations.

"Wizzos are worse than closet queens," Matt ragged Haney. "All you want is a chance to come out and tell the world what you really are—something respectable like a pilot." The lieutenant relaxed into his seat; he had turned Haney into a decent pilot, able to fly the jet if anything should happen to him.

"Air off, Matt," Haney shot back. "I applied for pilot training, but when the Air Force found out my mother was married to my father, they made me go to navigator training." They fell silent and Haney nudged the throttles and stick, rooting the fighter in position. The boomer on the tanker tried to fly the boom into the refueling receptacle located behind the fairing that streamlined the inboard leading edge of the left wing into the fuselage but missed. Matt hummed a few bars of "Try a Little Tenderness" over the UHF radio. On the third try, the boomer slid the nozzle down the ramp into the receptacle. It popped back out.

"Recycle your system," a woman's voice commanded over the radio.

"Shit," Matt muttered. "Some broad getting on-the-job training as a boomer." He reached for the fuel control panel, cycled the Fuel switch from open to close to open, and scanned the receptacle door. It was open. He glanced back at the tanker. All the visual clues were perfect and Haney had kept the fighter in a tight formation. "Not our problem," Matt grumbled.

"Cut her some slack," Haney said, "we all got to start some place." This time the boomer made contact and six thousand pounds of fuel were quickly pumped into the Eagle. Haney easily compensated for the change in weight and kept the jet in position. Then they were finished and cleared off.

"Nice goin'," Matt conceded and took control. Haney grunted and went to work, calling up the low-level part of their mission that he had loaded into the navigation computers. The map on the Tactical Situation Display (TSD) in both cockpits cycled and the electronic moving map started to scroll, showing them their position and new route. The command steering bar in the Head Up Display (HUD) in front of Matt slued to the right, showing him the new heading to the first steer point that entered them onto the route that twisted and turned through the desert and mountains of northern Arizona and Nevada.

Matt dropped the fighter down to two hundred feet above the deck and coupled the autopilot to the Terrain-Following Radar while Haney used the mapping function of the Synthetic Aperture Radar to double-check their positions. Satisfied that the laser ring gyro in the inertial navigation system was not drifting outside acceptable limits, he hit the EMIS switch that limited their electronic emissions and went into silent running. The two men were a loose, but well-coordinated team.

They overflew the low-level entry point and the system automatically programmed to the next steer point and, again, the command steering bar slued to a new heading. The autopilot followed and loaded the F-15 with four g's in the turn onto its new course. Matt visually checked their position and calculated they were running three hundred meters abeam of their intended track. He glanced inside the cockpit and checked the TSD. The multicolored moving map on his center screen held them at the same position. The system was accurate.

While they were on the low-level part of their mission rooting around in the rocks and weeds, Matt would constantly double-check the systems in the aircraft, ready to go to a backup mode if one failed. If pressed on the matter, Matt would admit that he did not fully trust the Terrain-Following Radar and was reluctant to use it below two hundred feet.

If they had to, he and Haney would pull out maps they had

prepared and resort to old-fashioned map reading and dead reckoning as the primary means of navigation. But that had never happened on a mission, only in the simulator. When the systems worked as advertised, Matt felt more like a passenger than a pilot when they flew the rigidly constructed mission they had flight-planned on the ground. He was slightly bored and secretly wished that something would go wrong to spice up the flight. He hated routine.

At predetermined points they had picked during day before for the penetration-type mission, Haney would hit the EMIS switch, bring the APG-70 radar to life, and do a few sweeps of the area before returning to silent running. The high-resolution radar would send a wealth of information through the processors and create detailed, picturelike images of the area. Haney would freeze the pictures, making patch maps so he could refine and, if necessary, update their position in the nav computer. At the same time, he was constantly double-checking the systems. As long as the autopilot and Terrain-Following Radar were working, the wizzo was much busier than Matt.

On the third leg, a short eleven-mile dash across an open valley, Haney hit the EMIS switch and swept the area with the radar. "Two hits at one-three-five degrees, fifty-five miles," he said, calling out two unidentified aircraft.

Matt mentally cursed for missing the two airborne targets that were to the southeast of them. He locked the lead return up with the radar and got an altitude readout—three thousand feet. You're getting sloppy, he warned himself, a sure way to get your ass in a very deep crack. He broke the radar lock. The target Matt had locked on to was now displayed on the TSD as a red aircraft symbol. Then the Eagle jerked onto a new heading and flew up a canyon that would lead to the next valley.

"Didn't think we'd have any company out here," Matt mumbled, now fully alert and paying attention. He was thankful that his squadron commander, Lieutenant Colonel Jack Locke, had paired him with the strongest wizzo in the squadron. It never occurred to him that Locke had matched them up for a reason.

The Terrain-Following Radar and autopilot worked perfectly and lifted them over a ridge at the head of the canyon before slamming them back onto the deck, keeping them at their set clearance limit of two hundred feet, and turning them to the south. Now they were on a new heading down a long valley, pointed in the general direction of the two unknown aircraft.

"Going to take another look for those two bogies," Matt said. "I haven't got a visual on 'em yet." Even though they were flying at two hundred feet above the ground, well under the two aircraft, neither of them was interested in reporting a near miss. Again the radar came to life. This time a third target appeared. "Got another bogie out there in front of the other two," Matt said. "It's coming down the valley straight at us."

"Jesus H. Christ," Haney said, "he's below us!" The wizzo had his number three screen programmed to show the pilot's HUD and had seen the altitude readout when Matt locked up the third bogie. It was well below a hundred feet.

"Rog," Matt replied, much calmer than Haney. He disengaged the autopilot and lifted the F-15 up to seven hundred feet. "No tally." He was straining to visually acquire the three aircraft. "I'm doing another sweep. Don't want to be sandwiched."

"This ain't a limited emissions profile anymore," Haney groused. "What the hell," he rationalized, "don't want to run into any lost touristas out here." This time the radar stayed on.

Now Matt had a wealth of information to work with and toyed with the idea of using the Eagle's capability to instantly switch from a low-level, long-range interdiction mission to an air-to-air role. It was what made the F-15E such a potent weapons system. He punched up the air-to-air master mode that readied them for an engagement. He drove the cursors on his air-to-air radar scope over the first target, locked it up, and looked through the target designator box on his HUD. "Tallyho," he told his backseater, now seeing the target closest to them. "Got the slow mover—comin' right at us." Matt kept the ground speed riveted on 480 knots. "Don't let me overfly the next turn point."

"Damn, we ain't out here to engage anybody," Haney cautioned.

"Like the boss man says, 'Treat any unknown target like a potential threat and you won't have a bad day.' " Matt rolled the Eagle up onto its right wing when they passed over the slow-moving aircraft passing underneath them. "That guy is really down in the weeds. Wonder if he even saw us? Did you ID him?"

"Civilian, twin-engine. Looks like a Cessna Four-oh-six. What the hell is he doing out here?"

"Too big for a Four-oh-six," Matt told him. The lieutenant's eyeballs and aircraft recognition were good and he had caught a few small differences when they flashed by. "Tally on the other two. Shit hot! They're F-Fifteens." Now the pilot could see the other two northbound aircraft. He dropped their jet back down to five hundred feet above the ground to pass well underneath. "Why in the hell they screwing around out here?"

Haney had already asked himself the same question and had been analyzing the information on the scopes in front of him. "They were set up in a racetrack pattern, each one on opposite legs. I'd bet they were in a radar search pattern. Now they're flyin' slow in a scissors pattern behind the slow mover—like they found who they were looking for. Oh shit, they're . . ."

"Got to honor the threat," Matt growled as the two other F-15s passed over, twenty-five hundred feet above them.

"No way!" Haney shouted over the intercom. Matt was no longer just bending the rules—he was shattering one of the more important ones. An air-to-air engagement with the $29-million F-15E had to be carefully planned and prebriefed so no one would do anything stupid.

The engagement developed quickly. Matt pulled his Eagle into the vertical and stroked the afterburners, pulling six g's as he hooked up behind the two F-15's, maneuvering into their six o'clock position. Their headsets filled with the characteristic growl of a Sidewinder missile as the infrared seeker head on the training missile they were carrying started to track. The lock-shoot lights on top of the canopy bow were flashing. Matt mashed the communications switch on the left throttle with his thumb, transmitting over the UHF radio, "Fox Two on the northbound F-Fifteen on the right." It was a standard radio call telling the F-15 that Matt had simulated a Sidewinder missile shot—at him.

"Come off right!" Haney roared as the two fighters split apart, taking evasive action, honoring the threat Matt had presented to them. The jet Matt had called a simulated infrared missile shot on had pulled into the vertical, pirouetted to get a visual on his attacker, then pulled his nose back after the slow mover on the deck. His wingman broke down and to the left, reversing course to the south. When he had a visual on Matt, he pulled off to the west and rejoined on his flight lead, ignoring Matt who had peeled off to the east as Haney had called, disengaging. Then Matt and Haney regained their original track, flying their low-level mission, back in a bombing role. The impromptu diversion had taken less than a minute and Matt was feeling much better.

The wizzo had twisted around in his seat, following the two F-15s. "They're still tracking that Cessna," he told Matt. "Jesus H. Christ, didn't you see the Sidewinders they were carryin'?" Haney had caught a glimpse of the two air-to-air missiles hung under each wing of the other F-15s. Silence from the front cockpit. "Them puppies were white." He didn't need to remind the lieutenant that training ordnance was painted blue and that live missiles were painted white. "We bounced two alert birds. They were probably on a scramble going after a smuggler, a druggie."

"I thought they were out just messing around," Matt said. "You think they got our tail number?"

"That's why they turned on us but it doesn't matter," Haney shot back. "Just how many other E models you think are roarin' around out here?" The Air Force only had two hundred copies of the supersophisticated, dual-role version of the Eagle. "Damn, we really stepped in it this time."

A laugh came from the front cockpit. "Probably. Not to worry."

Avi Tamir let himself into the family's apartment and dropped his briefcase by the door. Sometimes he wondered why he still carried the old battered bag around for there was no way he could bring any work home from his laboratory. Nowadays the bag rarely held anything other than lunch and a newspaper. "Shoshe?" he called. No answer. "Not home," he muttered and looked around for the note that he knew would be somewhere. She never left it in the same place. He found it in the kitchen, next to the refrigerator. He chuckled to himself. Shoshana always left the note in a place where he would naturally see it as he went about the routine of coming home after being gone for the week. She was never wrong.

The note was a simple "Beach with Yoel. Back at five," scrawled in her bold, open handwriting. "No doubt in her new swimsuit," he grumbled. "Yoel will like that." He poured himself a glass of club soda, threw in a slice of lemon and two ice cubes, and lumbered out onto the balcony. He leaned on the railing and took in the view of Haifa that spread out below him. He loved their big apartment in the "Hadar," the old residential area halfway up the hill above the old bustling city on the broad bay.

He thought about his daughter for a moment and tried to visualize her in the latest swimsuit she had brought home last weekend. At first, he had been pleased when she announced it was a one-piece—that is until he saw it. Why couldn't she be more modest and less clothes-conscious. You're getting old, he told himself, when you go tut-tut instead of wowie. He rubbed his bald head, amused with his predicament at fifty-two years of age. So you lost your hair and want to be a grandfather, he thought. Well, maybe the bathing suit will move Yoel off dead center. He caught himself tugging at his beard and made himself stop. "Now that's acting too old!" He laughed aloud.

"Faah-ther," Shoshana called from inside, "I'm back." Tamir turned and waited for her on the balcony, a smile playing at the corners of his mouth. His daughter joined him, still wearing the old shirt she used as a beach wrap. She gave him a kiss on the cheek and settled onto a chaise longue, stretching out her long legs. They talked about the usual things a father and daughter share—his work in Tel Aviv that took him away during the week; her new job with a citrus fruit export firm—all safe and pleasant subjects.

"Did you wear your new swimsuit today?" he finally asked. He mentally berated himself for acting like the father of a teenage girl. It was no longer any of his business what she wore. But he couldn't help it. He managed a smile, still trying to keep the conversation light and easy.

"Of course," she laughed, knowing the way he was. She stood up and shed her wrap. "It's not that bad," she teased him. His smile faded when he saw it. "I had hoped you'd like it," she said, modeling the latest in swim wear, a one-piece suit that was severely cut to her waist, showing all of her back and too much of her breasts for his taste. It was cut high on her hips, forming a deep V that accentuated her legs.

A sadness crept into his brown eyes, for he was looking at a twenty-six-year-old woman, vain about her looks and not the young, overweight, ungainly daughter he wanted to preserve forever. Like him, she stood exactly five feet ten inches tall and was big-framed. But unlike him, there was not an ounce of fat on her. Still, she was exquisitely feminine and graceful; her well-shaped legs were not those of a model, but developed and reflected her Dutch heritage; her full hips tapered to a narrow waist and she was big-busted. She turned around for him, smiling over her shoulder. "Yoel likes it," she said.

"I don't doubt it." He glanced at her flawless back, perfect bottom, and sighed. "When are you going to get married?" It was the old argument, but they had both learned to control it and keep it in bounds. Tamir knew that Yoel spent every night in Shoshe's bed while he was away during the week in Tel Aviv. At least, he consoled himself, they maintain appearances when I'm home.

She spun around and put the old shirt back on and gave him another smile, completely disarming him. "Soon enough Father, soon enough." It was her face and hair that did it, so much like her mother's—high cheekbones, doe-shaped brown eyes, a full mouth and perfect teeth, and thick, shoulder-length black hair that she pulled back off her face—a beautiful face. Tamir had long ago seen how Shoshana could stop traffic even though she was not fashionably thin. She was pretty in a way the fashion magazines would never accept. Shoshana was a big woman and could have modeled for Rubens. Looking at her, he smiled, for she was also a thoroughly modern sabra: born in Israel, intelligent, independent, and tough. And he loved his daughter. If Miriam, her mother, were still alive, life would be perfect.

"Where's Yoel?" he asked, wanting to stop thinking about his wife.

She sat down and started to brush out her hair. "Home. Big family dinner tonight. We're invited."

"Must we?" Tamir would have preferred spending a quiet dinner alone with his only child. He watched her work the brush through her hair, again seeing her mother, and he remembered how Miriam's hair, her long and glowing black hair, had first caught his attention when he was a young man working in a kibbutz.

"Faah-ther!" She pursed her lips and blew a strand of hair away. "You're the one that keeps talking about marriage. That does involve other families, you know."

"What time?" He knew when he was defeated.

The young man who had covered the chief of staff's office during the night had sorted the mail, message traffic, briefs, memos, and whatever else had come into the White House for the President's attention into three piles. Since it was Saturday and the three stacks were relatively small, Melissa Courtney-Smith was able to quickly review the priority he had given each item. "Good work, Tim," she said, dismissing him. The woman watched him retreat out the door, picked up the most important stack, and carried it into the inner office.

She followed a well-established routine and aligned the pile of documents and folders on the chief of staff's large mahogany desk, making sure the left edge of each was lined up with the left margin of the document below it, creating an orderly, staggered pattern. Melissa Courtney-Smith gave the desk one last check before she left. Her boss, Thomas Fraser, was a perfectionist. Her practiced eye swept Fraser's office—everything was in the proper order and the coffee was made.

It was by chance that she glanced at Fraser's collection of small pewter soldiers displayed in a cabinet and was shocked that they were not lined up properly. She rushed from the office, rummaged through her desk until she found a ruler, and ran back into the office. A quick look at the clock told her it was 7:59 A.M.—she had less than a minute. Quickly, she measured the distance between the figurines, spacing them evenly along the shelf. The woman made a mental note to speak to the cleaning supervisor. Someone had fouled up when they cleaned the office during the night and it wasn't a mistake that Fraser would tolerate. The staff did have to take care of each other.

Melissa was finished and barely back in her office when the door swung open. Thomas Patrick Fraser, the chief of staff, rushed through. He grunted at her in passing. She went to the silver coffee urn, drew exactly two thirds of a cup, and stirred in one level teaspoon of sugar before she followed him into his office. Saturday or not, the daily routine had started. She sighed, wishing she had time to go for a long bike ride. But it was the price she paid for being the chief of staff's first assistant, a job that was as close as Fraser would let her get to Matthew Zachary Pontowski, the President of the United States.

Fraser was hunched over his desk, scanning the PDB, the President's Daily Brief, the top document on the stack. "Goddamn it all to hell," he snapped at Melissa. "Tell the analysts who put this piece of shit together to get it right or I'll squash some fucking heads." He threw the thin, twelve-page document at her. "No way I'm going to send intelligence based on pure speculation to Zack." He was one of the few people who still presumed to use the President's nickname and it grated on Melissa's sensibilities.

She thumbed through the professionally printed brief that contained the best and most exclusive intelligence available to the United States. It was considered so sensitive that it was sealed and only twelve people saw the final product. And Melissa and Fraser were two of them. She found fresh red marks slashed across the section on the Middle East. Her eyes scanned the offending paragraphs until she found the name of the analyst at the bottom—William Gibbons Carroll. "Carroll's the best analyst we've got on the Mideast," she told Fraser. "He's got an impressive track record and the President knows it." She paused, letting him digest this information.

"The President is *very* knowledgeable about the Middle East and you know how he works." Melissa waited impassively, carefully hiding her dislike for the fifty-eight-year-old man. During the campaign, she'd come to understand Fraser's importance to Pontowski, what with his political connections, ability to tap unlimited sources of campaign contributions, and links to the corporate world. She just wished that the President had given him an ambassadorship to an out-of-the-way place in Africa or the South Pacific, rather than made him his chief of staff, but rumor had it that Fraser demanded this position because the Senate would have rejected his appointment as an ambassador. His reputation as a wheeler-dealer matched his slicked-down, grossly overweight appearance that even expensively tailored suits could not hide.

Fraser glared at her, wanting to fire her on the spot. He

didn't like the way she argued. "What's your point?" he demanded.

"If he reads something in the PDB that doesn't track with what he's reading and hearing from other sources, he just might call Carroll in."

Fraser gestured for the brief and reread what the analyst had said about the current developments in the Middle East. "This is pure crap about the Arab masses seeing Saddam What's his name as a martyr and forcing their governments to unite to finish his work or that Iraq is secretly rebuilding its military strength. Hell, Iraq is still digging out of the rubble—economically and politically. And I certainly don't see any signs of growing tension between Syria and Israel. Zack might get the idea that Israel is not able to handle the situation, that things are getting out of control."

"Things change," Melissa said. "It's the job of intelligence to stay on top."

"Get a fresh copy," he demanded. "I'll send it up this time." He picked up the next folder in the stack and started to read. Then he looked up over his reading glasses at Melissa's retreating back. He made two mental notes: Fire the bitch as soon as possible and get with the director of central intelligence to make sure the party line was reaching the President.

Be careful, he warned himself. The broad has some sort of pull with Pontowski. He had tried repeatedly to find out what it was and at first had simply chalked it up to sex. Beautiful women did come with the job and, even at forty-five, Melissa Courtney-Smith was gorgeous. But in all the years he had known Zack Pontowski, Fraser had never detected the slightest extramarital indiscretion. The President liked women, associated easily with them, and when he found a competent one, relied on her skills and listened to her opinions. But he never took advantage of them. "Humph," Fraser grunted aloud. It didn't make sense that a man of the President's generation would treat women like he did men. Fraser knew exactly how he would have used the woman if she wanted to flit around the edges of real power. It was beyond his way of thinking that Pontowski valued Melissa simply because of her years of loyal and competent service on his staff.

"For Christ's sake!" he yelled when he read the third

folder. "Melissa, get the wing commander at Luke Air Force Base on the phone. Matt's back at it again."

"Shoshe, why didn't you tell me sooner?" Tamir was watching his daughter go about the business of packing. His fatherly instincts warned him that she was lying and they were going to argue.

"You would've only been upset sooner," she replied, padding barefoot through the apartment, wearing an old, half-opened, baggy shirt over her briefs and nothing else.

"Must you dress like that?" he asked. He couldn't help it. He wanted his daughter to be a good Jewish girl. Why are we stuck at the same place we were when she was seventeen? he asked himself.

"Faah-ther," she said in exasperation, sounding like a teenager, "there's only you and me here and I am packing."

"You should have told me sooner," he repeated. "Going on a vacation on such short notice—I don't like it."

"I told you, it's a working holiday. The company is sending me on business. Otherwise, I could never afford it. Not on my salary."

"Why would a fruit export company be doing business in southern Spain? It doesn't sound right."

She took a deep breath, tried not to let her annoyance break through, and kept her voice calm and reasonable. "I'm checking on new packing and processing equipment. My company has got to stay current if we're going to compete in world markets."

"Shoshe . . ." He wanted to confront her with his suspicions, to lay it out, to satisfy his inquisitive nature. Because of his work in the government, he had heard that Shoshana's company also fronted for Mossad and he strongly suspected that his only child, his big, beautiful, beloved, raven-haired daughter, worked for Israel's Central Institute for Intelligence and Special Missions.

"Shoshe . . ."

"You sound like a stuck record." She smiled at him. "I've got everything I need packed so I can change now. I'll cook dinner. Just the two of us. You can drop me at the airport in the morning on your way to work."

Five minutes later, she was dressed and in the kitchen, singing and cooking. Well, Tamir thought, now she knows how to handle me and avoid an argument. He settled into his favorite chair and looked out the open French doors that led to the balcony. The lights of Haifa were coming on below them. It was the end of the Sabbath. She would not have told me anyway, he consoled himself. They never admit it when they work for Mossad. It is one of their strictest rules—the first one they learn.

"I'll drive, Father," Shoshana said, loading her two suit-cases into the trunk of the family's Volvo. Tamir grunted and settled into the passenger's seat. He was worse then a bear coming out of hibernation early in the morning. She pointed the car down the hill and joined the light Sunday morning traffic.

He was surprised by how smooth a driver she had become. "You are driving much better," he mumbled, still not fully human. "I remember the last time I rode with you . . ." He dropped the subject and relaxed into the seat for the seventy-mile drive to Ben Gurion Airport. "The car's running better," he said, yawning.

"I had it tuned up," Shoshana replied, glancing at him. "Asleep. Good." She floored the accelerator and wove smoothly through the light traffic. The car was silent as they left Haifa and headed south.

The sharp staccatolike bark of an AK-47 shattered Tamir's sleep. Panic jerked him fully awake when he saw two cars in front of them crash together, blocking the road. Instead of hitting the brakes, Shoshana went straight at them, aiming for a gap between a stopped bus on their left in the oncoming lane and a light-green car parked against the curb on the right. He gasped for air when she wrenched the steering wheel to the left, into the bus. At the same time she stomped on the gas, breaking the rear end loose and skidding them side-ways through the gap. He was vaguely aware that gunfire was coming from the parked car.

"Whaa . . ." was all he could manage and a bolt of fear shot through his stomach as the wrecked cars in front of them burst into flame and two bullets slammed into the back of the Volvo. He was certain they were going to roll or skid into the flames.

"Get down!" Shoshana shouted. She eased off the accel-erator, still keeping them in the skid as they slowed. Now they were through the gap. Again she mashed the gas pedal and they rocketed around the rear of the bus in a tight U-turn. They accelerated back down the road toward Haifa, keeping the bus between them and the parked car. He could see flames coming from the bus as more gunfire poured into it from the other side. Metal and glass fragments rained down on them. Then they were clear, barreling to safety. "Terrorists," Shoshana said, her voice amazingly calm. "They were in the parked car." She pulled into a service station and jumped out of the Volvo, demanding to use the telephone.

Tamir stumbled out of the car still breathing hard and in a state of shock. Now the sporadic terrorist attacks that plagued Israel had touched him and threatened his family. Before, it had only been an incident recorded on TV. Now it was reality. He examined the two holes in the rear of the car, one in the deck and the other in the rear window. Both had passed completely through the car at an angle and exited out the right side. Slowly it came to him that Shoshana had saved his life by throwing the car into a skid and taking the gunfire in the rear; otherwise, the slugs would have plowed through his door.

He followed her inside and found her on the phone reporting the incident. He listened, aware of a growing thirst. He wanted a cool drink—badly. "Yes," she said, confirming the location of the attack. "There were three of them, two men and a woman. General impressions only, young, Arab-looking, not European or Oriental. I saw two AK-Forty-sevens. Nothing else. They were in a light-green Renault." Tamir listened as she reeled off the seven digits of the license plate. "There was a different number plate on the front. I didn't get it all; the first two numbers were four-seven." She identified herself and then hung up. "We can go now," she announced. "They'll call you if they need more information."

Back in the car, he stared at her. "How did you see all that? And the driving. Like a professional race car driver."

"Oh, Faah-ther." The seventeen-year-old was back. "I don't know. I just did. It was luck. The only time I've ever been in a skid was when I took driving lessons. You remember, I told you about that."

He wanted to believe her; he wanted to be certain that his daughter was telling the truth and just going on a nice business trip to Spain. But his years of training and work as a scientist had conditioned him to evaluate the evidence he saw, to divorce emotion and wishing and hoping from cold logic. Then he looked at her and she tossed her head, throwing her hair to one side, just like Miriam. She saw him watching her and gave him that beautiful smile. The father in him won and he believed her.

Shoshana concentrated on driving, picking her way through back roads until she rejoined the main highway, well clear of the terrorist ambush, heading toward the airport. Please stop asking so many questions, she thought, keeping her silence. I'm doing the same thing you are. She thought about her first field assignment—to make contact with one Is'al Nassir Mana. She had only been told why Mossad was interested in him, not how to exploit their relationship. But she knew what she had to do.

"This is good stuff," Mike Haney said. "My wife is guzzling her third one. What's it called?" Matt Pontowski's backseater helped himself to another dose of the punch Matt had brewed for the party.

"Tell her to go easy," Matt warned. "It's called a French Seventy-five. It's sneaky and can really do a number on you. According to my, ah, sources"—Matt almost said "grandaddy" but he didn't want Haney to think he was name-dropping—"it first saw the light of day in World War One and was named after a famous French artillery piece. Believe me, it can be lethal." The lieutenant smiled as he recalled how his grandfather could go on endlessly, spouting trivia from what he called the Great War. The elder Pontowski's interest in World War One made sense, considering the President of the United States was born on November 11, 1918, the day the war ended.

Matt checked the bar again, satisfied with the way the squadron party was going. It was the first time he had used the big recreation room at the condominium where he lived in Phoenix, Arizona, and it was a perfect party place, the way it opened out to the pool and spa. There was a sauna in a back room and he liked the large freestanding fireplace that formed a pillar in the center of the room.

The squadron commander, Lieutenant Colonel Jack Locke,

and his wife were leaving and came over to Matt. "Nice party," Locke said.

Gillian Locke extended her right hand for Matt to shake. "I really enjoyed it and don't want to leave. Baby-sitters, you know." Her British accent charmed him and she gave him a beautiful smile.

Locke turned and looked around the room, wanting to stay. But he could see the younger troops wanted to get rowdy and were only held in check by his presence. It was one of the reasons squadron commanders left early. He remembered when he was a bachelor lieutenant. Now he had to play the squadron commander. "Take good care of the drunks." He smiled, his way of saying not to let anyone drive under the influence.

"Roger, sir," Matt said, all business. "We got designated drivers and I'm keeping them stone-cold sober. Poor bastards." The Lockes said a few more good-byes and disappeared out the door. Matt breathed a sigh of relief.

"Oh, oh," Haney said. "Looks like one of the ladies is getting ready to do it." A small crowd was gathering around a corner of the freestanding fireplace in the center of the room. A girl wearing a tight skirt was looking up at the beam ceiling twelve feet above her head. The bricks did not form a smooth edge, but stuck out. The way they overlapped and alternated made a ladder effect that the girl was going to test. She hiked her skirt above her thighs and scampered up the corner of the fireplace like a human fly.

"Woo-ie!" she called at the top, tapping a beam in the ceiling. She started to work her way down.

"Hope someone catches her if she falls," a soft voice said behind Matt. He turned to see the condominium's owner standing in the doorway.

"No way I'm going to stand under her," Haney said. "My wife would skin me alive—claim I'm turning into a dirty old man and looking up women's skirts."

"I think," Matt said, "there's plenty of volunteers to catch her, Mrs. Mado." He handed her a cup of his punch.

Barbara Mado returned his smile and sipped the punch. "French Seventy-fives. Wicked."

Matt caught the gleam in her eye. "Why don't you stay and get acquainted, Mrs. Mado." Matt had heard the rumors about her and knew a party animal when he saw one.

"Please, it's Barbara. And I will if you don't mind. Sounds like fun." She smiled and joined the crowd.

"Is she really a general's wife?" Haney asked.

"Yeah," Matt said. "A three-star. Lieutenant General Simon Mado. A real asshole. He traded his first wife in for her a couple of years ago. Figured it would help his career."

"I can see why. Great body. She could pose for *Playboy*. How old you think she is?"

Matt shrugged an answer. "I'd guess late thirties. Rumor around the condo has it she was a Las Vegas showgirl in a prior life before she started buying real estate. Apparently she made a bundle before marrying Mado. She still shows up now and then; takes good care of the place."

Haney moved behind the bar and helped Matt while the party got noisy and rowdy. From time to time, Matt noticed Barbara Mado and started to worry about her repeated trips to the punch bowl. Most of the married couples had left and someone had turned the music up when he heard a squeal from the pool. Two lieutenants were launching Barbara into the air. He heard a splash and shrugged. Three more splashes followed in short order.

The girl who had climbed the fireplace came up to the bar, gathering a few well-deserved comments. She was only wearing a wet teddy that left nothing to the imagination. She threw her soaked dress at Matt. "Please do something with that," she laughed.

Another chorus of shouts marked Barbara's entrance from the pool. She was fully clothed and dripping wet. "Unzip me, please," she said, turning her back to Haney.

He did as he was told. "Man, I got to leave," he said. "Too wild for an old married man like me." He went in search of his wife.

"Chicken," Barbara called at his departing back and stepped out of her dress. She kicked it into a pile against the bar and mentally compared herself to the young, half-dressed girl. Matt sucked his breath in. Barbara Mado was spectacular in her wet black lace bra and sheer matching bikini panties. She might as well have been naked.

He leaned across the bar and did his best W. C. Fields routine. "Well, well, my dear, anyone who drinks French Seventy-fives and runs around dishabille can't be all bad."

"You like," she laughed and moved off to the punch bowl. He could hear a promise in her voice.

"Never made it with a general's wife," he muttered, thinking about his prospects when the party was over.

A few minutes later, Haney came back, leading his wife. "I found her in the dressing room." The young woman had obviously been sick. "Too much of a good thing." Shouts from the fireplace caught their attention. "Oh, oh," Haney said. "Time to split. Like now." Barbara was climbing the chimney. Halfway up she stopped and kicked off her shoes before climbing again. At the top she patted the beam. Then she reached behind and unsnapped her bra, dropping in onto the faces below her. The shouting grew louder and more encouraging.

Matt turned to Haney looking for help, but he was gone. Standing in the doorway were two policemen, staring at the ceiling. Matt followed their gaze. Barbara was still up at the top of the fireplace, kicking off her panties.

"We got a noise complaint," one of the cops said, not moving his eyes from the beam. "Your party?"

Tamir found a place near the back wall with the others who had been called in to watch the exercise. "The prime minister has heard about your little bit of excitement yesterday," the man standing next to him said.

"News does travel fast," Tamir allowed. His eyes moved over the room, searching. Finally, he found the short, bald-headed, newly elected prime minister, Yair Ben David. "Has he ever been down here before?" Tamir asked. They were crowded into the command room of a concrete bunker buried two hundred feet in a hill outside Tel Aviv. The warren of tunnels, blast doors, and rooms that made up Israel's wartime headquarters was the most restricted and well-guarded complex in Israel—even more than the underground nuclear facility at Dimona where Tamir spent much of his time.

His neighbor shook his head. "Few have. I think our new prime minister Ben David is going to have his eyes opened this morning."

"Ben David knows we have the bomb," Tamir said.

"But not how many or the way we control it," the man replied. Tamir could hear cynicism in his voice, an indication of what he thought of politicians.

For the next three hours, Tamir stood silently, making notes as a possible wartime scenario was spun out for Ben David. Finally, they reached the stage where the Syrian forces opposing them in the north resorted to the use of chemical weapons. The Israeli civil defense sectors continued to report in, detailing civilian casualties to both blistering and nerve agents. One computer display showed how the stockpiles of gas masks, protective equipment, antidotes, and medical supplies necessary to counter gas attacks were scheduled to be distributed. Another computer with a war-gaming program listed breakdowns in the distribution net due to the confusion and destruction of war. Reported civilian casualties started to skyrocket.

Ben David stood up and turned to the generals surrounding him. "Stop this nonsense. You have taken this scenario too far. The Iraqis never used chemical warheads and I seriously doubt the Arabs will *ever* use chemical weapons against us. They understand how we would respond." He was a tough old man who had lived his life on the edge of conflict and had definite ideas about his enemies and how best to deal with them.

The minister of defense, Benjamin Yuriden, stood up beside him and placed a hand on his prime minister's shoulder. "Yair," he counseled, "a war does not stop. We will not be prepared if we refuse to consider worst-case scenarios. That's why we're here." He gestured at the order of battle board that listed the enemy units facing them. "We know the Syrians, Iraqis, Libyans, all have chemical weapons and are trained in their use. It is logical that when they are losing, like in today's scenario, they will use them against us."

"Are you saying," Ben David shot at Yuriden, "that we are victims of our own success? We cannot win a decisive military victory because the Arabs will retaliate with chemical weapons on our people?"

"It is a situation we must consider," Yuriden answered.

"Then my answer is simple." Ben David's blocklike hands cut through the air, his combative instincts in full play. "They use chemical weapons and we escalate. We'll continue with the exercise. Stand down from combat the aircraft we need to upload all our nuclear weapons." The prime minister's jaw was rock hard and his lips were compressed into a tight line.

The minister of defense took the decision calmly. This was

an exercise. "Are you sure you want to upload all our aircraft-delivered weapons at this point. We are winning the ground war."

"I said all."

"Standing down that many aircraft will seriously hurt our conventional offensive operations."

Ben David glared at the general. "How many aircraft does that require?"

"Eighty-seven."

Ben David's knees gave out and he sat down. "We have that many atomic bombs?"

"That's only aircraft-delivered weapons," Yuriden told him. "We also have thirty-five tactical nuclear weapons that can be fired from one-hundred-fifty-five-millimeter howitzers and fifteen warheads for our Jericho Two missiles."

Then a strange calm came over the prime minister. He wanted details. "Which are the smallest?"

"The artillery-delivered weapons—two kilotons."

"The largest?" Ben David was fascinated. Like all Israeli politicians, he knew that his country was a nuclear power, but until now, he had no idea of what that meant in the harsh reality of making war.

"The aircraft-delivered weapons—thirty kilotons."

"We may not be able to win," Ben David said, "but then neither can they. I want to see how this scenario plays out. Order one of our largest bombs dropped on Damascus. Have our ambassador at the UN relay the warning that we will use more unless the gas attacks stop immediately. We will not be driven into the sea." Then another thought occurred to him. "What casualties can the Syrians expect?"

"Approximately a thousand times the number of ours from gas attacks," Tamir said quietly from the rear of the room. The stunning announcement drove a wedge of silence across the room as his estimate was repeated to those who had not heard.

The prime minister spun in his chair and glared at Tamir. "Too high."

"No, probably too low."

Ben David knew Tamir. "How can you be so sure?"

"I tested the weapons." It was a simple statement of fact, the expert telling what he knew.

"Then we will use a smaller weapon to demonstrate our

resolve," Ben David announced. "The Arabs understand power that comes from a sword."

"The destruction on a city will still be terrible," Tamir said. "I don't think Israel can live with the political consequences."

"You're now an expert on political consequences?"

Tamir lowered his head and spoke quietly. "Syrian civil defense is a shambles. They do not have the rescue or medical facilities to handle the casualties even a small weapon will cause. They will throw open their country to every reporter imaginable and let them record the destruction for the world to see. The facts will condemn us." Tamir raised his head and his voice. "It is a major escalation, a holocaust of our making. The Soviets and the rest of the Arab nations that have stayed out of the war will enter against us. The war will become an uncontrollable fire that will consume us."

"You assume too much, Tamir," the prime minister said.

"I tested the weapons," was his only reply.

Ben David turned his back on Tamir. "What is our smallest weapon?"

"Two kilotons," came the reply.

"We will drop one such weapon on Damascus."

Tamir left the room, sick to his stomach. In the corridor, he leaned against the wall, taking deep breaths. This is only an exercise, he told himself. "I never thought . . ." he whispered to himself, barely audible, "never believed"—his despair was growing and twisting inside of him—"that it could go this far."

2

The strident tones of the Klaxon had jolted Matt and Haney into action. It was a "Smoke" and he and Haney ran for the cockpit.

"I'm up." Haney's voice came over the intercom, cool and

collected, the moment Matt slipped into the seat and jerked his helmet into place. They were patched together by communication cords that ran from the ceiling of the bunker to their helmets. The same com cord connected them to the command post whose call sign was Dogpatch. After an engine start, they would go on internal power, unplug the cords, and establish radio contact with Dogpatch.

Matt glanced at the set of command lights mounted in the ceiling above the open blast doors. All three were red. If the bottom light had been green, he would have started engines and held in the bunker. If the middle and bottom light were green, he would have taxied for the runway and held to await a takeoff order. If all three were green, he would have launched for a holding orbit to await a coded strike message that would send him and Haney into a nuclear war. Matt thumbed his transmit button. "Dogpatch, Romeo Zero-Four. Standing by for words." His voice was amazingly calm.

"Roger, Romeo Zero-Four," Dogpatch answered, "continue to hold." They could hear chatter in the background as other alert birds checked in on status.

The wing had deployed to its Colocated Operating Base at RAF Stonewood in the United Kingdom as part of a Reforger exercise the United States mounted every September. Near the end of the active phase of Reforger, the political situation in the USSR had turned into a shambles as contending factions struggled to gain control of the decaying empire. Finally, the hard-line military clique had gained control and started to make ominous moves in the forward area and reoccupied Poland. NATO had responded by increasing its state of readiness, which in turn had triggered a harsher response by the Russians. Then Matt had found himself and his backseater, Mike Haney, sitting Victor Alert at Stonewood, ready to man a nuclear-loaded F-15E that was parked in a hardened bunker. Frantic political maneuvering had reduced tensions and the day had started out as just another routine tour of alert duty.

The bottom command light flicked to green, the order for an engine start, and Matt pulled the T handle of the Jet Fuel Starter at his right knee. Before the small starter engine could spin up, the middle command light changed to green. Now they were cleared to taxi. Matt could see the image of the Security Police truck that was parked in front of the bunker as a block to an unauthorized taxi move out of the way. "Looks like a go," he mumbled under his breath, waiting for the engines to spin up and the inertial nav system to align.

The top command light changed to green, ordering a launch, as the command post controller transmitted a coded strike message. "All Victor aircraft, this is Dogpatch with a Zulu Yankee message . . ." Both Matt and Haney copied the coded message down.

"I copy a valid strike message," Haney said, much faster than Matt in decoding the transmission.

"Roger," Matt answered, not bothering to finish his own decode. Trusting Haney, he gunned the throttles and taxied for the runway.

Forty-five minutes later, they had reached their departure point over Denmark and were dropping down through a thick ceiling to start their low-level ingress into hostile territory. At five hundred feet, they broke out of the overcast and could see approximately five miles in front of them. "Better and better," Matt said. He flipped open the small map booklet that traced their route and used it to double-check their position, which was also on the Tactical Situation Display. "I hold us on course, on time," Matt said.

Haney confirmed Matt's call with a hasty "Roger." He was sweating and breathing hard. A bright light flashed off to their left, momentarily causing their gold-tinted visors to go opaque, saving their eyesight from the searing light of a nuclear explosion. Then their visors cleared and they could see again.

"Damn," Matt yelled. He had been hand-flying the jet, not relying on the autopilot, and had inadvertently ballooned to seven hundred feet when his visor blanked out his vision. He slammed the F-15 back onto the deck. Two surface-to-air missiles flashed by over the canopy and exploded behind them.

"Oh shit!" Haney yelled from the pit. "Master Caution light." They had taken battle damage.

"Fire warning light on number two," Matt told him.

Haney started to read the emergency checklist for Engine Fire or Overheat. "IP in two minutes," he warned Matt. Now they were running the emergency checklist, shutting down their right engine and double-checking all switches, making sure the nuclear weapon they were carrying was armed and would release. "Break right!" Haney yelled. "Bandit four o'clock. On us."

Instinctively, Matt reefed the fighter to the right, trusting Haney's call. He called up the air-to-air mode on his HUD and selected an AIM-9L Sidewinder missile. The plan form of a MiG-29, the Soviet equivalent of the F-16, flashed in front of him, turning away from the fight. Matt turned hard after the MiG, the G meter reading five g's. A reassuring growl came through his headset—the seeker head on the Sidewinder was tracking. He hit the pickle button, sending the missile on its way, and wrenched his jet back to the deck, dropping below two hundred feet.

"Hard left!" Haney yelled. "Bandit . . ." Before Matt could react, the cockpit shook violently and a loud explosion deafened them. Smoke filled the cockpit. From memory, Haney yelled out the Smoke and Fumes checklist. Matt reached and pulled the emergency vent handle and the cockpit cleared.

"What the . . ." Matt gasped, surprised by the toxicity of the fumes. He hadn't expected that. He scanned the sky for the bandit. No joy. It had been a hit-and-run attack. They had most likely been hit by a Soviet Aphid, a decent air-to-air missile.

"Keep coming left," Haney ordered. "IP on the nose."

Matt could see the railroad bridge that was their Initial Point. They were seven miles out from their target, a Soviet Army headquarters. Another flash from a nuclear explosion sent their visors opaque and again Matt inadvertently ballooned the jet. But this time, there was no reaction from the defenders. The detonation had been too close. The F-15 rocked from the shock wave, the needles on the G meters bouncing, registering a 3.

"Son of a bitch!" Matt yelled. "The CAS is tits up." The Control Augmentation System that electrically adjusted inputs into the aircraft's control surfaces had malfunctioned owing to battle damage from the last hit they had taken. Now the pilot had his hands full just flying the aircraft.

"My screens are out," Haney shouted. The four video screens in front of the wizzo had gone blank. He jerked his map booklet out of the map case and flipped open to the target run page. "It's gonna have to be visual with an emergency release." The backseater could not believe how tired and thirsty he felt. Still, he kept talking, telling Matt to come right or left, when to roll out, as they bore down on their target. Streams of tracers filled the windscreen as Matt jinked back and forth. The defenders were fighting for their lives. Then Haney shouted, "Pull!"

Matt honked back on the stick and hit the emergency release button on his weapons control panel. They felt a slight shudder as the bomb separated cleanly, arcing high into the air—a standard toss delivery for an airburst. Matt slammed the F-15 into a descending left-turn escape maneuver. He pushed the throttle of his one remaining engine into full afterburner in a desperate attempt to gain separation distance.

Again, their visors went opaque as their bomb exploded behind them. The F-15 started to buck uncontrollably, sending signals that it wasn't going to fly much longer. But they had done their job and gotten their weapon onto target. "Matt," Haney said, his voice again calm and resigned. "We're gonna have to eject."

"Hold on," Matt said. "Preejection checklist."

"Whaa . . ." Haney said. He had never heard of that emergency procedure.

"Preejection checklist," Matt answered. "Remove helmet. Spread legs. Bend over. Kiss your ass good-bye."

The simulator at Luke Air Force Base gave two hard jerks as the instruments indicated they had impacted the ground. The TV screens surrounding the mock-up of the cockpit went blank and the lights in the big room came up. The pilot from Standardization and Evaluation stuck his head out from behind the control console. "Very funny, Lieutenant, very funny." There was no humor in his voice. "It was a decent check ride until the last wise-ass remark."

"Miss Temple." Gad Habish's voice cut through the clamor surrounding the baggage turntable at the Málaga airport. "Here please." Shoshana turned to see a paunchy, balding, middle-aged man holding her two suitcases. It was her case officer. So far so good. "LaziDaze Travel arranged for your transportation," Habish added, confirming he was her contact. Shoshana followed him out to a waiting car, leaving the rest of the passengers who had flown in from Montreal, Canada, on the KLM flight with her still searching for their bags. "How was the flight?" Habish asked as he wheeled the car into traffic and headed south for the town of Marbella on the Costa del Sol.

"Long and tiring," she said. "But no problems." Habish only nodded his head. He didn't ask any more questions for she had told him all he needed to know—Shoshana had made the roundabout journey through Paris and Montreal without incident. As planned, she had made contact with a Mossad operative in Montreal and exchanged her Israeli passport for a Canadian one along with a batch of credit cards, health insurance card, a social security card, a California driver's license and a U.S. Resident Alien card. All said she was a Canadian citizen named Rose Temple living and working in California.

"Why Rose Temple?" Shoshana asked, not liking her cover name.

Habish hid a grimace. She was obviously new at this with much to learn. "Easy to remember. Shoshana means 'rose' and Temple is very similar to your last name." He didn't remind her how an agent, even a very experienced one, could forget a cover name at an inopportune moment.

They drove in silence to the Atalaya Park Hotel. Habish deposited her at the entrance with a few instructions. "Take a few days to learn the town. The hotel has visiting privileges at the Marbella Beach Club so sunbathe and swim there. That's the only reason we've booked you in here. Remember, you're on an expense account. Use your credit cards when you can—keep a receipt for everything else. You'll have to justify every penny. You're not on a vacation. I'll contact you in a few days."

Shoshana's spirits lifted and her fatigue yielded a notch when the bellboy escorted her through the large hotel to her room on the fourth floor. The small room had a balcony with a stunning view of the hotel's gardens and the Mediterranean. She unpacked before changing into the swimsuit that had so upset her father. She thought about wearing the old shirt she used as a beach wrap and then about the casually undressed guests she had seen in the lobby. "Time for some sun," she told herself. Then she tossed the shirt on the bed and left the room.

Every eye followed her progress through the lobby as she asked for directions to the Marbella Beach Club. So far, not bad, she decided.

* * *

"The boss man is gonna have a piece of us," Haney warned his pilot. The two were in the squadron's lounge at Luke Air Force Base, waiting for the squadron commander, Lieutenant Colonel Jack Locke, to call them into his office. "Stand Eval takes those check rides in the simulator very seriously."

"What the hell," Matt muttered. "We got the bomb on target. I thought that was the bottom line."

"The mission of Standardization and Evaluation is to conduct evaluation flights to insure all crews are proficient in flying and adhering to standard procedures," Haney parroted. "That's why we have to fly a nuke mission in the simulator before Stand Eval certifies us as fully mission-ready."

"Big ef-ing deal," Matt groused. "Just what chance is there that we would ever drop a nuke for real?" The squadron commander's door opened and the Exec came out. He motioned for Matt and Haney to enter and closed the door after them.

Locke leaned back in his chair and kept the two young officers standing at attention while he studied the Standardization and Evaluation report on their check ride in the simulator. "Interesting," he began. "You worked your way through exceptionally heavy defenses and still got your weapon on target, on time." Locke raised his head and fixed Matt with a hard look. He does look like his grandfather, he allowed, sizing up the lieutenant—tall, sinewy, slightly hawk-nosed, fair complexion, sandy brown hair and possessed of the brightest blue eyes. "But you made some mistakes . . ."

"Yes, sir," Matt interrupted. "We took a SAM hit when I ballooned the jet after a nuke blast. But that was a goat rope—a bad call by Stand Eval. No way a missile could track us in that environment."

"Perhaps . . ." Locke wanted to say more, to get involved in a detailed discussion of weapons and tactics. But this wasn't the place or time for that. The squadron commander kept comparing himself to the lieutenant, remembering when he had been young, full of piss and vinegar, and confident—exactly like Pontowski. But was the lieutenant a good stick with the potential to make him worth saving?

Matt sensed the hesitancy, mistaking it for weakness, and decided to press his advantage. "Sir, we did what we set out to do. We smoked the bad guys, made 'em glow in the dark. And that's what it's all about.''

"It would've been nice if you had brought the jet back," Locke said.

Before Matt could say more, Haney interrupted. "Matt, shut up."

But Matt wouldn't let it go. "Damn it, Colonel. We should have passed that check ride. Those Stand Eval pukes haven't got a clue—"

Locke cut him off with a cutting chop of his right hand. "Wrongo. *You* haven't got a clue. You assumed you flunked. Stand Eval passed you with a 'marginal.' They did comment on your attitude and that's what's got me worried. That's why you're in here." He paused for effect, to let the news sink in. "Haney, you got high marks for your rapid decode of the message." Locke threw the two message forms they had used in the simulator in front of them. "And for the IP-to-target run. The Stand Eval 'puke' claimed it was the best he's ever seen. You''—he pointed a pencil at Matt—"didn't even bother to finish decoding the message. That was dumb because two-man control and verification of release messages is critical to the way we operate. Luckily, your wizzo was right. Haney, disappear while your nose gunner gets his attitude adjusted." The young captain saluted and beat a hasty retreat out of the office.

"Let's get something straight, Pontowski," Locke said, leaning back in his chair. "You passed that check ride because of your wizzo and the fact we need to get all our crews nuclear-mission qualified."

"I'm not asking for any gifts, sir."

"You're getting a small one because the squadron is moving to England and picking up a NATO commitment. We need every body we can get. The bottom line is that you're mission-qualified—barely. Normally, I don't accept a 'marginal' and put a crew back into training until they are 'satisfactory.' "

Matt was stunned by the news. "I didn't know we were moving . . ."

"That's close-hold information, Lieutenant. I'm telling you because it will be officially announced tomorrow. Keep it under your hat until then. There's another thing . . ."

Matt braced himself.

"You give a new meaning to the term 'double bang,' " Lock began, not enjoying what he had to do. Damn, Locke raged to himself, I remember when I was on the receiving end of a chewing-out like this one. But the young man standing in front of him was different. He had weight behind him. Hell! How much more backing could a fighter jock have than the President of the United States? Locke thought. The wing commander had forcibly reminded him of that two hours ago when he dumped the problem of Matthew Zachary Pontowski III and his wild ways into Locke's lap. The wing commander's words had been a simple "Work it out, Locke. Keep the kid under control and don't get me involved."

"Just how much farther do you think you can push the system?" Locke asked, switching his approach.

"Beg pardon, sir?"

"Let me put it another way, Pontowski. If any other swingin' dick in my squadron had jumped two alert birds scrambled on a drug smuggler or had a general's wife running around stark starin' naked at a party, he'd be long gone. Your political connections are saving your ass . . ." Suddenly, Locke was tired of the young man in front of him. Tired of his casual attitude and self-confidence that were ample evidence he wasn't worried about anything his squadron commander could do to him. And Locke knew he was right.

"Years ago," Locke said, "your personnel file would have had a big PI, for political influence, stamped on it. They don't do that anymore. In your case it wouldn't matter."

"That's not fair, Colonel—"

"Just listen, Pontowski. You're walking away from jumping the F-Fifteens clean as a whistle because of PI in the shape of one Thomas Fraser, your grandfather's chief of staff. Fraser is running interference for you and pinging on our wing commander. The Old Man can't take that sort of heat. Also, I've got other things to worry about, like a squadron move, and haven't got time for you." Matt started to interrupt, stung by Locke's hard words. But Locke cut him off. "Are you also hard of hearing? I said, 'Listen.' At least allow me one prerogative. All I can ask you to do is to try and act responsible and not kill anyone else in these games you play."

Matt was standing rigidly at attention, biding his time until he could escape. "One last thing," Locke continued, his voice flat and unemotional. "No political influence, no cosmic backseater, no fuckin' false bravado is going to save your ass when a MiG pilot has outflown you, outthought you, out-fought you, and is at your six o'clock hosing you down.''

"With the ruckus in Iraq over, that's not likely to happen, now is it, Colonel?" Matt was smiling when he said it, all his self-confidence back. He was getting bored.

"You'd better hope not," Locke said, thinking about his own experience in that particular war. "But in England you will be just that much closer to MiG drivers, won't you? Now get the hell out of here so I can do some productive work."

Matt saluted and left. Haney was waiting for him outside the office, wearing a worried look. He followed the pilot down the hall. "Are we gonna be okay?"

"Yeah," Matt reassured him, totally unaffected by the chewing out he had received. "Not a hell of a lot they can do to me. Stick with me kid and you'll be okay." The relief on Haney's face was obvious. "I gotta get out of this chick-enshit outfit for a while," Matt continued. "Maybe take some leave." He thought for a moment. "I know where there's one hell of a party going on." The young pilot turned abruptly into the administration office, grabbed a leave form, and filled it out.

The administration clerk checked the completed form. "Colonel Locke has to approve foreign leave," she told Matt.

"No problem. He'll sign it. Probably be glad to get rid of me for a while."

"Where you goin'?" Haney asked.

"Spain. See you in England." He ambled down the hall, leaving a perplexed Haney in his wake.

Shoshana sat at a small table in Marbella's main square, en-joying a late-morning cup of coffee and reading a two-day-old copy of *The New York Times*. She found the old town with its picturesque streets, small shops, and masses of flow-ers fascinating and, after three days, was spending more and more or her time there, mostly in dress shops. She dropped the newspaper in her lap and thought about the boutiques she would explore later on. A familiar voice brought her back to reality with a jolt.

"Don't turn around," Habish's voice said behind her. She did anyway and saw her contact sitting at the table immedi-ately behind her. He was reading a newspaper, seemingly unconcerned with her presence. "This is not a vacation. Spend more time at the beach club. We've arranged for you to attend a party there tonight. The club manager has an invitation for you."

Habish had been busy making contacts and opening doors for Shoshana's entrance into the more rarefied strata of Marbella's social life. Since the Mossad did not use local Jews for its operations, refusing to compromise their status or allegiance to their own country, Habish had to ferret out his own contacts and bring in two more agents. Luckily, Marbella was a tourist trap, although a very high class one, that required workers—hairdressers, waiters, receptionists—fluent in many languages. Habish had found a young Moroccan working as a hotel's assistant manager who was hired because he spoke Arabic. The young man was also Jewish and a Zionist. He had readily volunteered to help Habish, willing to become involved without knowing details. Secretly, the Moroccan hoped Habish was on the trail of another Adolf Eichmann. Shoshana would never know that three Mossad agents were backing her up, laying groundwork, watching her every move, and only getting above five hours of sleep a night. Gad Habish was a tired man.

"The dress boutique you were in yesterday," he continued, "the one near the fountain, go back this morning and talk to Gabriella. She'll help select a dress for the party." The sales clerk was another immigrant worker that one of the agents had recruited.

"I can't afford anything in there," Shoshana protested.

"Use a credit card," Habish snapped, cutting off any further conversation.

Twenty minutes later, Shoshana was trying on dresses, shocked that she would be buying anything with such a price tag. "You must be more relaxed and natural," Gabriella counseled. "Don't worry about the prices." She surveyed the young woman, analyzing her, trying to decide how best to showcase her natural beauty. "Black is your best color," she decided. "Try this one." The woman handed Shoshana a black, full-length gown, strapless except for two thin spaghetti straps over each shoulder and slit high up the right side, revealing most of her leg. The dress seemed to shimmer and flow over her body. "Yes, that will do perfectly."

Shoshana took stock of her reflection in a mirror, shocked at what she saw. "It looks like a nightgown . . ."

"Not quite. But that *is* the idea."

"What kind of bra do I wear with this? And look at the panty line!"

"Don't wear either."

Shoshana was ready for her first skirmish.

A gentle breeze moved in off the Mediterranean, cooling the large patio where the beach club held its parties, rocking the lanterns, and casting a moving pattern of light and shadows over the rich, famous, infamous, and hanger-ons that made up the "glitterati" of Marbella's society. Matt was sitting at the patio's bar just outside the French doors that opened into the main lounge taking it all in when a tall, Nordic young man walked through the doors. "Hellmut," he called, catching the newcomer's attention, "I'd given up on you."

"Never miss a party like this one, my friend," Hellmut Wisser, the son of WisserChemFabrik's general director assured him. For the next few minutes, the two old friends brought each other up to date on what they had been doing since they last met at Gstaad, Switzerland, for a week of skiing. Their friendship went back to the time when Matt was a cadet at the Air Force Academy and had accompanied his grandfather on a junket to visit NATO bases in Europe. They had met at a stuffy reception and had become instant friends when they discovered a shared interest in pretty girls, fast cars, skiing, and partying—not necessarily in that order. They had escaped from the elegant castle on the hillside overlooking Bonn where the reception had been held and for the next three days, pursued three of their four common interests, sorry that it was the midst of summer.

The friendship had grown on its own over the years and received positive encouragement from Hellmut's family when they learned that Matt's grandfather might become the President of the United States. For one short summer, the Wissers had hoped that something might develop between Matt and Hellmut's younger sister, Lisl. But nothing came of it, for other than a lustful enjoyment of each other's body, Matt and Lisl had nothing in common. They still slept together whenever they met.

They were talking about skiing when Shoshana walked onto the patio. "Who," Matt said, very interested, "is that?"

"A new face this year," Hellmut told him.

"And a new body," Matt allowed.

"Her name is Rose Temple. I had the company run a background check when one of our"—Hellmut paused, searching for the right words—"more influential clients expressed an interest. She's a Canadian working in California. Over here for a vacation and staying at the Atalaya Park. Some money in the family—ranching and lumbering."

"I hope," Matt said, "that she's one of them 'wimmen' my granddaddy warned me about."

Hellmut shook his head, an amused look in his eyes. He knew when Matt was about to give chase. "We would, ah"—again he sought the right words—"rather you'd not. There is an engineer here who we would like Miss Temple to meet." He nodded toward a dark, pudgy young man, Is'al Nassir Mana, standing next to Hellmut's father.

"Is this business?" Matt asked.

"Of course." Hellmut saw no reason to tell his friend that Mana was from Iraq and that his company was doing business with that country again. Americans could be incredibly naive about some things.

"Then he's going to have to take his chances with the rest of us," Matt said. He stood up and headed toward Shoshana.

"Matt," Hellmut called after him, "Lisl is here." The pilot paused before he rolled in for a reconnaissance run on his latest target.

Shoshana turned her head, cast a long gaze at Mana, then glanced away. He had seen her looking at him. Good. Slowly she returned her gaze, a slight smile on her lips. It was the classic, time-honored come-on—an interested look and a smile. Now the ball was in Mana's court. Would he take the few steps over to her and say something? No matter what he said, it would be well received. The Iraqi engineer was saying something to the elder Wisser. Then he started to walk toward Shoshana.

"He's not the one for you," a voice said. She turned to see Matt standing behind her. Now Mana was walking away. Matt's self-assured style cast a circle of strength and confidence around him that intimidated competition at a distance and that women found attractive and alluring. Mana could sense that he was already beaten. For a moment, Shoshana was flustered, not knowing what to do. A warm feeling welled up and pulled her toward the American. "Hi," he continued, keeping her off balance. "I'm Matt Pontowski."

She glanced back at Mana, who was watching them. Shoshana gave him an upward shrug of the shoulders with a smiling, perplexed look as if to say, "I can't help it," or "Save me." Mana smiled back then rejoined the Wissers. All was not lost.

"Oh, ah, Rose Temple." She looked away, sending an obvious signal that she was not interested. Her training had been most thorough in this area.

But Matt was not about to be put off. "Sorry, I didn't mean to scare off your Arab friend. I seem to do that all the time." He was establishing his territory, offering her protection if she wanted it and the tugging inside Shoshana grew stronger.

She was saved when a slender, self-possessed woman passed by. "Matt!" the newcomer sang out, her voice warm and friendly. "Hellmut said you were here." Lisl Wisser stopped less than six inches from Matt and reached up, touching his cheek. She was establishing her own territorial claims. For a moment, the entire room was aware of the trio, watching them. The two women stood in a stark, beautiful contrast to each other; one fashionably slender, a golden blonde, the other a dark, mature beauty with a glowing sensuality. Most of the guests knew who Matt was. Two men commented on the choice Matt would have to make. A third speculated that knowing Lisl Wisser, Matt wouldn't have to make a choice—if he was lucky.

Shoshana ended all speculation by excusing herself and walking away, determined to leave the party and salvage whatever she could. Matt watched her go. Lisl gave his cheek a friendly pat, recapturing his attention. "Tonight?" she asked, making sure Shoshana heard.

Outside the beach club, Shoshana asked the doorman for a taxi back to her hotel. A dark car driven by Gab Habish pulled up and she waited for the doorman to close the door before she said anything. Quickly, she recounted what had happened at the party. "You did well by leaving," he told her. "We've arranged for you to join a water-skiing party tomorrow at Porta Banus. Mana will be there. Wear your black bathing suit.''

"I can't wear that and water-ski," she protested. "I'll fall out of it." Habish only looked at her. She got the point—that was the idea.

"I'll have you picked up at eleven tomorrow morning," Habish said. He was looking forward to a full night's sleep. "And avoid Matthew Pontowski."

"Who is he anyway?" she asked.

Habish let his irritation with her show. "Start doing your homework and learn all you can about the people you associate with. His grandfather is the President of the United States.''

Shoshana felt a warm confusion tug at her again.

3

The black Mercedes Habish had dispatched to take Shoshana to Porta Banus blended perfectly with the other cars in the small, exclusive resort town that hugged a harbor overflowing with yachts. The driver deposited her at a dock where she joined a small group of people. Much more observant after Habish's sharp rebuke about doing her ''homework,'' she noticed that most of the crowd was made up of the younger set from last night's party. She also counted the armed uniformed guards that strolled casually through the waterfront and along the docks. She carefully noted the type and condition of their weapons.

Two luxury speedboats were ferrying the waiting guests for the water-skiing party out to a massive yacht that was too long to enter the harbor. A man in a white linen suit took her name and spoke into a small radio, checking her invitation before he let her board one of the speedboats.

Once on board the yacht, she was pleased that the baggy white shorts and cotton safari shirt she had chosen to wear over her swimsuit matched the casual dress of the other guests. Hopefully, she thought, Habish won't be too upset when I tell him that I didn't wear *the* bathing suit. Instead, she had donned a modest athletic tank suit with two bright fluorescent panels. Her instincts warned her that it would be more acceptable to Mana and less provocative to the likes of Matt Pontowski.

"Miss Temple," Hellmut called out when he saw her, "so glad you could make it." The heir apparent to the Wisser fortunes guided her by the elbow to his small group gathered around the taffrail at the stern of the ship. A waiter scurried up with a tray of Bloody Marys while Hellmut introduced her around. Is'al Nassir Mana extended his hand when he was introduced and she shook it, finding it warm and soft like his brown eyes. He spoke a few words and Shoshana thought of the teddy bear she loved to cuddle as a child. He did not match the stereotype she had created in her mind when she had studied his file.

Laughter and playful screams drifted up from the boarding platform as the first group of water-skiers took off, cutting across the wake of the Ferrari-powered ski boats. Shoshana was leaning against the rail, talking and smiling at Mana, actually enjoying the conversation when the high-pitched wail of four approaching jet skis demanded their attention. Lisl Wisser and Matt Pontowski were standing on the lead ski, cutting graceful arcs back and forth in a scissors pattern with another jet ski. Lisl was topless. "Ah, I see your friend from last night casts a wide net. But then, that is expected of a fighter pilot."

"Oh, please," she laughed, finding his Oxford accent pleasant, "save me from fighter pilots!" She noticed that Mana did not take his eyes off Lisl. Shoshana was wearing the wrong swimsuit.

Lisl set the style on board for most of the women who promptly went topless within minutes after her arrival. Two younger girls were sunbathing nude on the forward deck. Much to Shoshana's confusion, Mana was following Lisl around like a puppy, captivated by the half-naked woman. According to Mana's file, he preferred her type to Lisl's. Could the file be wrong?

"Arabs like blonds," Matt said, joining her. "But don't worry, Lisl will throw him back."

Shoshana didn't like the American knowing she was trying to attract the Iraqi and reprimanded herself for being so obvious. Tall, tan, and muscular, Matt was certainly a contrast to Mana. Clothes hid Matt's well-conditioned body and the muscles that rippled under his smooth skin when he walked or moved. She suspected he was very vain and spent hours working out in a weight room. You are probably something else in bed, she thought, disturbed by the man's magnetism. She peeled down to her swimsuit, deciding to do some water skiing. "How long does she play with her prey?" Shoshana asked.

Matt liked the sound of her voice. "In this case, I'd guess about thirty minutes." He gave her a thorough look. "Like your swimsuit," he said, meaning it. "Perfect for water-skiing. Want to give it a try?"

Shoshana caught a playful change in his voice, almost as if he were shifting gears. She shrugged her shoulders and climbed down the boarding stairs to the floating dock to wait for her turn. Matt stood beside her carrying on a light banter. Within minutes, they were sitting on the edge of the float as the ski boat played out their towlines. Then they were up, gliding and skipping across the bright blue water. Matt would roar with laughter as he cut back and forth across the wake of the expensive towboat. Shoshana found she was enjoying herself immensely.

On a tight pass around the yacht, she noticed that Mana was standing alone at the rail. Suspecting that Lisl had found someone else to play with, Shoshana gave a cutting motion with her hand across her neck, signaling she wanted to drop off. The towboat slowed and she threw her rope clear and coasted to a halt by the dock. "Enjoyed it!" Matt yelled as the boat accelerated away. Strange, Shoshana thought, he wasn't coming on at all. He only wanted to play.

She climbed back up the ladder, sure she now had a clear shot at Mana. She knew how to soothe wounded male pride. He was watching her as she worked her way through some dancing couples. "Americans," she fumed, joining him at the rail. "I can't get rid of him." The smile that lit Mana's face told her she had hit a responsive chord.

"They can be persistent," he said, still smiling.

Shoshana caught his last word and decided to play it. "I prefer them to be nonpersistent and nontoxic."

Mana looked at her in surprise. The words had a special meaning for him.

Don't stop now, she warned herself. "There I go talking shop," she explained, laughing, enchanting him. "I work for a commercial insecticide company and I guess it comes out when I'm fighting off bugs."

"So do I," he said. "Well, in a manner of speaking."

"Then that's why you know the Wissers." He only nodded. She pressed her opening. "Would you mind riding with me back to the port? Otherwise the American"—she cast a glance toward Matt who had finished skiing and was climbing the stairs—"will swarm all over me."

"It would be my pleasure." His formal way of speaking amused her.

Shoshana made sure they were engrossed in a conversation when they brushed past Matt so she could ignore him. Matt watched them leave. "Aced out by a fucking raghead," he muttered. Then he laughed. "Well, it has to happen once every five hundred years." He shook his head and went looking for Lisl. He found her sunbathing nude on the forward deck.

On the boat ride into the harbor, Shoshana sat close to Mana, their thighs touching, and kept him talking about himself. The young man waited with her as the black Mercedes, now driven by Habish, pulled up. "Would you be kind enough to join me for dinner tonight?" he asked, his English still formal.

"I'd love to." She smiled at him. "I'm staying at the Atalaya Park."

"Yes, I know. Shall I pick you up at eight o'clock?" Shoshana nodded in agreement. "Please wear the black dress." He almost was blushing when he said it.

"If you wish." She gave him a promising look as Habish pulled away.

"You wore the wrong swimsuit," Habish growled. "You were going after the Arab, not the American."

"It worked, didn't it?" she protested. "I *am* going to dinner with him."

"That was luck. You attract Americans by being provocative at first and then becoming very reserved. They have a basic prudish streak in them. With Arabs, it's show all the way. Get them panting and keep them that way."

"But Mana was a perfect gentleman . . . reserved . . . polite . . ."

"That's a protective disguise Arabs adopt when they travel. The perfect Western gentlemen. They revert to type when they are home and become egotistical, domineering bastards. Listen to me next time. You won't have so much trouble."

Shoshana sank back in the seat. She had much to learn.

Brigadier General Leo Cox ambled down a corridor of Arlington Hall Station, the Defense Intelligence Agency's annex located three miles from the Pentagon. A sharklike grin split the cadaverous face of the Air Force one-star general when he stopped at the office door of his best Middle Eastern analyst, Lieutenant Colonel William G. Carroll. "Bill, you busy?"

The analyst glanced up from his work and immediately shot to his feet. Unlike many of the personnel assigned to Arlington Hall, Carroll liked Cox. When the general had been assigned to run Arlington Hall by the DIA he had swept through it like a vengeful banshee, clearing out the deadwood, bringing in fresh talent, and changing it from a dead-end assignment into a top-notch analytical organization. Fools and paperpushers did not last long around Cox and he picked his key men with care. Carroll was one of the "spooks" whom Cox relied on and was far from being a deskbound paperpusher.

"Whose toes did I tread on this time, General?" Carroll knew that Cox liked to drop in on his subordinates unannounced, bypassing the chain of command. It was a habit that kept the higher-ranking milicrats, the military version of bureaucrats, in the DIA stirred up and their lower-ranking protégés afraid for their careers. The working troops loved it.

The general shook his head and closed the door behind him. "Sit down and relax, Bill. I've got a problem." Cox stretched out his skinny six-foot-four-inch frame in the only decent armchair in the office. "I sent your last analysis about Iraq and Syria showing signs of kissing and making up over to the CIA to be included in the PDB. Hogan bounced it right back with some scathing remarks about us being out to lunch. I won't repeat what he said about your linking the

Iraqis with the economic negotiations going on between Egypt and Syria.''

Carroll's mouth twisted into a rueful grimace. Hogan was the staffer in the CIA who compiled the President's Daily Brief, or PDB, and it was widely rumored that he wrote it up with a crayon. Supposedly, the PDB summarized the best intelligence the United States had for the President, and since the CIA had sole direct-reporting access to the President, all intelligence had to go through the CIA. ''The troops over at the CIA think we're too pro-Israeli.''

''Don't tell me, Bill.'' Cox smiled, raising a hand. ''I know that not a single one of those shit-for-brains over there speaks Arabic.'' Carroll was fluent in Arabic and Farsi; and could, in a pinch, get along in Berber.

''Someone had better tell the President what's going down or we're going to get our asses in the proverbial crack—again,'' Carroll said. Cox valued the slender and youthful-looking lieutenant colonel because his linguistic and analytical abilities were backed up by an outstanding record in the field. Carroll was one of the most highly decorated Air Force officers on active duty and wore the Air Force Cross for his role in rescuing 280 prisoners of war.

''I couldn't agree with you more,'' Cox said. ''But no one else, most of all the CIA, is reading the signals the way you do. I floated your analysis by General Howard and he almost threw me out of his office.'' Lieutenant General Howard was the Army three-star general in command of the DIA and Cox's boss. ''No one is buying your analysis that Saddam has become a martyr to the Arab people and could be a rallying point against the West. The Agency boys believe that we stomped Saddam hard enough to keep everybody in line and that the Arab claim that they have the men and money to change their third world status and only lack the will to do it is just so much hot air.'' Cox held up his hand to keep Carroll silent. ''Bill, I agree that Iraq is secretly rebuilding its military much like Hitler did in Germany in the 1930s. A nation learns more from losing a war than from winning it. We know they've gotten back all their planes from the Iranians. But that goes against the party line that the Iraqis are now rational actors and that the Mideast is stabilizing.''

''So what else is new?''

''I need to get the attention of the President or the National

Security Council," Cox said, "but I'm out of ideas and air-speed. If I can't do it through normal channels, it'll have to be looked to the media."

Carroll studied the pencil he was holding. He gave a little snort and shook his head. "That's a bad choice . . ." He understood the general's problem. Everyone in the administration was hailing the current negotiations between Egypt and Syria for an economic and mutual assistance treaty as a harbinger of peace and stability in that shattered area of the world, as everything the allied forces had fought for. But Carroll had discovered something else. At first, everything he had seen supported the accepted view of the treaty. Then a Mossad contact had passed him a top-secret protocol an Israeli spy had discovered buried deep in the negotiations. The protocol fused the Syrian and Egyptian military command and control systems and established communications links with Iraq.

After blending it with other intelligence, Carroll had come to one simple and overriding conclusion: The Egyptians, the Syrians, and possibly the Iraqis, were using the treaty to prepare for a major war and there could only be one target—Israel. Cox also had a contact in Mossad, one much higher than Carroll's, who had passed along the same intelligence to him.

"The Israelis know what's going down, so why doesn't the Israeli ambassador warn our State Department?" Carroll asked.

Cox shook his head. "Lots of reasons. Too many congressmen and senators would claim the Israelis are crying wolf. Their new prime minister is one cocky son of a bitch. Yair Ben David thinks Israel can take on all the Arabs as long as they keep their powder dry. He isn't worried, so his ambassador isn't worried. Everyone over here is happy because that supports our administration's position that the Israelis are on top of the situation, Iraq has quit lusting after its neighbors' oil, and that peace and prosperity are just around the corner. People only see what they want to see."

The general gave vent to his deeply ingrained cynicism. "What we've got here is a classic case of double whifferdill inverted rectalitis where everyone is looking up everyone else's asshole and seeing light at the end of the tunnel."

"Right." Carroll grinned. "And feelin' cool because the wind is in their face."

"Bill," Cox said, looking at his feet, "I can't leak it."

"And you want me to?"

There was no answer as the general disappeared out the door.

Just watching Shoshana move across the hotel lobby as they met for their dinner engagement excited Mana and he could feel the start of an erection. He willed it to go away as he joined her, exchanging ritualistic small talk. Up close, it was easier to take his eyes off the dress that promised so much. He was certain she was wearing nothing underneath and became even more excited when she entered the backseat of his limousine and flashed a bare leg.

Inside the car, the dress seemed to move over her, outlining her figure and then hiding it away. He was a flustered young man. "I . . . I hope that you will like the restaurant," Mana stammered. "It's a small place, very exclusive, with a quiet garden."

"It will be fine if we can talk," she said and reached out and touched the back of his hand. She was following Habish's instructions to the letter—get him panting and keep him that way. Shoshana felt sorry for Is'al.

The two-block walk from where the van pool dropped Carroll helped break the tension generated by the DIA and the daily grind at Arlington Station. He was relaxing into the peaceful routine of suburban Virginia when he turned up the walk to his house. He waved at his neighbor, a bureaucrat in the Department of the Interior who got off work much earlier, and braced himself. His son, a two-and-a-half-year-old bruiser, flew down the steps and bounced into his arms, demanding to be caught.

"Daddy, do you know what this is?" Brett Carroll challenged. A picture of a red stop sign was clutched in his small hand.

"Looks like a stop sign to me," Carroll replied. He knew how to hedge his answers.

"It's an octagon, Daddy." Condescension was apparent in his voice. He wiggled out of his father's arms and ran past his mother, off on the important business of two-year-olds.

"He's into shapes today," Carroll's wife told him. Mary Carroll was a tall, slender woman, a former Air Force officer and one of the POWs that Carroll had helped rescue from Iran. She kissed him and they walked arm in arm into the house, talking about the trouble their son had been in during the day. Mary caught the signs immediately that something was bothering her husband. She waited through dinner, knowing he would soon tell her.

Brett finally had run down and, with howls of protest, had been put to bed at seven-thirty. An unusual calm settled over the house. Mary settled onto the couch next to her husband and waited. "Mary," he began, "I've got a problem . . ." When he finished talking through his conversation with the general, his wife sat for a minute, studying the problem and her husband's face.

"Bill, you don't have to leak it if you can back-door it to someone upstairs. I have an old friend who might know someone who can help. Why not talk to her?"

"If I get caught off base, they'll crunch my head big-time. That means the end of this." He looked around the room, thinking about Brett and their home. It was a good life. "But Cox thinks this is important."

"Why doesn't he do it? Why pass it off on you?"

"The general is too well-known, too controversial, too pro-Israeli," Carroll answered. "If he leaks it to anyone, they'll either name him as their source or disregard it, figuring he's grinding some ax. But I trust him."

Mary sighed and stared across the room. She didn't want to put her home, her family, in jeopardy. Lower-ranking officers got stepped on hard when they played outside the established rules. Then she rose and walked to the phone, her decision made.

Two hours later, Bill Carroll was sitting in a parked car, telling what he knew to Melissa Courtney-Smith.

"I love the beach at night," Shoshana said, slipping off her shoes. She almost lost her balance and stumbled into Mana. "Sorry. Too much wine."

He smiled at her and took off his shoes. "I've never done this before. It's just like in the movies." Shoshana took his hand and led him down to the water's edge. The dinner had been everything Mana had promised and, much to her dismay, she found she liked the Iraqi. He was shy, eager to please, and so unsure of himself—just like so many Israeli boys she knew. That's it, she decided, he's still a boy. Habish's warning about Arabs reverting to type in their own country came back to her.

"Come on then," she said and pulled him into the water.

"Rose," Mana said. "You said you worked for an insecticide company in California." They were walking through the gentle lapping surf.

"Oh, Is'al, please don't talk business. I'm only a scheduler and just tell the plant foreman when to run a batch, how much, and where to ship it to." She reeled off some of the details Habish had given her to memorize about her cover story. "It's boring."

"You know I also am in the chemical industry." She could feel him looking at her, his brown eyes pleading. "I thought we might have much in common."

She leaned against his arm, letting him feel her breasts. "We do." She gave him a low laugh, full of promise. "But let's not talk about business. It's almost light. Please walk me back to the hotel."

The concierge on duty ignored them when they walked across the hotel lobby to the elevator. "It's all right," Shoshana assured him. "Be natural. Relax." She was amused by how proper he was trying to act. He had even put on his shoes before entering the hotel. Inside the elevator, she gave him a kiss, aware that even barefoot, she was taller than he. "That's nice," she said. "I like the way you kiss." She rubbed against him, feeling his erection. The elevator stopped and he drew back, blushing furiously that they might be seen in an embrace. "Oh, come on," she laughed, taking him by the hand down the deserted hall.

Outside her door, she fumbled for her key, let one of the gown's straps fall off her shoulder, and deliberately dropped the key. "Oh," she whispered and bent to pick it up. The low-cut dress opened provocatively and she could hear him breathe more rapidly. She stood and opened the door before turning to him, again brushing against his chest. "Thank you for a lovely evening," she said, putting her arms around his neck and pressing against him. She gave him a long and leisurely kiss and felt him respond. She pulled back, ran her right hand down his chest and pulled a shirt button loose.

She reached in and stroked his chest as she kissed him again, pushing her tongue into his mouth.

Then she rubbed up against him and again, her fingers moved down his shirt, almost accidentally dropping lower. As she did, she felt his erection pulse through the fabric and saw a stricken look in his eyes. A premature ejaculation. Mana stood there, not knowing what to do. Suddenly, she hated what she was doing. "Come inside," she told him. "You can use my bathroom." She caught a glimpse of Habish watching them through a slightly opened door down the hall.

Time to get rid of the bimbo, Thomas Fraser thought as he watched the young woman go through the motions of making coffee. But, damn, she's good in the sack. Fraser settled into an elegant wing chair, appreciating the expensive, immaculate apartment. This place is too classy for her, he decided, no reason for me to keep her here.

The President's chief of staff was a very contented man, enjoying the prerogatives of power and money. A buzz at the door chased any pleasant thoughts away and brought him back to reality.

The woman checked the TV monitoring the hall and gathered her peignoir around her. "It's your chauffeur," she said.

"Well, open the goddamn door." He didn't care that her wrap was almost transparent. She did as he ordered.

"Mr. Fraser," his driver said, "I got a call from the office on the car telephone looking for you. They say you haven't been answering your page and need you immediately."

"Who called?"

"Don't know, sir. A woman."

"Probably Courtney Smith," he growled, searching for his pager. He found it under the couch where he had kicked it when the girl had teasingly undressed him the night before. "Goddamn it!" he roared, blaming the young woman. "You stupid bitch, why were you screwing around with my page? Get out and be long gone before I get back."

Well, he decided as he waddled to the elevator, that solves one problem.

Melissa Courtney-Smith was standing by at her desk holding a neatly assembled file when Fraser burst into his office in the west wing of the White House. It was 7:58 in the morning and he was two minutes early. "What the hell's happening?" he shouted.

"The President," Melissa calmly replied, "called for a meeting at eight o'clock in the Situation Room with the National Security Council."

Fraser grabbed the file and bolted from the office, furious that a meeting had been scheduled without his consent. "Why wasn't I told?" he snapped.

"We've been trying to contact you for an hour," she said, easily matching his pace down the steps to the basement.

"What shit has hit what fan?" he demanded.

"Sorry, sir," she lied, "the President doesn't confide in me." Melissa had slipped a one-page memo from Bill Carroll into Pontowski's read file the night before. She had attached a note saying she thought he would be interested and initialed it with her distinctive "M." The President rose early every morning and read the file while he took his first cup of coffee. At seven o'clock, Zack Pontowski had walked into her office, handed her the memo and ordered the meeting for eight o'clock. She ran the memo through the shredder at her desk.

Fraser was the last person to enter the room and the Marine guard closed the door behind him. Inside the windowless fifteen- by twenty-foot room with the President, Fraser switched to a calm and genial personality. "Sorry, Mr. President, I just heard. Got to give my staff credit for tracking me down so fast." It was what President Pontowski would have wanted to hear.

"Glad you made it, Tom. Okay, gentlemen, I want to take a hard look at what's happening in the Middle East. I'm seeing things that disturb me and I don't want to be caught by something coming at us from out in left field. We may have to work out some new policy initiatives."

The director of central intelligence exchanged a puzzled look with the national security adviser, the man who headed the National Security Council. Neither of them was aware of any unusual activity in the Middle East. Still, the President had sent them a distinct signal that he was worried. Why else the hastily called meeting? Since the DCI was the overseer and coordinator of all United States intelligence functions, he took the lead. "Sir, we haven't monitored anything unusual or threatening. Our analysts are on top of it. Perhaps if you could tell us what's bothering you . . ."

"I want to know exactly what's going on between the Syrians and Egyptians," Pontowski told him. "I suspect there's more to that mutual assistance treaty . . . I want to know if Iraq is a player . . . We've worked too hard to create a stable Iraq and deny them any significant military capability . . . And I would like some answers by this afternoon."

The secretary of state chimed in. "Our observer at the negotiations reports all is in good order." Pontowski only looked at him. The secretary got the message. "I'll cable him to start digging and get his staff in gear."

Fraser's jaw was rigidly clamped and he worked not to grind his teeth. Nothing, he raged inwardly, was happening in the Middle East to warrant this much attention. Or was something going on he didn't know about? Who had gotten to him? What were his sources? Don't get paranoid, he cautioned himself. Pontowski does read three or four newspapers every morning. Maybe he stumbled onto something there. Rather than betray his irritation, Fraser decided to cool it and let others take the lead until he could control the situation.

Admiral Scovill, the Chairman of the Joint Chiefs of Staff, caught Pontowski's attention. "Sir, I'll get the DIA over here and find out what they've got. If there's anything unusual going on, they'll know."

"Oh come off it," the director of central intelligence protested. "The Defense Intelligence Agency gets its information from the CIA and the NSA. What would they have that's so damn unusual? And if they've found something, why haven't we all seen it?"

"Good question," the admiral answered. "Let's shake the tree and see what falls out." A warning kept tickling at the back of his mind that the Middle East was going to become unhinged again. The admiral had played a key part in the logistics buildup that helped force Iraq out of Kuwait and had later counseled that the drawdown of forces from Saudi Arabia following the successful conclusion of the war, leaving only a small trip-wire force in Kuwait and massive military stockpiles in the Saudi desert, was premature. But the current Iraqi government had sent strong signals through the CIA that they would live in peace with their neighbors. The strength of the CIA's endorsement suggested that the "boys from up the river" had an insider's knowledge of what was going on. The United States and the world were all too ready to abandon the shifting political sands of the Middle East deserts for the safe bedrock of domestic politics. Situation normal, Admiral Scovill thought, all fucked up.

Fraser looked up as if he had received a sudden inspiration. "Mr. President, is there some person you'd like to talk to, a recognized expert in the field?" Maybe there's a clue there, he thought.

Pontowski shook his head and stood up. Every eye was on him as he paced the room, a sure sign that he was upset. "I want peace in the Middle East," he said, his voice controlled and gentlemanly. "The surest way to bring that about is to create stability and prosperity in the region. That's why I'm so hopeful about the Syrian-Egyptian moves toward mutual assistance. With stability and prosperity, we can encourage all the parties, and that includes Israel and Iraq, to sit down and hammer out a solution to their problems. But until they do sit down and talk, we've got to protect any progress that's been made toward that goal or we're right back to square one. But I'm not so foolish as to forget that when Syrians and Egyptians got together in 1973 they started the Yom Kippur War. I don't want that happening again."

The DCI folded his hands and spoke quietly. "There is a degree of uncertainty that we have to live with when dealing with Arabs, and I might add, the Israelis. I'm referring, of course, to the Israelis' recent scientific tests in the Kalahari Desert with the South Africans."

A feeling of relief swept over Fraser—the DCI had just raised a peripheral issue that should distract Pontowski from cozying up to the current Israeli prime minister.

"Don't get distracted," the President said. "We don't know the exact contours of the relationship between Israel and South Africa or what they're doing in the Kalahari. For now, focus on Egypt, Syria, and Iraq."

Fraser didn't want to let the subject die. "I think the South Africans are using the Israeli lobby to push their case with Congress."

Pontowski nodded in agreement. "We've seen the results of that effort before." He pointed at Fraser. "Tom, I want you to stay on top of this and have some answers by this afternoon. Don't leave a single stone unturned." He walked out of the room, cutting off any further discussion, leaving a hushed and stunned group behind him.

The secretary of state broke the silence. "He's worried."

Fraser stood up and glared at him. "Obviously. We've got to sort this one out—and fast." For the next few minutes, he demonstrated the organizational skill that made him such an asset to the President. Finally, they were ready to leave.

"Okay," the Chairman of the Joint Chiefs of Staff asked, "who presents it to the President? I'd suggest we let General Leo Cox do it. He's the most knowledgeable man I have on the Middle East."

Everyone readily agreed, more than willing to let the Defense Intelligence Agency handle this one. "No," Fraser said. "I want the CIA to present it." No way I'm going to let that son of a bitch get to the President, he thought, stomping out of the room.

Back in his office, he threw the papers he was carrying at Melissa and slammed his door behind him. Once in the privacy of his own office, he paced the floor, rage and fury boiling through him. "Damn," he growled, "I control access to the President. I set the agenda. Someone's getting around me." Slowly, he regained control and the shooting pains in his stomach quieted, leaving only an occasional echo to remind him of his ulcer.

The light for his private line on the phone bank flashed at him. He sat down and hesitated before answering it, making sure he was in total control. It was B. J. Allison, the CEO of one of the largest oil corporations in the United States. Allison was also a heavy contributor to any cause or campaign Fraser might suggest and heavily invested in Middle Eastern oil. "B.J."—he forced a smile into his voice—"we've got to get together for lunch or dinner." He paused, listening to the voice on the other end. "Yeah, I got rid of the bimbo. Tomorrow night would be fine."

4

Zack Pontowski was sitting by his wife's bedside reading and drinking coffee when she woke up. She studied her husband for a few moments, not wanting to disturb him. We've been through so much together, she thought, and now you've got to watch me die. For a moment, she fought back her tears, not because lupus was again ravaging her body, this time attacking her skin, but because she couldn't help him now that he had reached the pinnacle of his career. She cried because he had to carry the burden alone. When she was in firm control and the tears conquered, she moved, letting him know she was awake.

"Sleep well, Tosh?" he asked. It was the same question he always asked her. She smiled at him as he laid down the thick read file that waited for him every morning, removed his glasses, and placed a hand gently over hers. Pontowski had caught her first waking movements and had concentrated on his reading until she was in control.

"You are so vain," she chided him. "You never let anyone see you wearing glasses." He humphed in response. "Probably just as well," she allowed. "Don't need to hide those steely blue eyes." He waited until a nurse had helped arrange her in a sitting position before handing her a cup of coffee. "Well, then," she continued, "have you solved the world's problems or will that take until lunch?" She believed in keeping him humble.

"Should have that done by tomorrow. Looks like a decisive power struggle is going on inside Russia." He always told her what was occupying his attention and she had a way of keeping him focused on what was important. "Lots of turmoil inside the Kremlin."

"Will that affect what's going on in the Middle East?" He had shared Melissa's memo with her the night before.

"Hard to say. It does look like Rokossovsky is in deep trouble. The old guard is fighting his economic reforms tooth and tong."

"Tooth and toenail," she corrected him. They both laughed although it was far from a laughing matter for Viktor Rokossovsky, the young and energetic Soviet premier.

"We got a letter from Matt," he announced, handing her the envelope. "He's in Marbella on vacation, whooping it up, I expect."

"Just like his father," she said. Pontowski waited while she read the rare note from their grandson. It was an occasion when he wrote, for Matt was like his father an unrestrained fighter pilot, eager to party, chase women, and fly whenever he got the chance. Zack Pontowski and his wife both shared the unspoken hope that he would not die in a fiery crash like his father did—that combat would not claim the last male descendant of the Pontowski clan. "Now this is different," she said. "He mentions a girl, a Rose Temple from Canada. Do you think our ne'er do-well grandson may be getting serious for the first time in his life?"

"Well, he did write a letter." Again, they both laughed.

Patience was not part of Fraser's personality and the delay ate at him. Still, he forced himself to sit quietly in the receiving room of the mansion in the rolling hills of western Virginia that B. J. Allison called home. Even for a private dinner at home, Fraser knew that B.J. liked to make an entrance. Some "home," Fraser decided, calculating its worth at around $19.5 million. He had missed it by less less than $200,000.

He was not disappointed by her entrance. Five minutes later, B. J. Allison swept down one of the spiraling staircases wearing a simple floor-length gown and a single diamond pendant with matching earrings. Fraser was impressed, not by the gown or diamonds, which he correctly estimated to be worth $2 million, but by the five minutes. B.J. kept governors and senators waiting seven minutes and was on time only for the President of the United States or royalty.

"Tom!" she sang out, her voice a beautiful contralto. "You do avoid me too much." Fraser couldn't help but smile as she took his arm and escorted him into the drawing room, the first stage in the journey to dinner. Only the eccentric

with strong self-destructive tendencies or the extremely powerful willfully avoided Barbara Jo Allison. Charles de Gaulle
had reportedly managed it successfully.

No one knew B.J.'s exact age, nor did they discuss it pub-
licly, for it was the one thing the petite and elegant woman
was sensitive about. Reporters could describe her as a witch,
bitch, or anything else within the realm of journalistic de-
cency with impunity. One young reporter had mentioned the
rumor that she was so politically conservative that she considered Attila the Hun a flaming radical and that she had a
swastika tattooed on the right cheek of her fanny. B.J. had
sent a note to the reporter's publisher telling him that the
swastika was tattooed on the left cheek because it was a lib-
eral philosophy, however misguided and amusing. The reporter's reputation and career were made.

The one TV commentator who had speculated about her
age had disappeared into obscurity within three days and later
committed suicide. Fraser was wildly off when he estimated
her age at sixty-six.

B.J. led Fraser through dinner with the grace and charm
she had learned from her mother in Tidewater Virginia and
regaled him with Washington gossip and delightful rumors. It
was only in the intimacy of the library over coffee that B.J.
turned to what interested her the most—oil and politics.
"They tell me the President is going to press Congress to
reduce the offshore oil depletion allowance. Now I think that
would be most unwise, don't you?" He readily agreed and
promised that he would do what he could to change Pontowski's mind. Neither of them mentioned that, thanks to
Fraser, Allison had thrown her weight, influence, and campaign contributions behind Pontowski in the recent election.

"And the Middle East, I do find that worrisome, don't
you?" Again, Fraser agreed, wondering what she was leading to. "Is it true that someone is telling the administration
that the Syrian-Egyptian treaty is more than an agreement to
spur on economic development in those two poor countries?"

Fraser almost dropped his cup. How had she learned that?
What were her sources? The briefing the CIA had given Pontowski the day before was classified top-secret. He knew better
than to lie. "Yes, that's true. The Israeli secret service—"

"Yes," she interrupted, "I know about the Mossad. I do

wish they would quit meddling in my business. Secret agents, penetrations . . ." She stomped her foot in frustration. "Why, you'd think I was a foreign power threatening those poor unfortunate people."

"What nonsense. If you want, I'll tell the President that the Israelis are harassing American companies."

"I wouldn't trouble him for the world." She laid on her soft southern accent, creating an illusion of helplessness. "You mustn't listen to the ramblings of a silly old woman."

"I should be so old," Fraser lied and quickly changed the subject. "Mossad did pass a warning to us that the treaty is a cover for a military alliance between Egypt and Syria with a possible link to Iraq. Some of our analysts think Israel is the only logical target."

"Ridiculous," she snorted. "I know many Arabs and they all want peace. Why just the other day I was talking to Sheik Mohammed al-Khatub, you know, that charming man from OPEC, and he assures me that they all want peace. The Israelis are using that as a scare tactic to get more money and arms out of us." She paused before continuing. "Tom." She laid her hand on his arm. They had come to the crux of the meeting. "I do wish that President Pontowski and Congress would recognize that we have many other friends in the Middle East besides Israel. And I do think it's time we let Israel sink or swim on its own, don't you?"

Gad Habish was tired when his flight from Amsterdam landed at Málaga. The return journey from Israel had been an ordeal and he had spent hours transiting through four different airports in four countries as he switched passports and changed identities. "All for twenty minutes with the Ganef," he complained. The team's number two man, Zeev Avidar, who had met him at the airport said nothing; he understood only too well Habish's feelings. Everyone in the Mossad knew their leader was habitually ill-tempered and irascible, but they also knew he was a genius who had learned his craft in the Warsaw ghetto as a teenager in World War II.

"What horse is the old Ganef riding these days?" Avidar asked.

"Money. What else. Claims we're spending too much of it. He had a fit over the dress until I showed him the pictures.'' Habish gave a snort that passed for a laugh. ''That shut him up. I think the old bastard actually got a hard-on.''

''Impossible.'' They were quiet for the rest of the ride into Marbella.

Shoshana was following the routine Habish had established for her to make contact. She started out by visiting a certain gift shop downtown and then pausing for a late-morning coffee on the main square. After that, she would visit a few more shops before dropping into Gabriella's dress boutique thirty-five to forty minutes after she had finished the coffee. Someone was always there to meet her. This time, it was a red-eyed Habish who was waiting.

''How's the relationship with Mana progressing?'' he asked.

''Satisfactory.'' He could hear an icy chill in her voice. When Shoshana chose, she could freeze a person with her haughty, reserved manner. But Habish was no ordinary person.

''Out with it,'' he demanded, cutting right to the heart of the matter.

''I don't like being watched by voyeurs,'' she replied, turning the temperature down a few more degrees. ''You are nothing but a frustrated—'' She cut the words off. ''I do not like what I am doing to Is'al and prefer not to be gawked at when I must . . . must seduce him.''

''Say it like it is,'' he snapped. ''When you must 'fuck' him.''

Her anger flared. ''We haven't gone that far yet. He has a problem.''

''Yes, we know. Premature ejaculation.''

''Must you do this to him?'' A pleading had crept into her voice.

''My God! You've fallen for one of the clients.''

''No. But I do like him. He is so vulnerable and unsure of himself.''

Habish motioned for her to sit down while he checked the hall for security. Only Zeev Avidar was there. He sat next to her and spoke in a soft voice, explaining the ''drill'' to her.

''Yes, we do watch you. You are under constant surveillance, twenty-four hours a day. It is not easy but it is necessary.'' She started to protest that it wasn't necessary, that she was perfectly safe with Mana. Again he anticipated her. "Believe me, you are in constant danger. This is the only way we can guarantee your safety. Did you know Mana has bodyguards and they have taken pictures of you and him together? Including that tender scene in the hall where you had him twanging at E above high C." Shoshana was shocked.

Habish pressed his advantage. "Is'al Mana is an Iraqi chemical engineer who right now, as we speak, is negotiating with WisserChemFabrik for highly specialized machinery that could be used to manufacture a new nerve gas. You know the most likely target of nerve gas—Israel." He stood up, his words now filled with emotion. "Shoshana, we are protecting our people, making sure that nothing like the Holocaust will ever happen again. No one *likes* what we do, least of all me. But there is no choice between the Manas of Iraq and the safety of our families. I wish there was another way."

His words had stirred memories deep inside and she remembered that Sunday long ago when she had cut her hair and visited Yad Vashem with her grandmother and aunt and uncle. "You're right." Her voice was her apology. "I had let my personal feelings cloud my judgment. It won't happen again."

"In our work," Habish said, "you must put your personal feelings away. But always remember where you hid them. You will need them when you're done with this filthy work. That is the way you remain a human being." He let her digest his words, judging her about ready for the purpose of his hurried visit back to Israel. She nodded and he knew she could continue.

"An agent reported the Iraqis are constructing a plant to make a new and much more deadly gas—one that we have no defenses for. He paid for that information with his life." He paused. "Shoshana, there is a connection between Mana and that plant. We want you to go inside, into Iraq, and find out what that nerve gas is."

Satiated, saturation, disgust. The three words rolled around in Matt's head, much like a tune that wouldn't go away. "Damn," he muttered, not knowing why he was so discontented. He was lying naked on the deck of a thirty-six-foot sailboat, another one of the many Wisser possessions, off the Greek island of Santorin. He rolled over, careful not to put any pressure on his crotch, and searched the beach for Lisl.

He didn't have any trouble finding her. She was the nude, golden-haired nymph running through the surf. "Exhibitionist," he grunted.

Lisl's brother, Hellmut, had sensed that Matt's growing attraction for Shoshana might complicate the negotiations with the Iraqis if the pilot stole her away from Mana. Rather than take any chances, Hellmut had suggested that the two of them leave Marbella and fly to Mykonos to pick up the boat for a few days' sail around the Aegean. Matt had readily agreed, seeing an easy way to end the games he was playing over Shoshana. He didn't like being aced out by an Arab.

Gingerly, he stood up and climbed down the companionway to find something to eat. He was standing in the galley when the boat rocked as Lisl climbed up the boarding ladder. "Not again." He made a promise to stop talking to himself. Rather than let Lisl trap him below for another round of lovemaking, he went back on deck. She was waving at another sailboat that was mooring beside them. Two couples waved back and they started an animated conversation in German.

"They'll be coming over when they finish mooring," Lisl told him. The two women on the other boat had already shed their clothes.

What in the hell is the matter with you, he thought. I'm in a teenager's paradise, screwing my eyeballs out and I've had it. For the first time in his life, he understood the difference between fucking and making love. And he knew whatever he and Lisl had been doing, it wasn't making love.

"Lisl, what's the date today?" She shrugged and called across the water, asking the new arrivals. He knew enough German to understand the answer. *"Scheise."* The German obscenity got her attention. "I'm AWOL. Got to get going." He explained that he had overstayed his leave and would be in a barrel of *Scheise* if he didn't get back to his unit. The news didn't bother Lisl, her four new friends would keep her occupied for a while. Her father would send someone to pick up the boat.

Two hours later, Matt was at Santorin's small airport. When he reached the counter, he almost booked a flight through Málaga, but decided against that. He couldn't waste two more days looking for Shoshana and had to get to his new base at Stonewood. He wished he hadn't gone sailing with Lisl and lost track of time—and Shoshana. He tried to write her off as just another passing fancy. But her face kept appearing like a beautiful melody that kept playing in his mind.

A light dew gave a freshness to the early morning as Habish started the car. Zeev Avidar, who specialized in forged documents, was packing his unique equipment into the trunk for the trip to the airport at Málaga. "I'm getting tired of this drive," Habish told Avidar. But there was no choice, his other agent was watching Shoshana and Avidar had to start the circuitous route that would take him to Baghdad.

Once inside Iraq, Avidar would keep the team supplied with all the fake documents a team needed to survive in that hostile country. It was no easy task, for he could not take the documents with him and would have to make them on the spot. During his journey, he would pick up the cover of a computer salesman and repairman trying to hawk his product inside Iraq. Like any good salesman, he would have samples of his product and, like a competent repairman, he would take his tools and spare parts with him. Avidar would go through the motions of setting up a computer business, taking his time as he worked through the masses of paperwork and the bureaucratic maze of the Iraqi government to get a business license.

Another agent, posing as an artist, had already smuggled in the unique types of paper and ink they would need. They would join up and Avidar would write a detailed program to load into a computer that would turn his laser printer into a most unique printing press. Their documents were so good that when experts compared Avidar's forgeries with the real thing, they always picked out the legitimate documents as the fake. But setting up the operation took time.

While Avidar was making his journey, the artist would make contact with an operative who was working with the Kurds, a minority fighting for their independence from the oppressive Iraqi regime. Through the Kurds, he would receive small, lightweight, .22-caliber Walther automatic pistols for each member of the team. The Walthers had been highly modified and used special, low-powered, German ammunition. When fired, the weapon made a soft *phut* sound and they did not need to use bulky silencers. It was a short-range assassination weapon. This was perhaps the most dangerous part of the operation and if he was caught with the weapons, it meant certain torture, execution, and compromise of the operation. Because of that, the weapons problem had to be resolved before anyone else entered Iraq.

Habish and two other agents would enter Iraq separately about the same time as Shoshana. She would have to travel without a backup and be on her own for a time. Once inside Iraq, the team would have to go to work with a vengeance, relearning the local customs, checking current police methods, and how the procedures at harbors and airports had changed since the last team was in Iraq. Then they would have to rent or buy at least three safe houses. Each agent would try to rent or buy a car, a difficult task in Iraq. While all this was going on, they would establish a communication system, make escape arrangements, develop hiding places, and pass out equipment. Avidar and the artist would work twenty hours a day, churning out the fake documents so an agent never had to use the same identity for doing two separate tasks. Habish would use the same driver's license for renting a car and while traveling. But he would never carry that driver's license when he was strolling from café to café, keeping in contact with his agents.

At a certain point, Habish would establish contact with Shoshana through the language school where he had told her to take lessons in Arabic. He would then move her into the operation, telling only what she needed to know, never revealing the entire operation or the identity of another agent to her. As the daddy rabbit for the operation, Habish was critical to the security of the entire team and he had promised himself long ago that he would commit suicide before being captured. Then Avidar would have to pick up the pieces and try to get everyone safely out of Iraq.

Habish knew what was ahead of him when he drove Avidar to the airport at Málaga. It was going to be up to him and one other agent to maintain a watch over Shoshana and he didn't look forward to the next few days. For now, he needed to get as much rest as possible until Shoshana wangled an invitation from Is'al Mana to visit Baghdad.

There was little doubt that Mana was totally infatuated with Shoshana. He followed her around like a puppy and sent her gifts every day. She encouraged the attention but refused to accept a single present and kept telling him that their relationship had nothing to do with material things. After a while, he believed her. Then Habish noticed that Mana's bodyguards no longer followed them around and used the time Shoshana and Mana were together to take a break.

Mana repeatedly tried to talk about his work to impress her with his talents and abilities. Again and again, Shoshana would put him off, claiming she didn't want to discuss business while on vacation and only wanted to spend more time with him. If he became too insistent in talking about chemical equipment, she would stroke and pet him, totally distracting him until a premature ejaculation sent him back to his villa for a change of clothes. Mana was in love.

Habish reprimanded her once for not letting Mana talk about his work. She froze him with her icy stare. "I believe the proper technique is to keep him 'humming' at E above high C." She liked Mana much better than Habish.

Finally, the negotiations between the Iraqis and Wisser-ChemFabrik were finished and Iraq had the last of the equipment it needed to complete its nerve gas plant. Habish had met her in the main square while she drank coffee and said that Mana would be returning to Iraq within the next day or two. She paid her bill and got ready to leave. "I know. He told me. We're having dinner tonight at his villa."

"Then he must ask you to go with him tonight."

"He will," Shoshana promised.

"How can you be so sure?"

"I've been doing my 'homework' and reading about Is'al's problem." She picked up her bag and left.

From the moment Mana picked up Shoshana at the hotel, he could not take his eyes off her, which was exactly what she wanted. The top three buttons of her white silk shirt were undone and her black, straight-legged trousers snared her small waist and hugged her ample hips and well-shaped rear.

They ate dinner on the balcony of his villa that overlooked the Mediterranean. When Shoshana judged the time was right, she suggested they go inside. Mana obediently followed. Inside, she stood in front of a mirror and checked her hair. "Is'al," she called, "this is a funny mirror. What's wrong with it?"

A bright crimson blush spread across the Iraqi's face as he told her there was a VCR camera hidden behind it. His honesty was painful.

"Do you take pictures of us?" she asked. He nodded. "Do you like watching them?" Again, he nodded. "Then I don't mind if it will remind you of me." She studied the mirror, not able to see anything behind it. "Is'al, ask one of the servants to bring in a bowl of ice cubes. Then dismiss them." He did as she asked and after the maid had left, she playfully kicked off her shoes and walked toward him. Her hips and shoulders swayed provocatively and Mana watched her breasts move under the silk blouse. He sucked in his breath when she undid the buttons down to her waist. She stopped in the middle of the room and beckoned for him. "Bring the ice," she commanded.

They met in the middle of the room and she took the bowl from him and set it on the floor. She turned so her back was to the mirror. Then she rapidly stripped his clothes off. Mana stood there perplexed, growing soft, losing his erection. Quickly, she undid her belt and shed her trousers and blouse. She was wearing nothing underneath. Mana was erect again, growing excited. She knelt in front of him and took him in both hands, feeling him pulse. It was almost over. Then she scooped up a handful of ice and clapped it over his penis. He gasped for air and visibly cooled.

Shoshana looked at him and smiled. "I think we've solved our problem." She picked up the bowl of ice and led him into his bedroom.

So this is what a whore feels like, Shoshana thought, loathing herself. She kicked her legs out of bed and looked across to Mana. He was sleeping peacefully, a childlike look on his smooth face. She didn't hate him—she couldn't bring herself to that. And he had been so grateful the night before. Then they had made love again, at least it was love for Mana. For her, she decided, it was more like two dogs mating in a plush garden. The second time, Shoshana only had to use the ice once. The third time, it had been normal. It was Mana's first successful sexual experience.

Shoshana walked across the huge room and drew the curtains back from across the picture window that overlooked the Mediterranean. The morning sun streamed in, flowing over her. It was the same sun that had waked Israel first, over two thousand miles to the east. She stood there, staring out to sea, toward her home.

"Rose," Mana called from the bed.

The use of her alias brought her back to reality and a bitter taste filled her mouth. She was using her body to get what she wanted and that made her a whore. She walked back to bed and crawled in next to him.

"Our vacation is almost over," she said and drew a fingernail down his chest and scratched his stomach. "I'm going to miss you very, very much."

"Rose," he said, still at the beginning. "I don't want this to end. Please, will you marry me?"

She wanted to cry but there it was. "Oh yes." Tears filled her eyes. "No, I can't."

"Why not? I love you." He was pleading.

"Oh, Is'al, you know how I feel about you"—she stroked his cheek and laid her breasts against him—"but there are so many problems." He started to protest but she hushed him. "There is your religion and, well, I'm really nothing. I don't speak your language and must learn it first." Now she was rubbing his crotch and drawing her fingernails along his erection. "And this is very important, Is'al. I will only marry you if your family approves."

"They will love you," he promised. She stopped him from talking with a kiss and they made love again, but she had to use the last of the ice.

Afterward, they lay together. Then: "Please come with me to Baghdad and meet my family."

5

It was a retake of the same scene Matt had starred in the last time he had seen his squadron commander, Lieutenant Colonel Locke. Only this time, the setting was different. Instead of standing in Locke's Spartan office at Luke Air Force Base in Arizona, he was at RAF Stonewood in England and the office was a shambles. The noise and activity of a tactical fighter squadron settling into his new home was a constant distraction. Matt wondered how long Locke would keep him standing at attention before chewing him out. Come on, he thought, get it over with. Just what the hell can you do to me? I was only eight days late and what the hell, no one needed me for anything.

Matt Pontowski would not have been so cocksure of himself if he had known what the look on his commander's face meant. It was the rock-hard look of determination that froze his features when he went about the business the United States Air Force paid him for—combat. The last time Locke had worn that particular expression he had killed seven men. But those men had never seen his face in the impersonal and antiseptic arena of aerial combat. They were lucky.

"Lieutenant," Locke finally said, his voice measured and calm. Matt stifled the grin that wanted to break out. He wasn't particularly worried about what the man could do to him. Hell, he mused, this guy is a lightweight. Locke caught the smirk on Matt's face and correctly interpreted it. "It's too bad you take your commissioning oath so lightly. This may come as a shock to you, but the President of the United States does place a special trust and confidence in you."

Matt wanted to laugh. "I think I know much better than most what the President of the United States expects of me." He had made his point and almost added, "Now do your damnedest, Colonel, do your damnedest."

Locke did. He was tired of the irresponsible young man in front of him who thought rules were for others. His voice never lost its reasonable tone and his face did not change. "Right. You overstayed your leave eight days and made no attempt to report in. A telephone call was in order. You should have contacted the squadron and extended your leave."

"Excuse me, Colonel," Matt interrupted, "but just what phone number was I to call? The squadron was moving."

"Apparently, you can't read either. Read your leave slip. The phone number to call in case of emergencies or requests for extension is on the front." Locke handed him his leave slip. Matt read it and felt his self-confidence starting to erode. "Now that we have *that* small matter straightened out, is there anything else you wish to say in your defense before we continue?"

"Colonel, you're making this sound like a court-martial."

The lieutenant was still trying to reassert his position, gain an unspoken dominance over the man.

"You'll have your chance for a court-martial in a few moments." For the first time, Matt understood how serious Locke was. Then he saw the look in the older man's eyes and was suddenly worried. "As of now, you are grounded while I initiate the paperwork for an Article Fifteen."

Article 15, nonjudicial punishment under the UCMJ, the Uniform Code of Military Justice, was much like a traffic ticket but with much more harmful fallout for an officer. Good sergeants were expected to get at least one as they made the system work, but it was the kiss of death for an officer. Article 15s were handed out by commanders as punishment for breaches in discipline. Officers were expected to give them, not get them, and were rarely promoted if they had one in their file.

"That's coming down pretty damn hard."

"No problem, Lieutenant. You don't have to accept it." Matt breathed a sigh of relief. He had forgotten that an Article 15 had to be voluntarily accepted in place of punishment under a court-martial—much like plea bargaining. "If you choose not to accept it," Locke continued, "that leaves me two options, I can drop the Article Fifteen and we're back to square one or I can initiate court-martial proceedings." The look on Matt's face told Locke that the lieutenant didn't believe he'd do the last. Too bad.

"Also, you were on the promotion list for captain. I redlined you. You're going to stay a lieutenant for a while longer—until you start acting like a captain and stop screwin' around."

"Colonel, this sounds like overkill." Matt was still trying.

"Then go for the court-martial, Lieutenant, go for it."

Matt got the message. "If I accept the Article Fifteen, what punishment are you going to lay on me?"

"Six weeks' restriction to base."

"Anything else?" The tone in Matt's voice indicated he thought it was pretty steep.

"Well, to keep you busy, you'll be in charge of the self-help project we've got under way here making the squadron building suitable for human life."

"Self-help? Where we paint and fix up the squadron instead of Civil Engineers? That's their job. Shit, Colonel, self-help is just an excuse for the Civil Engineers' not doing their job.''

"Lieutenant Pontowski, you're not reading my lips. Try it. It'll save a lot of confusion on your part. You're about to become the best construction engineer in the United States Air Force in Europe. Dismissed.''

"Colonel, I—''

"I said, 'Dismissed.' Also have the flight surgeon check your hearing. If you can't hear me, we may have to ground you permanently.'' Matt saluted and beat a hasty retreat.

"You've had it, you fucking meathead,'' Matt muttered, leaving the squadron and searching for a telephone to make a private call. Twenty minutes later he was talking to Melissa Courtney-Smith.

"Matt, I'm sorry,'' Melissa told him, "but Mr. Fraser clears all telephone calls to the President and he isn't in yet. It's still early in the morning here.''

"Melissa, I have to talk to Grandpop.'' She relented and put him through, aware that Fraser would try to fire her if he found out.

Zack Pontowski listened to the recital of Matt's troubles. He smiled when Matt told him that his squadron commander was holding up his promotion to captain and "offering" him an Article 15 all because he overstayed his leave. Just like his father, Pontowski thought. "Matt, you wanted to be an officer in the Air Force and fly. Well, in my book, that means you take the good with the bad. Sounds to me like you've got some *bad* headed your way.'' He listened to more protests before he cut him off. "Do you remember when you came home from school, I think it was the seventh grade, claiming your teacher had punished you unfairly for pouring water down a girl's back?''

Matt remembered only too well. The elder Pontowski had said that he had gotten into trouble by himself and he could get out by himself. Then he had grounded Matt for a month when he learned what had really happened and about all the other trouble the twelve-year-old had been in.

"Your grandmother's quite ill,'' he told Matt. "I'm in her bedroom and . . . right, here she is.'' He handed the phone over to his wife and picked up his read file. That boy's been up to something else, he decided. He's on his own now. He made a mental note to tell Fraser not to intercede on Matt's behalf.

"Passport," the Iraqi customs official demanded, threatening Shoshana with a hard look. She pulled the bogus Canadian passport out of her handbag and tried to look unconcerned as she handed it over. It was her first test and her heart was pounding. The man thumbed through the passport, studying the visa stamps. Habish's warnings about Arabs reverting to type in their own homeland came back. The customs man glanced up at her then back to her passport.

Shoshana tried to act nonchalant as she waited. She glanced around the customs area in the Baghdad airport. A bit on the seedy side, she thought. She forced herself to concentrate. He'll ask me some question, try to trick me. She went over the details in her passport. She was thankful for the cover name Habish had chosen for her—it was easy to remember.

"Name!" the official barked.

"Rose Louise Temple." She had anticipated his question! Her confidence soared, shattering the doubts and fears that were showering over her.

"Religion?" He was still acting skeptical.

"Protestant."

"Denomination please." He was somewhat mollified and not so aggressive.

"None," she answered. The man looked at her, confused. Then Mana joined her and stared at the official who quickly validated her passport and dashed his initials across the entry stamp. "Welcome to Iraq, Miss Temple. I hope you enjoy your stay." He forced a smile and looked at Mana, not at her. He had made a bad mistake. The Mana family was not to be trifled with in Iraq.

Nothing about Baghdad surprised her as they drove from the airport. The streets were dusty, the buildings on the seedy side, like the airport. The same Arabic music she had heard in Israel assaulted her ears when she rolled the window down at a stop light. And then it hit her—she could have been in East Jerusalem. The sights and the sounds were the same. Again, her confidence climbed. The change in Is'al did bother her, though; he was much more aggressive than in Spain. But in the chauffeur-driven car his family had sent to meet him, he reverted to the original Is'al. She hoped Habish was wrong.

"This is Sa'adon Street," Is'al told her. The car stopped in front of an elegant old hotel. "And this is the Baghdad Hotel."

Inside, the Baghdad Hotel reminded her of an old movie. It was exactly as she imagined a luxury hotel in an Arab city. None of the run-down look invaded the lobby. The room was true to type: high ceiling, spacious, with large windows that opened onto Sa'adon Street. The bathroom was old-fashioned but immaculate. "Oh, Is'al," she beamed, "I love it."

"Rose, I must tell you now that I probably won't see you for a few days. I must attend to my family and arrange for your introduction." She smiled at his formal, stilted English. Only in the most intimate moments did he become relaxed. "I'll call you as soon as I can."

"I don't mind waiting, but please don't stay away too long. I brought some books to read and"—she paused as if a thought had just hit her—"can you arrange for a tutor to teach me Arabic? I must learn your language." He nodded, a pleased look on his face. "And I can do some sightseeing and shopping." His frown told her she had said the wrong thing.

"You must stay in the hotel until I call."

Has he reverted to type? she thought. I've got to establish some independence or I can never make contact with Habish. "Oh, Is'al." She smiled at him and touched his cheek. "You know how lonely I get." He knew no such thing but she felt no need to be rational. "Let the hotel arrange a guide and car for me." He only shook his head. "Please"—now she was wheedling—"I do need the exercise. Otherwise, I'll have to spend all my time at the swimming pool." A shocked look crossed his face. He knew the stir she would cause in Baghdad society once she was seen in a swimsuit. "Is'al," she breathed his name, "I want to find the most exquisite bowl to hold the ice." He crumbled and beat a hasty retreat, promising to arrange something.

The next morning, Mana telephoned, telling her that his sister, Nadya, had agreed to be her guide and teach her some Arabic, but that formal lessons were out of the question. She told him that was perfect and hoped they could meet today. Mana arranged for his sister and aunt to meet her for lunch at the hotel. For the next two hours, Shoshana dressed carefully, picking out her most conservative clothes. She was certain Mana wanted her to be carefully chaperoned and watched—a definite problem.

At exactly one o'clock, Shoshana's phone rang and the clerk announced that Nadya Mana was waiting for her in the lobby. Shoshana resigned herself to the ordeal in front of her and went downstairs. "Miss Temple?" a voice called the moment the elevator doors opened. A beautiful young girl of perhaps twenty was waiting with an older woman, an obvious chaperone. Nadya Mana tried to act very Western as she extended her hand and Shoshana could tell by her expensive Parisian clothes that she was the Mana family's pampered and spoiled pet.

Lunch proved to be delightful and before too long they were giggling and carrying on like two schoolgirls. Afterward, they went to Shoshana's room to examine her wardrobe. "Is'al," Nadya said in exasperation, "should have bought you tons of clothes. Oh, these are beautiful," she added hurriedly, not wanting to offend Shoshana, "but he should have." She stomped a dainty foot to emphasize her point.

"He wanted to," Shoshana explained, "but I wouldn't let him."

"Why?" Nadya was incredulous.

Shoshana led her by the hand to the bed and set her down. "You must understand, I love your brother very much. Of course, I can't tell him that." Nadya nodded in understanding. Now they were conspirators. "In my country, a woman only accepts expensive gifts from a man if she is his mistress or his wife. I will not be Is'al's mistress."

Again, Nadya nodded. "But in my country it is different. Here, a man must show his wealth and how much he cares for you. Come, we're going to buy you many clothes and Is'al is going to pay for it all!" They laughed like conspirators and hurried to the waiting car, the aunt still in tow.

Nadya's chaperone was asleep, snoring loudly by the time they reached their first stop. They left her in the car and went into a boutique that would have done a Parisian couturier proud. The two women who ran the shop chased everyone else out and fawned over Nadya. Within minutes, Shoshana was in a back room trying on the many dresses Nadya had thrown at her. Shoshana appraised herself in the mirror, decided she liked one, and went out to show Nadya. But she couldn't find the girl. Suddenly, the women did not speak English at all. Puzzled, Shoshana went back to the fitting room. She heard a low moan from a room down the hall and walked back, checking to be sure she was alone and careful not to make any noise. The door was slightly ajar and she pushed it open to see inside. Nadya was locked in an embrace with a young man, her skirt up around her hips and her panties on the floor.

Terminally frustrated was the only way to describe Matt. Locke had promised him that he would become the best civil engineer in USAFE, United States Air Force in Europe, and he was determined to prove his squadron commander wrong. But not being able to fly was what hurt the worst, for Locke had grounded him during his forty-five-day confinement to base. He had reluctantly "accepted" the Article 15 Locke had "offered" him after talking to a lawyer. The lawyer had reviewed his case and simply said that he would rather represent the Air Force in Matt's upcoming court-martial. He got the idea that Locke was serious.

On the first day after the Article 15 had been administered, Matt had shown up in the squadron building at exactly 7:30 in the morning in a clean flight suit. He dropped in on mission briefings and listened to what the crews were planning for their flight. But he had to stop that, for it was a form of pure torture that was pushing him into a pit of despair. Then he hung around the scheduling desk drinking coffee and watched the crews go out to fly. That made him feel worse. At the end of the first day, his flight suit was still clean.

The routine repeated itself for two more days and Matt slipped deeper into a sour funk, wallowing in self-pity. On Thursday, Locke stopped him in the hall and asked for a "How goes it" on the self-help project.

"Sir," Matt admitted sourly, "I haven't got a clue."

"That's a true statement," Locke said, looking around the squadron. Nothing had been done for three days. "It's going to be a long forty-two days." He walked away. Matt's first thought was to strangle Locke, but instead late that afternoon, he found himself knocking at Locke's office door, determined to restate his case and at least get back on flying status.

"Damn it, Colonel Locke," he protested. "Rumor around the squadron has it that you raised all sorts of hell when you were a lieutenant. Why are you coming down so hard on me now?"

Locke motioned for him to sit down. For a moment, he looked into his own past and a sadness came over him. "Because I was going down the same road you're on right now." Matt started to interrupt, his case made. Locke held a hand up. "But the best officer who ever strapped on an F-Four saved me from myself by letting me sweat out a pretrial investigation for a court-martial. He knew I was going to get out of it because of a technicality—but I didn't. One other thing; I deserved to be court-martialed. I was guilty." He let it sink in. "That officer was Muddy Waters."

Silence hung in the room. Waters was one of the Air Force's legends, the man who had taken the 45th Tactical Fighter Wing into combat in the Persian Gulf and died getting them out. Now Locke's squadron was part of the 45th.

Locke leaned forward over his desk. "Waters taught me the meaning of leadership. Without leadership, a fighter puke isn't worth shit. And the key is a sense of responsibility—I didn't have it then—and you don't have it now." The silence came down hard.

"Sir," Matt finally said, "may I ask you a question about Waters?" He had overhead the old heads BS in the bar and every now and then, the legend of Muddy Waters would come up. "Did he really give you his call sign just before he bought it?"

Locke stared at him—hard. The memories were painful. "Yeah. He made me Wolf Zero-One just before he was killed surrendering the base." Another long pause. "He gave me the responsibility of bringing the Forty-fifth home. I did."

"It was different then," Matt protested. "The Mideast is all sorted out now. I'll never fight a war—"

"That's what I said."

Something turned inside Matt. Locke followed Waters into hell and came out forever changed. Long ago, Matt Pontowski had admitted to himself that Locke was probably the best pilot he would ever meet. And now he knew that Locke was a true rarity—a leader. "Sir, I want to be a leader, but what in the hell can a lieutenant do?"

"Leadership for a lieutenant means doing the best job you can and taking care of your people."

"And who do I take care of?" Matt asked, bitterness in his voice.

"Your backseater. Don't kill him. I happen to like Haney."

"And not me."

"There's nothing to like. Sure, you're a charmer and the ladies think you're God's gift to studdom, but there's nothing to you."

Locke's hard words cut into him. A hard resolve came over him to prove Locke dead wrong. "Colonel, about this self-help project, I don't even know where to start."

"Talk to the best NCO you can find." Locke looked and then nodded at the door, his way of telling Matt that the conversation was over. Matt stood up, saluted, and left.

The next morning, Matt found the NCO he was looking for, Master Sergeant Charlie Ferguson. Ferguson was the squadron's senior-ranking sergeant and considered himself the unofficial "first shirt" for the squadron. He knew how to make the Air Force system work and, within hours, the lumber, plaster, and paint they needed were in the building. For help, Ferguson went to the "Detention Facility," Air Force-ese for jail, and had six inmates released to his custody for a work detail.

Matt was learning a lot about construction and how the Air Force worked. He had never realized that there was so much involved in just putting up a simple wall or doing a little electrical wiring or plumbing even though he had majored in civil engineering. He also learned how to bypass most of the Air Force bureaucracy's paperwork. But he could not avoid all of it. He was getting the job done and would have been all right if it hadn't been for the ceiling in the lounge.

Ferguson and his convict crew of laborers were almost finished with the lounge. They had installed a kitchen area and a bar, paneled the walls, and were ready to mount indirect lighting against the ceiling. But the ceiling was too high and Matt thought that they should drop it about two feet. He and Ferguson went on one of their "requisitioning runs." The military contracting system generates tons of surplus and Ferguson found what they needed buried in a pile of junk that had been tagged for disposal. One the way back to the squadron building, the colonel who served as the base's RM, the resource manager, stopped them. They explained that what they had found was surplus and that they were using it for a self-help project in their squadron. When they couldn't produce the paperwork, the RM had them return it all.

The next day, Ferguson ginned up the required forms and Matt took them over to the RM's office for an official signature. But he couldn't get in to see the RM because a crew of workmen were installing a new dropped ceiling in his office using the same large acoustic tiles and hangers that Ferguson had unearthed. Matt was furious. That night, he and Ferguson's crew of six convicts visited the RM's office and did a quick bit of midnight requisitioning. By the next morning, the ceiling was safely installed in the squadron's lounge.

The RM had a very strong suspicion about what had happened to his ceiling and was in the squadron before eight o'clock in the morning. For a moment, Matt was certain the man was going to have a heart attack when he saw *his* ceiling. Before they had lifted the large tiles into place, two of Matt's "helpers" had dropped their trousers and bent over. A coat of paint was applied to the buttocks of each in the squadron colors of black and gold and each tile was pressed against the makeshift templates. Now the ceiling was decorated with a mass of black and gold butt prints. The RM sputtered and, at a loss for words, stormed out of the squadron lounge.

Matt and his crew were busy turning the tiles over when Locke came into the lounge. He shook his head and told Matt to report to his office. Once there, Matt paid for the ceiling with a chewing out of legendary proportions. Locke considered the matter closed but the RM had other ideas. Within hours, Matt was under investigation by the Office of Special Investigations for theft of government property. Ferguson came to his rescue two days later when he produced a bill of sale from a local civilian supplier that stated they had bought the ceiling tiles from him. Matt was off the hook but in the bad graces of every colonel in the wing. With the exception of the NCO Club, the squadron building had the best interior decoration of any building on base.

* * *

Romance and clothes-dominated Nadya Mana's life and nothing else seemed to interest her. Shoshana was shocked when the girl mentioned she would celebrate her eighteenth birthday next month and Shoshana realized that she was dealing with the mentality and impetuousness of a spoiled teenager. On most outings, they met with three of Nadya's friends who were also chaperoned by older women and Shoshana found herself swamped by giggly girls, all talking about boys and clothes, exactly like her friends when she was thirteen.

Shoshana was amazed how the girls plotted to break away from their chaperones to meet their latest boyfriend until she realized the older women deliberately looked the other way. But the rules didn't apply to her and Nadya's aunt stayed attached like a leech.

Panic started to build when she realized that she was being carefully watched and would never be able to establish contact with her team unless this changed drastically. Mana provided the key when he visited her one night and told her that she wouldn't be meeting his family.

"I'll not be your mistress!" she screamed at him and started to pack. Mana tried to stop her but much to her surprise, she discovered she was stronger. Like most of his class, Mana had never engaged in physical exercise or hard work. His muscles were as soft as his face. Then she turned playful, physically dominating him while they made love, using pain instead of ice to control his response. He screamed in agony and begged for more. Later, before he left, it was agreed that she could find a tutor to teach her Arabic but that Nadya and her aunt would have to accompany her.

Nadya sulked when she accompanied Shoshana to meet her tutor, a small wisp of a woman, one of the struggling Iraqi middle class who ran a language school for foreigners. The girl would sit huffily in a corner of the room while her aunt would go to sleep, snoring loudly. "Nadya, I feel so bad about you having to wait for me," Shoshana consoled her. "Why don't you visit one of your friends while I'm at my lesson? Your aunt can take me to you if you're not back." Nadya eagerly accepted, seeing an opportunity to meet her boyfriend. It worked perfectly, Shoshana would go into her lesson, the aunt would go to sleep, and Nadya would disappear. Just before the lesson would end, Nadya would reappear with new makeup and freshly combed hair.

One day, the woman who normally instructed her was sick and Shoshana had a substitute—Gad Habish. The woman who ran the school was Mossad's Baghdad station chief.

Nothing in Fraser's face or actions betrayed the cold fury that was rolling through him as he scanned the switchboard's computerized telephone log that listed every phone call the President made or received. He could not control the outgoing calls, for it was his job to do the President's bidding. But he was determined to control the incoming calls and the log was clear—a call had reached the President without his okay. He noted who was on duty at the time of the call. Melissa, he fumed to himself. That bitch had stabbed him in the back! He jabbed at the intercom button on his communications panel and ordered Melissa Courtney Smith into his office.

"Melissa," he began, his voice calm and businesslike, "I noticed a call reached the President without my okay. You know anything about it?"

Melissa looked at the offending entry in the log. "I cleared that one. It was a personal call from Matt. You weren't in yet."

Fraser's lips pursed into a thoughtful moue. She had done the right thing. If the President found out he was withholding personal phone calls . . . well, he preferred not to think about that one. Zack Pontowski's anger never surfaced, but the results were something to behold. "Okay, next time memo me, though."

"Sir"—she gave him a confused look—"I think I did. Let me check the files." She hurried out of the office and was back with a memo in a few minutes. Nothing was ever thrown away; everything was carefully filed and stored as a record of the Pontowski administration. "It did come across your desk." She didn't mention that she had buried it in a pile of low-priority memos that Fraser often ignored and farmed right back to her for action.

"Okay, next time make sure I initial it." His face and tone were all reasonableness. "Melissa, you know the success of a presidential administration rests on the flow of information to the President. I cannot let him get inundated with trivia." She nodded and left. They were still at a stalemate. Fraser wanted to fire her and lock up the office of the presidency in his control. Melissa had other priorities and, when she was honest with herself, she would admit that she loved Zack Pontowski and wanted to protect him.

Thomas Patrick Fraser was power-hungry. He longed for it like some sought money or fame. He had money, gained in a slash-and-burn career organizing corporate takeovers. But what he had always wanted was power over people—the ability to call the shots and make others jump at his bidding. And that ultimately meant politics. He was a realist and knew that while he had the wealth and connections to be elected a senator, he did not have the charisma or the long-term staying power to reach the ultimate pinnacle—the presidency of the United States. So he chose an alternate road; he would be a kingmaker and become the chief aide and adviser to the man he would make President. The man he had selected to back was Zack Pontowski. It may have been a mistake.

Normally, a chief of staff is the President's chief adviser, but in the case of Zack Pontowski, there was no one single adviser, for he listened to many sources and then made up his own mind. Perhaps his wife came as close as any to being his principal adviser, and while he always listened to what she had to say, he still made up his own mind.

Goddamn it, he swore to himself, I made Pontowski and I will control him. His intercom buzzed. It was the President.

"Tom, I want to meet the delegation when they arrive and let them know this is a friendly meeting." A group of three congressmen and two senators who were sometimes called the Israeli lobby were scheduled to meet with the President in fifteen minutes.

"Good idea," Fraser agreed. "Want me at the entrance with you?"

"Not necessary. But I do want you at the meeting. Bring the briefing books." The briefing books were the thick three-ring binders that were constantly updated and held all the information needed to review a subject. In this case, the subject was Israel and the Syrian-Egyptian treaty.

Fraser was waiting for the President and the delegation when they entered the Oval Office. He said nothing and took notes during the meeting. His mind raced as he listened, ferreting out the implications of what was being said. The delegation was worried about the latest signs of cooperation between Syria and Egypt and saw an inherent danger in the treaty for Israel. Pontowski agreed with them, and then he dropped the bombshell. "We have intelligence reports that the treaty contains a secret protocol fusing the Syrian and Egyptian military command and control systems." He didn't mention the suspected Iraqi connection. That would have sent the delegation into orbit.

The delegation's worst fears were confirmed and they demanded to know what the President was going to do about it. Pontowski assured them that the State Department was talking to the Israeli government but that the Israeli prime minister was not overly concerned at this time.

"Mr. President"—it was the junior member of the delegation—"we are also concerned about Iraq. We have learned that they are once again purchasing equipment from a German firm, WisserChemFabrik, that could be used in the manufacture of nuclear arms."

Fraser grabbed the Iraqi notebook and flipped to the armed forces section. He handed it to the President. "That machinery is earmarked for a petrochemical plant outside Kirkuk," he said, sotto voce, loud enough for the delegation to hear. "The embargo against anything that could be used for nuclear weapons or any significant weapon system is still in force." Pontowski adjusted his reading glasses and scanned the notebook. When he was certain that the notebook contained no references to CIA activities in Iraq, he handed it to the junior congressman.

"Worrisome," Pontowski agreed, "but not critical at this time. We are certain that Iraq is being denied anything that could be used to make an atomic bomb. Besides, Iraq has received stern warnings not to even think about nuclear weapons. We don't believe this equipment can be used for nerve gas production. We're watching it."

"Mr. President"—the young congressman was relentless—"nerve gas is the poor man's nuclear bomb—"

"Which neither we nor the Israelis," Pontowski interrupted, "believe the Arabs will use against Israel."

"May I ask why?" The junior delegate wouldn't let it go.

"Because that could invite the Israelis to respond in kind or even go nuclear," Pontowski said. Loud protestations broke out from the delegation declaring that the Israelis only had protective equipment for nerve gas and that it was unfounded speculation about them having a nuclear capability and that, even if they did, they would never use it.

Pontowski waited patiently until the hubbub subsided. "Gentlemen, can I interest you in an intelligence briefing on the current situation? I'll send General Cox from the DIA with a team of briefers over to you for an update."

Fraser almost interrupted and recommended the CIA give the briefing, but that would have overstepped his bounds and upset Pontowski. He kept quiet and calculated his next move. Why did the President specifically say Cox? After the congressional delegation had left, the President sat thoughtfully. "Tom, what do you think?"

Now Fraser had to play it absolutely straight and give him the best advice he could. "I don't think the Iraqis are a factor at this time. But we need to watch the entire situation and start considering alternate scenarios." Fraser was suggesting that the President assemble a task force of his people to start playing what-if games and come up with suggested positions for the United States. "Also, we need to hear from the other side."

"Who did you have in mind?"

"Some CEOs from oil corporations have asked to see you. I've been stalling them. Talking to them might be a good way to show that you're striving to maintain the status quo in the Middle East."

"Oil. It always comes down to that." Pontowski didn't expect an answer. Even now, the United States was importing over half of its oil supply and much of that came from the Middle East. He knew that the oil industry simply wanted to keep it flowing and avoid another Arab oil embargo like that of 1974. "Okay, arrange it." Fraser felt a surge of triumph; he was still getting what he wanted.

"I suppose"—the President smiled—"that Mrs. Allison is among the group."

"She's heading the delegation."

"Please tell B.J. not to be late."

6

After a month, Shoshana considered herself a fixture of the Baghdad Hotel. She had settled into a comfortable routine and while Mana's family did not label her his mistress, neither was she seen as his fiancée. Little by little, Mana loosened the reins and she was allowed more freedom to move about on her own. She was careful never to break her established pattern because when she went out alone one of the family chauffeurs always drove her. At least she had met his older brother, a brigadier general who was rebuilding the Iraqi Air Force, so there was some progress toward meeting his father. She was willing to wait. She sighed out of boredom and called the desk, summoning the chauffeur. The highlight of the day's activities was her language lesson. She sighed again.

Gad Habish had become a regular at the café off Rashid Street and the waiter automatically brought him a cup of coffee and a newspaper. Habish made no pretense at being an Iraqi but used the cover of a German businessman in the café. Since he tipped well and insisted on speaking Arabic, he was readily accepted and welcomed. This morning, the agent who posed as an artist was waiting for him with news. They chatted for a few minutes before the agent mentioned the chemical factory located near Kirkuk.

"It's complete," the agent said. Habish talked about the weather. "A technician from WisserChemFabrik says they will be testing a new insecticide in the next week or two," the agent added as Habish talked about the unusually cool weather for September.

Habish left the café first and strolled back to his car. He drove to the safe house Avidar worked out of and changed his identity cards, becoming a substitute teacher. He left the

93

car behind and rode the dilapidated bus system to the language school. Substitute teachers did not drive cars in Iraq. He was waiting for Shoshana when she arrived for her lesson.

"When did you last see Mana?" he asked.

"Last week. He spends a lot of his time in Kirkuk where the chemical factory is being built. He should be back today or tomorrow."

"Does he still talk about his work?"

"That's all he talks about now," Shoshana told him. "He tries so hard to impress me."

"Why?" Habish demanded.

For a moment, Shoshana hesitated, not wanting to confide in her case officer the nature of their sexual relationship and Mana's total subservience to her. "He needs to prove his worth to me," she said. Then she slowly told him how she dominated him in bed. Habish wanted to know every detail and questioned her relentlessly.

When Habish was certain he knew everything, he carefully weighed Shoshana's position. "If he starts to talk about the new plant at Kirkuk the next time you see him, become very interested."

"Why? It would be a change in our relationship."

"Because the plant is finished and they are testing a new nerve gas next week. Find out as much as you can."

"He'll become suspicious if I press too hard."

"I don't think so. Given a chance, he'll talk endlessly. Just listen."

"Then what do you want me to do?" she asked.

Habish looked straight at her. "The next time he goes to Kirkuk, go with him, learn all you can." He stood up and left. Outside the building, he lost himself in the crowd and worked his way back to the safe house, making sure he wasn't being followed.

Shoshana returned directly to her hotel room and drew a bath. She felt dirty for the way she was using Mana. She turned her feelings for him over and over, examining them. She smiled when she thought of his boyish eagerness to please her. Reluctantly, she admitted that she was fond of the Iraqi engineer and didn't want to see him hurt. The smile faded when an image of Habish threatening Mana materialized. Because of their intensely intimate relationship, she had unwittingly developed strong protective feelings for the Iraqi and she feared what Habish might do.

The phone rang. She grabbed a towel and hurried to answer it. It was Mana. He had just returned from Kirkuk, was still at the airport, and wanted to see her immediately. She told him to hurry for she did miss him.

She hung up, sat down, and cried, hating what she had become.

The squadron self-help project was finished and Matt was basking in compliments from his fellow pilots and wizzos. Even Locke seemed pleased. Charlie Ferguson, being a grizzled old master sergeant, took it all in stride and only saw it as business as usual. For Matt, it had been a lesson in accomplishment and he took pride in what he had done. Then his name appeared on the schedule for a "ride" in the simulator to refresh his emergency procedures. He was going back on the flying schedule and he saw an end to his troubles.

Afraid he had grown rusty, Matt hit the books, reviewing every procedure, rule, and regulation that applied to F-15s. Then he turned to weapons employment, refreshing his memory on delivery parameters and techniques. Contrary to popular opinion, flying fighters is more than strapping on a jet and taking off for a few fun-filled minutes roaring around the sky. It takes hours of constant study, review, and planning on the ground, and as long as Matt flew high-performance fighters, it would never stop.

After the session in the simulator, he flew a requalification flight with Locke in the backseat before he was teamed with his old WSO, Mike Haney. Locke noted with satisfaction that Matt had his attitude on straight, was going by the rules, and had all the promise of being an outstanding fighter jock. He decided that Matt had finally earned his captain's bars.

Early one morning, when Matt was sleeping in after a night flight with Haney, an Inspector General team hit the base for an unannounced Operational Readiness Inspection—an ORI—the make-or-break test of a peacetime unit. For four days, the IG team would throw a series of wartime tasks at the wing, demanding they demonstrate their proficiency in everything from mass casualty exercises to emergency buildup of weapons to flying planned wartime sortie rates and simulated combat missions.

Matt's first indication that the ORI was under way came when a pounding on his BOQ door woke him. A voice told him to report to the squadron ASAP, that an IG team was on base, and that a "recall" was under way. Like everyone else, he did not shave, brush his teeth, or wash because the IG team would want to see a "sense of urgency." A freshly shaved face during a recall said somebody did not have the proper sense of urgency. But the team that had hit Stonewood liked to play catch-22 games and zinged the wing for lacking in military appearance.

Less than an hour after the start of the recall, the squadron was fully manned and configured for its wartime mission. The crews waited patiently in the squadron as Maintenance finished uploading live ordnance on their aircraft. Then a crew would run out to its assigned aircraft, perform a pre-flight, and check in on status with the command post, ready to launch. However, no aircraft would actually takeoff loaded with live ordnance. Matt and Haney were not assigned an aircraft and had to wait in the squadron building while the frenzied activity went on around them. Neither liked being a spectator. Because they were in the squadron and not in a bunker manning a jet, they were among the first to hear the rumor—the wing had already failed the inspection.

Slowly, fact replaced the rumors. One of the inspectors had noted a mistake in the command post when the on-duty controller decoded the first alert message. The controller had sent the wing into a more advanced stage of readiness than the message called for. The IG team claimed the wing had automatically failed the ORI. The wing commander was arguing that merely jumping to a higher state of alert only meant the wing would be ready sooner to meet its wartime mission. A general from headquarters was called in to render a decision and the ORI was put on hold.

Charlie Ferguson explained it all to Matt. "It was a legit hit," the grizzled old sergeant said, "but not worth busting an ORI. Looks like we got a chickenshit team doing the inspection."

Later on, Matt complained to Locke about it, sensing a gross injustice. "What the hell does this have to do with hosing the bad guys down?"

The squadron commander looked Matt square in the eye.

"Not a thing, Captain. Not a single goddamn thing." He handed Matt his captain's bars, turned, and walked away.

Headquarters United States Air Force in Europe sent Brigadier General Donald "Bull" Heath to RAF Stonewood to determine if Matt's wing had indeed failed its Operational Readiness Inspection. General Heath was scathing in his rebuke of the Inspector General team chief when he reviewed the technicality the IG team had based its decision on. He lived up to his reputation and nickname when he told the unfortunate colonel heading the team that he had his head so far up his ass that he needed a Plexiglas window in his stomach to see where he was going. By the time Heath left the base five minutes later, a case of Plexiglas cleaner, commonly known as "whale sperm," had magically appeared in the offices the IG team was occupying during the inspection. Master Sergeant Charlie Ferguson claimed to be totally innocent and that he had been in the area on legitimate business.

The morale of the wing skyrocketed and the inspection was back in full swing. No matter where an inspector went, he or she was bound to see a bottle of "whale sperm." On the last day of the inspection, the weather deteriorated and all of the low-level and gunnery-range missions had to be canceled. The IG team was still smarting from the constant sight of Plexiglas cleaner bottles and wanted to find a reason to bust the wing. Frustrated, they tasked the wing to fly an excessive number of high-altitude missions, hoping that Maintenance or Operations would screw up. But the wing met the challenge as the inspection ran out. Finally, the last mission was laid on Matt's squadron. Jack Locke shook his head when he saw the last mission being grease-penciled up on the scheduling board. His squadron was tasked to fly a one-versus-one, basic fighter maneuvers (BFM) mission. He called his superior, the wing's deputy for operations, to confirm what he saw. "Boss, is that chicken Colonel Roger 'Ramjet' Raider, the IG's gift to the tactical fighter community, who's going along for a ride in the backseat of number one?" he asked.

"One and the same," the deputy for operations told him.

"Why my squadron? The guy's a clueless wonder."

"It's an unannounced check ride," the DO told him. "The IG is still gunning for us and I want you to lead it. Keep it simple and put one of your best sticks in number two." The DO broke the connection as Roger "Ramjet" Raider walked into the squadron building. Locke puzzled for a few moments over whom he would tap to fly the second jet. A BFM mission was relatively undemanding but he wanted his best pilot. He told the scheduler to get Matt and Haney into the briefing room while he blew some hot air for Ramjet to suck on.

The mission briefing Locke conducted was a masterpiece of standardization, starting with a time hack and continuing through every required item on the briefing checklist. Matt and Haney exchanged unbelieving looks when they noticed the colonel was making too many notes on his Mission Data Card. Ramjet was writing down information that he should have automatically memorized. A fighter jock's number one tool is his brain and Ramjet wasn't using his.

The flight itself proved to be routine as Locke and Matt worked through a series of basic fighter maneuvers. Haney was bored silly in the pit of number two and had little to do. Matt was enjoying the mission. "Talk to me, babes," he told Haney as they set up for their last engagement.

"We're the defender on this one, the Old Man is the attacker. He'll convert to our six, do a quarter plane and zoom and fall in behind us. He'll drive to lag and try to herd us around the sky." Haney paused. Matt could tell from the tone in his voice he didn't like being a target. "Before he does all that to us, why don't you reef hard into him while he's still converting to our six and force him into a scissors. That ought to get Ramjet's attention."

"Aah, I don't know," Matt said. "Maybe we ought to keep it simple and let Locke eat our shorts."

"A scissors is a basic fighter maneuver, the boss briefed it, and he did say to do it if the situation was right."

"Sounds good," Matt allowed. "Let's do it if we can."

"Colonel Raider," Locke said over the intercom in his jet, "I'm going to quarter plane and zoom on this engagement. But I'm going to make a deliberate mistake and give the defender just enough room to counterturn on me and enter into a scissors. But he's got to be damn good to see it. So don't be surprised if you see his nose pitch back into us when we're still ninety degrees off his heading." Locke was worried about the heavy breathing he could hear coming over the intercom. Come on, Ramjet, he thought, this is no biggy.

As briefed on the ground, the two jets positioned and Locke slashed down onto Matt, rapidly closing to his six o'clock position and almost ninety degrees off Matt's heading. To kill his high overtake speed, Locke pulled his nose up and traded his airspeed for altitude before rolling and pulling his nose back to Matt's six o'clock. But Matt saw that Locke had given him enough room to counterturn and reefed his fighter into a hard upward turn, bringing his nose onto Locke. Now the two were climbing as they repeatedly turned nose-to-nose and overshot each other. Both pilots were decelerating as fast as possible, each trying to get his nose behind the other's tail.

"Shit hot!" Locke yelled over the intercom. "He caught it!" The heavy breathing coming from his rear cockpit grew more rapid as their airspeed fell below 200 knots and Locke pulled over thirty units of angle of attack. "Now watch this," Locke said. "We're going to get in the phone booth with him." The veteran pilot closed to a thousand feet. "Damn, the boy's good," he muttered as Matt timed a rolling reversal perfectly and gained a slight advantage.

"Too close!" Ramjet shouted.

"Still a thousand feet separation," Locke told him, trying to calm the colonel. "The regs say we can close to five hundred before knocking it off. Pontowski can handle it." Locke hardened up the scissors, slowing down to 160 knots and bringing his nose up, increasing the angle of attack. "Screw the phone booth, time to get into the coin return." He closed to inside six hundred feet.

The angle of attack indicator was bouncing around thirty-five units and Ramjet lost sight of Matt's aircraft under the nose. At the same time, he felt the onset of a slight buffet that would increase as they slowed the fight and increased the angle of attack. Ramjet saw it all and it hurt—he wasn't used to flying in the pit of an F-15E and watching a close-in fight from that perspective.

Locke was pleased with the way Matt handled the maneuver. He decided to disengage, eased off the stick to separate, and transmitted a cool "Knock if off" over the radio. He was smiling.

But Ramjet panicked at that same instant. He desperately wanted to get a visual on the other aircraft and drowned

Locke's radio call with a shouted "Knock it off! Knock it off!" as the two F-15s joined together in a midair collision.

The forces generated by the two aircraft, each weighing over twenty tons, when they smashed into each other were horrendous. The G meters in the cockpit spiked to the max and froze, unable to sense the full impact. Matt's left wingtip slashed into the canopy of stretched acrylic on Locke's F-15, killing both colonels instantly. Most of Matt's left wing and horizontal stabilator were ripped off as his jet tried to shed the wreckage of Locke's F-15. Fuel and hydraulic lines ruptured as the engines sucked debris into their turbofans. The delicately balanced blades came apart, becoming instant shrapnel, igniting the fuel the high-pressure pumps were still forcing toward the engines. The rear of Matt's aircraft exploded.

But the engineers and workers at McDonnell Aircraft Company had done their job well and the Eagle refused to die. The titanium bulkheads and the heat-bonded joints held and Matt and Haney were still alive after the initial impact. Haney pulled at both ejection handles on the side of his seat and started a dual, sequenced ejection. The canopy flew back into the slipstream and Haney's seat went up the rails first. In less than half a second, the rocket sustainer under his seat kicked in, sending him well clear of the jet and directly into a piece of their left aileron that was fluttering to earth. It looked like the aileron lightly brushed the top of Haney's seat, but again, the impact forces were horrendous. Haney's seat lost stabilization and tumbled earthward, its parachute shredded.

Haney separated manually from the seat and pulled his ripcord. But nothing happened. He was conscious for the full three minutes before he hit the ground.

Thomas Fraser looked up from his seat and well-ordered desk and smiled at the two Air Force officers Melissa had escorted into his office. No look or word betrayed the frustration that was souring his day. "General Cox, good to see you again." Fraser stood and extended his right hand, all his Irish good nature up front. Deep inside, he wanted to order Cox to leave the White House and never come back.

"Mr. Fraser," Cox began, "I'd like you to meet Lieutenant Colonel William Carroll. Bill's our premier expert on the Middle East.''

"So, you're the man whose reports on what's happening over there have gotten the President's attention,'' Fraser said as he shook Carroll's hand. He waved the two officers to seats and settled into his own chair. "General Cox, is this the first time you've briefed the President?'' Fraser was furious that he could not control all the information reaching the President and wanted to learn what the DIA was going to tell him in advance. It was a matter of damage control.

Cox smiled. ''I brought Bill along so he could brief the President directly. Straight from the horse's mouth—so to speak.''

"Most unusual, but then Admiral Scovill did tell the President you were producing some great work at the DIA.'' Fraser made a mental promise to even the score with the crusty old admiral who chaired the Joint Chiefs of Staff and never cleared what he was going to say with Fraser first. "Just what will you be reporting to the President this morning?''

"Essentially, Bill will be presenting a detailed update of the summaries you've seen in the President's Daily Brief. Should take sixteen minutes if there are no questions.''

That's not likely, Fraser thought. Pontowski always asks questions. Fraser did not like the way the President insisted on personally hearing opposing viewpoints on every major issue. He liked it even less that a young-looking, bright lieutenant colonel was briefing him. He felt his control slipping away. Michael Cagliari, the national security adviser to the President, walked into the office. "Okay, gentlemen,'' Fraser beamed, "you're up. Keep it short. The President has a full schedule today.'' He escorted Cagliari and the two officers into the Oval Office and found a chair in the corner, his stomach churning in frustration.

Cox introduced Carroll and let him do all the talking. Pontowski sat silently, taking it all in. Carroll's message was a simple one: Iraq and Syria were patching up their long-standing feud and Carroll linked it with the Egyptian-Syrian mutual assistance treaty. "In short, Mr. President,'' Carroll concluded, "we are seeing Egypt, Syria, and Iraq preparing to fight a war.''

"And the target?'' National Security Adviser Cagliari asked.

"Israel," Carroll answered.

"I'm having trouble accepting Syria and Iraq finally getting in bed together after all the years they've been at each other throats," Cagliari said.

"Iraq has always been one of the hard-line confrontation states and regards itself as in a state of constant war with Israel," Carroll explained. "But distance and short wars kept Iraq out of the fighting so far. By the time Iraq could get itself organized to logistically support participation in an Arab-Israeli shooting match, the war was over. The main points of disagreement between Iraq and Syria have been over Syria's support of Iran during the Iran-Iraq war and of Kuwait in the 1991 conflict. Now the Syrians are reevaluating their position, trying to find an accommodation with Iraq."

"So you are convinced Iraq is now aligning with Syria militarily?" Pontowski said.

"Yes, sir, I am," Carroll replied. His answer carried conviction. "Also, Iraq wants to settle a very real score with Israel."

Fraser's head shot up; his face did all but shout, "What score!"

Pontowski laughed at his chief of staff's abrupt reaction. "Tom, Israel has been the primary support behind the Kurdish rebellion that has plagued Iraq for years. It's a basic element of faith among Iraq's leaders to punish Israel for keeping the Kurds stirred up. Cooler heads who argue for an accommodation with Israel disappear into the cellars of Al Mukhabaret."

"Al Mukhabaret?" Fraser asked. He had never heard that name.

"The Iraqi intelligence service and secret police." Pontowski liked to surprise his staff with what he knew. "Mike," he said, choosing his words carefully, "put a team together to watch the situation and come up with some concrete proposals to back up Israel."

Fraser wanted to interrupt and say that there was no confirming evidence and that they should stay focused on the United States' primary goal in the Middle East: to keep on the friendly side of the Arab oil interests and keep the oil flowing. After all, it was simply a matter of good politics—and business. He said nothing and a pain shot through his stomach.

"Also," Pontowski continued, "we need to develop a comprehensive plan now on how we are going to handle another Arab oil embargo like 1973. And get the word to the oil companies that we won't tolerate the excessive profits they made during the last crisis." He sat thinking for a moment. "Colonel Carroll, I'd like you to move over to Mr. Cagliari's office and work for him." He smiled at Cox. "I know. I'm stealing your top talent. But I want to stay on top of this. I hate being in a reactive mode." He turned to Fraser. "Tom, make it all happen."

The door to the Oval Office opened and Melissa walked in unannounced. It was too much for Fraser and he stood up, about to tell her to leave immediately. Damn! he raged inwardly, the stupid bitch hasn't figured it out yet. I control access to the President.

"Mr. President," Melissa said, not caring that she had interrupted or what the consequences would be. "I just received a phone call from the Pentagon. . . . Matt's been involved in a crash. . . . No word on survivors. . . . Nothing else at the moment."

7

Avi Tamir folded the latest letter from Shoshana and placed it in his old battered briefcase with the other postcards and letters she had written. He tried to concentrate on his latest project: creating a hydrogen bomb by the gaseous boosting of lithium-6 into an atomic bomb. But he couldn't focus on his work.

Reluctantly, he pulled the postcards and letters out and spread them on the table, rereading each. The father in him wanted to believe the picture they painted—Shoshana was on an extended business trip, mixing business and pleasure as she toured fruit packing and processing plants in southern Spain. But the scientist in him won out and he saw another pattern. All the cards and letters had been written at the same time with the same pen. And while the handwriting on the cards appeared to be the same, the dates were written with a slightly different pen. A magnifying glass confirmed his suspicions.

The pieces all fit together; his daughter was working for the Mossad and was on an assignment. His beautiful and only child—his only tangible link with Miriam, his long-dead wife. A sick feeling swirled through his stomach and he prayed Shoshana was safe in Spain and not somewhere else.

He berated himself for not attempting to work and put the letters away. "I only want my daughter home safe and sound," he said to himself.

"Don't worry," Mana told Shoshana, "the villa is very nice."

Shoshana kept looking at the dusty landscape and simple one-story buildings along the road that led from Kirkuk's airport to the villa and Iraq Petroleum Company furnished for visiting guests. She wondered how any luxury could exist amid the poverty and destruction she saw. The driver turned the big Mercedes down a paved road. Around a bend and out of sight of the main highway, they entered a canopy of trees. A high whitewashed wall appeared in front of them and a heavy wrought-iron gate swung back as they approached. Inside, a magnificent garden swept up to a large mansion.

The majordomo was waiting for them at the entrance and escorted them to their rooms on the second floor. Servants scurried to hiding places and kept out of sight, but always ready to serve. Mana only smiled and nodded condescendingly. It was everything he had promised.

That afternoon, he took Shoshana on a tour of the new chemical plant the Iraq Petroleum Company had built thirty kilometers west of Kirkuk. She could sense the professional pride he took in showing her what he had accomplished and made numerous mental notes about the layout of the plant. She carefully marked the one heavily guarded building he studiously avoided.

Over breakfast the next morning, Mana hurriedly explained how he would be gone most of the day as they were conducting tests and that he had to be present. Shoshana asked what they were testing and Is'al beamed as he related how they were testing a new insecticide. "Everyone thinks it is a gas," he explained, "but that's totally wrong. It is really a liquid dispersed in a vapor that forms droplets on contact with a surface. And it's most persistent."

She put on an act of forced interest while her mind raced with the implications of what he was saying. Twice she tried to change the subject, but Mana kept on talking. Everything he said only revealed that the "insecticide" he kept mentioning was meant for humans. "It sounds dangerous," Shoshana said. "We ran a batch of new insecticide where I worked in California and some of it escaped before it was diluted." She reached out and touched his hand. "Please be careful." He promised her he would. "Can I go sightseeing today?" she asked, again changing the subject.

Mana frowned. "That's not possible, please stay here."

Some spy, Shoshana thought as she walked him to the waiting car. I won't learn a thing cooped up here.

The construction staff of foreign engineers was waiting for Mana's arrival at the guarded building he had avoided on the tour with Shoshana. They led him through the freshly completed building, reviewing every detail involved in the manufacture of binary nerve gas munitions. The concept behind a binary nerve gas is simple: Two harmless agents are kept separated until they are employed; then the two agents are mixed together either in-flight or just prior to use, forming a deadly mixture. While the idea is simple, the production of a binary system is no easy task. But it had to be a binary system, for the scientists had provided the Iraqis with an additional capability. When mixed, the new nerve gas mixture was highly corrosive and capable of penetrating the protective clothing and gas mask filters the Israelis used.

After a break for noon prayers and lunch, a small group of Iraqi and foreign engineers and scientists escorted Mana deep into the third basement where tests were conducted. Six guards were waiting for them with two prisoners.

"That one"—the plant's general manager pointed at the woman—"is an Israeli agent. And the man is her Kurdish contact. We captured them six months ago." Both were wearing the protective clothing issued to Israeli soldiers for NBC (nuclear-biological-chemical) warfare. The manager growled a command and the guards removed the handcuffs from the prisoners and dropped gas masks at their feet. "Put them on," the manager ordered.

Zakia, the Israeli agent, glared at the men and adjusted the straps of the mask and jerked it into place. She blocked the exhalation valve and blew, clearing the mask. Her quick deft motions proved she was familiar with the mask.

Kamal, the Kurd, asked, "Zakia, is this right?" She reached up and adjusted the straps. "I've never worn one before," he explained as the guards shoved them toward the pressure chamber. Suddenly, he threw a hard left jab into the guard nearest him. The blow glanced off the guard's right cheek. Two other guards rushed up and threw him into the chamber, slamming the heavy door behind the two. Kamal shouted at them in Kermanji, his native tongue, calling them all the English equivalent of "pig shit." The double doors were sealed and checked for leaks while the team watched through view ports.

"Now we release the nerve agent," the manager explained. He paused before turning the valve and looked to Mana. "If you wish . . ." Mana's face lost all color at the thought of releasing the nerve gas. He gave a slight shake of his head and the manager turned the valve.

Now a scientist started a running explanation. "Normally, the subjects of such an experiment would be perfectly safe encased in their protective equipment. Please note how the droplets form and coalesce on contact with the material of their clothing and neoprene of their gas masks. It appears as if the droplets are evaporating on the material when in fact they are penetrating through to the skin." Mana felt his stomach contract. The scientist could have been discussing a high school chemistry experiment.

The nerve gas was slow in penetrating the protective gear and for a few minutes, both prisoners felt a surge of hope. Then the first droplets penetrated Zakia's suit and came in contact with her skin. The nerve agent was rapidly absorbed into her blood and sought out its target, the body chemical cholinesterase. Now the nerve agent immediately bonded with the cholinesterase, stopping it from breaking down acetylcholine, the body chemical that causes muscular contractions.

Zakia started to breathe rapidly as the cholinesterase in her body was made ineffective and acetylcholine rapidly built up.

Her nose was running and she fought down a powerful urge to rub it. She had been trained as a doctor and knew what was coming next.

"Zakia," Kamal shouted through his mask, "what's wrong? My chest . . ." They were both feeling a tightness in their chests, making it hard to breathe. But it was much worse for Zakia.

Outside the chamber, the scientist took an obvious pride in his work. "Ah, the onset of the symptoms. You can see they are both experiencing difficulty in breathing." A sour taste welled up in Mana's mouth and he felt sick. But he could not take his eyes off the two people inside the chamber.

"I'm going blind!" Kamal shouted. He looked at Zakia to help, but there was none she could offer. Her pupils were much further dilated and her vision very dim. Now both were wracked with uncontrollable spasms. Together they ripped their masks off in a vain effort to breathe. Mana gasped and drew back from the viewing port. They were drooling from the mouth as nausea swept over them. The woman started vomiting first as the onset of nerve gas was more rapid in her body. Mana turned his face away from the view port, not able to watch them twitch, jerk, and stagger about. Sick revulsion swept over him as he faced the end result of his work. He was afraid that he too would vomit up the rich lunch he had finished less than an hour ago. But he could not turn off the scientist's voice.

"By now they have both urinated and defecated. . . . Ah there, the final symptoms." The scientist's voice droned on.

Mana could not help himself—he turned to look. The woman was on the floor, comatose. Spasms wracked her body.

"And now," the scientist said. "The antidote." He hit a button and a small tube rolled out onto the floor of the pressure chamber. He spoke into a microphone. "Take the caps off the tube," he instructed Kamal. "Hold it in your fist and press the open end against your thigh. Press the button on the other end with your thumb. You will give yourself an injection that will save your life." The man did as he was told and within minutes his spasms stopped.

"What you see is the antidote to the nerve gas," the scientist told Mana. "We put it in a double-needle syringe modeled after the Dutch combo pen NATO uses for atropine."

The scientist smiled. "Of course atropine is ineffective as an antidote for our new nerve gas. But the combo pen is an excellent device." He passed out combo pens to the group. "Please put these in your pocket and have them ready in case any nerve gas escapes when we open the chamber. You know what the symptoms are and how to use the antidote."

The plant's manager gave orders and an engineer evacuated the chamber. When the atmosphere tested free of contaminants, he gave another order and a guard threw open the double doors to the chamber, drew his pistol, walked in, and shot Kamal in the head. Then he fired a shot into the head of the woman.

"We need to perform autopsies to determine the full effects of the nerve gas," the scientist explained.

Mana threw up and had to be rushed to a lavatory where he passed out.

Shoshana heard the commotion when Mana returned. She rushed to the front hall and sucked in her breath when she saw him. He was staggering and the front of his normally immaculate suit was stained with vomit. She chased the servants away and half carried him up to their rooms. There, she stripped his clothes off and bathed him with a damp cloth as he lay exhausted on their huge bed.

Slowly, he recounted the entire day, every detail, trying to purge himself of what he had seen. "It was so much more horrible than anything I imagined," he told her, trying to justify his actions. "I only wanted to protect my country . . . my people . . . from the Zionist threat." Sobs wracked his body.

Revulsion twisted inside Shoshana and any feelings she may have felt for Is'al, the boy, were driven out by a fear of Mana, the enemy. Her resolve hardened. "Oh my God," she whispered. "How terrible, how frightening for you." She stroked his head until he fell into a fitful sleep. Then she slipped out of bed and rifled through the pockets of his coat. She found the combo pen he had mentioned and hid it in one of her suitcases. Then she ordered ice from a servant and after it arrived, undressed and crawled into bed beside him.

The next day, they returned to Baghdad.

* * *

Hassan Derhally had presented a business card, much as a Western businessman would have when he entered Is'al Mana's plush office. Unbidden, he had settled into a chair next to the ornate desk and waited, completely at ease. When he spoke, his words were soft and respectful but there was no doubt in Mana's mind that Derhally was powerful and dangerous. Too many whispered tales made the rounds of Baghdad society about the sudden disappearance of individuals after talking to Derhally. Not even Mana's family could protect him from Hassan Derhally of Al Mukhabaret, the Department of General Intelligence that fronted for the Iraqi secret police.

"How may I be of service?" Mana asked. An obvious quiver caught at his words.

"This is really nothing," Derhally replied, "merely a minor thing." He watched Mana's Adam's apple move. He was getting the response he wanted. "From time to time," Derhally sighed in resignation, "we must track down misplaced material. Such a waste of time, but I suppose necessary. Don't you agree?" Mana agreed, fearing the man's bland stare.

"I understand you were present during a recent test at the Iraqi Petroleum Company's headquarters in Kirkuk," Derhally continued. He did not wait for Mana to confirm his information. "While there, you were given a device called a combo pen to use in case there should be an emergency. All but one of the combo pens were returned and we were wondering if you might still have it." He watched Mana's face. The man's a fool, he thought. "As you can see, a minor matter."

"I don't recall . . ." Mana stammered. "Oh yes, I put it in my coat pocket. But I was taken ill and rushed to a lavatory. It must have fallen on the floor there."

Derhally stared at Mana. After a short pause that seemed hours long, he shook his head no. "Ahh, then I can't imagine . . ." Mana's desperation was obvious. "It must still be in the pocket of the suit I wore. Perhaps one of my servants found it. They all steal me blind, you know." Derhally stood up and fear shot through Mana. He felt dizzy.

"Come," Derhally said. "Let's talk to your servants and end this matter." He paused and smiled for the first time. "If it's not there, perhaps your Miss Temple can assist us. I assume she's at her hotel."

"She never leaves without my permission," Mana said, trying to show he was in control of his private affairs.

"Really? I doubt that," Derhally replied, destroying the last of Mana's self-confidence.

The missing combo pen was not at Mana's home and the eagerness of his servants to answer questions left no doubt as to where to look next. The servants thrilled when they heard Derhally order Mana to take him to his mistress—their master was finally being humiliated. Then worry replaced any sense of elation they felt at Mana's misfortune. They knew how deep Al Mukhabaret could cut.

Shoshana was in the gift shop of the hotel when she saw three men escort Mana through the lobby to the elevator. She recognized Derhally immediately from the description Habish had given her. She had learned to do her homework. The dark suits and sunglasses the other two men wore were ample proof of their profession—government security. Are we that obvious? she thought.

She fought down the panic that wanted to consume her and turned her back to the lobby, forcing her mind to work the problem. Obviously, the Iraqis were on to her. But how? What had she done wrong? That's the wrong problem to work on now, she berated herself, focus on the objective. And the objective was in the bottom of her purse—the small tube that contained a double hypodermic needle that automatically injected the antidote to the new nerve gas into a victim's body. She had wrapped a brightly colored aluminum candy wrapper around it, making it look like a popular candy.

Gently, she stroked a potted flower and then slipped the tube into the branches. It was very obvious. Then she carried the pot to the shopgirl and scribbled a happy birthday note and tucked it next to the tube. She paid for the flower and gave the clerk an address. "Please deliver this sometime today," she instructed.

Shoshana strolled out the main entrance of the hotel and turned down Sa'adan Street, giving no hint of the turmoil boiling through her. Twenty minutes later she was at the dress boutique Nadya Mana had taken her to the first day they met. After looking through a dress rack, she asked to use the phone. She dialed a number and let it ring four times before hanging up. Then she immediately redialed and let it ring once. It was the emergency signal for one of the team to meet her.

After leaving the shop, she walked to Rashid Street, where she shifted her handbag to her left shoulder—the signal for a pickup. A car pulled to the curb and the rear door swung open. "Miss Temple?" She did not recognize the voice but a surge of relief to be in contact with her team propelled her into the car.

The two men in the front turned to look at her. For the second time that day, Hassan Derhally smiled.

Gad Habish and Zeev Avidar sat in their car, watching Derhally drive away with Shoshana. "Where do you think he'll take her?" Avidar asked.

Habish only shrugged and fell in three cars behind Derhally. "At the first stop, get out and start drying the operation up. I want everyone moving. Use your safe house for a point of contact. Be there when I call you. If we can't get the girl out by tonight, we go." He didn't tell Avidar that he would leave a two-man watch team behind to try to rescue Shoshana. If the Iraqis could not break her and used torture. . . . Well, he didn't think about the options open then. Habish hoped she could hold out long enough for him to get the team out of Iraq and then spill enough information to save her own life. Perhaps a prisoner exchange in a few years . . .

At a stop light, Avidar hopped out of the car and moved through the traffic to the sidewalk. He disappeared into the crowd. Habish scanned the traffic to see if Derhally had a backup car in trail. He found the other car almost immediately. A single agent was sitting in a gray Lada directly behind him. "Sandwiched," Habish grumbled to himself. But it was obvious that the Iraqi was not aware that Habish was trailing the lead car. He knew the danger signals only too well. His problem was to follow Derhally and not be observed by the backup car. All his training and experience, and every gut feeling he possessed, told him to rescue the girl now, before the Iraqis got their act together.

The problem solved itself when Habish saw the single agent behind him talking on a radio as Derhally pulled to the curb in front of the dress boutique. "Retracing her route," Habish said to himself. He pulled around the corner and slowed, anxious to see what the backup car would do. The gray Lada also turned but pulled to the curb and stopped. Habish almost smiled as he turned into a dusty alley and parked. He got out of his car and walked back to the gray Lada. The Iraqi was surprised when Habish opened the door and slipped in beside him. "Derhally said to stay with you." Habish's Arabic was faultless and the agent had a confused look on his face when Habish shot him.

Without any sign of haste, Habish got out of the car and walked around to the driver's side. He opened the door and pushed the body into the passenger's seat. He got in and drove into the alley behind his parked car. There, he stuffed the body into the trunk of the Lada, left the ignition key on the front seat in case anyone wanted to steal the car, and threw the trunk key on a roof. Some enterprising Iraqi car thief would dispose of the body for him.

Habish returned to his car, slipped on sunglasses and the dark coat of his suit. He combed his hair back and decided he looked close enough to an Iraqi goon from the secret police. He drove around to the boutique and parked directly behind Derhally's car.

The two women who ran the shop glanced at him nervously when he walked in. He gave them a hard stare—a man in charge—and swept the room with a practiced look. They were alone. If Derhally had been in the shop, he would have been an innocent customer who would beat a hasty retreat. But now, he was another agent. "Is Inspector Derhally here?" he asked in a low voice, nodding to the rooms behind the shop. The women blabbered an answer. "Good. Please close the shop and leave. Do not tell anyone we are here. Do you understand?" They understood perfectly and were out the door in less than a minute.

Habish drew his pistol and pulled the slide back, charging the chamber. He slipped into the hall and waited. He could hear a man's voice coming from the rear office.

"Miss Temple, please. No more games." It was Derhally talking.

"Call the Canadian embassy," Shoshana demanded.

"In time, in time," Derhally said. "And how will you prove you're a Canadian citizen? You don't have your passport."

"You know the hotel holds the passports of all foreigners until they get an exit permit. I am a Canadian citizen." Shoshana was sticking to her cover.

Habish waited until he had an idea of where the three people were seated inside the office. Then he holstered his pistol and pulled out the fake Canadian passport he carried. He knocked on the door and entered. "I'm from the Canadian embassy," he announced. "I've been told a Canadian citizen, Miss Rose Temple, is here and needs assistance."

Derhally took the passport and scanned it. "This is not an official passport."

"Oh, sorry. Wrong one." Habish reached inside his coat and drew his pistol. In one quick fluid motion, he stepped to one side, went into a shooter's two-handed crouch and shot Derhally in the head. The other agent had his pistol half drawn when Habish shot him. Without hesitating, the Israeli methodically shot each man in the head again.

"Anyone else?" he asked Shoshana. She shook her head no. She was sitting in a chair in the corner, her wrists tightly manacled with plastic flexcuffs. Her hands were already red and starting to swell from lack of circulation. It was the first step in an Iraqi interrogation. Habish cut through the thick white plastic with a small penknife. "Did they contact anyone?"

"They made two calls on the car radio," she said. "One was to a backup. His name is Fahad. I think he's driving a gray Lada and is parked outside. Also, they checked in with their control. I heard them use my name and refer to the hotel. That's all I could understand." Habish was impressed. She hadn't panicked and kept her eyes and ears open.

"Where's Mana?"

"I don't know." Shoshana rubbed her hands, trying to stimulate circulation, and told everything that had happened. She left nothing out.

"So you sent the combo pen to your language teacher disguised as a birthday gift." Habish was impressed with her quick thinking. He made a phone call, contacting Avidar with new instructions. "Help me hide these bodies and clean up this mess. We've got to get out of Baghdad tonight."

The waiting was a grueling endurance contest. Shoshana envied the Mossad agent who used the language school as her cover for she went about her business as if everything was normal. Shoshana couldn't match the teacher's cool facade and her agitation kept breaking through as the minutes dragged.

"The flowers will come," the petite woman assured her.

"Where's Habish?" Shoshana wondered. "I thought he'd be back by now."

"Like the flowers . . ." They fell back into their waiting.

The clock read 5:32 when Habish returned. He was all business. "We're rolling up our operation here," he told the two women. "Avidar is putting the final touches on the new passport and exit visa you'll need. I'm working on the assumption that Al Mukhabaret has got yours from the hotel and instructed the desk clerk to report anyone asking about you." He looked at the woman who ran the school. "Can you get out on your own?" The woman nodded and left. Neither Habish nor Shoshana knew how she would leave Iraq. They assumed she would use her contacts with Kurdish rebels to move her through northern Iraq and into Turkey, but if Habish or Shoshana were captured, they could not reveal where she went. Likewise, she did not know how they were escaping out of Iraq.

"We've got to move fast," Habish said and handed her a Walther exactly like the one he carried. Shoshana checked it over as he talked and dropped it into her handbag. "There's only one flight leaving tonight in three hours. SwissAir. You're on it." For the first time, she saw a hint of nervousness play across Habish's face. "We've got to get that combo pen out."

The minutes now flew by as the scheduled departure time approached. Finally, Habish could wait no longer. "The clerk in the gift shop will probably deliver the flowers herself after the shop closes. Too late."

"Why don't I go pick the flowers up?" Shoshana volunteered.

"Too dangerous. Someone might be waiting for you."

Shoshana thought for a minute. "Maybe not. Derhally really thought I was a Canadian citizen." Habish gave her a quizzical look. "I heard them mention Canada three times over the car radio and when you walked in, he did believe you were from the Canadian embassy." Habish was almost convinced. "I've picked up enough Arabic to understand some of what they were saying and I think they were still sorting this out, not sure of what they were on to."

Habish bought it. "It's worth a try. Zeev should be here in a few minutes. We'll leave him here to wait for the flowers if they arrive while we go to the hotel. I'll put on my Canadian official act at the front desk and ask for you. If anyone is watching the hotel, that should cause a distraction. You go into the gift shop and check on the flowers."

Ten minutes later, Shoshana was walking out of the gift shop carrying the flowers with the happy birthday card and combo pen clearly visible. Habish was still talking to the desk clerk when she ran into Mana.

"Where have you been?" Mana asked. He was excited and shaking. His eyes widened when he saw the brightly wrapped tube stuck in the flowers. "What is going on?" He snatched the combo pen out of the flowers and peeled the aluminum foil back. The dark olive green tube stood in dark contrast to its bright wrapper. He grabbed her upper arm and, for once, Shoshana was surprised by his strength.

Adrenaline, Shoshana thought, I hope he isn't thinking too clearly. "Is'al, it isn't what you think." He stared at her in disbelief. "I am a Canadian and work for a firm that specializes in industrial security. Your government contracted with us. . . . But I never thought I would fall in love with you. . . . Up in my room . . . the proof . . ."

Mana wanted to believe her and nodded dumbly. She could feel the strength drain from his grip. "Come," she said, breaking his grip and moving toward the elevator. "Let's go to my room." She caught Habish's attention just as the elevator doors closed on them. Smiling at Mana she lightly drew her fingers over his crotch. "Perhaps afterward?" It was a mistake and she could see the doubt flare in his eyes at the obvious sexual ploy. They rode in silence. Mana still had not said a word when she opened the door to her room. "You'll see," she promised.

The Iraqi barged past her into the room. She closed the door behind them after making sure no one was in the hall. Her travel clock beside the bed said she had less than an hour to reach the airport. Time had run out. "What you need is in the stationery box," she said, pointing to the dresser. He jerked a drawer open and spilled the contents on the floor. She reached into her handbag and grabbed the Walther Habish had given her. She didn't pull it out but walked across the room to Mana. "It's in the next drawer," she told him. Again, he jerked a drawer open.

His back was to her and his head bent over when she dropped her handbag and freed the Walther. In one quick motion, she raised the weapon and pulled the slide back, chambering a round. It was the motion she had practiced over a thousand times while in training and the words of her instructor came back, dominating her actions: "You pull a gun, you've blown your cover. So you shoot. When you shoot, you kill."

The last sounds Is'al Mana heard were the click of the slide ramming a shell home and a *phut*. Her instructor had repeatedly shouted at her, "Always shoot twice." She did as she had been taught.

Habish was standing in the hall when she locked the door behind her. "Where did you hide him?" he asked.

"In a closet behind some clothes." She had covered him with the same black dress she had bought in Marbella to seduce him.

Habish nodded. That might give them a little more time before a maid discovered the body. He could see tears in her eyes. "Don't let up now," he cautioned.

In the lobby, Habish phoned Zeev Avidar at the language school and made some vague references to buying a replacement computer. Avidar understood that he was to meet them on the road outside the airport with new documents and the luggage Shoshana would need to get through immigration.

The traffic on Abu Nuwas Street was jammed up for three blocks as cars and trucks fought to cross the Jumhuiya Bridge over the Tigris River. Habish turned down a side street and headed for the Ahrar Bridge, a kilometer upstream. The traffic was insane, trying to cross the only two bridges that had been repaired after the war. Once across the river, they had to double back to make contact with Avidar. Fortunately, the traffic was now light and Habish was able to make good time. A half kilometer short of the airport, the traffic piled up again and there was still no sign of Avidar. Habish checked his watch. "Thirty minutes," he muttered.

"There he is." Shoshana had turned around and picked him out behind them in the stopped traffic. She jumped out and ran back to his car and piled into the backseat just as the cars started to move. By the time they reached the entrance to SwissAir, she had changed clothes and scanned the new documents. She was now Abigail Peterson.

"Peterson entered the country three days ago," Avidar explained, "and Passport Control might have your old name and orders to stop you."

Avidar carried her bags as they hurried toward the immigration counters. Three other late arrivals for the SwissAir flight were still in line and she caught her breath as Avidar dropped her bags and disappeared. When the last person in front of her moved away from the counter, she bent down to pick up her bags. She looked up into the deadpan face of the same immigration official who had cleared her into Iraq.

"Miss Temple," he said, recognizing her immediately, "we've been waiting for you. Your passport and exit visa please." He held out his hand, enjoying his power over her now that there was no Is'al Mana to intimidate him and Al Mukhabaret had issued orders to detain her.

"Of course," Shoshana replied. She reached into her handbag and touched the Walther. Then her mind was made up. She clenched the pistol and glanced at the exit to her left. Just maybe she could avoid capture long enough to pass the combo pen off to Avidar. She would have to be the decoy to let Avidar escape. This was not the way she had planned to die.

"Passport!" the man demanded. He was staring at her handbag. Suddenly his head snapped up and he came to attention. "Sir!" Habish was standing directly behind Shoshana wearing his dark suit coat and sunglasses. He looked exactly like an Iraqi ape from the secret police and he was waving an identification card that established him as an inspector. Avidar had done his work well and the ID card was a perfect copy. The Iraqi was trembling.

Habish grabbed Shoshana by the arm and jerked her toward the exit. The force pulled Shoshana's hand free of her handbag and the contents spilled on the floor. Habish kicked the Walther toward the counter. "You're a fool," he snarled. "She would have shot you and I should have let her. Now, pick everything up." The man hurried to do as he was told. "Give it to me." He took the handbag and rushed Shoshana through the exit leading to the street.

Avidar was right behind them with Shoshana's suitcases. "Hurry," he urged, "two real agents are at the counter."

* * *

The Safety Investigation Board was convened at RAF Stone-wood in less than twenty-four hours after the crash. Matt was amazed at the efficiency of the base and the board in starting the investigation. The wing's Safety Officer had guided him through the first hectic hours. Sensing trouble, Matt had asked for a lawyer, but the Safety Officer explained that the Safety Board took no disciplinary action and none of its findings could be used in a court-martial. The board simply wanted to determine the cause of the accident to prevent it from happening again. If the Air Force wanted to hammer Matt, it would convene an Accident Investigation Board to conduct an investigation and gather evidence independently of the Safety Board.

Seventy-two hours after the accident, the Safety Board had issued a preliminary report on the accident. While the report said the cause of the accident had yet to be determined, every experienced fighter jock knew what the final verdict would be—pilot error. And all eyes were looking directly at Matt. He gave up going to the casual bar in the officers' club when he overheard a pilot and wizzo talking about the accident.

"You think Locke screwed up?" the wizzo asked.

"No way," the pilot answered, "Locke was too good for that."

The memorial service in the base chapel for the three men was a gut-wrenching experience for Matt. He sat alone at the end of one pew, avoided by the men of his squadron, and concentrated on what the chaplain had to say. Then a two-star general, Rupert Stansell, stood in front of them and delivered the eulogy. The general asked them to look at Locke's life and draw lessons from his example. Stansell's final words rang true when he offered a prayer: "Please take this man and judge him fairly, for he was among the best we have."

The mourners gathered outside the chapel and waited. The roar of distant jets could be heard and three F-15s overflew the chapel in a missing man formation. Then three RAF F-4s passed over in the same formation, their roundels catching the setting sun. Matt had heard that a British air marshal, a Sir David Childs, had ordered the flyby. He looked at the high clouds that were turning from hues of pink to blood-red and knew that Locke's influence had reached deep. Not knowing what to do, he followed a basic instinct and sought out Locke's British wife. He found her standing with friends, holding the hands of her two small children.

"Mrs. Locke, please accept my condolences . . ." He felt like a rigid fool.

The woman raised her chin and looked at him. Her eyes were dry and clear. She had done her crying in private. "Yes, thank you." He knew he was dismissed and walked away.

Matt did not escape without hearing a muttered "He's such an asshole," when he crossed the street, heading for his BOQ room.

"Yeah, and his family will bail him out," another voice said. "You won't see an Accident Board on this one." He recognized both voices and knew they meant him to hear.

A week later, the Accident Board finished their investigation and issued an interim report: Nothing new had been discovered and the cause of the accident would have to wait further analysis of the wreckage. Matt found that no one in the squadron would talk to him. He was in limbo. That afternoon he went to the Class VI store and bought a bottle of Scotch, determined to hang on a colossal drunk in the privacy of his BOQ room.

The next morning he walked into the squadron building, still feeling the aftereffects of the Scotch he had swizzled the night before. That's not the answer, he told himself. He tried to sneak by the scheduling counter when he recognized the pudgy major talking to the sergeant on duty.

"Captain Pontowski," the sergeant called. "Major Furry here wants to talk to you."

Matt stifled a groan. Major Ambler Furry was the wing's weapons officer, a distinguished graduate of the Air Force's Fighter Weapons School, and Locke's old backseater. Furry's career stretched back to F-4s and he was one of the original cadre of the 45th who had served under Colonel Muddy Waters. Matt cursed his luck for being associated with legends of the Air Force. In any other unit, he could have sunk into welcome anonymity.

Furry pointed to an empty office and left the counter. Matt followed him. Normally, men built like Furry tended to waddle, but Matt noticed the wizzo had a rolling gait that shouted self-confidence. Furry closed the door behind them and motioned for Matt to sit down. "How's it going?" Furry asked.

"Not good. You'd think I had a case of the plague that could be caught by standing inside fifty feet."

"Sounds more like you're still feeling sorry for yourself." Furry didn't wait for an answer. "Look, it's always hard getting over an accident."

Matt turned away and looked at the white wall board that still had the sketch of an air-to-air engagement on it. "I'm not sure I can fly anymore . . . I haven't flown since the accident. I don't even want to. I look at an F-Fifteen and I see trouble. . . . Hell, I'm not even sure what caused the accident."

"I doubt if it's a permanent condition," Furry said. The wizzo had seen it before—Matt was suffering a massive case of self-doubt. If he was to have a future flying fighters, Matt would have to find his self-confidence; the belief that he was the meanest, toughest, best fighter pilot on the block and any comers had best know it.

The pilot said nothing.

"I understand you haven't been matched with a new wizzo. You want me in your pit?"

Matt couldn't believe it. Locke's old wizzo, one of his best friends and probably the best backseater in the wing, was now volunteering to be his wizzo. What was going on? then it came to him—his grandfather's influence. Matt wasn't going to have it. "Why?" he challenged. "A phone call from some general in the Pentagon?"

"You think I work that way?" Furry shot back. "Then fuck off." He started to leave.

"Why?" Matt was confused. "I've got to know."

Furry stopped. "I was talking to Jack the day before the accident. He said you were one damn good stick." Furry paused, recalling the conversation, controlling the emotion he felt. "He claimed you're a rerun of him and living proof of what the Tactical Air Force is all about."

"And what's that?" Matt asked.

"Fighting and fucking, everything else is a surrogate."

"Colonel Locke said that?" Matt was incredulous.

"It's not original but yeah, he said that." A rueful look played across Furry's round face as he thought about his old friend. "There's one other thing I can't get past—Jack wouldn't have picked you to fly as number two with Ramjet Raider along if he had any doubts about your ability."

"But why take a chance on me? Hell, like I said, I don't know what happened up there and everyone is saying I caused the midair."

Furry's face was impassive. "I don't think you did."

8

"Mr. Fraser," Melissa called, stopping the President's chief of staff as he hurried past her desk. "B. J. Allison called ten minutes ago and asked for you to call her immediately."

A worried look flicked across Fraser's face and he glanced at his watch. It was 6:32 in the morning. "What does she want so early in the morning?" he grumbled to himself and scurried into his office. Barbara Jo Allison was well known to be a night person, often working till four in the morning and then sleeping until noon. She would be at her bitchiest if she had been working all night.

Melissa saw the telelight for one of Fraser's private lines flash on her com panel. Fraser had left strict instructions not to interrupt him when that light was on. The light was still flashing six minutes later when the President called. "Melissa, don't you ever go home?" Pontowski asked. The warm humor that always floated underneath the surface whenever he talked to her was still there, enchanting her.

"I just got here, sir." It was a lie. She had been at work for over an hour. For her troubles, she was paid $53,000 a year, had no private life, and never had time for a vacation. She could feel the first twinges of cynicism sour her personality as menopause approached, and she realized she would never have a family. Yet, when she was honest with herself, she admitted she would have it no other way. Melissa Courtney-Smith loved Zack Pontowski and had long ago given him her loyalty, willingly devoting her life to his career. When she was younger, she often indulged in a fantasy that included her body in that devotion. But that fantasy had been laid to rest years ago. Part of Zack Pontowski's appeal was his faithful loyalty to his wife.

"Is Tom around?" Pontowski asked. "He's not answering his line."

"He's in his office, sir. He often turns the bell off when he's working. He probably didn't see the light. I'll get him." It was a minor snafu, the kind that Melissa often handled—smoothing out communications in a busy office. She didn't hesitate and walked directly into Fraser's office to tell him that the President was calling him on the direct line to his office. She deliberately did not knock, curious to see what was distracting Fraser.

"Damn it, B.J., I'm doing what I can . . ." He was still talking on the phone, his back to the desk.

"Excuse me, sir."

Fraser whirled around in his chair, furious at the interruption. Melissa pointed at his intercom panel. The light for the direct line to the President's quarters was flashing. "The President."

"I'll call you right back," he said and cut off B. J. Allison. Melissa closed the door as he glared at her.

Now what was that all about? Melissa thought. That's the third time this week Allison has called him.

Ambler Furry was not impressed with Matt's mission brief for their first single-ship, low-level mission. "Is that all you've got?" he asked.

"Yep, let's go do it," Matt answered, glad to see they had plenty of time for him to get a cup of coffee and relax in the crew lounge before the flight. He also wanted some time to screw up his courage and drive his self-doubts back into the shadows.

"Let's get a cup of coffee and then let me show you how I'd brief the mission," Furry said. It was not a request.

"Don't you think it's a bit stupid to go through the entire briefing guide just for a single-shipper? We both know what we've got to do and can talk about it in the air."

Furry grinned at him. "If it's stupid but works, it ain't stupid." Matt started to protest, but Furry just grinned. "That's one of 'Furry's Rules for Survival.' "

" 'Furry's Rules for Survival'?" The pilot was intrigued.

"I've got a whole list of 'em."

"What's the first rule?" Matt asked. He liked the wizzo's way of thinking.

"Never forget your jet was made by the lowest bidder."

"Okay, forget the coffee. You brief."

For the next twenty minutes, Furry machine-gunned Matt with procedures, techniques, options and what ifs. When they walked out of the briefing room, Matt knew that he had a hard-nosed professional flying in his pit who probably knew more about how to handle the sophisticated, multilayered systems in the Eagle than anyone he had ever met. "You make it sound so simple," Matt told him.

"The important things are always simple."

"Is that another one of your rules?"

"Yep. But it's got a tough partner—the simple things are always hard."

From the moment Furry stepped off the crew van that delivered them to the hardened concrete bunker that sheltered their aircraft, Matt could sense a change in the wizzo as he neared the F-15—his easygoing demeanor disappeared, his step quickened. Then Matt realized he was teamed with a professional killer, a man more than willing to enter the combat arena, risk his own life, and purposefully bring death and destruction on an enemy. Matt felt a sense of purpose settle over him as he started his preflight. He wanted to do it right.

"This is one healthy jet," Matt said. They had just come off a tanker after an air-to-air refueling and were letting down for a second low-level run. On this run, they would head south, working their way through the hills of northern England and onto an RAF range that sported a host of simulated Soviet air defenses. Their job was to get through a ring of simulated antiaircraft artillery (AAA, or triple A) and surface-to-air missiles (SAMs) that were backed up by very real radars and electronic jamming. Once through the defenses, they were to drop an inert laser-guided bomb on a mock-up of a Soviet command bunker.

"All systems are go," Furry told him. "Couple the TFR to the autopilot." Matt did as the wizzo suggested and set the clearance limit for five hundred feet for the low-level run. Deep inside, he did not trust the Terrain-Following Radar. Gingerly, he relaxed his hold on the stick, ready to "paddle" the autopilot off and hand-fly the jet. "Come on," Furry groaned, "five hundred feet ain't low. Take it down to at least three hundred. Nice picture on the Navigation FLIR."

Matt chanced a glance at his left Multi-Purpose Display (MPD) video screen where he had called up the Navigation Forward Looking Infrared picture coming from the LANTIRN (Low-Altitude Navigation and Targeting Infrared System for Night) pod slung under the right intake. The same pod also held the Terrain-Following Radar (TFR). The pod under the left intake carried a laser and a FLIR for targeting. Together, the two pods made the F-15E into the true all-weather, nighttime, dual-role fighter that had ruled the skies over Iraq. The infrared picture coming through the nav pod was almost as sharp as the visual picture he was seeing through the HUD (Head Up Display). It was very reassuring.

Then Matt looked at the right-hand MPD, where he had called up the TFR. The E scope presentation checked perfectly with what he was seeing on the Nav FLIR and through the HUD. Furry was trying to remind Matt of what the F-15 could do and rebuild his confidence after the crash. "Come on," Furry urged, "take her down. We got to get into the weeds if we're going to get onto the range undetected." The TEWS, or Tactical Electronic Warfare System, started to chirp, warning them that an acquisition radar was sweeping the area.

"Amb, I don't know about the TFR down this low. If it fails . . ."

"Then we've had a very bad day," the wizzo growled. "use the goddamn feature or someone *will* guarantee we get our asses hosed down."

"Jesus H. Christ, Amb!" Matt protested. "This is only a training mission."

"Train like you're going to fight," Furry snapped.

"Real original. Is that one of your 'rules'?"

"Damn right" was the only reply from the rear cockpit.

Matt set the clearance limit to three hundred feet and let the autopilot take them down. After a few minutes, he started to relax and concentrate on other tasks. His trust in the F-15 was coming back. The TEWS was doing its job and they were getting early warnings of the hostile radars ahead of them.

At one point, Furry reevaluated the threats in front of them and reprogrammed their route, bypassing a heavily defended point and flying down a low valley. The Tactical Situation

Display (TSD) that Matt had on his Multi-Purpose Color Display screen blinked and the new route came up on it. The TSD was a constantly moving electronic map that was synced with the laser ring gyro inertial navigation system and nav computer. The TSD showed them their current position and was overlaid with a wealth of navigation info. "We've got to get lower in this valley," Matt said and lowered their clearance limit on the TFR to two hundred feet. Furry only grunted in satisfaction. Matt was amazed how fast Furry could bring the APG-70 radar to life by hitting the EMIS Limit switch, sweep the area in a mapping mode to update their position, and then tell him to take command of the radar for an air-to-air sweep. Within seconds, Furry would hit the EMIS Limit switch again and they would be back to silent running, their powerful radar in standby.

"I wish we could use the jamming feature of our TEWS," Furry said. "That would water their eyeballs." In peacetime the crews were only allowed to use the detection part of the TEWS and not activate the system's jamming and deception circuits.

The chirping warning sound on the TEWS changed, becoming more insistent. "Airborne interceptors," Furry muttered. "I've got our position wired down to a gnat's ass so when I hit the EMIS Limit, do an air-to-air search for bogies." It was a crew coordination procedure the wizzo had talked about in the mission briefing. It went off without a hitch.

"Right on," Matt rasped. "Two hits, on the nose, forty-two miles."

"Probably RAF Tornados out of Five Squadron at Coningsby," Furry told him. "I heard they were using the range." A low laugh came from the back. "I know those toads. They're good but the Fox-hunter radar on the Tornado ain't worth shit. Try to sneak by 'em."

"Rog," Matt said, feeling much more confident. He made a mental note to ask Furry how he knew so much about the RAF when they debriefed. Probably another one of his damned rules, he decided, probably something about knowing the opposition better than what your wife wants in bed.

Then Furry's fangs started to grow. "What the hell," he said. "Even if they don't see us, let's engage. A kill is a kill."

Matt was feeling better and better as his self-confidence surged. "I'll simulate a head-on shot with an AMRAAM at the leader and after it would have gone on internal guidance, I'll take a head-on Sidewinder shot." Furry grunted an acknowledgment. The more they flew together as a crew, less chatter would be needed and they would become much more efficient. The AIM-120, or AMRAAM, was their medium-range standoff missile that was launched in a semiactive mode, homing on reflected radar energy from the F-15's radar. Close in, the AMRAAM's internal radar would become active and steer the missile to the target, allowing the F-15 to disengage. By launching a Sidewinder missile at short range, the target aircraft would have to defeat a second missile. Only this one would be guided by an infrared seeker head. Life would have been very complicated for the Tornado if the missiles had been for real.

"I'll blow on through and turn on the trailer," Matt said, "and Fox Two him." Fox Two was the brevity code for a Sidewinder missile. Furry grunted again. "Then I'll close a Fox Three." Fox Three was the brevity code for guns, their close-in weapon.

"No can do," Furry said. "Without a face-to-face briefing before the engagement, the ROE say one turn only on a defender and no closer than one mile." The ROE, or Rules of Engagement, determined just what they could do when engaged in combat. The ROE for peacetime were designed to keep fighter pilots alive.

"Rog," Matt acknowledged. "Now."

Furry hit the EMIS Limit switch and the radar came to life. Matt locked on the lead aircraft and simulated launching an AMRAAM. He keyed the UHF radio, transmitting on the frequency all aircraft using the range had to monitor. "Fox One on the northbound Tornado at twelve thousand feet." Fox One was the brevity code for a radar missile. He waited, watching the two aircraft split on his radar, taking evasive action. Matt pulled up and into them. The track-while-scan ability of the Hughes radar gave him an awesome capability. When the computer gave him a signal that the AMRAAM would have gone on internal guidance, he locked on with a Sidewinder and simulated launching it. "Fox Two on the same aircraft," he transmitted.

Now Matt searched for the second aircraft. He thumbed

the Weapon Select switch on the side of the right throttle full aft. Three things happened: The radar went into an air-to-air supersearch mode and locked on the nearest target, second, the 20-millimeter cannon was selected or made "hot"; and third, the sight picture in the HUD flashed to a "guns" display. Matt looked through the small target designator box on his HUD. As advertised, he could see the target and did not have to search the skies for a "tallyho," the visual sighting of another aircraft. He broke lock and zoomed into the sun, never losing sight of the Tornado. In the mission briefing, Furry had suggested that technique as a way to find the bad guy and then confuse him. The radar warning gear in the target aircraft should have warned the pilot that he was being tracked by the F-15's radar. When the signal disappeared, the pilot would be preoccupied with a visual search while they hid in the sun.

"Tallyho on the trailer," Matt shouted. At the same time, he moved the Weapon Select switch to the mid-detent position that called up a Sidewinder missile. Again, the system did its magic.

"Tallyho the leader," Furry said, much calmer. "Coming to our six, disregard him, we already killed him." The lead Tornado was converting to Matt's six o'clock position, eager to engage. But in reality, one of the missiles would have taken him out. In this game of cowboys and Indians, Furry figured this particular cowboy was dead and was going to ignore him.

Matt was still climbing straight up. He rolled and pulled his nose down, into a forty-five-degree dive, pointed directly at the second Tornado. "That's your one turn," Furry cautioned. The one turn allowed by the ROE did not have to be made parallel to the ground but could be made in any plane. Matt had made his in the vertical. The distinctive growl of the Sidewinder came through their headsets. The cooled, infrared seeker head on the Sidewinder was tracking the target. The Lock/Shoot lights on the canopy bow came on. "Fox Two on the Tornado in a hard left diving turn," Matt transmitted. He stroked the afterburners and continued his dive. The Pratt and Whitney F-100-229 engines responded crisply and they outran the Tornado that was at their six o'clock.

A clipped British voice came over the radio: "Fox One on the Eagle."

"He blows a lot of smoke for a dead man," Furry said.

"Thanks for the fun, troops," Matt transmitted. "Got to run." They were back on the deck, heading for the target.

"I want to update our position," Furry said. The wizzo called up the mapping radar on his right-hand MPD. The radar image was overlaid with symbols coming from the navigation computer. If the inertial nav system was totally accurate and had their actual position pinpointed, the turn points and target boxes that had been programmed into the navigation computer would be over the correct spot on the radar return. But life being as it is, they seldom agreed. He placed the radar cursors over the center of one of the target boxes, which should have been a small crossroads he had picked out during mission planning. He hit the Auto Acq switch under his right thumb on the right-hand controller and reduced the size of the box around his cursor. Then he hit the pushbutton switch with his little finger, freezing the picture. He was making a map. The system counted down for a few seconds and then unfroze. "Take command and search for bogies," he said.

Matt took command of the radar with the Auto Acq switch on his stick and did a quick search. "Done," he said. Furry hit the EMIS Limit switch and they were back in silent running. All the time the TFR had been coupled to the autopilot and guiding them along their route at 480 knots and two hundred feet above the ground.

While Matt was searching for more bogies, Furry had updated the nav system by refining his cursor placement on the crossroads (he picked the southwest corner) on the frozen radar map picture. When he was satisfied, he hit the castle switch on the right-hand controller and updated the system. In effect, he was telling the navigation computer that was where the center of the target box should have been if the system was totally accurate when it placed the box over the radar image. The computer worked backward and refined its internal alignment, taking into account the movement of the aircraft since the map was made. Matt saw the aircraft symbol on his TSD jump a fraction of an inch when the system was updated. The autopilot sensed the change in their position and made a slight heading adjustment, putting them back on track.

All of this took less than forty-five seconds, much faster than the first time they did it.

"Eat your heart out, Mr. Nintendo," Furry laughed. "Best damn video game in the whole world. We'll get faster." Silence. "Let's simulate battle damage from that last engagement. Aah, say we lost our radar, laser, and FLIR and have to do a backup delivery using manual only."

"Come on, Amb. I haven't done that in six months."

"What the hell, it was briefed. No time like right now."

"Give me a break!"

"Okay, okay, just an idea. We'll save that one for our next mission."

"Thanks a bunch." Matt was seriously wondering about the man riding in his pit. Furry wanted to push the aircraft, its systems, and themselves to an extent he didn't care to think about.

Matt took control of the aircraft when they overflew the IP (initial point) that was the last checkpoint that showed the way to the target. Matt flew around a low hill, squeaking them down to a hundred feet, using terrain masking to protect them from defenses around the target. Furry used the radar to slue the Target FLIR onto the target. An unbelievably clear infrared picture materialized and they were still eleven miles out. A computer generated target box surrounded a concrete bunker. The wizzo moved the castle switch on his left-hand controller aft and the box changed to a triangle—the symbol for the target. Satisfied that he had the correct target, he mashed the trigger on the same hand controller and the weapons delivery computer went to work, processing a wealth of information to put a bomb on that target.

"Designating," Furry said. With that one word, Furry told Matt they were working their target. Matt had the weapons system in full automatic, so he mashed the pickle button and held it. When the computer had reached a delivery solution, a bomb would come off the stub pylons automatically. They both felt the bomb separate from the aircraft. "Lasing," Furry said and mashed the pushbuttons at the bottom of his left-hand controller. Matt banked away so Furry could continue to lase the target. Through the Target FLIR, they saw the bomb fly right through the closed door Furry was illuminating.

"Strange way we make our living," Matt said and coupled the TFR to the autopilot for their egress.

* * *

The fatigue generated by the mission was demanding its price and Matt wanted to flop out on one of the couches in the new crew lounge and take a break. But Furry was heading for an open briefing room for a postmission debrief. He followed Furry down the hall because something inside of him felt good and he wanted to recapture all that they had accomplished. He ignored the two pilots standing by the scheduling counter trying to wangle an extra flight. "Hey," one of them called, "kill anyone today?"

Matt spun around. Anger lashed at him and splintered any satisfaction he felt about the flight. "Excuse me very much, fuckhead," he shot back.

A viselike hand clamped down on his shoulder. It was Furry. "Only turn to blow the meatball out of the sky," he growled. "Otherwise run away and fight another guy." He half dragged Matt down the hall.

"What the hell's that supposed to mean," Matt grumbled, his temper barely under control.

"This is not our day to engage," Furry answered and closed the door of the briefing room behind them.

"Another one of your rules for survival?"

"Goddamn right," Furry snapped.

The agony of waiting was back on Shoshana and she wanted to ask when Habish would return. Instead, she studied the four walls of the basement room of the safe house where they had gone after leaving the airport. Zeev Avidar looked up from his computer and sensed what was bothering her. "It helps if you can keep busy," he said and went back to his work. A few moments later, the laser jet printer whirred and a new ID card for Shoshana spat out the bottom. Avidar picked it up and examined it critically. "Yes, this will do," he decided. Then he fed the printer a sheet of paper that he had aged with chemicals and heat from the oven. The printer whirred again and he had an authentic-looking Iraqi identification card.

"Now we need a photo," he said. He posed Shoshana with a dark shawl draped over her hair and took a series of Polaroid photos. After each shot, he would change her makeup with a soft artist's brush. Finally, he had one that made her look like a farmer's wife. Then he treated the photo with a chemical, giving it an aged look, before he trimmed it and fixed it to the ID. He used a pen to add some finishing touches to the final product and handed it to her. Then he repeated the process, only this time making her into a college girl.

Shoshana watched him work, amazed at how calm he was. Avidar did not strike her as a world-class forger and could have been a merchant in any bazaar in the Middle East, for he was skinny, dark-skinned, and slightly round-shouldered. Only his soft dark brown eyes held the key to the real Avidar. He was an artist.

"When we leave, I'll have to destroy all this," he said. "Gad and I have four different sets of identification, so that's no problem. But I haven't had a chance to work up a complete set for you." He returned to his work.

"How much longer before he returns?" she asked, not able to contain her impatience. How to wait in a safe house had not been covered in her training.

"Not long. He'll call when he's ready."

"What is he doing that's taking so long?"

"That's not the kind of question you should be asking," Avidar said. Then he relented. "He's closing our operation down and has to get in contact with our people here. We can't leave them high and dry. He's got to make contact, pass on money, new identification papers, and instructions. It takes time."

"So you think the Mukhabaret is on to all of us?"

Avidar turned his baleful eyes back to the computer. "If not now, they will be shortly."

The phone rang, filling the small basement room and making Shoshana's nerves jangle even more. Neither answered it and after two rings it stopped. Avidar placed his hand over the receiver and waited. When the phone started to ring, he picked it up and said nothing, only listening. Then he hung up. "Habish," he said. "It's not good. He's being followed and had to ditch his car. We've got to pick him up near the University. We've got to hurry." They climbed up the stairs and moved a wall panel and wardrobe into place, hiding the door. It was one of the many changes Avidar had made to the house. They walked calmly out the back door and climbed into one of the cars Avidar had found for the team.

The traffic over the Jumhuya Bridge was unusually heavy for that time of night. Avidar mumbled under his breath and merged into the jumble, honking his horn and swearing in Arabic until they were clear and heading for Antar Square. "We make one pass," Avidar explained. "Habish either makes contact or we go on alone."

"We can't just leave him . . ."

"Yes we can. Our first priority is to get the combo pen out of the damn country. We've got to be out of Baghdad tonight. Under the dash, feel around until you can feel the Uzi clipped there." She nodded when she felt the small machine gun. "Good. Be ready to use it."

They turned down a narrow street that led off Antar Square. "I see him," Shoshana said. "On the right, beside that building. He's seen us."

"Got him," Avidar grunted. "There's two men on the other side of the street." He stomped on the accelerator. "Get the Uzi," he ordered. He was going to use the car to block the two men who were moving out of the shadows toward Habish. Shoshana bent forward only to have her face smashed into the dash when Avidar mashed the brakes and skidded the car to a stop. She ignored the pain and grabbed the gun. Before she could raise up, four shots rang out from the left and she heard Avidar groan as the car stalled. He was hit. Habish jerked the right rear door open and piled into the backseat. She leaned across Avidar and stuck the snout of the Uzi out his window and sprayed the street.

"Go!" Habish shouted from the rear. Shoshana shoved Avidar against his door and half sat on him to get at the controls and start the car. She shifted into what she thought was low gear and let the clutch out. She was in third and the car lurched forward, almost stalling. She jammed the gearshift into first and accelerated away. Two more gunshots slammed into the back of the car, one grazing her neck. Habish returned fire from the backseat. "Got the bastard!" Habish yelled as she turned the corner. "Stop the car." Before the car had come to a halt, Habish was out and disappeared around the corner.

Not knowing what Habish wanted her to do, she jumped out of the car, ran around to the driver's side and pulled the wounded Avidar out of the driver's seat. She was shoving him into the backseat when Habish came back. He jumped behind the wheel and they drove off. "They're both dead," he said and handed her a radio he had taken off one of the bodies.

He didn't have to tell her that he had shot both of the wounded men in the head. "Listen for radio traffic," he commanded, "and make sure we're not being followed."

Somehow, Shoshana managed to plug Avidar's wound and stop the bleeding while she rotated through the four channels on the radio and scanned the road and sky behind them for pursuers. Then they were back at the safe house. Together, they lifted Avidar out of the car and placed him in the back of a dilapidated truck Avidar had bought from a farmer.

Inside the house, Habish told Shoshana to burn any scrap of paper that might help the Iraqis. While she fed the fire, Habish hooked two electrical leads from a wall outlet into the computer. When he made contact, the circuitry started smoking. Smoke and fumes filled the room. Then he did the same to the printer. When he was satisfied that their circuits were fused, he lifted a circular hatch out of the basement floor. "The well," he told her and dropped all their equipment down the hole. "They'll find it—eventually."

He led her upstairs to a bedroom and threw some old clothes at her. "Time to become a farmer," he said. "Hang the combo pen between your tits like a pendant and tape it down." While she did as he ordered, Habish started to load the truck with food and cans of water and gas that had been stashed in the basement.

When Shoshana was changed, she rushed downstairs and helped him load the truck. "Do we have a first aid kit?" she asked.

"In the truck . . . beside Avidar." While he changed into the worn clothes of a farmer, she climbed into the back of the truck. A flashlight and the first aid kit were lying next to the wounded man. Then she realized that everything they had been doing at the house had been planned and probably rehearsed.

"Avidar, I need to examine you," she said. "Were you hit anywhere else?" He shook his head weakly. She broke the kit open and wished she had paid more attention during her first aid training.

"Stop the bleeding first," Avidar whispered. The irony of it hit her; the wounded telling the nurse what to do. "Then clean the wound as best you can." She rolled him over and examined the small hole in his left side. Blood was still oozing out around the handkerchief she had shoved into the wound.

Habish climbed into the back of the truck and held the flashlight, watching her work. "Move over," he said and handed her the flashlight. She watched him as he deftly removed the handkerchief, examined the wound, stopped the bleeding, and bound Avidar up. "You shouldn't have stopped," Habish gently scolded. "Your orders were to pick me up only if it was safe." A weak smile crossed Avidar's face and then disappeared. "You always were a fool," Habish said, returning the smile. "Okay, time to go."

They climbed into the cab and Shoshana was surprised at how quickly the engine started. "Avidar worked on it," Habish grunted. "You should have known how to take care of his wound."

The reprimand cut deep into Shoshana and she didn't know what to say. But Habish was right, she should have known what to do. "Where are we going now?" she finally asked.

"Kirkuk."

The four men waited for the President's reaction. Michael Cagliari, his national security adviser, glanced at the notes he had made and found nothing encouraging. Admiral Terrance Scovill, Chairman of the Joint Chiefs of Staff, relaxed into the comfort of the couch in the Oval Office and ran possible questions through his head that Zack Pontowski might ask him. Bobby Burke, the director of central intelligence, said nothing. He did not like being the bearer of such ominous news when he had no idea of what was going to happen next. Tom Fraser sat in a chair off to the right and felt a surge of relief. This, he thought, will take Pontowski's mind off the Middle East and planning for an oil embargo for a long time.

"Are we reading the signals wrong?" Pontowski finally asked.

"There is always that possibility, Mr. President," the DCI answered. "But it correlates with too many other items coming out of the Kremlin. And we haven't seen or heard from the general secretary for over three weeks."

"They haven't come close to solving their economic problems," Cagliari added. "There is growing unrest, mostly in the Ukraine, Moldavia, Georgia, and Azerbaijan. Even the

Baltic States are joining in. Which, considering the way the Soviet Army has been setting on them since they declared their independence, is an indication of how had things are."

"Terry, what do you see?" Pontowski asked.

Admiral Scovill leaned forward. "We are monitoring a great deal of movement on the part of the Soviet Army. But it is all internal and toward the hot spots Mike just mentioned. None of it can be considered threatening to NATO or Western Europe. One other thing, Mr. President, they are being very obvious about it. The Soviets want us to know they are not threatening NATO."

Pontowski nodded and leaned back in his chair, glad that he had brought the three men over from the previous administration. They were turning out to be his best advisers, despite the serious misgivings Fraser had voiced at first. "So, it looks like Viktor Rokossovsky is about to lose his job as the general secretary of the Communist party."

"That in itself," Cagliari said, "isn't too much to worry about. It's how they are doing it. We had thought the Soviets had solved the succession-of-power problem and could do it peacefully. This is shaping up like an old-fashioned *putsch*. They're going to do this one with tanks and guns."

"It gets complicated," Burke said, "because we don't know whose side the army is on. Right now, we assume the generals are stirring the pot."

"So what do you recommend we do?" Pontowski asked. He wanted their honest opinions. He would make up his mind later after listening to his secretary of state.

Cagliari spoke first. "Right now, nothing. We must not do a thing the Russians could interpret as a threat or an attempt to mix in their internal affairs. We've got to keep things quiet."

Scovill and Burke agreed with him.

"Okay, gentlemen, that's it for now." The four men rose and started to leave. "Tom, hold on for a moment." Fraser held back until the men had left. "Well, what do you think?"

Fraser hesitated. It wasn't often that Pontowski asked his advice on foreign affairs. He knew he had to give it his best shot. "I agree with Mike, we've got to keep things quiet until the Russians get their problems sorted out."

"Is that all?"

Fraser shook his head. "The Middle East. I see problems

there that could spill over and frighten the Russians. That's not good when they are having internal problems. They used our response to Iraq's invasion of Kuwait as an excuse to crack down. I don't know what they would do if the Middle East became destabilized again.''

''What kind of destabilization would drive them over the edge?''

''I'm really the wrong man to ask that question. Why don't I call in Cox or that whiz kid Carroll?''

Pontowski smiled. ''Tom, I got the impression that you don't agree with them.''

Fraser was stunned. How had Pontowski cottoned on to that? ''Well,'' he stammered, ''I don't. I'm for a balanced approach in the Mideast and I think Cox and Carroll are too pro-Israeli. We need friends on both sides of that fence. But that isn't my job so I shut up.''

''What is your job?''

''To keep facts, options, ideas, opinions flowing to you.'' He paused and smiled. ''And to take care of all the damn paperwork.''

''Keep it up, Tom. Keep it up.''

Fraser knew he was dismissed and beat a hasty retreat to his office. Was the President sending him a message?

''Mr. Fraser,'' Melissa called when he passed by her desk. ''B. J. Allison called.''

He decided to ignore the message.

9

Discretion is a relative thing, especially in Washington, D.C., where almost everyone practices it to some extent, and the higher the orbit of the power circle a person whirls around on, the more vital it becomes to the survival of the practitioner. Thomas Patrick Fraser instinctively understood this and had become a master at the game. He relied on a pleasant, Irish-bred manner to charm people and a quick intelligence to stay at least two jumps ahead of any potential indiscretion. Normally, it worked well and to his advantage, covering up his sharklike nature.

But when Thomas Fraser lost his temper, his rough South Boston heritage broke through and he was anything but discrete with those who occupied a power circle below his. They received the full blast of his anger. But since Fraser was anything but suicidal, he never let those spinning above him see this side of his personality. And Barbara Jo Allison's constellation was well above his.

"Really, Tom," B.J. said, peering at him over her teacup, "I do not believe the President is honoring his commitment to me. After all, I did make substantial funds available to you during the last election." Her anger at having to summon him a second time when he did not respond to her first call was apparent in the acid tone of her voice.

"B.J., you knew at the time that I had to launder that money and that Pontowski didn't know a thing about it."

The petite woman took a sip of the herbal tea she drank before going to bed. "You led me to believe that you would be my friend at court."

Fraser used the break to drain his coffee cup. The summoning phone call from Allison had wakened him out of a sound sleep at three in the morning and he was still not fully awake. You bitch! he mentally cursed. How do you expect a man to think so early in the morning. "If he ever finds out," Fraser cautioned, "he'll appoint a special prosecutor and launch a full-scale investigation. I'll be the first casualty."

"And the scandal will rival Watergate." Allison smiled. "It will be the end of his administration." She had enough representatives in her pocket to guarantee that the House would at least convene a committee to consider impeachment.

Fraser fought down the urge to argue and tell her that Pontowski was a skilled and ethical politician. "Don't underestimate him."

"Come, Tom. We've been friends too long to fight over this." Now she was using her soft southern accent to charm. She was offering him a reprieve—if he chose to take it. She reached out a liver-splotched hand and touched his wrist. "I only want this silly talk about an excess profits tax on oil stopped. And the very idea of national emergency controls over all the oil corporations if there is another Arab oil embargo is too painful to think about. Why, you would think *we* did not have the best interests of our very own country at heart.''

Fraser knew exactly what B.J. had at heart—profits. Even he would have a hard time unraveling the creative bookkeeping her accountants indulged in, but his personal estimate was that B.J. doubled her profits any time there was a significant upward shift in world oil prices. What he didn't realize was that she could do even better if she knew a decline in prices was in the making. B.J.'s main problem was public relations. Public scrutiny of her business methods would probably raise such an outcry that the government would be forced by an irate electorate to nationalize the oil industry.

''I can only do so much,'' Fraser said. He wanted to quiz her about her sources. Highly accurate and confidential information was being leaked to her. ''My value to Pontowski is how well I run the Office of the Presidency for him. I am really an administrator, not a policymaker. He sent me a strong signal the other day.''

''Tom!'' Allison had popped to her feet. The vitality in the old woman surprised him. *''You''*—she stressed the word—''are not listening. I made an investment in *you* and *that* man. Now I want a return on the money I spent.''

Fraser fought down his anger. Normally, he would have ruined anyone that spoke to him that way. But this old woman was too rich, too powerful. ''Please, you must look at the problem from the President's point of view. He sees an oil crisis if the Arab-Israeli war breaks out again.''

''Then the answer is simple, isn't it?''

''I don't see an easy solution,'' Fraser replied.

''Oh, you men can be so difficult at times. Stop the war from starting. Any woman can see that.''

''Much easier said than done.''

''Yes, it is easy,'' Allison snapped, her voice hard and raspy. ''We only have to support our Arab friends and stop letting the Israelis determine our foreign policy. After all, how much oil do the Jews control?'' Now her voice became soft and wheedling again. ''Please, help an old friend who needs to go to bed and rest.''

Fraser stood, glad that she was dismissing him. "I'll do what I can."

"Yes, do that." The threat was obvious.

Melissa was sorting through a pile of documents and messages when Fraser stormed into his office. "Why the hell isn't my desk ready?" he barked.

"Sorry, sir," she answered and glanced at her watch. "I didn't know you were coming in this early."

"Goddamn it, it's your job to know. Look, lady, if you can't do this job right, I'll get someone who can." He ripped off his suit coat and tie and threw them on the floor. "Get me another suit and a clean shirt." He stepped into his private bathroom. "Get the fuckin' lead out!" he shouted.

"My, you are being a bastard this morning," Melissa said to herself. "Well, go right ahead and press the fire-the-secretary button. We'll see who wins that one." She deliberately chose the wrong color tie to go with the dark brown plaid suit she pulled from his closet. She passed them through to the bathroom and then walked down the hall to a deserted office. She found a private phone line, called the White House garage, and asked to speak to Fraser's driver.

"Hey," the young engineer said, "come take a look at this. It's the third time I've modeled it. The results are all the same." The senior engineer who had been working on the F-15 crash at RAF Stonewood bent over McDonnell Aircraft Company's most advanced design computer and studied the results of the junior man's work.

"Change the impact angle ten degrees and run it again," the senior engineer said. This was the eighth F-15 crash he had investigated and he had a strong suspicion what had caused the fatal midair collision involving lieutenant Colonel Locke and Captain Pontowski.

"The results aren't going to change," the junior man said. He ran the program again and the results stayed the same. "Only one way to get a shear angle like that on Pontowski's wing—Locke's aircraft had to strike it while in a downward rolling maneuver."

"Okay," the senior engineer said, "time to get flight test involved."

The two engineers picked up their computer printouts and

the VCR tape from Matt's aircraft that had survived the crash and walked over to McDonnell's flight test section. The test pilot they talked to could have been a computer programmer working for IBM. There was none of the flash, the dash, the straight teeth and crooked smile that went with the popular image of men who risked their lives advancing man's knowledge of the flight envelope. He was a thoughtful and highly intelligent engineer who also happened to be a superb fighter pilot at one time in his career. He also had every intention of dying in bed. He listened to the engineers and watched the VCR before he said a thing. "The last transmission from Locke's aircraft . . . I can hear two 'Knock it off' calls. We need to break them out."

The test pilot joined them as they drove over to another building with a sound lab. The engineer there listened to the tape and put it through his computer, splitting one voice from the other. Now they could clearly hear Locke's voice say, "Knock it off."

"No stress there," the test pilot said.

"Listen to the other voice," the sound engineer said. This time the rapid voice of Colonel Roger "Ramjet" Raider could be heard alone.

"That guy panicked," the test pilot said.

The four men looked at each other. "I guess this means the 'Gruesome Twosome,' " the senior engineer said. Now all four—the sound engineer was very interested and not about to be left out—piled into a car and drove to the flight simulator. The simulator McDonnell had built was a far cry from a normal trainer. The mock-up of the cockpit was suspended in the middle of a planetarium and a computer-generated picture was projected on the inside of the dome. The picture, not the cockpit, moved to commands from the pilot. It was unbelievably realistic.

Inside, they found the two young computer experts McDonnell had hired to run the system plotting some new dirty trick. They could perform magic in the simulator and took a great deal of relish in defeating budding F-15 pilots who tried to fly air-to-air combat in the sim against them. Larry Stigler was the oldest at twenty-eight, and looked eighteen. Stigler seldom said a word and resembled a stork. His junior partner, Dennis Leander, was twenty-three and looked like a very short overfed elf. But he had the personality of a gremlin.

Around the company, they were known as the Gruesome
Twosome.

The six men sat around the table and reconstructed the
accident, going over every detail. Stigler raised an eyebrow
in the general direction of Leander. "Colonel Raider came
through here about a year ago," he said, "and spent about
an hour in the sim."

"He crashed three times," Leander added. "He was ten
miles behind the aircraft with his head up his ass." He let
that sink in. It was a confidence he would never voice outside
the company. "I think we can reconstruct the midair with no
trouble."

The test pilot crawled into the front seat of the cockpit
while the senior engineer played backseater. The junior engineer stood on the narrow platform that surrounded the
cockpit. He was ten feet in the air. The three men could hear
talking coming from the control console until Stigler closed
the door, sealing them into the dome. The picture on the wall
showed them sitting at the end of a runway, ready to take off.
The pilot cranked engines and started his takeoff roll. The
runway flashed past them and then they were climbing out at
a steep angle. The pilot commanded a roll and the picture
moved around them. They heard a loud thump as the junior
engineer fell down onto the platform.

"Damn," he said, "I've got vertigo. Better get out before
I toss my cookies." Leander froze the sim, suspending them
just above a cloud deck. The door at the back flew open and
Stigler helped the sick engineer out.

Then they were "free" and "flying" again. The test pilot
flew two engagements, once as Locke then as Pontowski.
Leander played the opposite aircraft from the control console
and the image of his jet would flash past them on the walls
of the dome, exactly as it really happened. "Okay, freeze the
sim," the test pilot ordered. "Can one of you two fly this
puppy? I want to see it from Raider's position."

The sim froze again, the door opened, and a grinning Stigler crawled into the front cockpit while the test pilot took
Raider's position in the backseat. The test pilot was amazed
at how well Stigler could fly the simulator and wondered what
he would do in the real thing. On the first setup, the suspicion
came to him. "Stig," he said, "we need to switch cockpits." After they were repositioned, the pilot continued.

"When you hear me say 'Knock it off,' I want you to vote on the stick and push it forward, hard. The idea is that you want to lower the nose to see Pontowski's jet."

Again, they went through the setup and entered a scissors. Again, the angle of attack increased as their airspeed bled off. Finally, the exact position of the two jets was re-created. "Knock it off," the pilot said. Stigler did as he had been told and pushed the stick in the rear cockpit forward with both hands, palms open. But the pilot instinctively tried to hold on to the stick. The contrary resistance sent the stick sideways out of his grasp. The simulator rolled under and downward to the left, creating the same angles that had puzzled the junior engineer. The test pilot had learned what had happened. "Okay," he said. "That's enough."

Outside, the six men gathered around the table. The test pilot looked at them, a sad expression on his face. "From the backseat it looks hairy. They were flying at a low airspeed and a high angle of attack, but still had lots of control. They were not even close to departing controlled flight. The pilots had no trouble seeing each other but Raider would have lost sight of Pontowski's jet under the nose. For an experienced wizzo, no problem. But now listen to the VCR tape just before impact." He played the tape. "Just when Locke radioed for them to disengage with a 'Knock it off' call, Raider yelled the same thing. You can hear the panic in his voice. Then he voted on the stick, momentarily overriding Locke's control, and crashed them into Pontowski's wing." The test pilot paused. "The only other explanation is that Locke committed suicide."

"Is that a possibility?" Leander asked.

"No way," the test pilot said. "I flew out of Ras Assanya with him when he brought the Forty-fifth home from the Persian Gulf. I knew him."

The envelope was addressed to M. Courtney-Smith and waiting for her in the mailbox when she got home. Melissa checked the return address—it was the one she had been waiting for. Thanks, Joannie, she thought. An old friend, another secretary who had devoted her life to public service, had called from her office in the Pentagon and told her about the final report on Matt's accident. Melissa had asked her to mail it to her and bypass the normal six or seven bureaucratic layers that would edit and change the report before it was judged to be sent to the White House.

Inside her apartment, she made a cup of tea and settled down to wade through the document. Her cat, Caesar, jumped into her lap and purred. Outside of her work, Melissa was a very lonely person. She was amazed at the clear and lucid way the report was written. The conclusions were hard and unyielding. "No wonder the milicrats in the Air Force won't let these things go public," she told the cat. Instinctively, she knew that the report would step on too many toes and raise some hard questions about how the Inspector General system selected the officers who conducted inspections.

Like most Air Force reports, the details and meat of the accident board's findings were in the appendix. She flipped to the back and ferreted out details. The descriptions under the Cause of Death section brought tears to her eyes and she thought about the one man other than Zack Pontowski she had ever loved. Tom Dennison had been a Navy fighter pilot who had found a watery grave while making a night carrier landing in heavy weather. She remembered the way he had laughed when he told her, "Peacetime readiness inspections are like mess-hall cuisine—a contradiction in terms. No combat-ready unit ever passed an inspection."

"Well, I know two people who should see this," she told her cat. Then she thought about Fraser. "Perhaps, I should drop in on Mrs. Pontowski." Caesar purred his approval.

Ambler Furry wandered through the squadron looking for Matt. He finally found his pilot alone in the Intelligence section, his head buried in a report on the combat capabilities of the new Soviet fighter, the Su-27 Flanker. "The squadron still avoiding you?" Furry asked and flopped his bulk down on the couch beside him.

"Yeah, like the plague." Rather than talk about that, Matt changed the subject. "You know, the Intel weinies say I'm the first one in the squadron to read this." He waved the report at Furry.

"It does get your attention, doesn't it. Whatcha think?"

"It's getting tough out there. Better than the MiG-Twenty-nine Fulcrum. I think they've finally got a counter to the Eagle."

"Probably," Furry allowed, "but they won't use it right.

To match us, they've got to train like we do and that means their pilots would have to learn to think for themselves. There's no way the commissars will chance that. Hell, independent judgment goes against their basic doctrine and scares the hell out 'em.''

"They can't be that stupid," Matt said.

"Well, they have been so far. Kinda encouraging, isn't it?'' Matt agreed with him. "Speaking of encouraging, I think you should read this." Furry pulled a folded copy of the accident report out of a leg pocket on his flight suit and threw it at Matt. He sat and waited while the pilot read it. When Matt looked up, Furry was smiling.

"Shit hot!" Matt shouted. The report completely cleared him and laid the blame squarely on pilot error when Colonel Raider took unauthorized control of Locke's aircraft. The bitterness that had soured Matt's existence shattered as the self-doubts that had driven him to the edge of despair evaporated. He had not been responsible for the accident and there it was for all the world to see.

"Kinda encouraging, isn't it?" Furry allowed. He got up to leave. "I'll leave that copy for the squadron to read. Looks like you're home free."

For a moment, Matt was at a loss for words. "I think I'll take some leave now and go home. My grandmother's not well . . .''

"Can you hold off on that for a few days?" Furry asked. "We need to rub a few assholes in the dirt on an exercise we got coming up." A wicked look crossed the wizzo's face.

"I can do that."

Furry grunted and turned to leave.

"Amb," Matt said. "Thanks."

"I'm so glad you came." Tosh Pontowski smiled from her bed. She was sitting up and feeling much better. The surge of hope Melissa felt when she saw how much the President's wife had improved brightened her smile. "Don't be fooled," Tosh told her. "This damn disease comes and goes. Right now it's in remission." She patted the bed beside her, wanting Melissa to sit close. The last thing the President's wife wanted was sympathy. She considered her fight against lupus, which means "wolf" in Latin, her own personal battle.

The two women were old friends and for a few minutes

talked and laughed about day-to-day life around the White House. Melissa could see Tosh grow tired as they talked and fought back her tears, thinking how unfair it was that such a vibrant woman who had given so much was being ravished by lupus. "I heard some good news about Matt," Melissa said. She could see Tosh brighten. "The Air Force cleared him of the accident. A friend sent me a copy of the accident report. She thought we'd like to know right away. She said otherwise it would be weeks before we heard." Both women knew that the Pentagon would "officially" release the report only after several layers of military bureaucracy had "chopped" on it. In the process of gaining each office's approval, it would be heavily edited.

Tears glistened in Tosh's eyes. "That is good news. I would like to see him."

"I can arrange that," Melissa offered.

"No, please don't. He is on his own." Then another thought surfaced. Like her husband, Tosh Pontowski was a political animal and, even now, could not put her restless mind at ease. "Does Tom Fraser know about the report? That you're here?" Melissa shook her head no to both questions. "Please don't tell him. I would like to tell Zack." She sank back into her pillows. "I know Tom is an excellent chief of staff . . . but for some reason . . . I just don't like him. I'm being silly, I suppose."

Melissa shook her head no again. "At times, he can be a real . . ." she didn't finish the thought. "He is an excellent administrator, the best I've ever met. He works hard, very hard." Both women understood how the chief of staff lightened the load of the President. "I'm worse than you—I don't trust him. He wants something." The younger woman had confirmed Tosh's suspicions and she wanted to hear more. "Lately, B. J. Allison has been telephoning him a lot. Fraser's driver told me he drove him to her town house at three o'clock the other morning."

A rueful smile played across Tosh's lips. "I wish it had been for something illicit. But not with that old biddy. Do you know she still works until three or four in the morning?"

"Well," Melissa said, "rumor has it that was when she always did her best work—especially when she was younger."

"Come now," Tosh replied, "we mustn't speak poorly of our elders." Her eyes sparkled. "Especially one who is eighty-six years old.'' They both laughed. Now the President's wife grew serious. ''I cannot fathom how anyone can be so greedy and grasping.'' She reached out and held Melissa's hand. ''She sold her soul years ago to rise to the top of the oil industry and will do anything to protect her ties to the Middle East. I just know she wants to influence Zack's Middle Eastern policy. That must be the reason for her interest in Fraser.'' She fell silent, thinking. ''Now what in the world does she have on Fraser?''

10

The twin five-year-old girls, Megan and Naomi, burst into the room and threw themselves onto Furry's lap, each demanding a good-night kiss and hug before their mother hustled them upstairs to bed. A warm feeling came over Matt while he watched Ambler and his wife go through the nightly routine. He had seen it before and envied his backseater's domestic life. Furry caught the bemused look on Matt's face after the two little girls he called his Heckle and Jeckle scampered out of the room. ''Why don't I look forward to when they discover boys?'' he asked.

''No problem,'' Matt replied. ''Just buy a pair of matched shotguns and make sure every lusty stud that comes around sees 'em.''

''Ironic, isn't it,'' Furry said. ''In the not too distant future, I'm going to be discouraging boys from doing the same thing I was trying to do to some father's little girl when I was sixteen. One of the joys of being a parent, I guess.''

''Well, at least you know the opposition,'' Matt said.

''Not fair,'' Furry laughed. ''Throwing one of my own 'rules' back at me.''

''It does apply,'' Matt replied, ''I was thinking about that when I saw the operations order for Gunslinger Four.'' Gunslinger IV was the name of a NATO exercise their wing had been tasked to participate in.

"I was talking to Colonel Martin about that today," Furry told him. Matt shook his head at the mention of the wing's new deputy for operations. He didn't like the man. "He wants your squadron to plan our tactics," Furry continued. "I suggested that you do it since you just got checked out as a flight lead."

"You must have slipped a cog," Matt protested. "I'm not ready for that."

"You are and Martin bought it."

"Thanks for the favor." Sarcasm laced Matt's words.

"Hell, I didn't invite you over to eat my grub and guzzle my booze for nothing. We need to talk about it."

"Amb, let one of the old heads take it. I haven't got a clue."

"I remember when Jack Locke said the same thing." Furry waited while Matt wrestled with his emotions at the mention of Locke. "Muddy Waters—"

"Why does his name keep coming up?" Matt interrupted.

"Because Waters was a rare bird. He could lead men in combat and they would follow. He didn't let Locke off the hook and it paid off when the ragheads were pounding the hell out of us at Ras Assanya. Jack was the guy who planned the defense of the base." For the next hour, Furry retold the story of how the 45th Tactical Fighter Wing had gotten involved in the first Persian Gulf war and had to fight its way out. Matt listened, absorbing the lessons that Furry had learned the hard way. "Then it was Locke who helped plan the rescue of the men who were left behind and captured. Locke picked up where Waters left off."

A shattering pain beat at the pilot's defenses. "Why are you telling me this?"

"Matt, I'm not like Waters or Locke. It's just not in me. For that matter, I only know one person who is." He paused. "You."

Matt stared at his backseater and his pain yielded to disbelief. He didn't believe what Furry had said. "That's bullshit."

"Nope. Fact. Time you proved it."

Matt stood up and paced the floor. "What the hell is this? Some type of buck-the-kid-up session?"

"It's what the Air Force is all about," the major told him, not about to let the pilot off the hook. "We take our losses, learn from our mistakes, and get on with the job. Now it's your turn."

"Amb, I can't do it."

"You'll never know until you try."

"Look, it's late and I got to go," Matt said. Furry nodded and walked him to the door. His wife joined them as they stood talking and hugged him good-bye. They watched Matt retreat down the walk before closing the door.

"You really upset him," she said. "Can he handle it?"

"Yeah," Furry answered, "he can handle it. But he doesn't know it yet."

The next morning, Matt walked into Wing Intelligence and asked to see the operations order for Gunslinger IV. After wading through the dull document, he had one of the sergeants pin a large-scale chart of the exercise area up on a wall in the mission planning room and cover it with acetate. Then he sharpened a grease pencil and pulled a chair up in front. He straddled the chair backward, his arms resting on the back and looked at the chart, determined to make something happen.

"It's our hands," Shoshana said.

"What about them?" Habish replied as he fought the steering wheel and guided the truck along the rutted track that passed for a road. He tried to pick out the smoothest path, aware that every bump and jolt hurt Avidar.

"They're not hard and calloused like my father's. He grew up on a kibbutz and still goes there for vacations."

"So some people have funny ideas about vacations," Habish countered. "We need to find a place to spend the night."

"Our hands are too soft and clean. If we hit a roadblock, someone might notice."

"That's why we're on these back roads—to avoid roadblocks." The trail in front of them split and Habish stopped the truck. Shoshana automatically picked up the compass and one of Avidar's maps and got out of the truck. In Iraq, only the military and intelligence agencies were given accurate maps. But in the early days of the operation, Avidar had replaced the hard disk in his computer with a spare one he had brought in with him as a "repairman." The disk contained a cartographic data base and he was able to make maps that rivaled anything the Iraqis had. The map Shoshana and Habish were using included the web of dirt roads and tracks that crisscrossed Iraq and allowed them to avoid using the main highway from Baghdad to Kirkuk. But they had paid a price; it had taken them forty-eight hours to cover 125 miles and they still had 60 miles more to go.

Shoshana took a compass reading, oriented the map, and looked around to see if she could find a recognizable landmark for a bearing. Habish bent over the map and pointed to a spot north of the city of Tuz Khurmatu. "We should be about here." She agreed and climbed into the rear of the truck to check on Avidar. He was shivering, bathed in sweat and half conscious.

"Please," she whispered, "not this." She felt his forehead and almost panicked. He was burning with fever. "Gad! Avidar's fever is up."

"Bathe his head in water," Habish called from under the truck. He was rubbing his hands in the grease and dirt on the truck's differential. Within moments, he was bending over her shoulder. "See if you can get four aspirins down him," he said. She rummaged in the makeshift first aid kit and wished they had decent medical supplies. Not that it would do much good, she thought, I'm worthless when it comes to this. She shook four aspirins into her hand and held them to Avidar's mouth. "No, you fool," Habish said. "He'll choke. Crush them and dissolve them in water. Get him to sip the water." He climbed back into the cab and started the engine, pressing toward Kirkuk.

An hour later, they ran into their first roadblock. The two soldiers were surprised to see the truck grinding along the little used road and hurried to throw their rifles over their shoulders and block the road. Both were trying to act bored and dangerous. Habish took in the poor condition of their rifles and shabby appearance with a practiced eye. "Roadblock," he warned Shoshana.

The soldiers waved the truck to a stop and ordered Habish to get out. While the older of the two examined the tattered identification booklets Habish produced, the other stuck his head into the truck. A half sneer crossed his face when he saw only Shoshana. She had hidden Avidar under a blanket and behind some baskets. "Get out," he ordered and unlimbered his rifle.

Shoshana understood the simple command in Arabic and got out. "Your name," he barked. Fear paralyzed Shoshana. She understood what he had said but could not remember the name Avidar had given her on the false ID he had made at the safe house.

"Her name is Zanab," Habish answered.

The soldier shoved Shoshana toward Habish. "I asked her, pig-face." He jabbed the butt of his rifle into Habish's stomach and took a great deal of satisfaction in watching him crumble to the ground. Then he kicked viciously at Habish and forced him to roll under the truck.

"Farmers," the older soldier laughed, "care more about their goats than their wives. Leave him while we see what we have here." He grabbed Shoshana's shawl and ripped it away. "Very pretty for a farmer's wife."

"Too good for a farmer if you ask me." The leer that crossed the teenager's face hardened and aged him. "Make her undress." They both laughed. Shoshana did not understand what they had said and stood silently, determined not to say a word. The older of the two drew his bayonet and used it to poke at her clothes. He pulled the loose-fitting dress away from her body with the point and then shoved the bayonet through the fabric, ripping it away. "You're using the wrong bayonet!" the teenager laughed.

"Be patient," the soldier said and methodically cut the rest of her clothes away. When he was finished, both men were absolutely silent, astounded at their good luck.

Shoshana stood there and looked away from the man standing in front of her as he shucked off his equipment and pulled his pants down. She had thought about the possibility of rape before. She could feel the Iraqi's heavy breath on her as he fumbled at the combo pen between her breasts. With a vicious jerk he ripped the tube free and threw it at the other soldier. "Probably money," he said and turned his full attention back to Shoshana.

The words of one of her instructors in training came back. "Give them what they want, anything. If they want your money, give it to them. If they want your clothes, take them off. Give them your body. Give them your dignity. But if there is one thing you cannot give them, then you must either kill them or be killed.'' The soldier pushed her to the ground and forced her legs apart. She looked at Habish lying under the truck. He was staring at the soldier holding the combo pen—the one thing they could not give them.

The soldier slapped her hard and threw his weight on her, pinning her down. His head jerked around when he heard a loud *phut*. Shoshana bucked, threw the man off, and rolled free. Avidar was standing over the crumpled body of the young soldier and aiming a pistol at the half-naked man.

''No!'' Habish shouted. He rolled out from under the truck and stood up. He took the Walther from Avidar and shoved the muzzle under the soldier's chin, barraging him with questions in Arabic.

Avidar collapsed to the ground and Shoshana ran to him, not caring that she was naked. He was jerking convulsively and consumed with fever. She dragged him back into the truck and wrapped him in a blanket. In desperation, she wrapped another blanket around both of them, hoping her body heat would help. Slowly, the tremors wracking his body slowed, then stopped. His breathing was almost normal when she heard the Walther's distinctive *phut* from outside.

Then Habish was standing at the rear of the truck. ''I need your help. We need to make it look like these two deserted and took off.'' He turned away and went to work while Shoshana found another dress to wear. Not exactly like a farmer's wife, she thought, but close enough. She jumped out of the truck and found him digging a shallow grave.

''Maybe we ought to bury the bodies away from here,'' she suggested. Habish nodded and within minutes, they had buried the soldiers' equipment and loaded the two bodies into the rear of the truck and were moving again. ''We need to get Avidar to a doctor. I think his wound is infected.''

Habish concentrated on driving and did not answer. He stopped the truck in the middle of an open area and told her to look for a dip or gully in the ground that could not be seen from the road. ''They won't stop and search an obvious open area,'' he told her. Sixty meters from the truck, Shoshana found a slight depression, little more than a dent in the ground. She lay down in it and called for Habish. ''Where are you?'' he answered. When she stood up, he waved his approval. Within minutes, they had buried the soldiers and were driving away. ''Always remember,'' he said, ''the best place to hide is like that. Here,'' he handed her the combo pen, "hide this.''

She opened the front of her dress and shoved the tube between her breasts. ''That won't work,'' she said to herself. ''Stop the truck.''

She jumped out and ran around to the rear, reached under and rolled the tube over the differential, smearing it with grease and dirt. Then she climbed back into the cab and dropped it on the floorboards at their feet. Habish nodded in approval. ''We still need to find a doctor.'' She wouldn't let it go.

''The guard,'' Habish said, ''told me that the army has thrown up roadblocks all over the place in the last two days. They were told to stop and check everyone. Anyone who looked the least suspicious or foreign is to be detained.''

''What do we do now?'' Shoshana could feel the panic in her building.

''The obvious. We get on the main road and look like everyone else.''

''We'll run into another roadblock.''

''That's true,'' he conceded. ''But we'll be just another truck of farmers in a long line of trucks. Maybe the soldiers won't be so interested in rape if we're in a crowd.''

''They'll see Avidar and—''

''We tell them up front that he's sick—delirious and violent—and we're taking him to a doctor. If they get too curious, I'll tell them that he was bitten by a mad dog. They won't mess with a case of rabies.''

Shoshana brightened, feeling more confident. ''Maybe we can get directions to a doctor at a roadblock.'' Habish didn't answer and they drove in silence until they joined the main road and fell in behind a string of trucks moving toward Kirkuk.

Of all things available to Zack Pontowski, privacy was the hardest to come by and he was enjoying the unscheduled break in the day's schedule. He leaned back in his chair and closed his eyes, his fingers interlaced across his stomach, for all appearances asleep. It was the picture of an old man dozing on a park bench. But he was working. He sorted through the jumble of facts, opinions, and guesses that were piling up around the events taking place in Russia and the Middle

East, evaluating them with his own set of mental filters and prisms.

Pontowski had a view of the world created by long and hard experience and knew better than to try to interpret events by holding them up against a fixed belief of what should be. That was a sure formula for failure. Instead of lamenting about the perversity of a world that did not match the vision of a true believer, he relished the challenge of creating a foreign policy, a course of action for his country, that was as clever, varied, and devious as the world itself.

He also knew that the immense power he wielded from the White House could be checked in thousands of way he had never thought of. That didn't bother him in the least and he savored the chance to enter the arena of geopolitics and contest with the brilliant, stupid, greedy, fanatical men and women who moved on the stage of world power.

For a few moments, Pontowski allowed his mind to wander down the corridor of remembrance. A warm feeling of awe and pleasure surged through him when he recalled the time he met Winston Churchill during World War II. The scene had not dimmed with time and was clear and focused in his memory. That was when I started down this path, he thought, when I knew what I wanted to be. Winston, you old sea dog, I had no idea what you meant when you said, "The oceans we travel are storm-tossed on the surface and dangerous with shoals and barrier reefs. Yet with cunning navigation we can reach safe harbor. But the ever-changing seas move with a force beyond our feeble imaginations and you must contend with the sea as it is and not as you would want it to be." You must have been practicing a speech that day.

He gave a little snort and brought himself back to the problems at hand and hit his intercom button. "Tom, what's next on the schedule?"

"National Security Council meeting in the Cabinet Room. The CIA has an update on the fun and games going on in the Kremlin."

"Anything on the Middle East?" Pontowski asked.

"Nothing new there, Mr. President."

"Get Lieutenant Colonel Carroll to join us. I'd like an update."

The line was quiet for a moment. "Ah, sir, we haven heard of anything new for a while and things are quiet in part of the world. Besides, I doubt that Carroll could be ready on such short notice. And we are pressed' for time. You've got a delegation of CEOs from the oil companies scheduled in immediately after.''

"Have Carroll there. This is what he gets paid for." Pontowski cut the connection.

There was no sign that Bill Carroll had been unprepared when he wound up his presentation on the Middle East. The first thing he did every morning when he came to work in the basement of the White House office building was to prepare an updated briefing. But he was nervous. It was the first time he had briefed Pontowski alone. "Finally, Mr. President," he concluded, "we have monitored a joint command and control exercise between the Syrians and Egyptians. There is only one logical conclusion—they have now consolidated the command and control functions of their armed forces."

Pontowski leaned forward and looked at Fraser. "Then that part of the world is far from being quiet. Have the Soviets increased their support of Syria?"

"No, sir," Carroll answered. "Their level of support remains unchanged but they would like to increase it. Selling weapons to the Arabs is a good source of foreign credits, which they badly need. They did deliver some weapons to Iraq contracted for before the invasion of Kuwait—that was part of the deal that was cut with the Iraqi colonels who took over. That delivery gave Iraq an operational squadron of Su-Twenty-seven Flankers which are based at Mosul. It complements a squadron of MiG-Twenty-nines based at Kirkuk.''

"Have the Syrians or Egyptians kissed and made up with Iraq?" This from National Security Adviser Cagliari. He had keyed on the President's question and understood what he was getting at.

"I believe they have," Carroll replied.

Bobby Burke, the director of central intelligence, snorted. "My people don't subscribe to that at all. Besides," he quipped, "the Arabs always have a hard time figuring out who's the bride when they try to arrange a meeting." Laughter worked around the table. "Mr. President," he continued, "I know the mutual assistance pact between Syria and Egypt is strongly reminiscent of the relationship between Syria and Egypt before the Yom Kippur War in 1973. But things have changed.'' He glanced at Fraser. "First, Egypt is at peace with the Israelis and in spite of many disagreements with them is still honoring the peace treaty. Second, the situation in the Kremlin has the Soviets totally preoccupied. Until the Russkies sort out who's in charge, no one is going to start a shooting match in the Middle East. God only knows how the Soviets would react if Syria, their most important client state, was threatened. No sane person would chance that.''

Pontowski didn't comment on the saneness of the tribal politics of the Middle East. "Gentlemen, thank you for your time. Keep watching the situation in the Kremlin and I want no surprises coming out of the Middle East. That's it until next week.'' He rose and left the room with Fraser close in trail.

"Tom, bring on the CEOs. We need to talk about a national energy policy. Be a good chance for a photo opportunity.''

"Ah, Mr. President, could we slip that meeting five minutes. There are some papers I would like to have you sign.''

Pontowski paused before he entered the Oval Office. "Tom, is B. J. Allison late?''

Fraser nodded. "Sir, she is an old lady. . . . Maybe if we gave her a few more minutes?''

"Bring 'em in now.'' The President smiled. "And I want you there. Please tell Melissa not to disturb us.''

The sergeants who normally worked in the mission planning section of Intelligence had given up on Matt and tried to ignore him and the clutter around the room. The major who ran Intelligence yelled at them to get the place cleaned up in case one of the colonels with a well-developed anal compulsive complex dropped in and got bent out of shape over the mess around Matt. The sergeants relayed the message to Matt who ignored them. Caught between a rock and the Air Force belief that neat and tidy means good and efficient, they cornered Master Sergeant Charlie Ferguson and asked him to talk to Matt. Ferguson told them to lock the door to the mission planning room and put a sign up that restricted entrance to CNWDI security clearances.

"What's a CNWDI?'' they asked, almost in unison.

"A security clearance that allows access to Classified Nuclear Weapons Design Information.'' Ferguson grinned. "You

can't believe the hassle that goes with it. Nobody wants one.''
The sergeants did as they were told and Matt was left in peace
to work on Gunslinger IV.

Two days later, Ambler Furry saw the sign, gave a belly
laugh, and opened the door.

"What's so goddamn funny?" Matt said when he saw his
wizzo.

"You trying to work." He looked around the room. "This
place is a disaster area."

"Yeah. I've been living here trying to make something
come together. What a can of worms."

Furry walked over to the wall chart Matt had been working
on. "What's the problem?"

"It's the operations order. We're supposed to attack Ahlhorn Air Base in northern Germany."

"I've done that before," Furry said. "Poor Ahlhorn, it
always gets attacked 'cause it's smack in the middle of a low-
fly area. We can really get down in the weeds and root
around."

"Big deal," Matt said. "The operations order says we got
to attack from the northwest. We'll all be sitting ducks running in from the same direction. You'd think the Air Force
would've learned something from Vietnam and the raid on
Libya in '86. If we put our attacking aircraft on the same
route, we're nothing but cannon fodder."

"Use corridor tactics," Furry advised, still looking at the
chart. "There is a difference between opening a corridor and
flying the same route."

"We'll be up to our ass in air defenders trying to hose us
out of the sky. If we're in a corridor, they'll know right where
to find us."

"If you're up to your eyeballs in Gomers—you're in combat," Furry said.

"Another one of your 'rules'?" Matt asked. His frustration was building. "You got one for a goat screw like this
one?"

"Yeah. When in doubt, use industrial strength deterrence."

"On who?" Matt was now shouting, his frustration breaking
through.

"On the air defenders, who else?" Furry beat a hasty retreat out the door as Matt started throwing things at him, rearranging the litter in the room.

"You realize I'm violating my number one 'Rule for Survival,' " Furry said over the intercom. They were parked at the end of the runway getting a "quick check" before takeoff. Eleven other F-15Es stretched out behind them on the taxiway, all part of the strike package on Ahlhorn.

"Never forget your aircraft was made by the lowest bidder?" Matt asked.

"Nope. Never fly in the same cockpit with anyone braver than you are."

"You keep changing the order."

"Priorities are man-made, not God-made."

"Another rule?"

"Yep, and common sense."

"Keep the faith, babes, this'll work," Matt reassured his backseater. The raid plan Matt had finally devised was based on one of the Rules of Engagement in the operations orders. The defenders had to honor any threat the attackers presented, take evasive action, and follow a formula for attrition. Then Matt developed a way to open up the corridor and at the same time vary the flight routes into the target area. When they were near the base, they would use standoff tactics and simulate tossing GBU-24s, two-thousand-pound, laser-guided smart bombs with great glide capabilities.

The crew chiefs who were quick-checking the jets were finished and Matt called the tower for takeoff. Three minutes later, the strike force was airborne and headed out over the North Sea toward the Continent.

The defender's response to the attack developed much as Matt had predicted. The Dutch had scrambled six F-16s out of their base at Leeuwarden and established a combat air patrol, or CAP, over the North Sea. The Luftwaffe scrambled eight F-4s out of Jever into two CAPs, one high and one low, inside the low-flying area around Ahlhorn. It was going to be a tough day and the Eagles would have to fight their way in. But Matt had other ideas about getting out.

The Eagles were flying at two hundred feet above the dull gray waters of the North Sea. They were ingressing in elements of two. Each pair, or element, were in a combat-spread formation about two thousand feet apart and two miles in trail behind the element in front. From a high-flying bird's point of view, it resembled a ladder. But this ladder had fangs and snaked its way over the ground.

The Dutch CAP got the first surprise when Band Box, the call sign for the Dutch Military Radar Control Post, vectored the F-16s in pairs onto the low-flying F-15s. Like most single-seat fighter jocks, the Dutch pilots didn't really believe the Eagle was a true dual-role fighter that could instantly switch from a ground attack, dropping-bombs-on-the-bad-guy fighter-bomber mode, to an air-to-air role. They laughingly referred to the Eagle as the Mud Hen, claiming that dropping iron bombs was strictly "moving mud." The F-15 pilots thought the Fast Pack fuel tanks strapped to the sides of its fuselage gave the aircraft a slightly bloated appearance, earning it the nickname Beagle. But the Dutch pilots were about to discover it was no dog.

Matt and his wingman were in the lead and split apart when their radars picked up the fighters coming at them. Each engaged a separate pair of F-16s, and both simulated a launch of two AIM-120s, the AMRAAM, when they were still miles apart. Four AMRAAMs coming their way was too potent a threat to be ignored and the Dutch F-16s broke off their attack, taking evasive maneuvers according to the ROE. While Matt and his wingman rejoined and continued on their way to the target, the Dutch contended with the AMRAAMs. When they did get their act together, the ROE had cut their numbers in half and two more simulated AMRAAMs were coming at them. These two missiles had been launched by the third element of F-15s that were now in range. The ballet repeated itself and two remaining F-16s decided enough was enough and that they would engage the F-15s on their way back. Besides, they needed some time to think about the new tactics the F-15s were using.

Now the F-15s were coasting in, flying down the estuary of the Weser River. "I've seen this before," Furry grunted from the pit, remembering when he had been on a similar mission in the past led by Jack Locke. How many years ago was that? he thought. Furry had been a second lieutenant, the wing's basket case, barely able to scramble aboard the F-4 the 45th was flying then. And Locke had been an up-and-coming tiger, demonstrating his tactical skills on Ahlhorn. It had been the wing's final exercise before they went to war in the Persian Gulf. Many of those warbirds had not returned.

"Multiple hits, twelve o'clock at forty-five miles," Matt's wingman called over the UHF. He was painting the Luftwaffe CAP on his radar. But this time, Matt told the second and fourth element of F-15s following him to engage. Part of Matt's plan was to hide pairs of F-15s in the strike package that were configured strictly for air-to-air. The Luftwaffe F-4s were waiting for the F-15s to penetrate the low-flying area and were surprised when they heard their radar controller radio that four Eagles were surging out of the attackers at them. Suddenly, the eight F-4s found their hands full of missile launch calls and F-15s. It wasn't what they had expected and the F-4s lost interest in the strike package that sneaked past them on the deck. The TEWS in Matt's bird came alive with a loud howl of chirps and squeaks warning them of radar ground threats near the base. "Mostly Hawks," Furry said. He had a healthy respect for what the American-made surface-to-air missile could do and was glad they were using standoff tactics. Distance would offer them protection.

When they were within ten miles of the base, Furry had his target, the command post bunker, identified on the targeting FLIR and called, "Designating." Matt knew they were onto their target as his head twisted back and forth, looking for the Luftwaffe HICAP that was out there looking for them. "Shitfuckhate!" Furry yelled. He had a malfunction in the laser illuminator in the left LANTIRN pod. Now they had to use the Target FLIR for the primary delivery mode and not a highly accurate laser delivery. His fingers flew over the hand controllers and he drove the Forward Looking Infrared's cross hairs over the bunker and tried to lock on. No luck. He needed a sharper contrast on the target to get the system to lock on for guidance. "No lock, no lock. Drive in closer."

"The Hawks . . ." Matt cautioned. Closer meant they would be well within the envelope of that missile when they tossed their bomb.

"Damn it, closer!" Furry yelled. "We simulate turning on the TEWS and burn eyeballs out." Another peacetime restriction kept them from turning on the active electronic countermeasures in the Tactical Electronic Warfare System to jam radars. On exercises like this raid on Ahlhorn, they could only use the TEWS to warn them about electronic threats.

Matt continued to press the attack run. "Locked," Furry announced, triumph in that simple word. "Cleared-to-pickle."

Matt lifted the jet to five hundred feet. The TEWS exploded in sound, warning them of multiple simulated SAM launches—all at them. "Bomb gone," Matt said. In real life, they would have felt the bomb separate from the aircraft. Matt dropped back onto the deck and headed to the northwest while the other F-15s ran in from separate headings.

The F-4s that had been scrambled into a HICAP to defend Ahlhorn were entering the engagement, trying to nail the F-15s as they left the target area. Matt had rejoined his wingman and both pilots configured their systems for an air-to-air engagement. The F-15s that had been delivering bombs a moment ago were now ready for an air-to-air engagement, and there was no better weapons system for killing other fighters than the Eagle.

Matt's instructions to the aircrews for getting out of the target area had been simple, "We're not going there to defend anybody, so don't stick around to fight. Pull your fangs in when a bandit bounces you. Sort 'em out for one head-on missile attack and simulate a Fox One shot before the merge. Unload and stroke the throttles—blow on through 'em and keep heading for home. The next element behind you has a contract to do the same thing. The Rules of Engagement say the bad guys have to honor our missile shots and take evasive action. They're going to be up to their earholes and assholes just getting out of the way of our missiles while we get the hell out of Dodge."

And that's what happened as pair after pair of F-15s came at the defenders. Tail-end Charlie was flown by Colonel Mike Martin, the wing's new DO, the deputy commander for operations, a large and profane man with the personality of a gorilla in heat. He was upset because the Luftwaffe and Dutch had played by the Rules of Engagement and were making like dead men. More fighters were being scrambled out of both Jever and Leeuwarden, but they would be too late to engage the retreating F-15s. He snorted in frustration because he wanted to "kill" something or somebody. Then he gave a begrudging "Shit hot." He was looking forward to the debrief of the mission because Matt's plan had worked as advertised and violated Furry's "rule" that a plan is only good for the first thirty seconds of combat.

"Hey, Matt," a voice shouted when he and Furry walked out of the mission debriefing in the squadron. "We really knocked their dicks in the dirt on this one!" A chorus of good-natured shouts and obscene comments rained down on them. Another voice shouted, "The beer light's on in the lounge!" and the crowd moved in that direction. Furry gave Matt a friendly push and told him to get busy with the important things: "Drinking and bullshitting with the troops."

Matt stood for a moment, realizing he was part of the squadron and that he had earned it on his own. No, he told himself, that's not entirely true. He had earned it because Ambler Furry had encouraged him to keep trying and had kept faith in him when everyone else was dumping in his face. "Amb, why did you want to be my backseater?"

"Beats the hell out of me," Furry deadpanned at him, "I'm probably suffering from a bad case of the stupids." Then he relented. "I guess I saw a lot of Jack Locke in you. I flew another attack on Ahlhorn that he had planned. This one was better." He grinned at his pilot. "Come on, let's get to the serious stuff." He shoved Matt toward the lounge and the beer.

11

The wind gusted through the cracks in the door and sent waves of dust across the floor. Shoshana had tried to stuff the cracks with rolled-up newspapers, but nothing seemed to block the relentless wind. "I hate the wind," she told Avidar. The man only responded with a weak smile. "Where are you?" she mumbled to herself, wishing Habish would return. He had left them in the small one-room hovel on the outskirts of Kirkuk over twenty-four hours ago.

"He'll be back," Avidar said. She sat on the floor next to him and felt his forehead. The fever was building again. The antibiotics Habish had found after they had reached Kirkuk had broken Avidar's raging temperature but they needed more now. "Don't even think about it," Avidar cautioned. "No doctors."

"I know, I know," Shoshana told him, her frustration building. "The risk is too great." She bathed his forehead with a damp cloth and offered him water. "You saved Gad in Baghdad, you saved me at the roadblock, and now we can't do anything for you. If I was a nurse, at least—"

"But you're not." He squeezed her hand. "We all knew the risks before we started."

Shoshana tried to keep him warm as his fever surged and he slipped into unconsciousness. "Damn you, Habish!" she raged. "Where are you!" Tears streaked down her cheeks and she wanted to do something, anything to save this quiet man with the soft brown eyes. In her despair, she started to pray, something she hadn't done for years. "I can't even do that right," she told herself.

She sat with him until he died.

The makeshift shroud Shoshana was sewing together was almost finished when Habish came through the door. "You're too late," she said, not taking her eyes from her work. He knelt beside Avidar's body, no emotion on his face. "Well, say something, you bastard!" She was standing, shaking with anger.

"We need to leave."

Rage crashed through her, driving her anger and frustration before it like a windstorm. "Do we throw him in a ditch like those two soldiers? Or do we just leave him here for the rats to eat? Goddamn you, Habish. He saved our lives and I can never repay that. At least I can bury him."

"Shoshana . . ." He wanted to reach out and touch her, to tell her of his grief and sorrow. But he had to continue with what had begun in Tel Aviv when he started on this operation. And then against his better judgment, he gave in. "We'll bury him." He rose and brushed past her. "Stay here," he commanded and disappeared out the door.

He returned an hour later and without saying a word, picked up the body. He laid it gently in the rear of the truck and drove to a cemetery. Again, he carried the body and laid it gently beside an open grave.

"Why in a Muslim cemetery?" Shoshana asked.

Habish looked at her in disbelief. "Where else? Avidar was a Druze."

"He wasn't Jewish?" She was shocked by the revelation.

"Why do you think he spoke Arabic so well and blended in like he did?" Habish was slightly irritated. "He was not an *aqil*, one of the 'initiated' into the mysteries of their religion."

"I didn't know we could trust any Arabs."

"Muslims consider the Druze heretics and hate them as much as they do Jews. Avidar's people gave their loyalty to Israel in turn for protection. You need to know more about your own country." His voice hardened. "His loyalty speaks for itself."

She helped him lower the body into the grave and cover it with dirt. When they were finished, she knelt beside the grave and rocked back and forth in her grief. Slowly, the Hebrew words came as she rocked, "*Shma Yisrael* . . . In the beginning God created . . ." Habish's hand clamped down hard on her shoulder, stopping her. She looked around and saw a man in a white turban and long flowing black robes standing behind them—a mullah.

Zack stood in the doorway of his wife's bedroom, not wanting to disturb the moment. He was vaguely aware of the young, dark-suited Secret Service agent in the far corner of the main hall who was trying to blend in with the woodwork. They do try to give me space, he thought. But a President is never really alone. Zack accepted the inevitability of what that meant and knew the young agent would breathe easier if he went inside and closed the door behind him. I'll wait, he decided. They don't need me right now.

Sitting on the edge of his grandmother's bed, Matt was gently holding her hand in his and speaking softly. His voice had changed, not so strident and young. "I'm okay now, Grandmother. A good friend helped me get through . . . my wizzo."

A good friend? Pontowski thought. His wizzo? Before it had always been the girl of the moment whom Matt had talked about when bringing Tosh up to date on his private life. And he's wearing his class A uniform. He had never done that before and had always been in a hurry to get into civvies. My God, he does look like his father . . .

The image of Matt's father was now painted in large brush-strokes across Zack's memory. *You were on the way when Zack Junior was your age*, he thought.

"No." Matt smiled at his grandmother and answered another question. "There's no one special right now."

That was as close as Tosh will come to asking about your love life, Pontowski thought. *She wants a great-grandchild, hopefully a boy, to carry on the Pontowski name. Pontowski . . . a good Polish name that could trace its lineage back to a king. No doubt on the wrong side of the bedsheets, if the truth be known. The Pontowskis always were a lusty lot. Damn it, Matt, get with the program. You're the last of the line, almost the same age as your father when he was killed in Vietnam.*

"Will you make the Air Force a career now?" Tosh asked.

"Probably. I seem to have my act together now and . . ."

It is true, you do have your act together. Thanks to the Air Force. But at what a price. They tell me Locke was one of the finest officers they had, a superb pilot, a leader, a future general. Must we waste our best men? I've got to change that. Is there a price for Matt to pay?

"And, well"—Matt hesitated looking for the right words—"I'm good at it. I can fly the beast." He was serious now. "And I love the challenge. When I'm flying, I'm alive."

Now you understand yourself. Is that the beginning of discipline? Oh yes, I know about being alive, when food tastes better, love is sweeter. Someday I'll have to sit down with you and talk about the Big One, World War Two, when I was flying Mosquitoes for the RAF and met your grandmother. You can do both—be a pilot and a husband. Be honest, you want a great-grandson as badly as Tosh.

"Zack"—Tosh looked around her grandson—"come in and quit ignoring your family."

Zachary Matthew Pontowski, the President of the United States, savored the moment and felt a rare warmth work through him. *I suppose*, he thought, *that each of us is only given a few limited moments of happiness and contentment in this life. Are they the same? The secret isn't to wish for more of those moments but to know when you're having one.*

He walked through the door and closed it behind him.

* * *

"Oh, this is nice," the girl said as she looked around the elegant apartment that Fraser kept at the Watergate complex for such occasions. They had met at a dinner party that evening and after a show of interest on his part, the girl had easily gravitated into his circle. No one had objected, for Tara Tyndle was young, extremely well-endowed and gorgeous, and could carry on an intelligent conversation. She shook out her blond hair when Fraser took her wrap, creating the effect she wanted.

"I'm glad you like it. Drink?"

"Please. White wine." She walked around the room and touched the stereo. She gave him a look and arched an eyebrow. He nodded and she turned the stereo on. She knew exactly where to find the FM station she wanted. "I used to dance to music like this," she told him.

"I didn't know you're a dancer. Ballet?"

"Was a dancer. I gave it up, I assure you, this is not music for ballet." She could tell he was interested.

"That's too bad, I'd have liked to see you dance."

"It's not too late." She shook her head again, threw her hair to one side, and arched the same eyebrow. Fraser liked the way she communicated with him and again nodded.

Tara smiled and started to move with the music. She walked across the floor with the same sure step of a showgirl on a runway at a casino in Atlantic City or Las Vegas. Then she was behind his favorite chair, patting the high back for him to sit down. He did and she moved out in front. Now she was rubbing the sides of her hips, pulling her dress up her thighs. With an easy, practiced motion, she pulled the dress over her head and threw it aside, again shaking her hair out. Her movements slowed with the music as she teased him, slowly taking her bra off. Then her back was to him and she bent over, pulling her panties down, looking back at him. Slowly, she moved toward him and straddled his left leg, moving with the music.

Fraser's pager buzzed at him and she backed away, her sensuous movements blending with the music. She kicked off her high heels. He fumbled at the pager and glanced at the call number. "Goddamn it! What does that bitch want now!" B. J. Allison's phone number was flashing at him. He fought to control his breathing. When he was in control, he jabbed at the buttons of the phone next to him. His voice was pleasant and showed no traces of what he felt. "B.J., you do work late. How do you expect an old fart like me to keep up with you?" He listened. "Yes, of course. No . . . I don't mind coming right over. You called at a good time. I'm free."

The girl moved to the hall closet, took out his topcoat, and held it demurely in front of her. She was still moving to the music, swaying back and forth behind his topcoat. "Must you go?" she asked. He grunted and disappeared out the door. Tara walked back into the room and methodically searched it for bugs and a hidden VCR. It was clean. She sat down in Fraser's chair and crossed her long bare legs as she dialed a number. "Hello. Yes, it worked." She gave a low laugh, "Oh, yes. He's definitely interested but I won't be here when he gets back." She hung up and rapidly dressed. Just before she left, she scribbled her phone number for him to call.

Fraser knew Allison was sending him a message and that he would have to cool his heels for a while longer before she made an entrance. Of course she would bubble with apologies, but the message would remain—she was angry at the way she had been treated at the White House. After all, she had only been three minutes late for the meeting, and while it was a deliberate three minutes, Fraser should have smoothed things over with the President. Her money, power, and influence demanded that. She was determined to make that point with Fraser.

"Tom, you do spoil me." B.J. swept into the room, looking bright and cheerful for one o'clock in the morning. As always, he wondered how old she really was when he took her hand and tried to act courtly. She led him into the sitting room she used as an office and sat down. A secretary brought over a silver tea service and poured two cups. When he was finished, B.J. waved the young man and two other secretaries out of the room. "Now, Tom, we really must talk." Fraser braced himself for a brutal session.

"Doesn't the President know that *we* only have the best interests of our country at heart?" Her voice sounded wounded.

"No one doubts that, B.J. . . . ."

"Then why doesn't he show it? Oh, that man!" She stomped a small foot. "He must know we import over half our oil now and that most of it comes from the Middle East. *We*"—she kept stressing the "we"—"must do all we can to keep that oil flowing to us."

"I assure you, the President does understand that. But—"

"There are no 'buts,' " she interrupted. He could hear steel in her voice now. "The way he is encouraging the Israelis angers our other friends. Heavens, they might, if they are provoked, and who could blame them the way *he* ignores them, decide to create another oil embargo."

"Again, I assure you—"

"Assure me of what? That he is encouraging the Israelis in their own type of imperialism? That he doesn't care about peace in that part of the world? That he doesn't care about the concerns of our *true* friends? That Israel dictates our foreign policy? And now this talk of a national energy policy! Why . . . why"—she screwed up her courage to utter the dirtiest word she knew—"it's . . . it's . . . *socialism!*"

"He takes a broader view," Fraser tried to explain. "He sees our national energy policy linked to the Middle East situation, the problems in the Soviet Union, our balance of trade, the budget deficit." He regretted the last even as he said it.

"How dare he even think that *we* do not pay our fair share of taxes!" Allison believed what she was saying with all the fervor of a TV evangelist. She also believed in making a profit and knew how to turn an oil embargo to her advantage. She preferred to maintain the current way she did business importing oil, yet she did not want to be denied her profit-making options in case the Arabs decided to embargo the flow of oil. A national energy policy put too many limits on the amount of money she could make. It disturbed her that more and more senators and representatives in the U.S. Congress did not agree with her.

"B.J., please listen," Fraser begged. "I cannot change the President's view of the world."

"He must be listening to someone," she shot at him.

"Well, there is an Air Force lieutenant colonel, an expert on the Middle East, who recently came on board with the National Security Council."

"Tom, doesn't this remind you of that nice Marine under

President Reagan? Surely, he must be telling the President the truth.''

''He sees the situation much as the President does.''

''Then get rid of him. Get someone responsible to take his place.'' She pressed a button beside her chair and the young male secretary appeared almost instantaneously. ''Please get Mr. Fraser's coat,'' she ordered.

After Fraser had left, Allison twiddled her fingers, thinking. The door opened and Tara Tyndle walked in. She gave the old woman a beautiful smile, poured herself a cup of tea, and sat down. ''Well, Auntie?'' Tara asked.

''I can't believe how stupid *they* are.'' B. J. Allison lumped anyone who disagreed with her into a pile of ''theys.'' ''I do believe we are dealing with a hostile administration and Fraser does not have the influence with Pontowski that he led me to believe.'' She continued to twiddle her fingers deep in thought. Tara waited. She recognized the signs. ''Perhaps, the President needs something else to take his mind off the Middle East and his so-called national energy policy.''

Her fingers were at rest. B. J. Allison had made a decision. ''Do you remember the unfortunate Watergate affair with Mr. Nixon?'' Tara said nothing. ''Perhaps we need something like that to occupy Mr. Pontowski's time and energy. Are those two nice young reporters still working for that horrid newspaper?''

Tara arched an eyebrow. ''No. But there are others.''

Shoshana sat in the shade of the building next to the bus stop outside the new chemical factory the Iraq Petroleum Company had built near Kirkuk and concentrated on the activity around her. She judged the time to be after ten o'clock, which meant Habish was over three hours late. He should have come out of the chemical factory with the other workers at shift change. Shoshana fought down her impatience, hating the waiting, and wondered what might have gone wrong. The gates of the factory opened and a silver blue Mercedes drove out. She recognized one of the occupants from when she had toured the plant with Is'al Mana, but no one in the car even glanced her way.

A policeman made his way through the crowd at the bus stop and asked a man dressed in a fairly clean Western-style suit for his identification papers. The policeman scanned the papers mechanically and grunted. He handed back the papers, glanced at Shoshana, ignored her, and moved on past. My disguise is working, she decided. She watched the policeman approach Mustapha Sindi who was sitting nearby. Again, the policeman repeated his demand for identification.

Shoshana watched Mustapha as he handed his papers over. You are a cool one, she thought. Mustapha Sindi had a chameleonlike ability to change identities instantly. She remembered how convincing he had been at the cemetery when he appeared as a mullah. Even Habish had been fooled and he had told Mustapha to meet them there. He was reaching for his Walther when Mustapha identified himself. After that, Mustapha had taken them to a house in Kirkuk where they could hide. The sponge bath she had taken while a woman washed her clothes revived her spirits and she had established an instant friendship with a teenage Kurdish girl who had helped her wash her hair. A meal of grilled lamb, Arabic salad, and freshly baked bread had worked magic and she had slept soundly for the first time in weeks.

The next morning, she had joined Habish as they waited for Mustapha to return. Habish explained that Mustapha was a Kurdish rebel fighting for his people's independence from Iraq's rule. The Israelis had supported the Kurds in their fight and through that connection had recruited Mustapha to help Mossad.

When Mustapha returned, he had a new set of identification papers and a factory pass for Habish that identified him as a worker in the new chemical plant. Habish quizzed her about her tour of the place with Mana until he had a good idea of the factory's layout. Then he calmly announced that he was going inside.

"Haven't we done enough?" she protested. The two men ignored her and plotted how Habish would enter the plant as part of the night shift crew and come out the next morning. Shoshana and Mustapha were to be waiting for him at the bus stop. If nothing else, they could listen to the workers talk and hear any rumors if he was caught.

As planned, Habish had mingled with other workers that evening and entered the plant during shift change. Now it was late the next morning and Habish had not come out. After the policeman had disappeared, Mustapha got up and moved past her heading for the truck. "Walk away," he mumbled. "I'll pick you up down the road." She did as he said.

"What now?" Shoshana asked as they drove away in the truck.

"We come back tomorrow morning," Mustapha replied. The waiting was back, bearing down with its weight.

The crowd at the bus stop the next morning was buzzing with a low murmur. As more workers came through the plant's gates and joined the throng, the buzz grew and changed into a loud babble. Shoshana could catch enough words to understand that a massive search had been going on inside the plant. She fought down the urge to corner Mustapha and ask him what was happening.

Then she saw Habish come up to the gate with a large crowd of men. Each man had a slip of paper that the guards were collecting—an exit permit. Then it was Habish's turn. The guard studied his pass and the exit permit. She could see him ask a question and Habish shrug in reply. Something was wrong. The guard motioned for another guard to come over as a bus pulled up to the stop. The crowd being held at the gate behind Habish did not want to miss the bus and started shouting and pushing. The guard held on to Habish with one hand and frantically checked passes and exit permits while the other guard tried to push his way through the crowd.

Fighting to control her panic, Shoshana looked around for Mustapha. Then she saw the truck moving down the street toward the gate. Mustapha honked the horn as he eased through the men crossing the street to the bus stop. She fought down the urge to run as she walked out into the road and jumped into the back of the truck. She heard loud shouts from the gate and two gunshots. Mustapha hit the accelerator and the horn at the same time, adding to the confusion. Then Habish was at the tailgate scrambling to get on board. Another man was also trying to climb on the truck and escape the shooting. Mustapha drove faster, barging through the crowd.

Shoshana held on to the side of the truck and grabbed the back of Habish's shirt with her free hand, trying to pull him in. But the other man was in the way. With a vicious kick in the face, Shoshana sent him sprawling in the road. She heard a scream followed by a loud thump. They had run over a man not able to get out of the way. Then Habish was in the truck and they were clear of the crowd. "What happened?" she gasped.

"Mustapha shot the guard and I broke away in the confusion. Where's the Uzi?" Shoshana scrambled up to the cab and reached through the open rear window. She grabbed the small machine gun that was hidden behind the seat and passed it back to him. "They'll be after us," Habish predicted. "We need to ditch the truck and separate. I didn't get my ID back from the guard. It's got my picture on it. . . . So listen.

"They're in full production making a binary nerve gas at the plant. That doesn't make sense because binary systems are the devil to make—takes too much quality control. It would be much easier for them to make a normal V agent, like the Soviets do with their VR Fifty-five. Also, that building Mana never took you through is crawling with Europeans and Chinese. I got inside . . ."

"How did you do that?" Shoshana was amazed. "It was so well guarded."

Habish ignored her question. "I got as far as the machine shop before a guard found me. They're making a special casing for one part of the nerve agent." He reached into his pocket and pulled out a handful of shavings. "It's some kind of polymeric material." He gave her half of the shavings. "Shoshana, we've got to get out that combo pen, these shavings, and what's going on in there." He crawled up to the cab's rear window and told Mustapha they had to get rid of the truck and split up.

"You said a guard found you," Shoshana said when he rejoined her.

"I had to kill him. I stuffed the body in an air shaft but before I could crawl out of the duct, the next shift came on. I had to spend six hours in that air shaft with a corpse. Then by the time I got out of the building, I had to wait for the next shift change. Then with my rotten luck, some worker found the body and security started an ID check on everybody in the plant. In order to leave, you had to get your ID checked and pick up an exit pass. I 'borrowed' an exit pass from a worker."

"How?"

"God, you're naive. I had to strangle the bastard. Anyway, you saw what happened at the gate—the pass didn't match my ID."

"Habish. There." Shoshana was pointing to a sandy-brown-colored truck four hundred meters behind them. She could see a man standing behind a machine gun mounted aft of the open cab.

"Mustapha!" Habish yelled. "We've got a weapons carrier behind us." The Kurd floored the accelerator and started to weave through the traffic, putting four cars between them and the pursuing truck. The machine gun on the weapons carrier barked and a car behind them spun out and crashed, blocking most of the road. Mustapha gained a little more distance when their pursuers slowed to get around the wreckage they had created. "Just some bastard going about his own business," Habish said. He was staring at the truck that was chasing them. "They're probably talking on the radio. We haven't got long."

Now the weapons carrier was clear of the crash and accelerating. The three cars still behind them had heard the machine gun, seen the crash, and pulled over. The road was clear behind them. "He's gaining on us," Shoshana shouted. Again the machine gun raked the road. But the distance was still too great and Mustapha was weaving the truck back and forth. A bend in the road gave them a moment's respite.

Habish was lying on the truck bed beside Shoshana, still holding the Uzi. "We won't be so lucky next time." He crawled forward to the cab and yelled at Mustapha. Shoshana could not understand what he said and panic twisted through her when she felt the truck slow. Mustapha was pulling alongside and matching the speed of two cars they were overtaking. When they were abeam of the lead car, Habish stood up and held the Uzi over the side. He raked the top of the car with a short burst. Mustapha keyed on the gunfire and swerved the truck, smashing into the small car. Habish turned the Uzi on the following car and fired through its windshield, killing the driver. Shoshana caught a glimpse of a family inside as they sped away and Habish lobbed an incendiary grenade at the cars. She sickened when the two cars burst into flames.

For a brief moment, Shoshana seriously considered shooting Habish. Her humanity was in shreds and she could not accept the price others had to pay for their escape. "You fucking shithead!" she screamed. "You goddamned fucking shithead! You're killing innocent people! They're innocent!"

Habish slapped her hard, cutting her off, stopping the wave of condemnation.

"Look!" He was pointing back down the road. The two cars were totally blocking the highway and they could see the weapons carrier off to the side as it slowly worked its way past the wreckage. "They don't care if they kill their own people." He was snarling. "Why should we?"

"Because we aren't them." She stopped, at a loss for words. Habish ignored her when Mustapha called for him to come forward and talk. Shoshana could see the weapons carrier in the far distance moving after them again and yelled the news through the rear window of the cab.

"Up ahead," Habish shouted. "When we stop, you and Mustapha jump out. Follow him." He half turned his head toward her. "Do whatever it takes to get out of Iraq." He paused. "We've got to do this. We don't have a choice." For a fraction of a second, Shoshana thought she heard a trace of humanity in his voice. She didn't believe it.

They rounded a corner and Mustapha slammed on the brakes. Before the truck was fully stopped, Shoshana was out and running between two low buildings, and Mustapha was right behind her. She heard the gears on the truck grind as Habish sped away. Sooner than she expected, the weapons carrier shot by. "There's a car out back," Mustapha told her.

"What about Habish?" she asked.

"He knows what he has to do." The distant rattle of a heavy machine gun cut off his words. "Come," he said, "time to become a man and wife going about their business." He led her out to the car where the teenage girl who had helped wash her hair was waiting.

The girl frowned when she handed Shoshana her new papers. "You'll like being Mustapha's wife," she said as Shoshana got into the car.

Mustapha spoke softly to the girl and touched her cheek. Then he hopped in behind the wheel. "Meral is my wife," he explained and started the engine. "She's expecting our first child." Much to her surprise, Mustapha turned down the road in the same direction they had been going. "That is the way we want to go," he said. A few minutes later they were caught behind a string of cars, inching their way past the burning wreckage of Habish's truck. His escape had ended in a crash with another truck. A soldier waved them by and did not stop them for an identification check. Shoshana caught a whiff of burning flesh as they drove off.

12

Matt was standing at the scheduling desk in the squadron, getting ready for his first flight as an instructor pilot. He had been assigned to fly in the backseat with a new lieutenant in the squadron, one Sean Leary. He copied down the information from the big board behind the desk and grimaced when he saw the duty officer rub out his wingman's name and write in ''Martin.'' Mike Martin was the new deputy for operations.

''You'll love having Mad Mike as your number two,'' the duty sergeant said.

''I thought they called him Gorilla,'' Matt said.

''That's what he calls himself,'' Furry said. He had walked into the squadron and was standing behind Matt. ''Both names fit.''

''I wish you were going along on this one,'' Matt said.

''Then who would be sitting on whose lap?'' Furry laughed. ''You get to play backseater on this one while your student plays nose gunner. Come on, we need to talk about the lieutenant.'' He led Matt into a briefing room and closed the door behind them. ''What do you know about Sean Leary?'' Matt shook his head. ''His mother is a movie star.'' Furry mentioned a name Matt recognized instantly.

''I didn't know she was that old.''

''Yeah, kinda surprising,'' Furry continued. ''I was in his pit the last time he flew and recommended that he fly with an instructor pilot for a few rides.'' Matt waited to hear why. ''Basically, he's okay. But he has a tendency to get behind the aircraft.'' Matt was still listening. That was a problem but an experienced wizzo like Furry could sort that out. ''Also, he tends to bury the nose of the jet and get going straight down.'' The F-15 could easily handle that; might lose some altitude, but no big deal. ''And he gets too aggressive at the wrong times, especially when he's near the ground.''

''Why don't they team him with an instructor wizzo?'' Matt asked. ''You could handle all that in a heartbeat.''

''Why kill a perfectly good wizzo?'' Furry said. ''It's your turn to be a DM.''

''A what?''

''Designated mort. Welcome to the backseat of the F-Fifteen.'' Furry laughed and walked away.

''Stalwart fellow,'' Matt mumbled at his back.

Sean Leary was waiting in the briefing room when Matt walked in. Leary was a young version of Robert Redford and made Matt think of a young, eager Doolie at the Air Force Academy. Mike Martin came lumbering in and, much to Matt's surprise, Furry emerged from the DO's shadow. Furry grinned and said there was another last-minute schedule change and he would be Martin's backseater. Leary sat quietly, making the appropriate notes while Matt ran through the briefing for a one-versus-one BFM mission. At one point, Matt paused, remembering the basic fighter maneuvers mission he had flown with Jack Locke. He gulped and pressed ahead.

Once airborne, Matt discovered that Leary was a good pilot but too eager and aggressive. His timing was off and he would start a maneuver too soon and then run out of ideas on how to correct the situation he had gotten himself into. It was simply a matter of slowing him down. On the third engagement, Martin dragged the fight down to the bottom of the training area they were flying in. Their altimeters were hovering at 5,000 feet when the two fighters met head-on. Martin went into a horizontal turn and held it. ''Pull the nose up and use the vertical to counterturn on him,'' Matt said.

Leary pulled up into the vertical. ''Okay,'' Matt said, ''Martin's holding his turn. You can go on the offensive now and eat his shorts.'' The colonel was deliberately holding the level turn, his eyes glued to Leary's jet. He was willing to be a target at least once if the lieutenant could learn from it. ''Roll inverted and watch him while you come across the top,'' Matt said. ''Keep your eye on him until he's come through 180 degrees of turn. Drift a bit over the top and then pull down hard into him so you'll be in a lag position at his six o'clock.''

The maneuver was developing perfectly when Leary pulled hard down into Martin, stroking the afterburners. He was premature and should have waited about five more seconds. Matt had not been expecting the move and his head snapped to the right when Leary loaded the Eagle with four g's. Matt's helmet bounced off the canopy, momentarily stunning him. Leary was aiming them directly into Martin's flight path and had them pointed straight down and going through the Mach. Only Martin's rattlesnake-quick reflexes saved them from a midair collision as he pulled up, as Leary flashed by fifty feet in front, going straight down in full afterburner.

The first coherent thought Matt had was of the color brown filling the windscreen in front of him. The digital altimeter was unwinding in a blur and he could not read it. ''PULL!'' he shouted as he raked the throttles aft out of afterburner. He grabbed the stick, but it was already coming back.

''EJECT!'' Leary shouted over the intercom.

''NEGATIVE! NEGATIVE!'' Matt yelled. They were going too fast and outside the ejection envelope. The air blast would have crushed their chests when the seat kicked them out into the slipstream.

The nose of the Eagle came up as ''Bitchin' Betty,'' the computer-activated woman's voice on the Overload Warning System, announced they had an over g. Matt didn't worry about Betty. An over g was the last of their worries. The nose was pointed up but they still had a six-thousand-feet-a-minute sink rate. ''AFTERBURNERS!'' Matt yelled. He could not light the afterburners from the rear cockpit. The dash 229 engines kicked in when Leary jammed the throttles full forward.

They both heard a loud ''Oh fuck!'' over the radio as a cloud of dust enveloped them and, for a split second, Matt knew he was a dead man. Then they were flying again in an upward vector.

''Fire warning light on number one engine,'' Matt said as they climbed out. His breathing was ragged and quick. He called up the Overload Warning System on a video screen as Leary shut down the left engine. The screen read, ''10.5 g's, 130% overload.'' It was a major over g and the fire light was probably a result of the engine sucking something in. But they were still flying.

"We've lost utility hydraulics," Leary said, his voice also coming in pants.

"Okay, so fly the damn airplane. What systems have we lost and what do we do now?" Matt was still being the instructor.

"No brakes and we take the barrier," Leary said.

"Take your time and do it right," Matt told him. Slowly at first, and then with increasing confidence, the lieutenant ran the checklist for taking the barrier, the cable stretched across the approach end of the runway that would catch their tail hook and snatch them to a stop as in a carrier landing. Leary's voice was almost normal when he told Martin to look him over to see if any pieces of the jet were missing. Then he called air traffic control to announce that he had an emergency and would be taking the barrier at Stonewood.

The approach and landing went smoothly and Leary snagged the first barrier cable one thousand feet down the runway. When they were at a complete halt, Matt ripped off his oxygen mask and took a deep breath. He could smell urine. Leary had wet his pants. "We'll go to Life Support and change before we debrief Maintenance on the over g," he said. Leary was quiet.

When they had finished debriefing Maintenance about the over g, the fire warning light, and lost hydraulics, they went back to the squadron. Martin was waiting for them. "We got two fresh jets," he said. "Let's go and do it again." Leary visibly paled. "Get your ass out there," he snapped. "Now."

"What happens now?" Leary asked Matt.

"We kick the tires and light the fires and go do it again." Matt shrugged.

"Is that all there is to it?"

"No way," Matt explained. "We've got to help Maintenance do an over g inspection on the bird when we get down. We'll be up all night and at it most of tomorrow." He gave Leary a hard look. "This time do it right and eat Martin's shorts. Got it?"

The lieutenant got it and once they were airborne performed faultlessly. After they had landed the second time, a much more confident Leary walked into the squadron for the mission debrief. Martin and Furry both sat quietly while Matt recapped the mission in a briefing room. When he was finished, he asked if there was anything else.

Martin stood up and leaned across the table at Leary. "Lieutenant, you flew two ways today. The first time you had your goddamn head in the map case and almost pranged. You heard that 'Oh fuck' call over the radio?" He was jabbing his finger into the lieutenant's forehead. "That's the 'Oh fuck' I always use when I see some dumb shit diggin' a new hole in the countryside with one of my jets. We lost sight of you in the rooster rail of dust your afterburners kicked up from the ground. I prefer not to see assholes commit suicide, so the next time do it when you're alone.

"The second mission was nothing to brag about in the bar but at least you brought the jet back in about the same shape as when you got it. Now get the hell out of here and chase your body over to Maintenance and stay there until the over g inspection is finished." He glared at Matt. "You too, Fumble Nuts."

Martin stood there as Matt and Leary rapidly left the room. His lips compressed into a thin line. Then he threw Furry a hard look and gave a sharp nod with his head. "He'll do fine," he said.

"Leary?" Furry asked.

"No. Pontowski." He banged out of the room, careful not to let Furry see a crooked grin split his face. He headed for his office in wing headquarters, content with a good day's work.

Mustapha took his time covering the 160 miles to their next safe house. They worked their way down back roads, slept in the car, and avoided roadblocks and soldiers. Occasionally, they would double back to find a way around a checkpoint. But Mustapha always returned to their original course as they headed for the northwest corner of Iraq. On the seventh night, Mustapha found them a room at a makeshift inn outside the city of Mosul. He dropped into an overstuffed chair and fell into an instant sleep. Shoshana covered him with a blanket, concerned about his obvious fatigue, and then crawled into the narrow bed and fell asleep.

Loud voices outside the inn jolted her awake. She could barely see Mustapha in the dark as he rummaged in one of the battered suitcases that had been waiting for them in the car. Then he was sitting on the bed beside her. "Put this on," he ordered. "It's my wife's." She sat up in bed and peeled off her dress while Mustapha undressed. She fumbled at the nightgown he had thrown at her and then slipped it on. She was still trying to arrange it when he crawled into bed beside her naked and threw his arms around her.

"What are you doing?" she whispered.

"Quiet," he ordered. She lay there against him, her body rigid, and was surprised to feel his heart pounding. But there was no lust in the young Kurd, only fear. The voices outside grew louder and she heard footsteps echoing through the inn. The door to their room banged open and a young soldier, no older than Mustapha, barged in and turned on the light.

Mustapha jumped out of bed and yelled in Arabic, much too fast for Shoshana to catch the invective. The soldier laughed and called for his sergeant. Two other soldiers hurried over to the room and stood in the doorway and stared at Shoshana. She was sitting up in bed and the covers had fallen away. In the light, she could see the nightgown was flannel and very demure. Hurriedly, she pulled up the covers, afraid of the men.

An older man pushed through the door, obviously the sergeant in charge of the soldiers. "Identification," he snapped. While Mustapha dug their identification booklets out, he pulled the covers back from Shoshana, took a long look, and then ripped them completely away. He was more interested in her than the papers or the naked man standing in the middle of the room. Then Mustapha yelled in Arabic, dove at the open suitcase, and pulled out a small knife. He waved it around and shouted even louder. The sergeant started to laugh, threw their identification papers on the floor, and walked to the door. "We are good soldiers," he said. "Not like those other pigs." The look on the three younger soldiers indicated otherwise. Then he closed the door and they could hear him order the soldiers out of the inn.

Mustapha pulled his pants on, sank back into the chair, and took a deep breath. "I told them we had been married less than six months and soldiers had raped you twice. I swore that I wouldn't let it happen again."

"That was a foolish thing to do," she said, her voice soft and thankful. "But that knife against their guns?"

He looked at her and snorted. "I'm not crazy. I swore that I would kill you before I let it happen again."

The duty officer glanced up from his seat behind the scheduling desk when Matt walked into the squadron. "Call Major Furry at his office," he said and went back to reading the latest edition of *Stars and Stripes,* the newspaper published for the armed forces overseas. Matt used one of the phones at the desk to call Furry at wing headquarters.

"Hey, boy," Furry said, "you see the message that came in this morning from USAFE?" USAFE, United States Air Force in Europe, was their higher headquarters at Ramstein, Germany. Matt told him no. "Then you better chase your young ass over here 'cause it's got your name on it and Mad Mike is not a happy camper." Matt could hear amusement in his wizzo's voice.

Five minutes later, Matt and Furry were standing at attention in front of Martin's desk. There was nothing in the DO's face to indicate amusement. "You know what PI is, Captain?"

"Yes, sir. It's been explained." Matt was puzzled. He had been very careful to avoid anything that smacked of using political influence since the accident with Locke.

"This has got PI pecker tracks all over it," Martin said. He threw a message at Matt to read. Headquarters USAFE directed the 45th Tactical Fighter Wing, RAF Stonewood, U.K., to send one F-15E Eagle to Israel for a sixty-day exchange visit with the Israeli Air Force. The purpose of the visit was to demonstrate the capabilities of the F-15E weapon system. Captain Matthew Zachary Pontowski III was to lead the team.

"Sir, I had nothing to do with this," Matt protested. "I'd never pull—"

"Captain, if I had my way, you'd only pull duty as a nighttime latrine orderly. I suppose some paper-pushing, pencil-necked asshole on the staff at USAFE *just* happened to *pull* your name out of a hat." Martin was on a roll. "An exchange visit like this one is normally headed by a full bull, not a captain. Now you tell me how it happened."

"Sir, I don't know. I don't want the damn thing . . ." He heard a groan from Furry who did want to go. "Someone at

USAFE is playing politics and probably thought it would be a good idea to send me because of my grandfather.''

"Yeah." Martin was leaning across his desk, a shark about ready to tear his dinner apart. "That's a possibility. But I think it sucks." He shot a hard look at Furry. "Stifle yourself, Furry. You know I'm pushing formed crews and if Fumble Nuts here goes, you go.''

Martin had taken a cue from the Navy and was sold on the concept of formed crews where a pilot and a wizzo were teamed and always flew together. He was convinced that was the only way to exploit the full capability of the E model. It was proving to be a paperwork nightmare for the bureaucrats on the ground, but was showing positive results in the air. "There's no way I'm going to let you escape for two months," Martin told the wizzo. Furry was an outstanding weapons and tactics expert whom Martin kept hopping on special projects at wing headquarters.

"Sir"—this from Matt—"why don't you put all the crew's names in a hat and draw the lucky guy?''

Martin grabbed a cigarette and lit it. "Not bad. What do I tell USAFE?''

"Tell them that I decline because of personal reasons. No way they'll press to test that one. Leave my name out of the hat.''

Another groan from Furry. "Not fair," he protested. "Let me at the Israelis. In sixty days I can pluck their brains bare on every new tactic they've got. It's a rare chance, Colonel.''

"Okay, your names are in the hat too. Furry, arrange it for this morning.''

The main briefing room in the squadron was jammed as every pilot and wizzo crowded in for the drawing. Furry had turned it into an event and had a pretty civilian secretary there to pick the name. More than one rumor was passed around that she was the prize for the runner-up. With the proper amount of fanfare and hype from Furry, she reached into the hat and felt around. She pulled out a folded slip of paper and read it to the crowd. "Captain Pontowski and Major Furry," she announced.

Loud groans and accusations of a "fix" greeted the winners. "That's the name of the runner up, right?" Matt shouted. "Draw for the winner now." More good-natured shouts of "Scam" and "Fix" were heard as the crowd filed

out of the room. Furry joined Matt. "Well, old buddy," the
pilot said, "how's your Hebrew?"

"Duty's a terrible burden," Furry answered.

"Tall 'Uwaynot," Mustapha grunted. Shoshana could see
their destination in front of them, the isolated and dusty village of Tall 'Uwaynot. He had picked the village because it
was in the extreme northwest of Iraq and lay less than twenty-
five miles from the Turkish border. "I'll bribe some border
guards and smuggle you across," he said. He pulled up in
front of a walled compound on the outskirts of the village.
"This is our safe house. Stay inside and out of sight until I
can get it arranged."

Time became the enemy again as Shoshana waited for
Mustapha to complete the arrangements to get her across the
border. She had time to rest and wash their clothes, but no
amount of soap and water could wash away what she had
become. Bitterness burned inside her as she struggled to bank
that fire and forget that she was a murderer and whore. After
the initial shock of Habish's death had worn off, she felt a
profound relief at being free of the man. She stopped thinking about Habish altogether when Mustapha's young wife,
Meral, appeared one day, tired and dirty from the eighteen-
mile walk from the nearest highway. The next day, Shoshana
went with her to the village square and followed her around
as she shopped at the various stalls.

Two soldiers from the small army detachment that was assigned to the village stopped them, gave their identification
papers a quick glance, and handed them back. "They're only
farmers who were drafted by the government," Meral explained, "and probably can't even read." After that, the soldiers ignored them when they went to the square and the
gentle pace of village life reached out and enveloped Shoshana,
restoring a semblance of sanity to her life. Tall 'Uwaynot
was exactly what she needed.

Early one morning Mustapha woke her. "Come, I need
your help." He rushed her into the bedroom. Meral was lying on a sleeping pallet, awake but in obvious pain. The girl
was miscarrying.

"We're going to need a doctor or a nurse," she told Mustapha. He only shook his head and said they couldn't do that.
"Then get a midwife," she ordered. Again he refused,

claiming it was too dangerous to approach strangers. "Then I'll get one," Shoshana said and left the room. She had come to the end of her toleration for death and suffering.

Mustapha caught her outside and shoved her back into the house. "I'll go," he said and ran into the night. He was back in less than thirty minutes with an old woman who took one glance at Meral and started issuing orders. Mustapha would hurry to do her bidding while Shoshana sat in a corner and watched the old woman work. When she finished and Meral was resting comfortably, the old woman cocked her head to one side and studied Shoshana for a moment. Then she was gone.

"I told her you were my sister," Mustapha explained, "and that we had to take care of you because you're a simpleton and slightly crazy." He stared into the night. "I don't think she believed me. She'll gossip. The soldiers will hear and become suspicious."

"Then it's time to leave," Shoshana said.

"I'll see what I can arrange," he said and disappeared out the door.

Shoshana walked to the door and stood there. The distinctive *phut* sound of a Walther drifted back to her. She was still standing in the doorway when Mustapha came back. "There was no choice," he said. "She lived alone and won't be missed for a day or two. We must leave now." Shoshana stared at him. "I said there was no choice," he snapped. "Everything we do has a price. She was the payment."

Shoshana lay on the ground beside Mustapha's wife. The young girl was growing weaker and Shoshana had half carried, half dragged her the last three miles through the mountains until they reached their rendezvous point with Mustapha. Shoshana was sorry that they had to bring her along, but she would have never found the hidden niche without her. "At least I could carry her," she consoled herself, gasping for air. When her breathing had slowed and she felt some strength return to her legs, Shoshana crawled out from behind the rock where they were hiding and scanned the valley below them, looking for Mustapha. Nothing. She crawled back and lay down, glad for a chance to rest. "What is he doing down there?" she said, more to herself than to the girl, and dozed off.

A man's voice and a sharp guttural command in Arabic caught at the edges of Shoshana's consciousness and jolted her fully awake. For a moment, her heart pounded rapidly. Then she heard Mustapha's voice and her breathing eased. Again, she heard the same hard voice followed by a wheedling sound from Mustapha. Both of the women heard it and pulled back into the rocks and brush, trying to become invisible.

"They are hidden here," Mustapha said in Arabic. Two border guards climbed around the rock and stood in front of the two women. "Do I get a reward?" Mustapha asked from behind the two men. He was cringing and wringing his hands. A perfect toady.

"No, but I will," the border guard with the hard voice rasped. He swung his AK-47 down off its shoulder strap and jammed the muzzle into Mustapha's stomach, bending him over in pain. He knocked the Kurd to the ground with the butt of the assault rifle and then took aim at Mustapha's head. Shoshana closed her eyes, not able to see another killing. She heard a single shot and Meral gasp in surprise. Then she opened her eyes. Mustapha was still lying on the ground, but the lifeless body of the hard-voiced guard was sprawled out over him. The other guard was standing over them, an automatic in his hand. Blood, brains, and most of the dead guard's forehead were splattered over Mustapha.

"This is the man I bribed," Mustapha explained. "Unfortunately, this one"—he pushed himself free of the body— "could not be bribed." While Mustapha tried to clean himself, the guard stripped the dead man's uniform off and threw it at Shoshana. "Put it on," Mustapha told her.

"I'll never pass for a guard," she said. Mustapha grunted and rubbed more dirt over his skin and clothes. Shoshana hated the smell of the dead man's uniform. It reeked of stale cigarette smoke, sweat, and urine. It had not been washed in weeks. "What now?" she asked and stood for inspection.

"You go with Kermal here," Mustapha explained. "He'll take you to his checkpoint and you walk across the border into Turkey."

"And you trust him?" Shoshana was incredulous. "I won't fool anyone in this uniform."

"He wants the money and it'll be at night. You'll get across."

"Where will you and Meral be?" she asked, concerned about the young girl.

"Near here, waiting for Kermal to come back to get the last half of his money. If anything goes wrong, you come back here. We'll find you."

Meral pulled Shoshana aside. "Trust him," she whispered. "It's been arranged."

Shoshana did not like the casual way Mustapha arranged things. "Why don't I cross the border somewhere in the mountains where it's safer and away from the guards?"

"The Turks have many patrols on their side of the border," Mustapha explained. "If they pick you up without an entry stamp on your passport, they'll turn you back over to the Iraqis."

"Then how do I get an entry stamp?"

"Simple. The Turkish guards at Kermal's checkpoint have also been bribed and will stamp your passport. They are expecting you."

"So everyone has a price or we kill them," she said, disgusted with it all.

"We have no friends," Mustapha said, "so we must buy our allies." He jutted his chin down toward the border. "It's getting dark and time for you to go."

Shoshana touched Meral's cheek and followed Kermal down the mountain.

13

The small truck was waiting for the Eagle when it cleared the runway at Ramon Air Base. "That must be the Follow-Me," Matt said. Furry humphed an answer and got his camera out, ready to take pictures of the Israeli air base located in the Negev Desert. "Not much to see," Matt said. Most of the base was underground and the only worthwhile thing they could see was the control tower and the two jets sitting alert at the end of the runway. Both men were surprised at how fast the Follow-Me truck drove, demanding that they taxi fast to keep up as it led the way to the hardened underground concrete shelter where they would be parked.

The ramp was unusually quiet, and when they did see a truck or person, they were moving fast. At one point, the Follow-Me pulled off the side of the taxi path and stopped. Matt did the same and waited, wondering why the delay. Suddenly, four F-16 fighters erupted from the ramps leading to their underground shelters and taxied quickly to the runway. The big blast doors shut immediately behind them. The four jets slowed as they taxied onto the runway but did not stop. They took off in pairs with ten-second spacing between elements. "Did you see that," Furry said, wonder in his voice. "We'd never taxi that fast or do a formation takeoff without lining up on the runway." They were moving again.

"Yeah," Matt replied. "Well, we're taxiing that fast now. It doesn't look very safe to me."

"Depends on the way you look at it," Furry said. "They don't spend much time on the ground in the open. Probably figure they're safer in the air."

"You'd think they were in a combat zone." Matt didn't say more as they reached the ramp descending into the bunker. It was a massive structure with blast doors at both ends that were wide open. The Follow-Me drove quickly through the bunker and disappeared. A crew chief was waiting, holding his hands up and motioning them forward. Matt did as directed and then the crew chief crossed his wrists above his head, the signal to stop. He glanced at the nose wheel and shot Matt a look of disapproval. Matt was six inches off the mark. A crew boarding ladder was hooked over the left side of the cockpit and the two men clambered down, glad to be out of the cockpit after the long flight to Israel.

Men swarmed over the jet, refueling it from an in-bunker system. At the same time, other men were downloading the wing tanks. A disheveled-looking sergeant from Maintenance came up to them, asking if they had any problems and asking to see their maintenance forms. "No problems," Matt told him and handed over the forms.

"What the hell!" Furry yelled behind them. "They're uploading missiles." Matt turned to his jet and was surprised to see loading crews slipping AIM-9 Sidewinders onto the missile rails on the wing pylons. Four AIM-7 Sparrows were on a missile trailer, waiting to be uploaded under the fuselage.

"Hey, Barge," Matt yelled at the retreating back of the maintenance sergeant, "what the hell is going on?"

"It's a combat turn," a voice behind him said. Matt turned to see a young man his own age standing behind him. The rank on his epaulets announced he was a *rav seren*, a major. "Dave Harkabi," he said, extending his right hand. "I'm your escort officer."

Matt shook his hand, more concerned with what was going on with his jet. "Should they be uploading missiles?" he asked. They were not combatants, at least not that he knew of.

"We practice every chance we get," Harkabi explained. "They'll download when they're finished." He glanced at his watch. "Won't be much longer. If they take more than ten minutes, they'll be out here all day until they get it right."

"Jesus H. Christ," Furry said. "A combat turn in less than ten minutes?" He whipped his camera up and took a picture of the men swarming around the F-15. An armed guard stepped up and put his hand in front of Furry's camera and told him no photographs were allowed. "Oh, oh," Furry said. "I took some pictures when we were taxiing in."

"Give me the film," Harkabi said. "We'll develop it and return anything that's not classified. Please don't take any more photos around the base without permission." Matt noticed that Harkabi had a definite English accent and decided that Mad Mike Martin would have a field day chewing out any one of his officers who was dressed so casually. Harkabi's khaki shirt and trousers needed a pressing and his shoes hadn't seen polish in a long time. Rather sloppy and unspectacular, Matt thought. "Come on," Harkabi said. "They're finished." He led them out to a waiting car. The bunker's blast doors were cranking closed and Matt caught a last glimpse of his bird, still fully loaded for combat.

"Whatcha think?" Matt asked Furry as they climbed into the car.

"That combat turn was impressive."

"Can't say much about their uniforms," Matt allowed.

"The side with the simplest uniforms wins," Furry intoned.

"Another one of your 'rules'?" Matt asked.

"Yep. Also a history lesson." He stared out the window as Harkabi drove them in and studied the base. It was modern, heavily bunkered, and judging by the ramps, all important buildings were underground. "Take a look around," Furry said. "You probably won't see this again."

"What's that?" Matt replied, confused.

"A base at war."

Avi Tamir waited impatiently for his turn to see the prime minister, Yair Ben David. Normally, Tamir would have used the time to dig into one of the scientific journals he subscribed to and never seemed to have time to read. But today was different—Shoshana had called him that morning with the news that she was home. He had itched to leave his lab early and catch the train to Haifa. But Ben David's secretary had telephoned, telling him that the prime minister wanted to see him that afternoon. Reluctantly, he made the sixty-mile trip to Jerusalem.

"Yair will see you now," the secretary said. The atmosphere in the office reflected the traditional, egalitarian ways of Israel and every one was on a first-name basis. Tamir wasn't taken in for a moment; he knew who was in charge.

Ben David met him at the door and shook his hand, "Avi, glad you could make it on such short notice. I know you're anxious to get home."

The scientist wondered how the prime minister knew that.

"Please sit down." Ben David waved Tamir to a comfortable chair, sat down himself, and lit a pipe. The old, massive briar pipe was his political trademark. He puffed for a few moments, not inhaling. "Avi, I was talking to Benjamin Yuriden today." Ben David did not have to mention that Yuriden was the minister of defense and Tamir's boss. "We were wondering what progress you have made." Tamir was not surprised that the prime minister would talk to him directly about his work—things were kept informal in the Israeli government.

Tamir tried to make himself comfortable, but the subject Ben David wanted to discuss did not allow comfort. "There is progress. We should have a working model ready within the next three months."

"The triggering mechanism?"

"No," Tamir explained. "The entire system. My people have taken shortcuts using the information provided by Mossad."

"Ah yes," Ben David interrupted. He did not correct Tamir. The job of stealing defense technology from the United States was not done by Mossad but by another branch of Intelligence: the Scientific Liaison Bureau. Their agents operating in the United States had penetrated a lab at Sandia Corporation and "borrowed" classified nuclear weapons design information. The "borrowed" information had saved the Israelis years of research and led Tamir and his staff directly to the development of a thermonuclear, or hydrogen, bomb. "Time," the prime minister said, "time. We need more of it but the Arabs are denying us that luxury." Tamir waited, knowing there was more to come. "I need a fully operational weapon as soon as possible."

"But for what use?" Tamir protested. "Why would we need such a terrible weapon?" The closer he came to perfecting a thermonuclear bomb for his country, the more his conscience demanded to know why. "We have more than enough atomic weapons to destroy our enemies."

Ben David laid down his pipe, folded his hands, and looked directly at Tamir, drawing him in. "We live in a troubled world filled with hard choices. One of our agents has learned that the Iraqis are now producing a new binary nerve gas that can penetrate the protective clothing we use."

"That doesn't make sense," Tamir protested. "Producing a binary nerve gas is very difficult. Why would the Iraqis go to all that trouble when a more conventional method of production is all they need? And the claim that a nerve gas can penetrate protective clothing? Well, I'm more than a bit skeptical."

"Believe me, enough is going on around Kirkuk that we cannot ignore it. Two facts. We know they are using canisters that are made of a polymeric material that is difficult to manufacture—but extremely resistant to corrosion. Also"—Ben David was spitting out words like a machine gun—"they are producing a new antidote. Our agent brought out an injector needle that looks exactly like the combo pens we use. We are analyzing it now." Ben David paused for effect. "Our scientists cannot break down the antidote. We don't know what it is."

"But in time we will," Tamir said. "Then we can manufacture it for our own protection."

"True . . . In time. But time is the one thing we don't have. Arab radicals have made Saddam Hussein a martyr to Western imperialism and are using him as a symbol to force cooperation between all the Arab states. In defeat, Saddam has brought Egypt, Syria, and Iraq together in defiance of the West's "new order." So much so that we now have evidence of a renewed military alignment between Syria and Egypt. Also we are seeing signs of much more cordial relations between Syria and Iraq. If that happens . . ."

"Yes, I see. That means the Iraqis' nerve gas can be used against us. But they wouldn't do that. Surely, they must suspect we have the *bomb* and would retaliate. It would be Armageddon . . ."

"They do. But it hasn't stopped them from developing their version of 'the poor man's bomb.' The Arabs will be made to understand that using a nerve gas, any nerve gas, on us is unthinkable. The consequences would be too great. That's why we need a thermonuclear weapon."

The moral dilemma that had deviled Tamir since the first nuclear test in 1979 was back to torment him. Am I to be a destroyer of nations? he thought.

"I know you are anxious to get home," Ben David said. He rose from his seat and walked Tamir to the door. "Avi, each of us must do what he or she can to protect our people and our land." He clasped the scientist's hand tightly. "Go. See your daughter. And be proud of her."

The train ride to Haifa gave Tamir time to mull over what Ben David had said. He cursed his probing, analytical mind that refused to rest. "Damn," he muttered to himself, not wanting to think about the pieces that were fitting together. His daughter worked for Mossad and had been the agent who had brought out the latest intelligence from Iraq. It was just like the prime minister to give him enough clues to figure it out. But why? Ben David always had an ulterior motive. Was it to spur him on? Or did the prime minister have something else in store for the Tamir family?

Rather than walk from the train station in Haifa, Tamir caught a taxi to the family's apartment. From the moment he let himself in, he could sense Shoshana's presence. "Shoshe?" he called.

"Here, Father." She stepped through the French doors opening onto the balcony and stopped. The room separated them. She was wearing a simple dress, sandals, and no makeup. He hair was pulled back into a single, thickly plaited braid. Then she was in his arms and he could only smell the soft fragrance of soap, no perfume.

"I'm glad you finally decided to come back and see your old dad," he told her. There was no rebuke in his voice, only the old banter.

"I'm so glad to be home," she said and drew back to look at him. He wanted to hear her say, "Oh, Faah-ther," but it was gone forever. Even her voice was different and the last traces of the girl he had so loved were gone. This was a mature woman. His daughter had changed and he would never call her Shoshe again.

Shoshana insisted on cooking dinner for them that night and not going out to a restaurant. "I did enjoy going shopping this afternoon," she told him as they sat down.

"Did you see Yoel?" he asked. He knew her old boyfriend would be anxious to see her.

She shook her head no. "I don't think there's anything there. Not now."

"Well, tell me about Spain." He promised himself to keep up the charade. For the next few minutes, Shoshana told him a very convincing story about her trip. She's been debriefed well, he thought. I wonder how long she's been back?

Later that evening, Shoshana announced that she had quit her job with the fruit export company. Tamir only raised an eyebrow, not sure of what to say. "I'm going to enlist in the *sherut miluim* and train as a medic," she told him. *Sherut miluim* was the reserve component of Israel's defense forces. "After I finish training, I'm thinking of becoming a nurse."

Tamir said nothing, thankful that his daughter was home.

"Now what's happened?" Melissa said to herself as she hurried to the waiting car that had been dispatched from the White House garage to pick her up. It had to be important for the duty officer to call her at four in the morning and tell her that Fraser had ordered her to work and that a car would be in front of her condominium within minutes.

The driver gave her a noncommittal nod and handed her the final edition of *The Washington Post*. "It's on the front page,'' he said. She opened the newspaper to glaring head-lines and a lead story that told of massive amounts of money being fed into political action committees, get-out-the-vote organizations, and Pontowski's own election committee. The reporter related how a sophisticated money-laundering scheme had covered up the donors and bypassed political contribution disclosure laws. Most of the money had been directed into political action committees that had then en-gaged in a TV blitz of vicious mudslinging. It was claimed that the get-out-the-vote groups effectively bought votes. The reporter ended the exposé by quoting the Senate minority leader, William Douglas Courtland. ''This was a highly unethical campaign with too much money going to the right people at the right time. One person or group had to be con-trolling the shots and they violated just about every election campaign law on the books.''

''How much of it do you think is true?'' the driver asked.

Melissa only shook her head, trying to think of what to say. Of course, she wanted to believe it was a pack of lies or misinformation, facts twisted to make a story. She had seen it before and accepted it as part of the game of politics. But this was different, it had the ring of truth and the *Post* had too good a track record with their investigative journalism. Sure, the newspaper made mistakes, but not ones that in-volved the President of the United States. The reporter was onto something. There was no doubt in Melissa's mind that Zack Pontowski would never allow, much less condone, the use of illegal campaign funds. He would have been the first whistle-blower. But perhaps someone inside the election campaign committee had exceeded his or her bounds. Who? An image of Fraser talking on a telephone immediately came to mind.

A secretary told her to go directly into the Oval Office when she reached the White House and she was embarrassed at interrupting the meeting. Fraser was sitting next to the chairman of the election committee. The Vice President was standing, holding a cup of coffee, listening to what the speaker of the House had to say. ''Coffee?'' Pontowski asked when he saw Melissa come through the door. She smiled a thanks and poured a cup from the silver carafe on the table. ''Well, like I was saying, Mr. President,'' the speaker continued, "it's way too early to see what this has done to your political base in the House."

"What about the Senate?" Pontowski asked the Vice President.

The Vice President stared into his cup. "It's the same. Too early to tell." He gave a wicked grin. "But I can call in beaucoup markers."

"Not on this one," Pontowski told the Vice President. Fraser's head snapped up, but he said nothing.

Pontowski leaned back in his chair. "Okay, Frank"—this was for the campaign chairman—"can you recall any questionable money coming in from political action committees or our people getting in bed with the wrong characters?"

"We returned anything that looked like it came from a questionable source," the man said. "And we stayed well clear of the PACs and get-out-the-vote groups. Too much wheeling-dealing going on at the state level."

"Did you keep a record of all that?" Fraser asked.

"Of course," the campaign chairman said. Fraser frowned.

"Melissa"—Pontowski was looking at her—"did you see or hear anything questionable when you were working at the national campaign headquarters?"

"Every day," she answered. "But if it had anything to do with contributions, I forwarded it to Mr. Fraser's office."

"Did you keep a record or some kind of memo?" Fraser asked. Melissa shook her head no.

"Tom, what did you see?" Fraser had been responsible for the day-to-day running of the campaign, leaving the chairman free to concentrate on fund-raising and overall guidance.

Fraser smiled condescendingly. "Only what Melissa sent up to me. I handled it." There was condemnation in his tone.

"Did you keep a record?" Melissa asked sweetly.

Fraser glared at her. "It wasn't necessary." Now he took charge. "It's an exposé, the kind of thing that sells newspapers. We've all seen it before and the *Post* has been slobbering after another Watergate ever since I can remember. There's nothing there, so we should stonewall it and throw the ball back into their court."

"I don't think it will be that easy," the speaker of the House allowed.

"Without proof, what have they got?" Fraser was on the offensive.

"Okay, enough," Pontowski said, holding up a hand and stopping all discussion. "This has the potential to blow up in our faces. It's like seeing a rat—if you see one, you can be sure there's more hiding in the woodwork." He spoke quickly, without emotion. "Here's what we're going to do. Tom, you're in charge. First, draft up a press release and get it back to me before it's sent out. As of now, we are concerned and conducting a full-scale investigation. If there was any wrongdoing, we'll find it and prosecute those responsible, no matter who they are. Second, talk to the attorney general and get a list of recommendations for a special prosecutor. Third, get the FBI involved and have them contact and interview everyone connected with the campaign."

"Sir," Fraser protested. "Do you have any idea of how many people that is?"

"Some," Pontowski replied, "some. Fourth, contact the IRS and have them start checking on reported tax deductions to my campaign. It had all better track with our records."

"They won't like that one," Fraser mumbled.

"No doubt," Pontowski conceded. "Fifth, I want action today and an update before you go home tonight. Sixth, I want every reporter coming to us for information and anything they dig up on their own will be old news. Any questions?" There were none and the group started to file out. "Tom, what's first on the agenda for today?"

Fraser stopped and looked at his schedule. "Breakfast with a delegation from the hill at seven-thirty, Mr. President. Subject: the Middle East." He handed Pontowski a list of the three congressmen and two senators who would be there.

"Humm, the Israeli lobby," Pontowski said. "Well, we can get some work done before then."

Later, the breakfast started pleasantly enough but tension slipped into the conversation as talk turned toward the main concern of the delegation. "Mr. President," the senior senator said, "we are worried about current developments and see an ominous threat being directed at the security of Israel. We understand that the Israelis have asked for increased military aid." Pontowski nodded and encouraged the senator to continue. "We believe the administration should honor that request."

"We only received the request a few days ago," Pontowski explained. "We're still examining it."

"Mr. President"—it was the junior congressman's turn—"my constituents are very worried about the bellicose statements coming from the Arabs that they are uniting to continue the work of Saddam and think we should give the Israelis the squadron of F-Fifteen Es they have asked for."

"Your information is very detailed," Pontowski said. "Like I said, we are looking at it."

"Since your grandson is demonstrating an F-Fifteen E to the IDF can I tell my constituents that you are favorably considering the request?"

Pontowski looked at the man and frowned. "I didn't know Matt was in Israel. Please believe me, sending my grandson was a decision made by the Air Force and does not reflect my policies in the area."

"Mr. President," the junior senator said. "We understand that your policies are changing."

"My policies reflect the reality of the situation," Pontowski replied.

"And what are the realities of the situation, Mr. President?" It was the junior congressman again. He was challenging the President.

"Gentlemen"—Pontowski smiled—"I'll be glad to discuss my Middle East policies here but we are going to disagree and I would prefer we keep the conversation confidential. We only tell the press that we had a 'frank discussion.' Agreed?" That was a polite way of telling the press that a serious head-knocking session went on at the meeting. A "blunt and open discussion" meant they had all but come to blows. Nods and agreement went around the table.

"First, I have no intention of letting Israel be destroyed or suffer a defeat at the hands of her enemies." He could sense the delegation relax. "However,"—the tension was back— "I have no intention of supporting all of Israel's policies— policies that are creating problems of their own making."

"What problems are you talking about, Mr. President?" the junior congressman asked.

"Specifically, the occupation of Gaza and the settlement of the West Bank."

"Gaza and the West Bank are vital for the security of Israel, Mr. President."

"Perhaps. But because of that occupation, Israel has to make many choices." This was greeted by silence. "Is Israel going to be a South African-type state in the Middle East where Jews rule a sub-class of Palestinians? Or is Israel going to be a democratic and Jewish state that lives in some sort of peaceable accommodation with its Palestinian neighbors?''

"But the Jews have a historical right to Palestine," the junior Congressman protested.

"All of it?" Pontowski answered, his voice calm and measured. "And what about the Palestinian claims? Have they no historical rights?"

"Mr. President, you obviously don't understand the complexity of the situation." The junior congressman regretted saying it as the words came out.

But Pontowski only smiled, waiting for him to continue. Silence. "It's allowed to disagree with me," Pontowski said. He was telling the young congressman to fight fair and that he was willing to overlook one minor indiscretion—as long as it was in private. "I do understand there are factions in Israel who claim the Jews are entitled to all of Palestine and that other fractions are willing to limit the size of Israel and share the land with the Arabs who were also born there."

"Mr. President"—the congressman was like a bulldog and would not let it go—"the choices you mentioned can only be made by Israel. Why should an internal matter for the Israelis affect our policies in the area?"

The moment of truth had arrived. "Because, their choice will determine my policy toward them."

Melissa was in the hall when the delegation left. The junior congressman ignored her when he announced, "The oil interests bought him. Read all about it in the *Post*."

Matt was tired when he unzipped his flight suit and headed for the shower, shedding the rest of his clothes as he went. Furry was flopped out in an easy chair, unable to move. Occasionally, a groan would slip out. They had ended their sixth week of flying with Israelis and returned to their rooms after an early-morning flight. "I'm too old for this," Furry boomed across the room as he reached for another beer. "My bones hurt from pulling all those g's. But damn, we were good today."

"Yeah, we were," Matt conceded. He had been surprised to learn that he could hold his own with the Israeli pilots and, in every one-on-one engagement, best them. Furry had repeatedly demonstrated the bombing accuracy of the Eagle's systems on "first look" targets and impressed the Israeli observers no end. "They ain't much to look at on the ground," Matt said from the shower, "but once they strap a jet on, they are something else."

Furry pulled at his beer, thinking. And so are you old buddy, so are you. "Hey, you think they're doing a snow job on us?" he called. "These pukes are supposed to be the best in the world." Got to keep the boy humble, he thought. "We shouldn't be rompin' and stompin' like this."

"Could be," Matt allowed, as he stepped out of the shower. "But I doubt it. At least not in the air. Come on, get your bod in gear, Dave's going to pick us up in a few minutes."

Furry groaned and launched his bulk from the chair. Dave Harkabi was going to take them on a long weekend when he went home to Haifa. He had apologized for not having room at his parents' home and booked them into a hotel on the beach. Twenty minutes later, they were in Harkabi's car, headed north for Haifa. They broke the monotony of crossing the Negev Desert by talking shop. "Your Eagle is most impressive," Harkabi said. "We could use a squadron of E models."

"Yeah," Matt said, deep in thought, "the jet has definitely given us an edge we wouldn't normally have."

Harkabi said, "You've had input into that advantage. You make the Eagle fly like a demon."

"We've been lucky so far," Matt allowed. "Your pilots are on to us now and are going to start kicking some ass."

"You think so?" Harkabi asked.

"Yep. You're too damn good. Look at your combat record . . ."

Harkabi laughed. "You've been reading our propaganda." He turned and looked at Matt. "Yes, we are good. We carefully select our pilots and then train like hell. Every flight is a potential combat mission for us. Why do you think we upload all our birds with munitions after we land?"

"Even ours?" Furry said.

Harkabi took a deep breath and ignored Furry's question. The Israeli major didn't tell them that every night an Israeli aircrew had powered up their Eagle and had worked the systems. One night, they had even flown the bird. He changed the subject. "When you look at our combat record," he explained, "always remember who we are flying against. Look at the Syrian Air Force. They have seven hundred fifty pilots. Of those, fifty are as good as any in the world. We know them by name, what they fly, and where they are stationed. The other seven hundred are turkeys, cannon fodder, worthless. We are fortunate because there are none in between.

"We monitor their communications and use it against them. If any of those fifty good pilots take off, we know it. Because they fly like the Soviets and rely on ground control to vector their fighters, we know exactly where the 'man' is and—what do you Yanks say?—we double- and triple-bang him in an engagement."

"You mean you deliberately go after their talent and go three-on-one?" Matt was amazed.

"Exactly. We will let their turkeys enjoy a temporary advantage while we concentrate on eliminating the real threat."

"Nice guys," Furry mumbled.

Again, Harkabi laughed. "What do you say? 'A kill is a kill'?"

When they were out of the Negev and into the heart of Israel, Harkabi gave a running commentary about the countryside, a perfect tour guide. He drove fast, telling them he wanted to reach Haifa before the Sabbath began. "Israel grinds to a stop at sundown," he explained. "If you're not religious, Haifa is the best place to spend the Sabbath."

His timing was perfect and Matt and Furry were deposited at the hotel as Dave sped away. Inside, they learned that their rooms had been paid for in advance. After a brief discussion, they told the clerk that they would have to pay because they couldn't accept gifts from a foreign government. The clerk shrugged and quoted a very reasonable price, settling the issue.

The next morning, Matt woke up at five-thirty and couldn't go back to sleep. He wandered out onto the balcony and took in the sunrise before he pulled on a pair of shorts and his running shoes and headed for the beach, intent on a morning run. Two miles from the hotel, he saw a lone swimmer walking toward the water. A sense of déjà vu swept through him as he neared the woman who was now in the water—there was something familiar about the way she walked, her figure.

He gave a mental shrug and ran on past as she swam directly out to sea.

Then it hit him. It had to be Rose Temple, the Canadian he had met at Marbella and had lost to that Arab engineer. The coincidence was too much and he slowed, lost deep in memory. Then he buttonhooked and ran back down the beach until he was opposite her. She was swimming parallel to the shore, maybe fifty meters off shore. He kept pace with her, surprised at how powerful a swimmer she was. When she turned shoreward, he sat down on the sandy berm and waited. Any doubts vanished when she waded through the shallow water. The traffic-stopping figure, black hair, wide yet very feminine shoulders, the magnificent breasts and narrow waist could only belong to one person. But it was her eyes that he remembered best. Those dark pools of promise and beauty. It was Rose Temple.

She ignored him and started to jog back down the beach. He pushed himself up and ran after her. "Rose," he called. "Matt Pontowski. We met at Marbella in Spain." There was no response at first and she kept running. He stopped, afraid that it might be a case of mistaken identity. "No way," he mumbled to himself and started after her again. "Rose," he called at her back, "please stop."

The woman halted and turned to face him and all his doubts vanished. She stood there in her black tank suit, not the flashy, half-naked come-on she had worn to entice Is'al Mana, but the same suit he remembered from the yacht party. Her skin was wet and glowing and her thick plait of hair shimmered in the morning sun as she stood there, waiting for him. "My name is Shoshana and I'm an Israeli, not a Canadian." She turned and ran down the beach, leaving him dumbfounded.

He headed back to the hotel, confused by the feeling of loss that held him tight. "What the hell," he said, twisting to look back down the beach. Then he ran as fast as he could after her. It was not a case of mistaken identity. It had to be her. Who else would tell him that she was not a Canadian? But the beach was empty. He had lost her. Slowly he walked back to the hotel. Well, you know how you're going to spend this weekend, he told himself. He was going to find the woman who now called herself Shoshana.

Shoshana leaned against the back wall of a beach house,

waiting for Matt to run by. She clenched her towel tightly, fighting back the tears that were threatening her. You have no reason to cry, she berated herself. He means nothing to you. That's a lie and I'm finished with lies. Once I was attracted to him but now he's part of a past that has nothing to do with my future. Again, she chastised herself for being so weak as to cry. She vowed never to cry again.

When her breathing had slowed, she found her car and drove home to the safety of her family's apartment on the hillside. She let herself in and called, "Father, I'm back," surprised that her voice sounded normal. Avi Tamir came out of the kitchen, a worried look on his face. He nodded in the direction of the balcony and disappeared back into the kitchen. She walked through the French doors.

Gad Habish was standing there, waiting.

14

"He wants to see you immediately," the secretary said to Habish without looking up from her work. The "he" was the wizened curmudgeon who headed Mossad's operations—the Ganef. Habish walked directly into the thief's office.

"Will she do it?" the Ganef asked.

"I don't know. Shoshana hates me and everything we do." Habish waited for a reply. There wasn't any. "Do we need her?"

The Ganef gave a little snort. "Pontowski is the grandson of the President of the United States. Have you forgotten that?" He didn't wait for an answer. "This is a chance to establish a *liaison* we might turn to our advantage later. We don't pass up opportunities like this." He paused. The Ganef had carefully meshed the reports of Matt's morning runs on the base with Shoshana's morning swim. It was simply a matter of bringing them together. "Especially when it only cost us a phone call to Harkabi to bring him to Haifa for a weekend.''

"What about the hotel?''

A line crossed the Gunot's lips that Habish took for a smile. "The Americans are paying for their rooms, not Mossad.''

Why am I doing this? Shoshana berated herself as she swam by the same part of the beach as the day before. She had been pulled and turned a dozen different ways by her emotions after Habish had left the apartment and still wasn't sure what to do. A warm tugging feeling kept pulling at her, urging her to go to the beach. It was the same sensation she had experienced at Marbella when they had first met. Be honest, she told herself, you want to see him again. But a revulsion at the thought of working for Mossad turned her down dark corridors of self-loathing and disgust. She wasn't the same person.

Matt sat on the berm in the same spot where he had waited the day before and watched Shoshana swim in to shore. He caught his breath as she walked toward him and he remembered the Greek legend of Aphrodite, the goddess of love, who rose naked from the sea. Now I know what the Greeks were thinking about, he thought as he watched her wade the last few feet toward him. "I'd always thought Aphrodite was a blonde," he said, loud enough for her to hear.

Shoshana said nothing and sat down beside him. "My name is Shoshana Tamir and when we met I was an agent for Mossad.'' She forced herself to look out to sea and not to him. It was an effort that cost her dearly but she was determined to tell him the truth. "Do you know what Mossad is?'' Nothing from Matt. "It's our version of the CIA,'' she continued. "My objective was to seduce and exploit Is'ul Mana. And I did. He was my only assignment and I quit Mossad when I was finished. I'm training as a medic in Zahal and start nursing school next month.''

"Zahal?''

"A word we use for Zvah Haganah Le Israel—Israel Defense Forces.''

"Why are you telling me this?'' Confusion and pain caught at his words.

Silence. Then a slight shake of her head. "I don't know. After you saw me yesterday, a Mossad case officer came to my home and asked me to make contact with you. They arranged for you to stay at your hotel, hoping we would meet.''

"Why would they do that?''

She stood, ready to leave. Matt reached up and touched her arm, not wanting her to go.

For the first time, she turned and looked him fully in the face. She was on the verge of tears. "Don't be naive. They didn't tell me *why.* Your grandfather . . . They're looking for a connection . . . the Israeli connection. I don't know.'' Despair ate at every word but there were no tears.

"Why are you telling me all this?'' She still wouldn't answer the most important question. She couldn't, for she didn't know the answer.

Shoshana pulled away from his touch and walked away, not understanding herself and the driving need to be free of lies and deceit. He followed her and grabbed her arm, forcing her to stop and turn around. "Why?'' he demanded. Like her he did not understand what was driving him on and why he didn't leave and get her out of his life.

"Look at me!'' Self-hate drove her words. "I'm a whore. I used my body to get what I wanted.'' Her body trembled as she fought to control her ragged breathing. Then, almost a gasp: "I had to kill Is'al to escape.''

He dropped his hand and freed her. Every rational instinct he possessed was shouting for him to disengage and run for cover. But this was not combat. "Doesn't that mean anything to you?'' she demanded to know. "I murdered a man and there is no punishment for me. Nothing.''

"I was in a crash with another jet where three men were killed,'' Matt said, choosing his words carefully. "They say it wasn't my fault, but I was involved. If I had been a better pilot, maybe less aggressive—who knows? One was a good friend and another, well, after my grandfather, Jack Locke was the finest man I ever met. He had a beautiful wife and two small kids.'' They stood inches apart, not touching, silent. His hurt matched hers. "Remembering is the punishment.''

Only the sound of the surf washing at their feet filled the small space between them.

The headlines shouted, EMBATTLED PRESIDENT STRUGGLES TO SURVIVE. Melissa looked around her office and didn't see any struggling going on. In fact, it was business pretty much as normal. She read the lead story anyway to find out what should be happening around her. She almost chuckled as the reporter alluded to midnight conferences and the hint of a presidential cover-up. She looked up to see Bill Carroll standing in front of her, five minutes early for the intelligence update on the Middle East the President had requested. "You're early," she said. "Have a seat and I'll show you in when the President is ready." Neither gave the slightest indication that they had met before in a much more unprofessional manner when Carroll had first told her about his discoveries in the Middle East.

Exactly on time, she escorted Carroll into the Oval Office where four men were with the President. Zack Pontowski was his normal unflappable self; three of the other men appeared at ease and only Fraser seemed agitated or worried. You do look a little ruffled, she thought, enjoying his discomfort. "Okay, Bill," Pontowski said. "What have you got this morning? The PDB sounded grim."

So that's what's got to Fraser, Melissa decided. The President read something Fraser didn't want him to read. She left them and returned to her desk.

Carroll set his briefing charts on an easel so the group could see them, took a deep breath, and began. "Mr. President, gentlemen, the Syrians are moving their tanks and armored units in a way that constitutes an increased military threat to Israel." He detailed how the Syrians were positioning three large armored corps in a forward position facing Israel. The northernmost force consisted of at least a thousand tanks in the Bekáa Valley opposite Beirut and anchored on the Syrian city of Homs. The tanks could move south down the Bekáa, cross the Litani River, and strike into the northern part of Israel directly at Haifa. The Bekáa Valley was a dagger pointed at the northern border of Israel.

The middle force numbered approximately eight hundred tanks and was moving into position on the Golan Heights right up to the Syrian disengagement line. The 1,250-member United Nations Disengagement Observer Force in the Area of Separation was getting edgy and had asked the UN for permission to reduce the number of their observers in case fighting broke out.

But most ominous was the third force of at least fifteen hundred tanks clustered next to the Jordanian/Syrian border in the Jebel Druze highlands. A new highway linked the Jebel Druze to the Jordan River and allowed the Syrians to thrust directly at Jerusalem through Jordan.

"Where did the Syrians get that many tanks?" Bobby Burke, the director of central intelligence, snorted.

"Sir," Carroll replied, "they bought them from the Russians."

The President ignored the exchange and studied the chart. "So the Syrians could launch a three-pronged thrust at Israel," he said.

Carroll flipped to the next chart of the Sinai Desert. "And the Egyptians have moved the location of their annual defense exercise, Desert Star, that starts next week." He circled an area that extended from the Suez Canal into the Sinai.

"Military maneuvers in the Sinai are a violation of the Camp David Accords," National Security Adviser Cagliari said. "The Israelis would never let them get away with that, nor would the UN peacekeeping forces and observers stationed in the Sinai."

"Normally, sir, that would be a true statement," Carroll answered. "But the Egyptians have invited observers to monitor the exercise and have even asked the Israelis to participate. The Israelis have ignored the invitation and protested the exercise. But they keep looking over their shoulder at all those Syrian tanks on their northern border."

Admiral Scovill, the Chairman of the Joint Chiefs of Staff, studied the map. "Any indication that the Iraqis are involved in any of this?" he asked.

"None at this time," Carroll answered. Burke nodded in agreement.

"What's the Israeli reaction?" Cagliari asked.

"Apparently they are taking it very seriously and have declared state of alert Gimmel. There's only two higher states of alert. As of now, all military leaves have been canceled and certain reserve units called up. If the Egyptians do go ahead with Desert Star, the Israelis will see it as a potential threat. They'll have to mobilize and move forces into position in the Sinai and keep them there until the threat goes away. They simply cannot ignore a military exercise of that size so close to their borders."

"So what are you telling us?" Fraser asked.

Admiral Scovill answered, "A war is going to break out soon. A military exercise like Desert Star is a screen to move forces into position. Any fool can see that." He glared at Carroll as if he were personally responsible. "Who presents the biggest threat to Israel and what can we do about it?"

"The Egyptians, sir. Apply diplomatic pressure and get them to cancel the exercise. That will remove a threat from the Israelis' southern flank and allow them to concentrate their forces opposite the Syrians. No way the Syrians can take on the Israelis without Egypt tying up part of the IDF."

Pontowski nodded in agreement. The lieutenant colonel had reinforced what he was thinking. "Contact State," Pontowski ordered. "Call the Egyptian ambassador in today and let's have a friendly chat. Also, I want to send all the players over there a loud and clear signal that we are concerned and are not going to sit on our thumbs and let a war break out. Any other suggestions, Colonel?" Pontowski was testing Carroll, seeing how deep his analysis cut.

Carroll thought for a moment. "This might be a good time to practice Response Alpha of your new national energy plan."

Fraser was floored. "Sir, we don't need to start rationing gas because of this."

"Tom," Pontowski said, a gentle rebuke surfacing in his voice, "you need to read the plan. Response Alpha is the first step we take in case of an oil crisis. It calls for the government to set up the framework that makes it possible to quickly implement rationing and conservation measures." He paused, definitely liking the way Carroll thought. "By testing our system, we send a message that our diplomatic efforts to keep fighting from breaking out are not going to be held captive by a fear of an oil crisis or another embargo."

"But Mr. President," Fraser argued, "that means the oil companies will be subject to strict governmental control. That's politically hazardous—"

Pontowski cut him off. "We won't ration a drop of gas at this time or interfere with anybody's business. We are conducting an exercise to find out how well our bureaucrats have done their job."

Ten minutes later, Melissa glanced over the top of her reading glasses at Fraser as he marched into his office. "Get the chief of the Secret Service in here now," he ordered and closed his office door behind him. Melissa dialed the number and relayed Fraser's message. My, but he is upset, she thought.

A few minutes later, Stan Abbott, an athletic fifty-four-year-old, was sitting in front of Fraser. "Stan, thanks for coming up on such short notice." Outwardly, Fraser was calm and controlled. "I know you're aware of what the newspapers are saying about the President." Abbott nodded. "I have just come from the President and want to reassure you that there is no cover-up going on. In fact, we want to do everything in our power to keep that from happening. *We*"— again he stressed the "we," implying he was relaying a message from Pontowski—"are very worried about certain people who work in the Office of the President and . . ." Fraser hesitated to see how much Abbott would do without receiving direct orders. Abbott said nothing.

Reluctantly, Fraser continued, committing himself. "We want a fresh look at these people." He handed Abbott a short list of names.

"You want us to request a new background investigation on these people?"

"I was hoping your office could investigate them," Fraser answered. "Very discreetly of course, but thoroughly. We've got to know if there's any rot in our woodwork, if there is something, anything, that's been missed."

"I can arrange that," Abbott said. Fraser thanked him and he left the office. Outside, he glanced at the list Fraser had given him. It puzzled him why only two names were written down: Melissa Courtney-Smith and Lieutenant Colonel William G. Carroll. If there was anything about those two that posed a threat to the President, he would find it.

What a strange derangement, Shoshana thought. I'm worse than a teenage girl and not acting my age. I'm twenty-seven and moving around in a daze living from hour to hour, simply happy to be with him.

Matt's back was to her as he leaned over the rail of the apartment's balcony, taking in the view. The lights of Haifa were twinkling in the dusk, spreading out as night fell. They were both tired after three days of sightseeing and Shoshana was leaning against the doorjamb studying his back, trying to come to terms with the man. Roaming around Jerusalem with Matt had been a discovery for her. He had dragged her into East Jerusalem, the Arab section, and had charged down narrow passageways, eager to meet the Arabs head-on.

She had protested that it was dangerous, but Matt had ignored her and mingled with the crowds, another tourist spending his money. That constantly changing kaleidoscope of new and old, Western and Arab culture, that mingled and fused in front of them in delightful patterns drew him on. He had finally run down and dragged her protesting into a small restaurant where a friendly owner and his family served an excellent grilled lamb, salad, and homemade bread. The smells of the food, the family speaking Arabic, had triggered a barrage of memories for Shoshana and, for a split second, she was back in Iraq. Then Matt's voice brought her back to the moment and she had found warmth and protection in his shadow.

"What's for tomorrow?" Matt asked, breaking her reverie.

"Very little, I hope. My father will be home, I'd like you to meet him."

He turned. "Oh, oh. This sounds serious when you meet the family." Then he smiled. "I'd like to meet your father."

"We can go to the beach . . ." She hesitated. "It's the day after tomorrow I want to show you." He waited for her to continue. "It's Yom Hazikaron, our Day of Remembrance. At noon Israel comes to a halt and for two minutes, no one moves, and sirens wail. It's the way we honor our people who were killed in the wars. If you saw it, perhaps you might understand us a little better. Then at dusk it all changes and we start to celebrate our Day of Independence. Haifa turns into one big street party."

"Sounds good," he said and turned back to take in the view.

Shoshana! she warned herself. Don't look at him so much. Don't touch him. There is so much in him that has changed since we met in Marbella. He is more reserved and confident but there is still that same boyish eagerness. And why do I feel so safe around him?

Then she gave up and moved to him. "Matt," she whispered. He turned and she walked into his arms. He held her, gently stroking her hair. He felt a slight shudder run through her body.

"What's wrong?"

She wanted to tell him that falling in love with a gentile, a foreigner, was the ultimate self-indulgence for an Israeli. Instead: "I'm so afraid there's going to be another war. You don't read Hebrew . . . The stories in the newspapers about Syria and Egypt . . . we've seen this so many times before. We are caught in a thousand-year war with no peace. The Arabs will not rest until they have destroyed us."

"A map is a map, and the one I saw on TV this evening says the Syrian tanks are moving away from your border. And it's pretty clear that my grandpop is talking to the Egyptians. I think the whole thing was overblown and there's not going to be any shooting in the near future."

It was what she wanted to hear and she held him close, content with that for now.

15

"You are pleased with yourself," Tosh Pontowski said. She was out of bed and sitting in her favorite chair.

Pontowski laid down his read file and sipped his early-morning coffee. "Doesn't happen often. Let me enjoy it." His wife knew he wanted to talk. "Looks like the Middle East is settling down. The talks with the Egyptian ambassador are going well and he assures us that the Egyptians are going to cancel the military exercise in the Sinai."

"Is he reliable?" Tosh asked.

"Always has been in the past. Also, the Syrians are pulling back from their forward positions and the Israelis have relaxed their state of alert."

"What about the Russians?"

"The Kremlin Kapers are still in full swing. God only knows what's going on over there. We are sure of two things. Rokossovsky is in a heap of trouble because their economy is in a shambles. He's fighting for his life."

"What's the second?"

"The old guard led by the army is trying to kick him out and go back to the Brezhnev way of running the country."

"Tush, I'm worried about those stories in the newspapers . . ."

"I know, love. There's nothing the newspapers like better than a scandal to beat the President with about the shoulders and ears. I've got an investigation going but so far haven't found a thing. We've even asked the reporters about their sources so we can trace it all down, but they won't help. Whoever buried the evidence dug a deep hole."

"If there was any evidence to bury," Tosh said.

"I hope you're right. But I've got a tingling sensation that tells me it's out there, just waiting to be thrown on the table and stink." The phone rang and he picked it up. When he set it down, he rose and paced the room for a few moments. "It's coming apart . . ." Tosh waited. Years of living together had given her an intimate knowledge of her husband and she knew the news the unknown caller had relayed was bad, very bad. "The Syrians have stopped their withdrawal." He kissed her cheek and walked hurriedly from the room.

Matt's height gave him a slight advantage and he could see over most of the heads around him. He was caught with Shoshana and Avi Tamir in a slow-moving current of humanity that was heading up the narrow path that led up the hill outside Haifa and into the cemetery on top. The distinctive wail of a nearby air raid siren started to build and was joined by others in the distance. It was exactly twelve o'clock. The crowd stopped moving. Matt could see men come to attention and little children fidget beside crying mothers, not understanding what was going on around them. He glanced at Shoshana and Avi, surprised that she was not crying like her father. The strident pitch of the siren wound down to a mournful echo and then died. For a few moments, the crowd was absolutely silent. Then he could hear low sobs and the voices of mothers hushing their children as the crowd started to move again, quietly and slowly.

Shoshana sat on the ground next to her mother's grave while Tamir pulled at some weeds that had grown around the headstone that had been missed by the Arab gardener who tended

the cemetery. Matt waited patiently and Shoshana finally
turned to look at him. "I barely remember my mother . . ."

"Miriam was killed in the Yom Kippur War," Tamir said.
"Shoshana was six years old and they were at a kibbutz in
the Huleh Valley. Have you been there?" he asked Matt. The
pilot shook his head no. "You should see it, it is the jewel
of Israel. But it lies at the base of the Golan Heights and the
kibbutz was shelled by Syrian artillery. Miriam was rushing
children to a bomb shelter . . . she never made it." Tamir
stared off in the distance, seeing something in his past.
"Shoshana is so much like her."

In the silence, Matt looked into Shoshana's eyes and knew
that he loved her. He didn't fight or question it, he simply
knew. He would tell her later when the moment was right.

"They shouldn't be flying," Tamir said, gesturing at two
low-flying aircraft approaching the hill. Matt looked, picking
out the two fighters immediately. He estimated they were
flying at about five hundred feet when a long stick of a smoke
trial reached up toward the aircraft and one disappeared in a
bright flash. "My God . . ." Tamir whispered.

"MiGs!" Matt shouted. "Hit the deck!" He threw himself
on the ground next to Shoshana and rolled on top of her. The
lone survivor streaked over the cemetery as another Hawk
surface-to-air missile streaked above it, this time missing. In
the distance, air raid sirens started to wail and the retreating
fighter skimmed over the housetops of Haifa. "Bomb run,"
Matt said. He had seen four 500-kilogram bombs slung under
the MiG-23. "Syrian markings," he told them. In the distance, they heard the dull thuds of exploding bombs and saw
pillars of smoke rise above the harbor. "They hit something.
Got a secondary."

Now they could see more aircraft in the sky. The crowd in
the cemetery panicked and started screaming and running
down the hill. "Stay here," Matt ordered and pulled Shoshana to her feet. He pushed her against a tree and grabbed
Tamir, dragging him with them. "We'll be okay here," he
said. "The target's Haifa, not us."

From his vantage point, Matt watched the brief air battle
over Haifa as the first wave of Syrian aircraft struck at their
targets. The Israeli defenders were slow in reacting and he
could only count two Hawk SAM batteries in action. Then
the distinctive rhythmic beat of a Bofors antiaircraft cannon

reached them. "Here comes the second wave," he announced as more Syrian fighters roared over them. He was counting the attackers, timing the reaction of the Israelis, and trying to gauge the damage inflicted by the Syrians. "You're getting a break," he said. "They're not concentrating on their targets, only jettisoning their loads indiscriminately over the city." The first of two Israeli F-15s slashed down onto the attackers.

"This is a break for us? This is good?" Tamir was yelling at him. "Innocent people are down there . . ." Matt stopped him by pointing to a plummeting aircraft, twisting and falling out of the sky. A parachute was drifting down above it. In the distance, they saw another MiG explode as the Israelis worked the attackers over.

"Yeah," Matt said, his voice low and unemotional. "You got a break here. It was a well-planned surprise attack. Great timing and they penetrated your air defense system. But they blew it over the target area, and that's where it all counts. Most of the bombs were off target. You had better hope it was the same all over."

"But they killed people," Tamir protested, "innocent women and children—"

"And they missed their targets," Matt interrupted, determined to make his point. "You can still fight another day."

"I have work to do down there," Shoshana said, walking away from the two men. She stopped and turned. "Come. You can help me."

The American swept the sky, looking for other aircraft. He could see the plan form of six F-15s established in a HICAP over the city. The attack was over. He followed Shoshana down the hill, toward the fires burning below.

"Where is the main threat?" Ben David demanded. He was deep within the concrete bunker that served as Israel's wartime headquarters. The big situation map in front of him was etched on a clear glass plate and plotters wearing headsets stood behind, marking up information they received in grease pencil. Because they worked in the rear, they had to write backward.

Three large arrows out of Syria were pointed at Israel. One of the plotters moved the head of the arrow that represented the First Syrian Army coming down the Bekáa Valley from the north. The lead tanks were twenty-five miles closer to Israel and would soon cross the Litani River, the last major obstacle before they reached the northern border. The arrow for the Third Army pointed at the Golan Heights had not changed. But the arrow for the Fifth Army coming out of the Jebel Druze highlands kept inching its way southward, directly through Jordan and toward Jerusalem.

The minister of defense, Benjamin Yuriden, answered his question. "We are not sure at this time." It was not what Ben David wanted to hear and he said nothing, barely controlling his anger. Ben David fought his natural inclination to vent his fury and yell at the men in front of him. They had been surprised by an enemy that they had thought of as cowardly, stupid, and technologically inept. And it shouldn't have happened, not after the Yom Kippur War of '73. Ben David made a mental promise to destroy the career of the chief of military intelligence. Other heads would also roll if they got out of this.

What the Syrians and Egyptians had done was on the situation board in front of him. It was the reality he had to deal with and he didn't like what it did to his self-image. The Arabs had snookered him, outfoxed him and his advisers by showing the Israelis what they wanted to see and believe. The retreating tanks on the northern border had convinced the Israelis that the Syrians simply didn't have the will to fight, matching the cowardly image the Israelis had of them. All the while, a large part of the IDF was deployed opposite the Egyptians in the Sinai while the Israelis took a big sigh of relief.

And then the Syrians had pulled off an unbelievably complicated maneuver—they had stopped their massive withdrawal and reversed in place. That was something that had even Israeli tank commanders staring in wonder with their mouths open.

The evidence was plainly before him—they were facing a formidable enemy. Three voices assaulted him at once, each with a different opinion. Ben David stared at the board in front of him, somehow managing to listen to all three at once. Then he erupted in a series of questions.

"Do we have a blocking force at the Litani River?"

"Moving into position now," Yuriden answered. "They are in contact with the Syrians."

"How long can they hold?"

"Unknown. The Syrians have the mass behind them to force a crossing within hours."

"Situation on the Golan?"

"Exchanging artillery barrages. The Syrian counterbattery fire is proving very effective. The Syrian tanks are not moving yet."

"How far have the Syrians penetrated into Jordan from the Jebel Druze?"

"Forty-five kilometers and are opposite Nablus, still well within Jordan and headed straight for Jerusalem."

"What are the Jordanians and Iraqis doing?"

"Nothing. But the Jordanians are evacuating their people and protesting in the UN."

Ben David lowered his head for a moment. Then his decision was made. "Order air strikes against the tanks of the First Army trying to cross the Litani River and the Fifth Army moving through Jordan. If the Jordanian Air Force intervenes, destroy it." Then another thought occurred. "Can we hit any of the headquarters commanding those three armies?"

Yuriden's face was an impenetrable mask. He stepped onto the small stage and the stocky ex-air force general pointed at the Syrian city of Homs, north of Lebanon, just inside the Syrian border. "The headquarters for the First Army moving down the Bekáa Valley is located here, over two hundred kilometers behind to the rear." At least this fit the Israeli image of the Syrians.

"Destroy it," Ben David ordered.

Major David Harkabi sat in the cockpit of his F-16 and glanced at his watch. Fifteen seconds to go. He pointed at the crew chief standing by the switch that would open the blast doors to his bunker. When the second hand touched twelve, he shouted, "ZANEK!" the Hebrew word to go or launch. It was the Israeli Air Force's war cry. The sergeant hit the switches and the doors at both ends started to roll back. At the same time, Harkabi started the F100 engine, bringing the F-16 to life. He taxied out of the bunker and raced for the runway. He was leading three other F-16s, the small strike force from Ramon Air Base that would go against the command headquarters of the Syrian First Army at Homs, over 350 nautical miles away.

His wingman fell into place on his wing when he paused at the end of the runway. He snapped his head back against the seat's headrest and then gave a sharp nod forward, the signal for takeoff roll. The two F-16s rolled together and the second two took the active. They would follow in ten seconds. It was Harkabi's fifth mission that day and his fourth new wingman.

Matt handed the telephone back to the harried girl behind the hospital desk and went looking for Shoshana. He found her in a hall bent over a gurney, tending a badly burned woman they had pulled from a bombed-out store. "I still can't get through to anyone," he told her. "If I can't find Ambler, I'm going to have to head back on my own or get in contact with our air attaché." She ignored him and kept working on the woman. Finally, two nurses took over and wheeled the gurney into the emergency room.

"We can make another run," she told him and walked out the doors to the bread van she had appropriated as an ambulance. A dispatcher gave her directions and she climbed behind the wheel. Matt hopped onto the passenger seat and she wheeled the van back into the burning port area of Haifa.

The attack Dave Harkabi was leading had been laid on by the Citadel, the Israeli Air Force's headquarters in Tel Aviv. Now it was being controlled by a direction officer in the hardened command bunker at Ramat David Air Base. He was standing at his console monitoring the takeoff of Harkabi's F-16s from Ramon and two F-4E Phantoms from his base that the Israelis had modified to function as Wild Weasels. The F-4s had been packed with electronic gear and antiradiation missiles to counter hostile radars, surface-to-air missiles, and antiaircraft artillery. The F-4s could jam and deceive radar signals and, if need be, send a missile down a radar tracking beam and destroy the command guidance system of a hostile radar.

The F-4s had one additional feature that Harkabi's life would depend on. The Israelis had just installed a new black box designed to defeat the monopulse guidance and tracking radar of the SA-11 Gadfly surface-to-air missile the Syrians had deployed with their armies. The Soviet-built Gadfly had taken a heavy toll of Israeli fighters that day as the Mach 3 missile proved it could hit anything that came within its launch envelope. Each missile transporter had four 18-foot-long missiles mounted on a turntable that could traverse through 360 degrees. The specially modified tank chassis the missiles rested on could travel and shoot on the run as it moved along with an armored force.

Israeli intelligence had identified over a hundred of the new missile launchers that were providing an umbrella for the three advancing armies. Twenty-six Israeli fighters, more than a squadron, had fallen victim to the Gadfly any time they had come within eighteen miles of a missile and were higher than a hundred feet off the deck. Out of desperation—and out of new ideas—the IAF could only stand off from the tanks thrusting toward them and wait until the Syrians were within artillery range and counterbattery fire could suppress the deadly missiles while the fighters worked over the ground forces.

Intelligence had reported four SA-11 Gadfly tracks surrounding the target headquarters at Homs and now it was up to Harkabi to challenge the missile again.

The street Shoshana drove down was in the working-class section of Haifa, not too far from the docks. The strident tones of a Klaxon split the air as an ambulance demanded the right-of-way down the narrow street. Shoshana pulled onto the sidewalk and let the ambulance pass. Ahead of them, they could see smoke rising from a pile of rubble in the street. "Damn them," Shoshana said, "they didn't care what they hit." She slammed the makeshift ambulance to a halt in front of the smoldering rubble that had been the front of a building.

An old man wearing a fireman's coat came up to them. "We've transported all the survivors," he told them. "The fire's almost out but the building is collapsing. She"—he pointed to a hysterical woman two men were restraining from rushing into the building—"says her three-year-old daughter is trapped inside. We can't get to her."

Matt got out of the van and followed Shoshana to the weeping woman and listened while she spoke softly in Hebrew. Then Shoshana took the woman into her arms and held her. Matt studied the men around him. Like the fireman, they were all in their sixties and older. All the younger men had left to fight the war, leaving the women, children, and old men to rescue the survivors. "Where's the girl?" he asked no one in particular.

The mother understood English and pointed at a rear corner of the building. "In the basement."

"There's an unexploded bomb in there," the fireman said. "Probably a time-delayed fuse. Who knows when it will go off."

"I wonder . . ." Matt said as he recalled the pattern of the attack he had witnessed from the hilltop cemetery. The one fighter that had flown over him at low-level had been carrying four general-purpose five-hundred-kilogram bombs and he had counted the attacking aircraft and explosions. If each aircraft had been carrying four bombs, then as best he could determine, 80 percent of the bombs had detonated. That tracked with an intelligence report he had read that claimed Soviet-designed bombs experienced a 20-percent dud rate.

"They weren't using time-delay fuses," he said. Silence but no movement on the part of the man. "Give me your coat and gloves," he said.

"Matt," Shoshana said, "it's too dangerous. Don't do it." She had almost said that it was their battle and not his. Matt ignored her and pulled on the fireman's heavy coat and tugged on the gloves, eyeing the building as another part of the front wall collapsed.

"Strictly a professional interest," he growled. "Always wanted to see what the business end of one of these puppies was like." Carefully, he worked around the outside of the building, looking for a way in.

The old fireman followed him, keeping up a running commentary on the destruction inside. He pointed to an unlikely opening in the back wall. "I'd go in through there," the old man said. Matt nodded and dropped to his hands and knees and worked his way into the building. Twenty feet inside, a masonry wall stopped him. "It's a load-bearing wall," came from behind him. The old man had followed him into the building, relishing the chance to give advice over his personal safety. Matt could see his gleaming bald head behind him and wondered how he had squeezed his big potbelly through the narrow opening.

"Why the hell aren't you doing this?" Matt grumbled.

"I'm retired."

"Great." The pilot wiggled through a crack in the floor and found himself in an open space. "Now what?" he mumbled.

"You're sandwiched between the first and second floor." The old man was still behind him. "The second floor collapsed onto the first. Feel it shake? It's all going fall into the basement in a few minutes."

"Then you better get out of here, pops."

Matt could hear scrambling and puffing behind him. He pushed aside some plaster and framing and inched his way forward, still looking for a way into the basement. Then he heard the soft whimper of a child. A crashing sound deafened him and dust and smoke washed over him. He coughed and choked, trying to breathe. The old man was back and handed him a red bandanna. "Here, tie this over your face." Matt did as he was told. "You're going to have to break through the floor." Matt felt the head of the crowbar being pushed up beside him.

The collapsed floor inches above his head shook as a tremor rippled through the building. Another whimper. Now Matt was certain he had the location of the girl pinpointed as he crawled into what had been a stairwell. The building shook again. "You had better hurry," came from behind him.

"Would you get the hell out of here!"

What looked like the heavy joists of a subfloor barred his way. He shoved the crowbar into place and tried to pry a wooden beam aside. No luck. "Look up, schmuck." The old man was still behind him.

Matt did and saw an opening above him. He reached up and pulled himself up and over, dropping down to the other side. He found himself on the edge of a ten-foot drop into the basement. He reached for the flashlight in his coat pocket and shined it around the basement. Directly below him, he could see the hole the bomb had bored as it fell through the building and burrowed into the earth. "Where are you?" he yelled. Nothing. Then he heard the old man yell in Hebrew from behind him, on the other side of the heavy beams. Softly at first, barely audible, he could hear the girl's voice. It was coming from behind a pile of debris that filled most of the basement.

"Go get a rope," he yelled to the old man. He threw the crowbar into the basement and inched his body over the edge backward and hung by his hands. When his feet were planted firmly against the wall, he pushed off and jumped into the basement over the hole made by the bomb. He fumbled for the flashlight to help him get his bearings. He could smell something burning. He sniffed again and followed the pungent odor to the bomb. He directed his beam down the hole. Fifteen feet below him he could see the tail assembly of the bomb. The smell was stronger. "What the hell?" he mumbled. Did the Syrian bombs use some sort of acid fuse for a time delay? He couldn't remember.

Panic was eating at him now and he rushed over to where he thought the girl was buried. "Where are you!" he shouted. Again he heard the girl cry. He started to push the rubble aside, using the crowbar as a digging stick. Out of frustration, he turned around and started pushing with his feet. Finally, he broke through and could see an opening under a collapsed wall. He twisted around and crawled under, shining the light in front of him. Now he could see the girl. "Come on, honey," he said, reaching for her. Then a small hand was in his and he gently tugged, feeling the girl come free. He pulled her into his arms.

"Now where are you when I need you?" He shined the flashlight up to the ledge he had jumped off. A rope came tumbling out of the opening, obviously tossed from the other side of the heavy beams. He jerked at it.

"Wait a minute," came from the other side. "I've got to tie it down."

Matt shifted the girl to his back. "You've got to hold on and ride piggyback," he said. He could feel her start to slip when he let go of her legs. For a moment, he didn't know how he was going to get the girl up to the ledge and then himself without help. The old man would have to wiggle over the beams and joists that had barred the way. No way he could to that. "Think!" he raged at himself. He ripped the bandanna off his face and tied the girl's wrists together, her arms around his neck, but her weight wasn't enough to choke him. She started to cry and he grabbed the rope and pulled. It was secure. Hand over hand, he pulled himself out of the basement.

On top of the edge, he yelled for the old man to reach up

as he shoved the girl over the beams. He could hear the old geezer make soft cooing sounds as he cuddled the girl. Then he pulled himself over and dropped down beside the two. The old man handed the girl to Matt. "Let's get the hell out of here," Matt said. "I smelled burning coming from the bomb."

"Go!" the old man shouted, frantically pushing them forward.

Once outside, Matt shouted for everyone to run for cover. Shoshana jumped into the van and started the engine, waiting for them. Matt jumped in, still holding the girl. The old man crashed in behind him as Shoshana sped away. A loud explosion ripped the building apart behind them.

"So they don't use time delays?" the old man yelled at Matt.

The direction officer at Ramat David Air Base scanned the big plot board in front of him. Everyone in the room was quiet and only the gentle hum of electronic equipment could be heard. A keyboard operator typed a message into her communications computer and then stopped. In a darkened alcove at the rear, the greenish glow of three radar scopes could be seen, lighting the faces of their operators. The tactical director sat at the middle scope and noted that Harkabi's four F-16s had reached their turn point far out over the Mediterranean and that the two F-4s were in position. He notified the direction officer, who keyed his mike and transmitted a go to the aircraft.

Over the Mediterranean, Harkabi copied the go and lifted his aircraft up to two hundred feet off the deck and did a com-out turn with his wingman, turning directly toward the coast. Farther to the south, the second pair of F-16s did the same. High above them, a specially modified Boeing 707 turned on its electronic countermeasures gear and sent a mass of false signals out. The two F-4s that would challenge the air defenses around Homs so Harkabi's strike package could get in crossed the Lebanese border and ran up the coast toward Beirut. They were using the coastal face of the Anti-Lebanon Mountain Range to mask them from the Syrians who were moving down the Bekáa Valley on the other side.

Syrian early warning radar operators started talking to each other, confused by the mass of targets now appearing on their scopes. A young Syrian captain, recently returned from a year's training, called it correctly and sent out an attack warning to all stations. He warned that they had multiple targets but that only a few were real aircraft. They just didn't know which were the false targets. Then heavy strobes blanked out the Syrian radars. The 707 was now actively jamming.

The air defense commander of the four SA-11 Gadflies surrounding the Syrian First Army headquarters at Homs ordered his men to battle stations. On each of the tracked vehicles, the antenna for the Flap Lid radar slued toward its predetermined sector. Then he performed a radio check with his ground observers, who formed a spider web of observation posts around the headquarters. The observation post farthest to the southwest reported a visual sighting of two F-4s heading directly toward Homs. The turntables on top of two Gadfly transporters turned toward the reported threat.

Harkabi coasted in one hundred feet off the deck and at 540 knots airspeed when his tactical electronic warfare gear came alive, sending him urgent warnings of hostile radar activity. He was four and a half minutes out. His radio crackled with commands from the two F-4s ahead of him as they ran straight at the target. The lead F-4 detected radar signals coming from the Flap Lid radars and launched two homing antiradiation missiles. At the same time, the Syrians launched two missiles at each of the F-4s. The Gadfly missiles used semiactive homing, which meant the Flap Lid radars had to stay locked on the F-4s for the missiles to guide. It was a shootout in which the winner had the fastest missile or had launched first.

The lead F-4 fireballed as the Gadfly won. But the two missiles the Israeli had launched were still homing. The air defense commander immediately placed his Flap Lid radars in standby as the tracked vehicles scooted to another position. The antiradiation missiles went into a memory mode and continued toward the last source they had detected. But the Flap Lid radars had suffered from poor quality control during construction and the wave guide on one of the sets leaked radar energy. One of the Israeli-built missiles sensed the weak energy escaping from the radar and homed on it. The missile track exploded as the missile found its mark.

Harkabi heard the radio call of the second F-4 as it tried to escape after launching two missiles. Then silence. He was sixteen miles out. His wingman split off to the right as they hugged the deck and Harkabi worked his systems. He was going to toss a two-thousand-pound optically tracked smart bomb at the target. If he could identify the headquarters on his video scope and lock it up, he could launch the bomb and leave while the optical tracker in the head of the bomb homed on the target.

But he was too low at one hundred feet and had to increase his altitude to get a picture. He lifted up to three hundred feet, well into the Gadfly's envelope. His electronic warning gear warbled at him—he was in the beam of a monopulse radar—but he had a video picture of the concrete bunker. He drove his target cross hairs over the entrance that gave him good light and dark contrast and pickled the bomb off. The F-16 jerked as the bomb separated. Two missiles were coming directly at him. Harkabi's hand twitched on the stick and the agile F-16's nose came up, snatching eight g's. Both missiles committed to an up vector and Harkabi slammed his jet in a hard turn to the left as he dropped to a hundred feet. The missiles tried to follow him through the descending turn but their small fins could not handle the turn and one broached sideways while the other flashed by overhead.

Behind him he saw his wingman fireball and wondered if he had got his bomb off. He keyed his radio and told the two F-16s following him to break off the attack and not challenge the Gadfly. He was vaguely aware that he was flying over a ZSU-23 antiaircraft battery and that the quad-mounted gun had been firing at him.

Shoshana was in the back of the van, kneeling in front of the little girl who was safe in her mother's lap. Shoshana was smiling and speaking softly in Hebrew while she cleaned the child and checked for injuries. Other than a few small cuts and bruises, the girl was only dirty and very frightened. It amazed Matt how the harsh, guttural Hebrew became soft and tender as Shoshana spoke, comforting the girl. When they were finished, Shoshana told the mother to get the child a tetanus shot just in case.

Matt sat down beside her in the van, not touching, their backs against the side panel. They were both exhausted. She turned to him, not smiling. "Matt Pontowski, you are . . ."

She stopped, not completing her thought. Saying "wonderful" simply wasn't enough.

"Stupid," the old man finished the sentence for her. Matt grinned at him. "What a schmuck. I had to tell you everything." He climbed out of the van and walked away.

The two looked at each other and laughed, the tension shredding. And both knew that love was there.

"Shoshana . . ." Matt paused. "I've got to go."

"I know."

"I'll be back."

The lone F-16 entered the safe corridor leading to Ramon Air Base at its assigned altitude, flew the prescribed route, and squawked the correct IFF code. When Harkabi was certain the Hawk missile batteries surrounding the base had a positive ID on him and would not send one of the deadly missiles his way, he flew a short final to touchdown. Little puffs of smoke belched behind the main gear. Harkabi took the first high-speed turnoff and fast-taxied for his bunker. The doors rolled back as he approached and he taxied directly inside and raised his canopy. The ground crew swarmed over the jet, checking it for battle damage as they refueled and re-armed it at the same time. A crew chief hung a crew boarding ladder over the left canopy rail and waited for Harkabi to climb down. Another pilot was waiting to crawl into the cockpit for the next mission.

Harkabi sat in the seat, too tired to move. He had drained the two plastic water bottles he carried in the leg pockets of his g suit and still felt a raging thirst. He flopped one hand over the edge of the cockpit and pulled the bayonet clip that released his oxygen mask from the side of his face with the other. Every motion was an effort. Despair ate at him—four wingmen lost in one day. At least one F-4 had also been lost on the last mission—probably two. And these were just the losses he had witnessed. He didn't move.

The crew chief called for help and another ladder was placed against the right side of the F-16. They had seen it before. Five combat missions meant over five hours of flying that took everything a pilot had. Total concentration, fighting four to eight g's on every maneuver, dehydration, and stress took a ferocious toll. The two sergeants climbed the ladders, one on each side and reached in, unstrapping and disconnecting the pilot from the F-16. Then they gently lifted him out and passed him down to waiting hands. The waiting pilot scrambled up the left ladder and settled into the still-warm seat. His hands flew over the switches as he ran the before-engine-start checklist.

A sergeant helped Harkabi to the side of the bunker where he could sit and wait for transportation. Both doors to the bunker cranked open as the fresh pilot brought the F-16 to life and taxied out. The combat turn had taken less than nine minutes.

Harkabi staggered to his feet and managed to walk the short distance to a crew truck. He watched the F-16 pair up with its wingman and race for the runway. Which one will come back? he thought. How much more can we take?

The war was less than ten hours old.

16

The corridor outside the National Military Command Center (NMCC) in the Pentagon was jammed with lieutenant colonels and full colonels wanting to get inside to witness first-hand the reports from the Middle East reaching the command levels of the Pentagon. Most were there because they were professional warriors with an intense interest in combat. But the rumor that the President was inside had spurred quite a few to think of a reason why they should be on the main floor. It was a golden opportunity to shine.

The NMCC was the closest thing in the Pentagon to the popular conception of a "war room," the inner sanctum from which a war was supposedly conducted. Bill Carroll shrugged his shoulders when he realized he would never work his way through the crush of bodies in the hall and was about to leave when he ran into General Cox, his old boss from the DIA.

"Come on, Bill," the general said, "let's try the Watch Center. Not so much dust being kicked up by the high rollers.'' They descended into the basement and found room at the rear of the main floor of the Watch Center where they had a clear view of the computer-generated situation boards. Both men felt much more at home in the Watch Center because it was essentially a fusion point that processed and evaluated incoming intelligence for forwarding to the National Military Command Center. Without the Watch Center, the higher levels of command would be inundated with irrelevant information.

Cox and Carroll were in time to hear the latest situation update briefing on the outbreak of fighting in the Middle East. ''This is going to be bigger than the Yom Kippur War of '73,'' Carroll predicted as the latest intelligence reports were covered and their significance analyzed.

''I don't think so,'' Cox replied. ''So far it only looks like an attack by the Syrians, and the Arabs can't take on Israel without Egypt.'' He pointed out how the surprise attacks by the Syrian Air Force on selected Israeli targets had not knocked out the Israelis' Air Force or command and control structure. The center board flashed and a new map appeared that showed the latest disposition of the three Syrian armored tank corps that had been positioned on the northern flank of Israel. All three had stopped their withdrawal back into Syria and were now moving southward, directly at the Israeli border. The Israeli Air Force had struck at the three columns but had taken heavy losses.

''I don't like it,'' Carroll said. ''The Syrians have got their sierra stacked in neat piles to pull that one off.''

''What are you saying?'' Cox asked.

''Look what they've done. Stopping a withdrawal of that size and immediately reversing is a complicated maneuver for armor. They didn't do it with one army corps but three, and it had to be coordinated with the Egyptian exercise in the Sinai. This was well planned and rehearsed. And we haven't heard from the Iraqis yet.''

''But the Egyptians are not fighting and the IDF can concentrate on the Syrians,'' Cox argued.

''General, right now the Egyptians have stopped maneuvers and are making nice friendly sounds to the Israelis. But they haven't stood down. That exercise was planned to present a threat in the south that the Israelis had to honor. I'm willing to bet that the Egyptians will remain in place and the moment Israel withdraws the forces they had positioned to cover the exercise, the Egyptians will attack. That Egyptian exercise was meant to make the Israelis deploy part of their defenses in the Sinai to weaken the northern sector. You watch, the Sinai is going to be quiet while the Syrians try to crack open the northern part of Israel.''

"The Israelis can handle it," Cox predicted. "I think the Syrians are about to get their asses kicked in the next few days."

"Don't bet on that," Carroll said. "The Israelis have always planned for short, decisive wars. This one is going to turn into a slugfest with heavy attrition on both sides."

"I hope you're wrong," Cox said.

"Me too."

The opening attack on Haifa had caught Furry in downtown Haifa. He had been playing tourist and taking pictures of Israel's Day of Remembrance when the first MiGs dropped their bombs. He had snapped four pictures of the fighters before a policeman shoved him into a shelter. After the attack, he had returned to the hotel on the beach and tried, unsuccessfully, to contact Matt. Then he tried to phone the American embassy in Jerusalem but couldn't get through. In frustration, he left a note for Matt and jumped in the car he had rented and drove to the air base at Ramon.

The base was sealed tight and only after protesting vigorously and by getting himself arrested by the military police, one of whom recognized him, was he able to get onto the base. The squadron he and Matt had flown out of was a mass of activity and he was told to stay out of the way. He wandered into different rooms trying to get a handle on the action but the built-in Israeli penchant for secrecy worked against him and he found himself constantly shuffled around. Finally, he had gone to the personal equipment section, gathered up his and Matt's flying gear and hooked a ride out to the bunker where their F-15 was sheltered. At least, he figured, I can get us ready to get the hell out of here when Matt shows up.

Much to his surprise, he found their F-15 fully armed and two pilots doing a preflight inspection. "Just what the hell you think you're doing?" he yelled. They ignored him. There was no doubt in his mind that they were going to fly his jet and he scrambled up the crew ladder and jumped in the front seat. It was all he could think of to do.

One of the pilots climbed up after him, drew his pistol, pulled the slide back chambering a round, and pointed it at Furry's temple.

The security guard at the entrance to the White House office building stopped Carroll and told him that he couldn't enter because his security clearance had been temporarily pulled. Not knowing what to do, Carroll had called his old boss at the DIA, General Cox, to find out what was going on. But Cox was caught up in a series of conferences and meetings as the DIA tried to piece together what was happening in the Middle East. Out of frustration, he called Melissa Courtney-Smith.

Melissa promised Carroll that she would try to get it all straightened out and his clearance reinstated. Until then, she urged him to go back to his old office at Arlington Hall. "Without a clearance, I can't get in there either," he told her. "Hell, I can't do squat-all." He hung up the phone and headed for the personnel office in the Pentagon. Maybe, he thought, I can get some action there.

"Mr. Fraser," Melissa said, stopping the President's chief of staff as he left his office, "Lieutenant Colonel Carroll has had his security clearance pulled. We need to get it reinstated."

"I hadn't heard. Perhaps," he said thoughtfully, "it would be best if we let the system work, not get involved until we learn more." He rushed out, in a hurry, to a meeting with the President and the National Security Council. A slight smile cracked his mouth. Melissa watched him disappear and placed a call to Carroll's home in Virginia. She needed to talk to him.

The nineteen-year-old reservist who was driving Matt across the tarmac at Ramon kept up a constant wave of chatter, telling Matt about the two attacks they had beaten off and how his air defense battery had shot down at least one MiG and damaged another. They had to hold before crossing a taxipath as two F-16s taxied past. Overhead, he saw an F-16 and F-15 enter the recovery pattern. "What the . . . !" Matt shouted. "That's my jet!" He jumped out of the jeep and ran for the bunker where he had last seen his F-15E.

The pilot had to wait outside the buttoned-up bunker until the Eagle taxied in. Without the recognition code, the ground crew wouldn't let him inside. When the blast doors winched open, Matt ran inside, only to be thrown to the ground by two sergeants. "Knock it off!" he yelled. "You guys know me." They ignored him as the Eagle taxied inside and the doors closed. He was speechless when he saw Furry climb out of the backseat and scramble down the ladder.

The wizzo had a grin from ear to ear when he saw Matt still spread-eagled on the ground. "We got two MiGs and blew the shit out of a mobile command post," he announced. He squatted beside Matt. "Seems they've been checking out our jet while we've been rootin' and scootin' after the local talent in Haifa." Matt wanted to protest that he hadn't been skirt-chasing. "Anyway," Furry continued, "I got here just as they were getting ready to launch on a mission . . ."

"They can't do that," Matt yelled.

"Well, they did," Furry told him. "They need every airframe they've got. They're even flying trainers on combat missions with kids barely out of pilot training. Anyway, I figured the best way to get the bird back in one piece was to have at least one person in the cockpit who had a clue—me. I can't believe what I did."

"Probably got yourself a court-martial," Matt told him, "is what you did."

"I don't give a shit about that. Hell, I was on the receiving end of some bombs in Haifa and wanted to even the score. Can you believe I violated rule number one? I flew with someone a hell of a lot braver than me."

The pilot who had flown the Eagle joined them. "Your backseater is good, very good," he told Matt. There were few better compliments in the Israeli Air Force. He extended his hand and pulled Matt to his feet.

Fraser had no trouble following the discussion going around the conference table in the Cabinet Room of the White House. He sat at his usual place, against the wall and behind the President, slightly to his right, not part of the National Security Council, but handy if the President wanted him. Fraser felt the mood in the room was definitely on course and that the United States would not act in haste and throw all its support behind Israel without considering its other interests in that part of the world. B. J. Allison would be pleased if she could hear the secretary of state argue for a cautious and deliberate approach to the war. And he was more than pleased with the CIA's intelligence summary that saw no immediate threat to Israel's survival.

What bothered Fraser was that he didn't understand the motivation behind many of the men and women sitting around the table. To him, motivation was always a matter of the bottom line measured in dollars. Anything that reduced the size of the next quarterly return was, by definition, wrong and these people were reaching the right conclusions for the wrong reasons. His finely tuned intellectual skills had no trouble following their reasoning; he just didn't understand where they were coming from. He relaxed into his chair, certain that not having Carroll's input had helped keep everything on track. The Air Force lieutenant colonel had definitely been too pro-Israel.

"When do you expect the main forces to engage?" Pontowski asked.

"They may not," the director of central intelligence answered. "This may be only a maneuver on Syria's part to consolidate its position in Lebanon. Some of my analysts are predicting that those three Syrian armies will halt before they come in full contact and then enter into negotiations for their withdrawal."

"And what would they negotiate for?"

The secretary of state answered the President's question. "The Syrians agree to withdraw their forces from Jordan but take over most of Lebanon. That's predictable since Lebanon is one of their historical objectives. They'll also try for more autonomy for Palestinians on the West Bank and the Gaza Strip."

"Should we start to resupply Israel at this time?" Pontowski asked. "They are taking heavy aircraft losses."

Fraser leaned forward. They had come to a critical point. Discussion around the table was lively, about equally divided for and against. Michael Cagliari, the national security adviser, took a cautious approach. "At this time, it looks like the Israelis can handle the Syrian threat. True, they are taking some heavy losses, but they can absorb those. We need to adopt a wait-and-see attitude. And there is the Soviet reaction to consider—"

"Which we must not underestimate," the secretary of state interrupted. "We don't know what's going on in the Kremlin, and if the Politburo sees their clients getting waxed, the hardliners may prevail and throw more weight behind the Arabs. An easy Israeli victory followed up by an aggressive push into Arab territory could lead to a much wider war, becoming regional instead of local."

"And that's a line we don't want to cross," Cagliari added. "Who knows how the Russians would react to that."

Fraser breathed easier when he saw Pontowski's shoulders relax. "For now, we wait and see," the President said. "Have our ambassador to the UN get a cease-fire proposal in front of the Security Council. Put MAC on alert and get ready to start a resupply. Stay on top of this." He rose and motioned for Fraser to join him as he left the room.

"Where was Colonel Carroll?" Pontowski asked as they walked back to the Oval Office.

"I had to pull his security clearance," Fraser answered. "There's a hint of some impropriety and I want to check it out before he returns to work. He should be okay, but we don't need to be blindsided by problems in the NSC when the Middle East is coming apart and the press is looking for a club to beat our administration with."

"Get someone to replace him until it gets sorted out," Pontowski said, making a mental note to speak privately to Stan Abbott, the head of the Secret Service, about the matter.

The combat mission Furry had flown was the key and the two Americans found themselves accepted as trusted allies by the Israeli pilots. It didn't surprise them when Dave Harkabi asked them to join a mission briefing for another attack on the First Syrian Army headquarters. Recent intelligence had traced the headquarters as it moved south after Harkabi's attack. The one bomb the Israeli major had managed to get on target had convinced the Syrian generals that they should move closer to the front line.

Matt listened intently, interested in how the Israelis would defeat the Gadfly SAM that was causing them so much trouble. The crew of the second F-4 that had been on Harkabi's first mission was at the briefing. The pilot explained how they had taken heavy battle damage but had fought their way out and recovered safely. Their latest electronic countermeasures, the F-4 pilot explained, were not effective against the Gadfly.

"Why don't they go in under the Gadfly's envelope?" Matt asked.

"They do," Furry answered. "But the Syrians use ZSU-23-4s for close-in defense." Matt had read the reports on the ZSU-23 and understood how the 23-millimeter antiaircraft gun could track a low-flying fighter right down to the deck. The ZSU-23 and Gadfly protected each other and formed a tough defensive perimeter. "The Israelis use standoff weapons to stay outside the range of the ZSUs," Furry continued, "but that means they've got to get above a hundred feet to acquire the target. That's when the Gadfly gets 'em. A no-win game; too close and a ZSU nails 'em, too high and a Gadfly ruins their day."

A petite young woman who Matt gauged to be no more than twenty years old entered the room. The three silver bars on her epaulets identified her as a *seren,* a captain. "That's the woman I want to be the mother of my children," Furry said, sotto voice.

"You've got a mother for your children," Matt reminded him. But he understood Furry's interest. The slender young woman was beautiful with dark hair framing a delicate face and high cheekbones. Her eyes reminded the pilot of Shoshana's. The Israeli pilots fell silent and watched her update the big situation map at the front of the room.

"The Syrian First Army has forced the Litani River and is reinforcing its position here." She was speaking English, acknowledging Matt and Furry's presence as she drew a semicircle on the south side of the Litani River, a bump directly opposite a main Israeli force. "The Syrian First Army is made up of three armored division"—she glanced at Matt and Furry—"what you Americans call a corps. They are now in contact with our Northern Command here." She drew a jagged line below the bump. "Fortunately, the Syrians are strung out in a long tail on the north side of the Litani as they move down the Bekáa Valley. But they are building up their mass and could break out of their enclave within twelve hours."

A sergeant entered the room and handed her a slip of paper. She paused and read it, deep in thought. Then she stepped to the map and drew an arrow out of the bump pointing toward the coast. "The Syrians have broken out and have now reached the coast and are turning south. Their next objective is Haifa."

The distance from the head of the arrow to Haifa was less than thirty miles. Matt's face turned to granite.

"Which makes it imperative that we stop them now," the intelligence officer continued. "We have monitored heavy communications coming from this area"—she pinpointed a spot north of the river crossing, well inside Lebanon—"and the recce photo is less than two hours old." The room darkened and a slide flashed on the screen. A hodgepodge of trucks and vehicles were clustered around what looked like a small hill—a large camouflaged net. The captain pointed out three communications vans barely visible under the edge of the net. "This is your target," she said, "the headquarters of the Syrian First Army that is threatening Haifa." Then she pointed out six ZSU-23-4s and seven SA 11 Gadfly batteries. The room was absolutely silent.

"We'll take it," Matt said.

The phone call from B. J. Allison came much earlier than Fraser had expected. He checked his watch, surprised that it was only eight o'clock in the evening. Allison came directly to the point. "Tom, we're worried that the President will overreact—"

"B.J.," Fraser interrupted, feeling confident if she was so worried to call him this early, "I've got it all under control."

"Oh, I do hope so," she answered and while the words were charming, the tone in her voice carried steel. "We have heard that the President's grandson is in Israel. We do hope that is not an indication of his unqualified support."

"Now don't go worrying about that," Fraser soothed. "Captain Pontowski was there on a routine exchange visit and the Air Force is trying to get him out as soon as possible." He paused, waiting for a reply. Silence. "B.J., we could use a break right now and handle this crisis better if the press would get off our case about illegal campaign funds—"

"Why, I have nothing to do with that," she interrupted, laying on her southern accent. "Forgive a poor old woman,

Tom, but I do worry about what is going on and would be able to rest much better if I could be sure that we will not desert our *other* friends in the Middle East."

Fraser knew they were bargaining—she for influence, he for less pressure from the press. "Trust me," Fraser said, "the President will do the right thing if he can. You know how the media can influence political and *economic* decisions"—stressing the word "economic" was his way of turning up the heat—"especially during a crisis." Now get off my goddamn back, he added mentally.

"Tom, if I could only be sure." She went on for a few more moments and then hung up.

So that's the trade-off, Fraser thought, we secure her interests in the Middle East and she dries up the press's sources of information about illegal campaign funds. And how in the hell did she know about Matt?

"He's being difficult," Allison said after she had hung up. "He must have buried all that money I gave to their campaign very deep. I do wish I knew how he did that and what's going on."

"Do you want me to find out?" Tara Tyndle asked.

"That would be sweet of you," Allison said, smiling at her favorite grand-niece.

Bill Carroll worked his way through the food line of the restaurant in the basement of the Union train station. Teenagers and their chaperons on school field trips filled the place and offered him the cover he wanted to meet Melissa Courtney-Smith. His wife, Mary, was right behind him, wrestling with their son Brett. For all outward appearances, they were part of the spring tourist rush in Washington, D.C. They found two empty chairs at a table occupied by Melissa and two teenagers. Brett's activity soon drove the teenagers away and Melissa and Carroll felt it was safe to talk.

"I've been listening to Radio Cairo and Radio Damascus on the shortwave," he said. "It's much worse than it appears in the papers and on TV. This is not localized fighting between Syria and Israel."

"The CIA and State," Melissa told him, "are concerned but don't think the fighting will go on much longer."

"Don't bet on it. The Arabs are whipping their people up for a *jihad*. You should hear the radio broadcasts. I wish more of those turkeys at the CIA and the State Department could understand Arabic.''

"The President's trying to get the UN involved and negotiate a cease-fire," she said.

"It had better be quick because Iraq's going to come in and join up with Syria. The Egyptians will lie low until the Israelis are fully committed in the north and then attack in the Sinai. The Arabs could win this one.''

"No one has said anything about Iraq coming in," Melissa said. "That changes everything.''

"Iraq has been a prime mover in this from the beginning and has come up with an 'Arab solution' to the Israeli problem with them leading the pack. The President has got to be warned," Carroll urged.

"Bill, how can you be so sure? After all, you have been cut off from your sources. I can't pass on hunches or guesses.''

"The Mossad contacted me. I hope they passed it on to General Cox.''

"But the Israelis talk to the CIA all the time. Surely, they must have told us by now?''

"They did," Carroll answered. "But you know how the CIA works. The Middle East Division chief is in the driver's seat on this one and he doesn't believe the Israelis. There's a strong anti-Mossad faction in the CIA. Probably professional jealousy. Hell, everyone thinks Iraq is still in the Arab doghouse because of the Kuwait war. But Arab opinion and policies can change in three days. They just don't think like we do.''

"And you think the fighting is going to get worse?''

"Much worse.''

Melissa gathered up her handbag and umbrella and walked away. At a nearby table a man watched her go, sorry that she had sat with her back to him and that he had only been able to read Carroll's lips. He doubted that his partner overlooking them on the balcony picked the conversation up with his directional mike. A teenager's boom box was creating interference. They ought to outlaw those things as dangerous to national security, he thought. We've got enough here, he decided; time to take a close look at the activities of Carroll's old boss, one Brigadier General Leo Cox.

* * *

"Whatever happened to rule number one?" Furry mumbled into his oxygen mask as his fingers punched coordinates into the Up Front Controller's keyboard. It was one way to load the coordinates for the steer points, offsets, and target for their mission into the aircraft's computers. With the right computer and equipment like they had in the squadron at Stonewood, he could have cut a data transfer tape cartridge with all the information the Strike Eagle's computer systems needed for the mission. Then Matt could have simply shoved the cartridge into the Data Transfer Module on the instrument panel in front of him and programmed the computers almost instantaneously. Furry resigned himself to the task at hand and kept punching the numbers in until he was finished. "Okay, ready to taxi," he told Matt.

"Hold on," Matt said. He leaned out of the cockpit and checked on the two technicians who were still working on the black box that programmed their Tactical Electronic Warfare System. "I can't believe you let them get into the TEWS," he said.

"Why not?" the wizzo answered. "It's a lot like the one they got on their F-Fifteens and what the hell, we need every break we can get going against those missiles." The two technicians had been working furiously since the briefing when Matt had volunteered to go after the headquarters. It had been Furry's idea to use the information the surviving F-4 crew had brought back from Harkabi's mission to see if they could reprogram the Eagle's black boxes to counter the Gadfly. Within an hour, the two technicians with their specialized equipment had been flown in and after a lively discussion in which everyone talked at once, they had ripped into the system, scaring the daylights out of Matt.

Harkabi had reassured him that the Israeli Air Force worked like that and they accomplished wonders simply by getting the right people talking to each other and then getting out of their way. Still, Matt felt like they were serving as guinea pigs.

One of the technicians stuck his head out from under the equipment bay and gave them a thumbs-up signal. The other man buttoned up the panel and they were ready to taxi. "Can't believe they did that with engines running," Matt grumbled. He checked his watch and taxied out of the bunker, gunning the engines and racing for the runway. He had never taxied that fast before with a bomb load. A green light blinked at them from the concrete bunker that served as the control tower. Matt took the runway and stroked the throttles, rolling without coming to a full stop to run the engines up. The Eagle leaped into the early-morning dark.

The direction officer deep in the command bunker at Ramat David noted Matt's takeoff time. He scanned the plot board and checked the master clock. The raid against the First Army's headquarters had been carefully planned and coordinated with one single objective—to get Matt's F-15 on target. He queried his tactical director on the exact location of the support aircraft that would help Matt and Furry penetrate the air defense ring the Syrians had thrown up around their headquarters. He keyed his radio and transmitted the code word that started the operation.

Over the Mediterranean, the same Boeing 707 that had jammed the Syrians' radar and communications on Harkabi's mission copied the go order and went to work. At the same time, Harkabi and an F 4 started a low level run toward the coast. But this time, they flew much higher—four hundred feet above the smooth ocean.

The Syrians responded by triangulating on the source of the jamming and employing their own electronic countermeasures. Two Syrian early warning radars found the two low-flying jets through the jamming and plotted their track. Then the Israeli 707 responded with electronic countercountermeasures and the Syrians lost the radar paints on Harkabi's flight. The Syrians decided it was another attack on Homs. They congratulated themselves on the timely move of the headquarters and the way they had deceived the Israelis.

A ground observer team on the coast of Lebanon reported Harkabi's flight coasting in, still on track toward Homs. The Syrian air defense was looking exactly where the Israelis wanted them to look. One Syrian early warning radar reported a fast mover coming out of Israel directly for the Litani River beachhead.

A Syrian radar control officer evaluated the information in front of him and identified the lone fast mover as a reconnaissance flight.

"Sir," the radar operator responded, "they use drones for reconnaissance. This is too fast for a drone."

"I said it was a reconnaissance flight," the officer snapped, ending the discussion. Still, he alerted the SAM batteries along the Litani River about the lone intruder before turning his attention to the developing raid against Homs.

"Lots of activity directly in front of us," Matt said. He tried to concentrate on the TFR and Tactical Situation Display as they raced along the Jordan River at the base of the steep escarpment that rose a thousand feet above them to the Golan Heights. But the radar threats that kept popping up on the Multi-Purpose Display he had slaved to the TEWS worried him. "Never seen anything this heavy before." He had to turn down the audio warning so he could concentrate on other tasks and hear Furry talk.

"Just like last time," his backseater said. "Glad we're not going that way." This part of the route Furry had laid out took them up the Jordan River valley at the base of the Golan and pointed them straight into Lebanon. "Jesus H. Christ!" Furry roared. "Six Flap Lids are active!" The Flap Lid was the guidance and tracking radar for the Gadfly.

"Ready, ready, NOW!" Furry said as the command steering bar in Matt's HUD slued to the right, telling him to turn into the steep wall of the escarpment. Matt reefed the Eagle into a hard right turn and stood it on its tail as he stroked the afterburners. It had been a carefully planned maneuver and they crested the ridge leading onto the Golan with fifty feet to spare. The TEWS exploded as the air defense radars of the Syrian Third Army on the Golan Heights picked them up.

The Syrian officer responsible for the air defense of the First Army in Lebanon noted Matt's change of direction and passed him over to his counterpart for the Third Army who had already acquired the Eagle on his radars. Now the Eagle's TEWS came alive, not trying to jam the Syrians, but to send out false signals that would confuse the defense radar. The Syrians now identified Matt as a threat against the Third Army or Damascus.

On cue, the Israeli forces bunkered on top of Mount Hermon activated their jamming and electronic countermeasures. The Syrians were surprised by the intensity of the jamming coming from Mount Hermon and ordered a heavy artillery barrage against the Israelis. It was one of many vain attempts to neutralize the mountaintop bunkers that gave the Israelis an unrestricted view of the Golan Heights and the plain leading to Damascus.

Matt flew his F-15 directly into this confusion, flying under artillery shells arcing above him. Then the steering bar in his HUD commanded a hard turn to the northwest and Matt responded, flying his jet around the base of Mount Hermon and into the Anti-Lebanon Mountain Range, now heading back to the Litani River. It had been a well-planned feint at the Syrian capital of Damascus. The Syrian radar operators tried to find the F-15, and failing, hesitated. They should have immediately notified the First Army's air defense that they had lost the target. Now three reports came in from SAM batteries claiming kills, which were two too many for the number of targets. Again the Third Army delayed notifying the First Army on the Litani River. Matt and Furry had successfully exploited the seam between two commands. They were less than two minutes out from their target.

Matt was not even aware of the sweat pouring off him as he worked his way through the mountain valley that pointed at their target. The TFR and his Forward Looking Infrared (FLIR) sensor made it possible for him to penetrate the mountains and the night. The monochrome gray holographic picture on the HUD in front of him was coming from the Nav FLIR and let him see what was in front of him. He kept checking the TFR, not wanting to fly into the ground. He touched the Master Arm switch, double-checking it to be sure it was in the up position. Without thinking, he punched up the armament display on his MPCD video, glanced at it to be sure he was in bombs ripple, and punched the screen back to TSD for a quick double check of his position.

"Go Target FLIR," Furry suggested. Matt changed the HUD and was looking at the world through a greenish soda straw. The Target FLIR had a much narrower field of view and Furry had slued it to the target before Matt brought it up. But there was no target, just terrain in front of them. "Too low," Furry said. "We're seeing a hill in front of the target."

A wild warbling sound from the TEWS blasted their ears. "A Flap Lid's got us," Furry said, his voice high-pitched and loud. Matt checked his TFR—they were a hundred feet off the deck, at the bottom of the envelope where a Gadfly missile might be able to guide on them. But he couldn't get any lower in the mountainous terrain. They were less than a minute out and were still dry for a target. Tracers from a ZSU-23 reached toward them.

Dave Harkabi and his wingman broke off their attack run nine miles short of the target and turned back toward the coast. Both aircraft dropped flares and chaff behind them as they ran for safety. The Boeing 707 stopped its jamming and let every Syrian radar find the two retreating fighters. The Syrian First Army air defenders relaxed and congratulated themselves.

Matt was thinking in split seconds, instinctively taking in a wealth of information, evaluating it, and reacting correctly. Scholars, psychologists, and pilots in quiet moments call it situational awareness. Fighter jocks call it having a "clue." Not only did Matt know exactly where he was, which in itself was quite an accomplishment since they were moving at 900 feet a second through mountains at night, he had a mental map of the enemy threat around him. In combat, situational awareness is what keeps a fighter pilot alive. Matt knew he was too low to acquire the target through his Target FLIR, they were being tracked by a Gadfly's radar but were probably below the missile's minimum guidance altitude in mountains, the tracers from the ZSU were still out of range, and the TEWS was screaming at him. So he did the only thing possible if he wanted to get a bomb on target—he pulled on the stick and climbed directly into the engagement envelope of the Gadfly.

"Designating," Furry called from the rear. He had found the target within seconds, laid his cross hairs over it and locked it up. The weapons computer could do its job now. Matt eased the stick forward and they porpoised back down on the deck. Immediately, he brought the nose back up for a second porpoise so the weapons computer sensed an upward vector and could reach a release solution for the bombs and automatically pickle. The F-15 jerked as two bombs rippled off.

Four bright rocket plumes—Gadflies—were lighting the night and converging on them. Again, Matt headed for the deck but the jagged terrain kept him high. Now he turned into the missiles, certain that he could outmaneuver the first two and generate an overshoot. His situational awareness warned him the second pair were another story. Then all four missiles flashed, exploding short of their target.

"Shit hot!" Furry yelled.

"What the hell . . ." Matt said. Furry was laughing like a madman, relieved that they were still alive. He would explain after they landed how the last-minute change the Israelis had made to their TEWS had enabled one of the black boxes to capture the range gate of the Gadflies' radar and generate a false range cue which, in turn, caused the missiles to receive a premature detonate command.

Two explosions from their bombs lighted the night as tracers from a ZSU-23 passed behind them.

Furry read the safe passage procedures to Matt as they approached Ramon to land. They had to fly a hard altitude at 250 knots airspeed, stay in a narrow corridor, and squawk the right IFF code or the Israeli Hawks and AAA would treat them as a hostile aircraft. "They're weapons-free," Furry reminded him. "Weapons-free" made thing more dicey, for every aircraft was treated as a "hostile" unless positively identified as a "friendly." It was like being guilty until proven innocent. Matt wired the approach and circled to land.

Before completing their rollout, Matt turned off on the first highspeed taxipath and headed for their bunker at thirty miles an hour. He automatically stabbed at the eight-day clock and stopped the elapsed time hand. He could hardly credit it; the mission had lasted less than fifty-five minutes and they had never flown slower than 540 knots indicated airspeed or higher than four hundred feet above the deck. He pulled his oxygen mask away from his face and rubbed the sweat away with the back of his gloved hand. He could not believe how tired he felt or how wringing wet with sweat he was.

In the backseat, Furry was busy checking all his systems. "Looks like we're undamaged and healthy as a horse," he announced. They had survived their first combat mission as a crew and the Eagle was undamaged. The bunker doors opened as they approached and Matt taxied directly in and shut the engines down. Instead of a ground crew waiting to receive them, two men stood in the bunker. One was the Israeli base commander and the other was an immaculately uniformed but slightly overweight U.S. Air Force colonel dressed in class A blues. The silver cord of an aiguillette

looped over his left shoulder announced he was the air attaché from the United States embassy in Jerusalem.

"What the hell have you two cowboys done?" the colonel
shouted, his face rock-hard.

17

The Ganef had not left his office for three days as he drove
Mossad into a frenzy of activity. He was furious with himself
and his organization for what he knew was a basic failure in
intelligence. His agents had reported the Syrians were up-
grading the quality of their military but they had failed to
determine just how deep the improvements had reached. The
Syrians were performing miracles on the battlefield and the
Israelis were facing a well-trained and modern army. A knock
at his open door caught his attention and the old man lifted
his head. He leaned back in his chair, pushed his glasses up
onto his forehead and rubbed his nose. Gad Habish was
standing in front of him. "Well?"

"I'm turning the Pontowski case over to Mordechai. He's
been briefed."

"I'll take it over myself," the Ganef decided. "How's it
going?"

"It was going very well as of five minutes ago. Colonel
Gold, the U.S. air attaché found him just after he landed
from a mission."

"It would be good if he flew another mission," the Ganef
observed. Habish said nothing. They both believed that Matt
could best serve the interests of Israel as a casualty or prisoner of war. The worldwide publicity resulting from the President's grandson dying or being captured fighting for Israel
would unconditionally force the United States into Israel's
corner.

"Shoshana Tamir has proven most useful," the Ganef said.

"We need to make sure she and the young Pontowski meet again."

"Nature will take care of that," Habish said. "If we can keep him in Israel." Then he changed the subject. "I'm leaving in an hour. Everything is arranged."

The Ganef looked at the man who had served him so well. "I don't like this. Too rushed." There was more than a professional worry behind his words.

"It has to be done," Habish said. "The station chief in Cairo is onto something and needs help. Maybe we can feed the Egyptians enough misinformation to keep them out of the war."

"You two got to have hemorrhoids of the brain," Colonel Steven Gold groaned. The air attaché was stalking back and forth in the small office he had appropriated in Dave Harkabi's squadron building. Matt and Furry were sprawled out in chairs, both sucking on water bottles, their sweat-stained flight suits unzipped. "Look at you," he spat. "Have either of you ever read the manual on dress and appearance?"

"The side with the simplest uniforms wins," Furry intoned.

"What the hell does that mean?" Gold shot back.

"You ever flown in combat?" Matt asked. Combat had been a new, and in many ways thrilling, experience for the young pilot. He doubted that he would ever be the same again, and for the first time, he understood how he had changed since the day Locke had first dressed him down. He smiled to himself when he thought of how his old, self-assured attitude had planted one of the earth's axis firmly in his butt while the world rotated there about. That vision of his self-importance had been destroyed.

"What does that have to do with this?" The colonel was yelling, misinterpreting Matt's smile, and on the very edge of losing his temper. "Not only did you jeopardize a thirty-million-dollar jet—"

"Twenty-nine million," Furry corrected.

Colonel Gold fought for what was left of his self-control. "But you actively involved the United States on Israel's side. Do you have any idea of the repercussions if you had been shot down and captured? Especially you, Captain Pontowski."

Matt decided it was time to bite back. He had seen too many colonels like the one standing in front of him—desk jockeys good at pushing paper who didn't have a clue about the business end of the Air Force. "Came damn close, Colonel. They almost got us."

"Captain, you seem to have forgotten who your grandfather is. I was given specific orders to find you and make sure you get out of Israel. Right now, your presence here is a political liability—" Gold was interrupted when the young intelligence officer opened the door. He could only stare at her, struck by how such a beautiful woman could be caught up fighting a war.

"Matt, Ambler," she said. "We've got the results of your mission. Want to see?" She held the door open and gestured toward her office. "Colonel Gold, after you?" The air attaché didn't hesitate and quickly followed Matt and Furry out of the room.

"Is this the first time you've seen our squadron, Colonel?" the captain asked as she escorted him down the hall.

The air attaché only nodded. You damn well know it is, he thought. Gold had been assigned to the United States embassy in Jerusalem for two years and even though he was Jewish and spoke Hebrew, this was the deepest he had ever gotten inside the actual operations of Israel's Air Force. The Israelis cast a dark mantle of secrecy over their military and carefully shielded their capability from outsiders. They believed their security depended on it. Since air attachés are official spies sent by their governments, the Israelis were careful to show them very little. Gold had learned more on his short search for Matt and Furry than in the previous two years.

Israel's early warning and air defense net was one of their closest-held secrets and the air attaché would have willingly sold his soul to learn the details of the elaborate structure of orbiting aircraft, fixed and mobile radar sites, command bunkers, and how they were all linked together by a triple redundant system of computers.

The rotating planar array antenna on top of Mount Hermon was a critical part of that system. Because of constant artillery barrages, the Israelis had developed a fast erect/retract mechanism to protect the antenna and keep it feeding information to its processors and high-speed computers. A counterbattery radar would scan the area, and when it reported the area free of artillery fire, the antenna would snap out of its protective bunker and come to an upright position. From its elevation of 9,200 feet, the antenna would sweep the Damascus plain and the Transjordanian plateau as far south as Amman in Jordan on every ten-second rotation.

As Colonel Gold was following the intelligence officer down the hall to her office at Ramon, the Syrians unleashed a heavy artillery barrage on Mount Hermon. The antenna quickly retracted when the counterbattery radar reported incoming and the defenders hunkered down. The captain in charge of the radar site on Mount Hermon was perplexed by the barrage, for the Syrian Third Army stretched out below him had been relatively quiet. He keyed his computer and ordered the antenna to come erect during an interval between explosions. The counterbattery radar sensed a six-second window between the incoming shells and the planar array antenna snapped up and took a 110-degree sweep of the area below before it retracted to safety.

Inside the bunker, the computers processed the new information and sent out immediate warnings. Under the cover of the barrage, the Syrian Third Army was repositioning on the Golan Heights. Farther to the south, the Syrian Fifth Army had launched forty-six tactical missiles.

The air attaché had reached the captain's office at Ramon when the alarm sounded. On top of Mount Hermon, the captain commanded the radar antenna to come erect once more. Again, the antenna popped up and partially swept the horizon. This time, the computers were able to determine the trajectory of the tactical missiles, and since the ballistics of a missile are constant, the point of impact, the target, was determined. Eight of the missiles were headed for Ramon Air Base. Again, warnings went out.

Deep in the command bunker outside Tel Aviv, computers reported the attack. Intelligence officers scanned the information and noted the targets. At first, the computers determined the missiles to be Soviet-built Scud Bs. But since the distance to Ramon was 320 kilometers, well beyond the range of the Scud B, the missiles arcing toward Ramon were upgraded to Scaleboards. Another warning was sent out for Ramon to expect eight missiles with two-thousand-pound high-explosive warheads to arrive shortly. An Israeli general's lips compressed and disappeared as he punched the telebrief phone at his console. Someone was going to have to tell Prime Minister Ben David that the Syrians were using much more accurate tactical missiles and that the battle for the Golan Heights could start at any time.

The pretty captain disregarded the air raid warnings and handed a set of photos to Matt. She handed another set to the air attaché as Klaxons outside their bunker warned the base to take cover. "We're as safe down here as anywhere else," she told him. Sweat glistened on Gold's face as two of the missiles eluded the Patriots and hit the base. It was the first time that the violence of war had found the colonel.

Fraser sat panting in the bathtub, his face etched with sweat, still trying to catch his breath. His heart was still beating rapidly and he could feel his temples pound. My God, he wondered, how close did she come to giving me a heart attack? I'll never let her do that to me again. For a moment he tried to remember all that he had told her. It seemed the more he had dropped names and told her about the rich and powerful people he associated with, the more excited she became. He shook his head and promised himself that he would never crawl into a bathtub with her again.

Still, he couldn't take his eyes off her as she sat on the edge of the sunken tub, her legs arched gracefully over his big belly. He was fascinated by the way she handled the old-fashioned straightedge razor as she flicked it up and down her legs. "Where did you learn that trick?" he asked.

"My grandmother's sister. Quite a gal in her day." She reached for a bottle of fresh champagne and wiggled the cork, popping it free. He knew how strong her long fingers were. Then she poured the champagne over her freshly shaved legs. He knew how that felt. In fact, he knew many more things now than he had an hour ago. He had always thought of himself as a sexual sophisticate, one of the things money and power could buy, but Tara Tyndle had destroyed that self-image. He was amazed that a woman with her looks and class could be—he searched for the right word—a modern courtesan, he decided.

Tara splashed some of the champagne over her naval and let it run down. Then she swung one of her long legs over his head. "Want to lick?"

Later, when they were ready to go and drinking a last cup of coffee, Fraser marveled at her transformation. Tara had become a young society matron. Or was she a highly successful business-woman? or the pampered wife of one of Washington's power brokers? He couldn't tell. "Dinner tonight?" he asked, looking at her over his cup of coffee.

"Oh I'm sorry, I can't." She gave him a sad look. "I'm going out of town for a few days. Switzerland."

"Why Switzerland?" Fraser considered that country one of the more boring places on the face of the earth and he did not like the Swiss—especially their incorruptible, self-righteous bankers.

"Business. I need to make some arrangements."

Fraser understood immediately. Her business had to do with secret bank accounts and the transfer of money. If it involved the laundering of "black" money, something he was an expert at, he could help her. "If it involved banking," he ventured, "you don't need to go to Switzerland. I do have some contacts . . ." He deliberately let his words die.

"I don't see how I can avoid it," she said, a rueful look on her face. "I would much rather go to dinner with you." Her tongue flicked over her lips and he caught his breath. "But the sums are very large."

"Like I said, I know some people who might be able to help you."

"Thanks for the offer, but I wouldn't want to impose." She rose to leave, satisfied that he had taken the bait.

An hour later, Fraser walked into his office. He settled down behind his desk, still preoccupied with thoughts of Tara. He had convinced himself that she was a power groupie, one of those women who skirted on the edges of true power, exchanging the only thing they had for a chance to be among the influential. And in exchange for a little aimless chatter, he laughed to himself, it's all for free.

Steven Gold pulled a small Japanese camera out of his shirt pocket and looked at the intelligence officer. "Go ahead." She shrugged. "It is your airplane." He walked around the F-15 and snapped six pictures, recording the damage the jet had suffered in the rocket attack. Since no one stopped him, he walked outside and took a picture of the damage to the underground bunker. It was the first time he had been allowed to take photos on an Israeli air base. Well, at least authorized pictures. He managed to take two more of the area around the bunker as he slipped the camera back into his pocket. He hoped the two unaimed photos would come out. Then he walked back inside and joined Matt and Furry.

"What do you think?" he asked the two young officers.

Furry crawled out from under his aircraft and brushed his hands. "Obviously she ain't going to fly for a while, but she's fixable. Can you get the Israelis to do it so we can get the hell out of here?"

"I doubt it," Gold answered. "They're maxed out just keeping their own aircraft in the air."

"I can't believe it," Matt said. "This place takes a direct hit from a two-thousand-pound warhead and all it does is blow some concrete loose and part of the blast door away." He studied his Eagle, making mental notes. "Most of the damage must have been caused by the blast door shredding."

"And that hunk of concrete that fell out of the ceiling and tore the radome off," Furry added. He was examining the damage to the nose of the F-15. "With the right parts, a combat repair team should be able to fix her in about forty-eight hours."

"I'll see if we can get a team in here," Gold said.

"How in the hell did they build this puppy," Furry said, waving his hand at the bunker. "There should've been a fire, what with all the fuel lines they've got in here, and hell, they even store weapons over there." He pointed to a small metal blast door set in the side of the bunker.

"Can I look around?" Matt asked the captain. She nodded yes and watched him inspect the bunker. It was obvious that Matt had studied civil engineering at the Air Force Academy as he poked around the bunker. Then they were ready to go and she escorted the three Americans back to the squadron.

Gold seemingly ignored the F-16s taking off while he calculated the Israelis had repaired the runway in less than twenty minutes. He tried to be unobtrusive as his eyes swept the base. He caught the captain studying him. She knows, he thought. He was certain that the base had become fully operational within thirty minutes after the attack as four F-16s landed and fast-taxied past them. "We need to talk alone," he told the two Americans.

* * *

The air-cooled V-12 diesel engine in the American-built M60A1 tank ticked over and came to life when the driver, Nazzi Halaby, hit the start button. Without thinking, he sat and locked the throttle at 1,200 RPM. He stuck his head out of his hatch on the sand-gray-colored tank and listened to the engine as it warmed up. He decided it sounded good and that the repair team had done their job well. He laughed when the other three members of his crew had to scurry out of the way of the M88 recovery vehicle as it moved around to mount the left track they had thrown in the last seconds of the battle that had raged around them less than four hours ago. Another forty-five minutes, Halaby calculated, and we'll be ready to roll.

"Why's the Druze laughing at us?" the tank's loader, Amos Avner, snarled. Avner was glaring at the skinny, ratlike Halaby who was climbing out the driver's hatch. Moshe Levy scratched the heavy black beard he had been cultivating for months, ignored Avner's latest jab at their driver, and decided to report in on the M88's radio. The tank commander crawled up the side of the United States-built tank recovery vehicle that made him think of a ship's superstructure built on a tank chassis, thankful that the M88 had been around to pull them to safety.

Moshe Levy was a thirty-six-year-old veteran tank commander who had cut his teeth in combat against Syrian tanks in Lebanon during the summer of 1982. He stood barely five feet five inches high and his stocky frame fitted easily into the M60. He knew how lucky they were to still be alive after throwing a track and then taking a hit in the engine compartment with an RPG.

Damn, he thought, why can't I be as lucky with my crew. Nazzi Halaby was the best tank driver he had ever met and it wasn't his fault the track had come off. But Avner wouldn't believe it and, as usual, had used the incident to give Halaby hell. Only the tall and lanky gunner, Dave Bielski, had kept the driver and loader from ripping into each other. One of them has got to go, Levy decided. He couldn't afford to have his crew fighting each other harder than the Syrians. It wasn't much of a choice, the loader Amos Avner would be the easiest to replace and he would never find another driver like Halaby. Levy did not miss the irony of his decision. He was getting rid of the only Orthodox Jew on his crew and keeping the Druze—an Arab.

The three Americans were hunched over a light table in the captain's office at Ramon Air Base studying another set of photos a reconnaissance drone had taken an hour after Matt's attack on the Syrian headquarters. The high-resolution pictures chronicled the death and destruction the two two-thousand-pound bombs had caused and it reminded Furry of another mission he had flown years before. "Nothing but hot hair, teeth, and eyeballs in there," he said.

Gold was going over the photos with a magnifying glass and his face paled. What Furry had said was true and he could see three dismembered, charred bodies. Gold was very vain about his full head of dark hair, beautiful teeth that his parents had spent a small fortune on, and deep brown eyes that women loved. He could see himself in the photos. He shuddered when he realized the two men standing beside him could be so cavalier about the deaths they had caused. The tall colonel's only flying experience had been in MAC and he had never met the likes of Matt and Furry. Smooth and normal exteriors of the two men masked the rock-hard, highly competitive nature of two professional warriors.

"I'm going to need the details of all you've learned for a report," Gold said, eager to return to the antiseptic world of reporting intelligence. "There's a wealth of information here."

"I actually learned more on my first flight," Furry said.

"You've flown twice for the Israelis?" Gold was incredulous as Furry nodded in reply. The air attaché had to fight for his self-control. "No. Don't say a thing." He bit his words off in anger. "I'm going to see your ass court-martialed. This is too fucking much. Just who in the hell do you think you are?"

"What about me?" Matt asked. The colonel spun around to face the young pilot. "Look," Matt said, "court-martial us both if you want but first, I think you had better find out what we've learned."

For the next two hours, Matt and Furry briefed the colonel on all that they had observed and done. Furry sketched four pages of diagrams and equations for the colonel on the Gadfly missile and how the Israelis had successfully modified the

F-15's TEWS. At one point, Gold stopped to warn them. "You know all this can be used as evidence against you in court-martial."

"So?" Matt answered for both of them. "We're not going to lie or cover up what we've been doing here."

"Especially when it can save some other jock," Furry added.

The colonel leaned forward over the table, his hands resting on the photos, maps, and diagrams scattered there. "You two don't have a clue what's happening, do you?" The two officers were quiet, not following what he was saying. "Because of you two, I have more up-to-date, hard intelligence about the Israelis and their capability than we've learned in the previous four years. The information on their hardened bunkers alone is worth an entire squadron of F-Fifteens. Now I have to ask myself why have the Israelis decided to show you two all this? Why is our liaison officer the prettiest, sexiest woman I've met here?" In Gold's world, another type of situational awareness was essential.

Gold pointed at Matt. "I think the Israelis want to keep you here and would like nothing better than for you to buy it. Think about it, the grandson of the President of the United States killed while flying a mission for the Israeli Air Force. Some headlines."

"Then we've got to get the hell out of here," Furry said. "And quick."

"Maybe not," Gold said. "Two can play this game. The price the Israelis pay for you staying here is information, useful information. I'm going to see if I can get you two assigned to my office as official observers with diplomatic status. But no more flying."

"Can we learn that much?" Matt asked. "Is it that important?"

"Oh yeah," Gold answered. He bowed his head and stared at his hands. "I think Israel is going to get its ass kicked bigtime and the U.S. has got to know exactly what's going on if we're going to stop this shitty war."

Moshe Levy was standing in his hatch with a death grip on the turret as Halaby hurtled their tank at full throttle up the coastal road. Like most Israeli tank commanders, he preferred to stand in the open hatch because it gave him an unrestricted view and to his way of thinking, that was the difference between being a target and a tank commander. It bothered him that during their first three engagements, many of the Syrian tank commanders were doing the same and not buttoning up until the last possible moment. Ahead of them, he could see and hear a battle going on.

A sharp bump threw him against the hatch ring but his Kevlar flak jacket cushioned the blow. He thought about telling Halaby to slow down to a more reasonable speed but the urgent commands coming over his radio wouldn't allow that. Levy estimated they were moving at forty miles an hour, much faster than the design speed of the American-built tank. Israeli engineers had modified the tank by increasing the engine's output from nine hundred to over a thousand horsepower and taking the governor off.

A bullet ricocheted harmlessly off the front slope of the tank, a good indication they were getting close. Probably a sniper sent out to pick off tank commanders, Levy thought. He estimated the shot came from the front left and swung the machine gun mounted in front of him in that direction. Another ping. Now Levy had the approximate position of the sniper's hide. He raked the area with a short burst of gunfire. The sergeant did not expect to nail the sniper, he only wanted to drive him to cover until they were past.

The radio squawked again, telling him to hurry. Even though it was dark, Halaby didn't slow down. They had been up this road once before and the mix of Halaby's natural instincts and excellent memory for terrain gave them a decided advantage. Levy was thankful that the loader, Amos Avner, was keeping his mouth shut about the ride. Avner blamed everything that went wrong on Halaby. Levy readjusted his night vision goggles. He hated night operations.

The action Levy and his crew were joining was part of the ongoing battle to stem the Syrian advance coming out of Lebanon. The Israelis had been forced to give ground as the Syrians consolidated on the southern bank of the Litani River and launched a southward thrust toward Haifa. But as the Syrian armored units crossed the northern border of Israel, they moved out from under their protective umbrella of SAMs, artillery, and counterbattery fire and ran into the main force of two Israeli armored divisions, fully mobilized, dug in, and determined not to yield another inch.

Israeli artillery fire had reached out and suppressed the Syrian SAMs, and the Israeli Air Force had at last been able to pound at the advancing tanks. No longer were the Syrians able to keep moving forward but had to contend with Israeli tanks bunkered down in prepared positions and supported by artillery. Israeli infantry had moved into position and dismounted from their APCs, ready to cover their own tanks and take on the advancing Syrians. The Syrians had finally come within the grasp of Israel's combined arms.

Slowly, the Syrian advance ground to a halt and the battle swayed back and forth, turning into a slugfest as the two forces punched at each other.

A shielded light blinked at Moshe Levy and the tank commander ordered Halaby to stop. A soldier scrambled up the front of the tank to the turret and quickly gave him directions to his new position, pointing at a map and gesturing to a nearby hill. Then he was gone and Levy told Halaby to leave the road and head for the hill. Near the top, they found a bulldozer scraping away at a little fold in the terrain, turning it into a wide cut that led to the top of the hill. It was a prepared position a tank could hide in. When the combat engineer was satisfied with his work, he backed his bulldozer down the hill and disappeared into the night, heading for another spot to repeat the drill. Halaby nosed the tank down into the fresh cut.

A man appeared out of the dark and identified himself as their new platoon commander and quickly briefed Levy and his crew on their situation. Before he left, the second lieutenant gave them new tactical frequencies for their radios, their only link beyond the small world of battle that would soon engulf them.

The radio crackled with commands and Levy recognized the voice of the lieutenant he had just spoken to. Numerous tanks supported by armored personnel carriers were advancing up the slope toward the platoon's position. Levy counted them lucky that there had been no artillery barrage and spoke into his intercom. "Take her forward, Nazzi. Hull down." The driver inched the tank forward up the rut. Now the turret was clear of the rut but Levy still could not see over the crest of the hill directly in front of him. The sharp crack of a tank's main gun to his immediate left deafened him. Incoming whistled over them and exploded behind them on the lower slope.

"Go to the berm," Levy ordered. Halaby gunned the engine and shot the tank forward right up to the crest of the hill. The 'dozer driver had done his work well and now Levy had an unrestricted view of the slope in front of him with only his tank's turret and half of its hull exposed. Coming up the slope in front of him were at least twelve tanks in a rough V formation with eight or nine tracked armored personnel carriers—Levy identified them as BMPs—spread out among them. The point of the advancing V was off to his left and a Russian-built T-72 tank was twenty-five hundred meters directly in front of them.

He dropped down into the turret and banged the hatch closed over him, buttoning them up and yelling at the same time. "GUNNER—IMI—TANK FRONT!"

He had just warned the crew that they were engaging, that he wanted Avner to load with an antiarmor round they called the Imi, and that the target was a tank in front of them. Before he could get his eye to the sight at his position, Avner had rammed a round into the British-designed 105-millimeter gun the Israelis had mounted on the old M60 and the breech had slammed closed. Automatically, Avner moved clear of the recoil and made sure the safety was off.

"UP!" Avner shouted.

Less than five seconds had elapsed since Levy had seen the tank. The gunner, Dave Bielski, had reacted on pure instinct and had traversed the turret, aligned the cross hairs of the thermal sight on the tank in front of him, and mashed the laser range finder switch as Avner loaded. He could see the T-72's turret swinging onto them. The computer solved the ballistics problem in milliseconds and aimed the gun. Three quick yells echoed through the tank that sounded like one word, the syllables shouted by a different voice:

"IDENTIFIED!" (Bielski)—"FIRE!" (Levy)—"ON THE WAY!" (Bielski).

Little of the gun's crack-boom penetrated inside the tank, but the heavy recoil served as punctuation.

"BACK UP!" cried Levy.

Halaby had the tank in reverse and immediately backed down the ditch to safety. The abrupt motion jammed Levy's eye against the rubber eyepiece of his sight and he saw the muzzle of the T-72 flash in front of him. It had been a race between the quick and the dead as the Syrians' shell split the empty air immediately above the hatch. They heard the sharp crack of their shell as it hit home but didn't see the flash of explosion as the T-72 brewed up. Moshe Levy's crew may have been torn apart by internal bickering and personal hatred, but in combat they were very quick.

"FORWARD!" Levy yelled. "LOAD AND CARRY IMI!" This time the gun would already be loaded with the best projectile they had for killing another tank. Israeli Military Industries had developed a superlethal, hypervelocity, armor-piercing, fin-stabilized, discarding sabot that could knock out any tank it hit. They called it the Imi for short after its developers.

Halaby slammed the tank to a halt in the same spot as Bielski slued the turret to the right, in the general direction where he had seen another tank moments before. Again, the commands sounded as one word.

"GUNNER—IMI—TANK RIGHT!" (Levy)

"UP!" (Avner he reconfirmed what he had already loaded)

"IDENTIFIED!" (Bielski)

"FIRE!" (Levy)

"ON THE WAY!" (Bielski)

Again, they heard a muffled crack-boom followed by a heavy recoil that rocked the tank.

"BACK UP!"

Their total exposure time had been less than fifteen seconds and they were still alive. "Not again," Halaby warned from his steel foxhole in the front of the tank. Levy paused, considering what his driver had just said. In combat, the driver is a microtactician and must constantly be attuned to positioning of the tank. While Levy and Bielski had been preoccupied with firing the gun and killing other tanks, Halaby had been surveying the battlefield and was convinced that the Syrians had them pinpointed and would expect them to pop out of the same hole.

"Which side?" Levy asked. They were communicating in their own special shorthand and reconsidering their tactical position.

"To the left," Halaby said.

"Do it," Levy ordered. He could hear Avner grumbling loudly as Halaby backed out of the ditch and back down the hill. Almost instinctively, the driver worked his way back up to the crest in the dark, picking his way over boulders and through a ravine.

"If he throws a track now . . ." Avner groused.

"Shut up," Levy said. "LOAD AND CARRY IMI!" They were nearing the top and the tank commander obviously expected to take on a tank again. They crested the top of the hill sixty meters from the ditch and again the firing sequence repeated itself. This time, a Russian-built Sagger antitank missile flashed over them as they backed down the hill, paying out the thin wire that guided it. "They were looking for us in our old position," Levy told Avner. "Halaby just saved our lives." Avner snorted in disbelief.

The next few minutes seemed like hours as the tank fought along the crest of the hill, rushing up, taking a quick shot, then backing back down to relative safety on the lee side of the hill, away from battle. The first light of dawn was diffusing through the haze and smoke drifting up the slope when a cease-fire order came over the radio.

Levy halted the tank at the crest of the hill and scanned the slope through his sight and periscope before he popped the hatch. He had to push a thick patch of crisscrossed Sagger wires off the turret to free the hatch. How many of the missiles had been fired at them? Then he stood up and surveyed the carnage around him. He counted nine burning hulks of T-72 tanks on the slope in front of him and numerous destroyed BMPs. The smell of burning fuel and flesh drifted over him and he wanted to throw up. To his left, he could see two burning Israeli tanks, one a new Israeli-made Merkava and an old M60 like his. No survivors there.

He keyed the radio, trying to raise the platoon's lieutenant. Finally, a voice he did not recognize answered. "What happened to the lieutenant?" Levy asked. "I lost contact with him when the Syrians broke through."

"Killed," came the answer. "He led the counterattack. It was touch and go. Say your remaining ammunition and fuel state."

"Avner," he asked over the intercom, "how many rounds do we have left?" Silence greeted him. He glanced down into the turret and saw that both Avner and Bielski were sound asleep. He counted the rounds left in the ammunition locker just behind the breech of the big gun. Four rounds, he thought, and all high-explosive antitank. None of the more desirable Imis, the hypervelocity armor-piercing shells that could kill a T-72 with one hit, was left. It had been a close thing and he wondered if he would have been able to disengage and pull back to reload. The radios had been a madhouse during the battle but he had been able to keep most of it sorted out and follow the action going on around him. "Nazzi," he called over the intercom, "how much fuel left?" Again silence greeted him. He decided the driver was also asleep. Rather than disturb him, he reported the ammunition he had counted and told headquarters that they were down to their reserve fuel.

Then Moshe Levy fell asleep, still sitting in the open turret.

The men surrounding the prime minister were worried, for Ben David had not slept in over seventy-two hours and the strain was telling. His decision-making capability had to be seriously weakened. Still, he seemed fully alert as the latest reports from the north filtered into the command post. The reports from the Northern Command were encouraging and it looked like the Israelis had finally stopped the advance of the Syrian First Army just inside their northern border. One analyst pinpointed problems the Syrians were having with command and control since their command post near the Litani River had been destroyed. Both sides had taken horrendous losses. "I can't accept much more attrition like that," Ben David grumbled and immediately asked for the situation on the Golan Heights.

"Very quiet," came the immediate reply. "The Syrian Third Army on the Golan is remaining behind its fortifications and not venturing out from under their protective umbrella of SAMs and artillery." But the news was not all good. "However, we have monitored a forward movement of their SAMs, bridging equipment, and artillery batteries. We think an attack in the Golan is imminent. Probably within twenty-four hours."

"And the situation in Jordan?" Ben David asked. For a moment, absolute silence filled the bunker.

The minister of defense, Benjamin Yuriden, stood up. "Not good, Yair," he said. "We have slowed the advance of the Syrian Fifth Army, but they are still moving forward. Unless we can halt them, they will be within artillery range of Jerusalem in thirty-six hours. We are taking heavy losses and resupply is becoming a problem. Our supply trucks are being attacked by Palestinians when they move through the West Bank. We are moving in armed convoys to get safely through. It's slowing us down.'' The Israelis were up against the hard reality of modern warfare—the side that could pump the most men and material into the maw of combat would win.

Ben David stood up, his face flushed and fists balled into knots. He drove his knuckles down onto the table. ''I know how to deal with terrorists and Arabs,'' he growled. ''The next time one of our supply trucks is ambushed, level the village or town where it happens.''

''Our trucks are being attacked on the open roads, outside the villages,'' an army general told him.

''Then go to the nearest village and take ten prisoners. If they will not identify the terrorists, shoot them. The attacks will stop.'' No one questioned the prime minister's order. Fighting for his country's survival was taking its toll, and for the first time, Ben David was seriously considering his nuclear options.

''He always takes the easiest job, the lazy bastard,'' Avner grumbled as he took another round that Dave Bielski handed him through the turret hatch. Each of the shells weighed over fifty pounds and it was hard work loading the magazine to its capacity of sixty-three rounds. As usual, Amos Avner was complaining about their driver, Nazzi Halaby.

''Refueling is Nazzi's job,'' Bielski grunted and worked faster to shut the loader up. A flurry of activity surrounded the tank as a forward support team refueled and reloaded the M60 for battle. Levy had left and gathered with the surviving tank commanders around the tank that had become the company's headquarters. The crew was buttoning the tank up a few minutes later when Levy rejoined them, a troubled look in his brown eyes.

Dave Bielski caught it at once and sensed trouble. ''What now?'' he asked.

''They gave me a platoon,'' Levy told the three men.

A stricken look crossed Avner's face. ''They promoted you?'' Levy nodded in reply. ''A *segen mishneh?*'' Avner asked. Again Levy nodded yes. ''Oh, no,'' Avner wailed, his voice high-pitched and filled with lament. *"Shma Yis-real . . ."*

"Shut up," Bielski growled at him. "We're not dead yet."

Avner stopped his recital of the sacred words Jews uttered at a moment of extreme peril. "We might as well be," he moaned. "A second lieutenant we don't need." The high attrition rates the Israelis were suffering in the war had caught up with Moshe Levy and his crew. Levy had received a battlefield promotion to *segen mishneh,* second lieutenant, and would lead a platoon into combat. What had Avner so upset was that Israeli officers were expected to lead and they did just that. Second lieutenants experienced an intensely exciting, but somewhat abbreviated life in combat, and Avner wanted no part of it.

"Mount up," Levy said. "We're counterattacking." Loud whistles overhead announced the beginning of an artillery barrage, and in the distance, they could hear the rumble of jets. A carefully coordinated attack was starting that would poke and probe at the Syrians, looking for a weak spot the Israelis could exploit. A wicked grin split Nazzi Halaby's weasellike face and he blew a kiss in Avner's direction. The Druze driver scrambled up the face of the tank and lowered himself into the driver's seat. He was as frightened as Avner but was determined to show the stiff-necked Orthodox Jew that he would not run from a fight. One of Avner's most deep-seated prejudices about Arabs being cowardly was taking a beating.

The young woman in uniform pushed her way through the crowd of people hurrying in and out of the building in Tel Aviv, pressed by the urgency of war. Occasionally, a male head would turn and follow her progress, hoping that the captain might have business in his office. She was familiar with the building and took the stairs to the second floor, turned right down the corridor, and walked into the end office, the entrance to Mossad's headquarters in the basement.

The Ganef was expecting her and motioned her to a chair in his office. He tried not to notice her legs when she crossed them and decided the short skirt was very provocative, especially to Americans.

"Well?" he asked.

The Intelligence officer from Ramon gave a slight shake of

her head. "Neither of them has made a pass at me. I thought Furry was interested at first, but he's happily married and misses his twin girls. Why do American men insist on carrying pictures of their children in their wallets to show everyone?" A beautiful, wistful look played across her face. "And Pontowski only asked if I happened to know Shoshana Tamir."

"What about Colonel Gold?"

"Nothing," she answered. "He's all business and would be highly suspicious if I made a pass at him. He knows the game. Gold may look like a pompous ass but he's not. He's a tough one."

The Ganef sat quietly for a few moments considering his next move. "So, we need something more than sex to put the Americans in our pocket. What is the price?"

"More intelligence," the woman answered. "Pontowski must become one of the Americans' best sources. The more the Americans learn through him, the more they will believe him when he tells them what we need."

"Then we must pay the price," the Ganef decided. "We must convince Gold that his best source of intelligence is Matt Pontowski. He will beg the ambassador to keep him in Israel as an observer." And perhaps, he thought, the young man might fly another mission for us.

Moshe Levy sensed, rather than knew, that the carefully coordinated counterattack was falling apart as he led his platoon toward their objective, a ridgeline overlooking the coastal road right on the border. It had been an easy advance and his three tanks and four APCs had encountered little opposition. Yet he was certain something was wrong. The two F-4s that he had heard checking in on the radio had not received clearance into the area and were holding when they should have been hitting targets of opportunity. The artillery barrage that was supposed to roll forward of their advance wasn't and he wondered if the shells falling around him might be their own.

He tried to look through his periscope but the bouncy ride and dust kept him from focusing through the small prisms. Levy wished the tank had the original commander's cupola with its ring of vision blocks, but the Israelis had replaced it with a low-profile cupola. He had no idea if there were friendly tanks or APCs to the left or right of his platoon. In fact, he couldn't see much of anything buttoned up in the turret and didn't even know where the enemy was.

Levy had to make a quick decision if they were to continue. He threw his hatch open, stuck his head out and scanned 360 degrees around him before he hunkered back down in the tank. The hard metallic ping of bullets ricocheting off the turret echoed inside. Tank commanders have a very limited view of the action around them when they are buttoned up and the smoke, haze, and dust that engulfed Levy's tank had blinded him. The quick peek had confirmed his worst fears: His platoon was rolling along totally unsupported on its flanks. "Nazzi," he half barked, half coughed over the intercom, "head for that low ridge off to your right and try to find a hull-down position."

Halaby did as ordered and veered the tank to the right. He could hear the rapid ping of bullets ricocheting harmlessly off the front slope of the tank, the most heavily armored part. Then Halaby saw the machine-gun nest; it was dug in at the top of the ridge directly in front of them. He tuned out Levy's barked commands as they engaged a Syrian tank and concentrated on where Levy wanted him to go. They were almost under the protective shadow of the ridge. Halaby expected the soldiers manning the machine-gun nest to break and run but they didn't. Now he could see another man wiggle into place beside the machine gun and aim an RPG at them. The tank was less than sixty meters away from the ridge when he saw the flash of the antitank weapon the Syrians had gotten from the Soviets.

The high-explosive warhead of the RPG-7V was traveling at a thousand feet a second when it hit the front of the tank and the shaped-charged warhead ignited one of the Blazer reactive armor plates attached to the tank. The explosion from the reactive armor canceled out the RPG. Halaby uttered an Arabic curse. The RPG could not have penetrated the front of the tank where the armor was the thickest. Now they had an open patch of armor where a Sagger could hit and penetrate. Halaby twitched on the T-bar he steered with and centered the tank directly on the men shooting at him. He buried his right foot in the big gas pedal and hurtled the tank over the top of the ridge and dropped its fifty tons of steel onto the three men in the machine-gun nest, grinding them into the rocks and dirt.

Without being told, Halaby reversed the tank, backing over the ridge. As they came down the slope, a wire-guided Sagger missile hit their front right track and exploded, blowing their track off the front idler. Halaby still had enough momentum and control to back the tank down a few more feet before they came to a halt.

The commands came quick and furious as Bielski traversed the turret and sought out the BMP that had launched the missile at them. Finally, the tank quieted and only the harsh noises of the radio filled the turret. Levy keyed his mike and spoke to his platoon before he popped the hatch and scanned the killing field in front of him with binoculars. Satisfied they were safe, he ordered the other tank commanders and squad leaders from the APCs to gather around his tank while he established contact with his company's command post. As expected, his orders were to hold and stand by for orders.

Bielski and Halaby were examining the battle damage to the tank when Avner slid down to the ground. "Where the hell are we?" he asked, trying to get his bearings.

"Apparently stuck in the middle of nowhere all by ourselves," Bielski said.

"Now what the hell are we going to do now?" Avner grumbled.

"Get a new tank," Bielski said. "This one is going to take some major repairs before it moves again."

Avner spun around and glared at Halaby. "Damn you! You were never ordered to go over the ridge. If you had stayed on this side, we would've never taken that last hit. You're a jinx, Halaby."

Nazzi Halaby shrugged, his way of fending off the heavyset, nineteen-year-old Avner. Then a thought occurred to him. "You're still alive, aren't you?"

Fraser was standing in front of the President's desk, waiting to escort him down to the Situation Room in the basement. Pontowski stood up and led the way as Fraser's short legs tried to match his long strides. "Who's giving the briefing today?" he asked.

"William Hogan from the CIA," Fraser told him.

"When will Bill Carroll be back?"

"He won't, Mr. President." Pontowski raised an eyebrow and Fraser knew an explanation was in order. It was the moment he had been waiting for. "We had him checked out and discovered he had an unauthorized contact with Mossad."

"Was he working for Mossad?" Pontowski asked.

"No, just talking to them when he shouldn't. Rather than take chances, we pulled his clearance and put him out to pasture. We're still watching him. By the way, another interesting connection showed up." They were almost to the Situation Room. "Carroll has been talking to Melissa."

Pontowski paused at the doorway and stared at Fraser. He humphed and walked through. Inside, the National Security Council, along with the director of central intelligence and the Chairman of the Joint Chiefs of Staff, were standing, waiting for him. The CIA briefer, William Hogan, was standing nervously beside a set of briefing charts. Pontowski nodded and sat down. Everyone but Hogan shuffled into his chair. "Mr. Hogan, I hope you have some good news for us," Pontowski said.

"I wish I did, Mr. President." With that, he started his briefing on the latest installment of the Arab-Israeli conflict. In a few words and with three charts, he summarized the situation. Fraser relaxed into his chair next to the wall and made desultory notes, easily splitting his attention. The Israelis are going to take a beating on this one, he thought. That should make B. J. Allison and her Arab buddies happy.

Matt's name caught Fraser's attention and he focused on the speaker, Admiral Scovill, the JCS Chairman. "Our air attaché has found Captain Pontowski and Major Furry and they are providing us with the best intelligence we have from inside Israel. It's all in Colonel Gold's latest report. We're talking a gold mine here." Scovill looked over his reading glasses. "Pun intended, sir. The intelligence is so good that our ambassador has requested that we make them official observers and give them diplomatic status."

"Too many political liabilities," the secretary of state said. "Your grandson as an official observer could be read as a personal commitment to the Israelis. And it is dangerous. If he were taken hostage or killed . . ." He let the thought trail off.

"Recommendations?" Pontowski asked.

The room was split evenly on the question. Finally, only the director of central intelligence, Bobby Burke, remained to be heard from. "I think they should stay in place. The

Israelis are famous for crying wolf to get more arms and aid. With a good source of intelligence, we can better judge what they really need and just how bad the situation is.''

"If the ambassador wants them, he's got them for now," Pontowski said. "If they are taken as hostages, nothing special." The men and women in the room could see the pain of that decision in the President's eyes. "Next item. Are we making headway in the UN to get the fighting stopped?"

The secretary of state knew the question was for him. "No, sir," he answered. "The Arab bloc of nations senses a victory and is stalling. Winning is a new sensation for them and they are collecting on every favor and debt owed them for support. There won't be any progress in the UN until the Israelis start to win."

Silence came down heavy in the room. "So the question is," Pontowski said, "should we start the resupply of Israel now?" This time, the room was unanimous that a resupply of arms had to begin immediately. Especially urgent was the need for more Patriot, TOW antitank, and Stinger surface-to-air missiles.

"Mr. President," the secretary of state counseled, "I agree that we need to start now. But, what we are sending Israel will be used against a very important client state of the Soviet Union. Given the turmoil going on inside the Kremlin, we had better tell the Russians what we're doing and send them reassuring words that we will not let Israel defeat Syria. God only knows how the hard-liners will react if they see a threat to their interests. We could be playing right into their hands and give the hawks in the Kremlin an excuse for a military coup. They're not above using an external threat as a reason for reestablishing a dictatorship. If they have their way, this fighting could jump the firebreak we've got around it now. We don't want to turn this into a wider, regional war."

Pontowski sat for a few minutes thinking about the options open to him. There was little doubt that the United States had to react now or that Israel would be overrun, and that he could not allow. But what were the Egyptians and Iraqis up to? Would they come into the war? What would the Israelis do once they were on the offensive? Yair Ben David was a tough old bird with a belief in vengeance and a deep-seated hatred of Arabs. What end game would the Russians accept? Was there anyone in charge in the Kremlin? Were the Syrians acting as a wild card on their own? Too many questions and no answers, he thought. Well, this is what I was elected to do, what I wanted to do.

"Mr. President?" It was the secretary of state. "Since the Soviet ambassador has been recalled home, may I suggest we use the Hot Line to establish contact and relay our intentions before we start resupply operations?" He pushed a sheet of paper across the table to Pontowski. "I've taken the liberty of drafting a message." The Hot Line was not a voice link with the Kremlin's leaders but a Teletype. "Also, perhaps we should send our own Russian translation with it so that . . . ah"—he sought the right diplomatic words but gave up—"the dumb bastards don't get it wrong."

The President read the message. It was concise, to the point, and made it very clear that the United States would cut off the flow of arms and material once the fighting had stopped and a return to the status quo had been achieved. "Get it translated and on the wires," he ordered. He rose and walked back to the Oval Office, mulling over how and when to tell his wife that Matt was still in harm's way.

"Sit down, Tom." Pontowski waved Fraser to the couch and slumped in his own leather-covered chair. He spun and looked out the window, not seeing the President's Park stretched out before him. This has got to be the loneliest job in the world, he thought. And it doesn't help with Tosh coming out of remission. Lupus was rampaging through her body, this time attacking her heart, killing his wife, his friend, lover, and best counselor. Suddenly, he felt very old.

"Mr. President?" It was Fraser bringing him back to the moment. Strange, he thought, how much I rely on Fraser and I don't even particularly like him. "Shall I order you some lunch?" Pontowski nodded. Before Fraser could pick the phone up, it rang. The President nodded and Fraser answered it. His face visibly paled as he listened. "The Hot Line is down," Fraser said, "no one is acknowledging our calls."

"That's not good," Pontowski said. He sank back into his chair, considering the implications. The crisis in the Kremlin had gone critical and he was making decisions in the dark, not knowing how the Russians would react, not able to cable them his intentions. "How many Russian advisers are there in Syria?" he asked.

"Over fifteen hundred at the last count," Fraser replied.

"Our weapons are going to kill some of them," the President predicted.

18

What I don't know will kill us, Moshe Levy thought as he watched his platoon consolidate their position. He had hated ordering one of the other tank crews to switch tanks with him, but as the platoon's commander he had to have mobility if he was to survive and get them to safety. His old tank was mostly hull-down behind the ridge and still capable of using its main gun. But if the Syrians attacked, it would be the first target. It amazed him how the other tank crew had readily accepted the change. Even Avner had commented on it and said that he would not obey that order. Levy had let it go.

The tank crews were finished with redistributing their remaining ammunition, and the squads in the M113 armored personnel carriers had dismounted and deployed along the low ridge that reached west out of the mountains and ran down to the sea to form the border between Israel and Lebanon. One of the squad leaders had suggested that they deploy recon/observation teams on the flanks and send a two-man scout team forward as soon as it was fully dark. Levy readily agreed. When he turned his attention back to his tank, he found Dave Bielski and another gunner boresighting the main gun. "The thermal sight is kaput," Bielski told him. Their night fighting capability would now depend on how good their backup infrared sight was. I wish the old crew had told me about that, Levy thought. I've got a lot to learn.

He checked on Halaby and found him alone under the tank, tensioning the tracks. It was a two-man job and Avner should have been helping him. Levy searched the growing darkness until he found his loader, eating behind a rock outcropping. He took a great deal of pleasure in kicking him into action and sending him over to help Halaby. I shouldn't have done that, he berated himself.

Darkness had settled over the ridge and Levy forced himself to maintain a listening watch on the radio. He badly wanted to check in and find out what was going on, but he knew that the longer the pause in fighting, the greater the chance of the Syrians' using radio direction finders to pinpoint his position. Then he could expect an artillery barrage. He rummaged around in the tank until he found his night vision goggles. I've got to get organized, he thought, but I don't seem to have enough time. He had never imagined that one of the main problems a commander had was time management. Why hadn't someone told him that?

When Levy had the bulky goggles that resembled a squashed set of binoculars strapped to his head, he scrambled to the crest of the ridge and scanned the slope in front of him. Nothing. Then he turned and looked down the reverse slope to check his own disposition again. To the south, behind them, he could see movement of greenish images. Were they surrounded? Isolated? For a moment, he would've sworn that his heart was in his throat. Then he saw the distinctive image of an M88 tank recovery vehicle emerge from the dust. He couldn't credit how gracefully the fifty-seven-ton monster moved, almost floating, then plowing over the terrain, leaving a feather wake of dust behind it. His heart found its proper place and he watched six Merkava tanks supported by a dozen of the heavily armored Centurion tanks that had been converted to APCs sweep toward him. It looked like an armored brigade was coming to the rescue.

Twenty minutes later, Levy was standing by the center hatch at the back of a Merkava tank as an *aluf mishneh*, or colonel, crawled out of the crew compartment. The colonel was in command of the brigade and using the Merkava as his command vehicle. "Congratulations," he said, pumping Levy's hand. "Our attack was turning into a complete disaster until you swung right and cleared this ridge. Apparently, the Syrians were going to use it to anchor an attack on our flank but thought better of it when you magically appeared."

Levy thought about how easily they had taken the ridge. "I don't think the Syrians were much sold on the idea," he said.

"Obviously, you changed their minds. Our latest reconnaissance shows they're pulling back, probably to reconstitute. We're moving forward until we come in contact to keep the pressure on them." He studied the map one of his staff handed him. "This looks like a good place for my headquarters. Moshe, you saved our ass on this one."

So now I'm a hero because of pure dumb luck, Levy thought.

"I've forwarded a recommendation that you be promoted to *segen*," the colonel said. "Division will approve when they hear what you did here."

Levy's mouth fell open. A *segen* was a first lieutenant and at the rate he was going, he'd make captain in a week. And that meant command of a company, which he definitely did not want.

The word that Tosh Pontowski was very ill again swept through the White House, casting a dark cloud over the entire staff. For those who knew what lupus could do, the news was especially grim and they struggled with their emotions, trying to soldier on as Tosh would have wanted. Even Zack Pontowski's political enemies, men who contested with him over every major issue and election, sent their best wishes and hopes for a speedy recovery to the White House. The President's wife was loved and respected.

Melissa Courtney-Smith had shed her tears in private and thought she was in full control when the President walked through her office. Without thinking, she stood up, wanting to say something, to offer hope. But the words weren't there. Pontowski nodded at her, acknowledging the unspoken words between them. He paused before leaving. "We need to talk." He nodded toward his office and she followed him. Once inside and alone, he motioned to a couch and sat down beside her. "Melissa, what have you and Bill Carroll be talking about?"

Her first impulse was to ask him how he knew about her and Bill. But Melissa knew he would not tell her. "About the Arab-Israeli war. Bill is very worried and claims the Iraqis will come in with the Syrians. He says the Arabs are whipping their people up for a *jihad* and if a cease-fire can't be negotiated within a few days, the Arabs might win."

Pontowski stared at his hands. "Why did he tell you?"

Melissa knew that they had come to the heart of the matter

and that by rights, the President should fire her for meddling in affairs that didn't concern her. But she wasn't about to lie or try to hide what she had done. "Because Bill doesn't think you're getting the full picture, that internal prejudices in the CIA and politics are filtering out key items."

"Where is Carroll getting his information from?" the President asked. Stan Abbott, the head of the Secret Service, had already supplied him with the answer. He was probing to see if she was playing the same type of games.

"From Mossad."

"Perhaps," Pontowski said, reassured by her honest answer, "the Israelis have their own special filters in place and want to feed us information to meet their own ends. Making sense out of the mass of information that floods into our intelligence agencies is a nightmare that I wouldn't wish on any sane individual. Someone has to interpret it all and try to put it into a larger framework. I suppose that's when a person needs an opinion—if you will, a view of the world—to filter and winnow facts."

He smiled at his favorite secretary. "I know you don't like or trust Tom Fraser and probably think he's pushing for the oil interests in all this. But have you ever thought why I selected him for my chief of staff?"

Again, he had surprised her. Melissa thought she had worked very hard to hide her dislike of the man. She shook her head. "I never did understand why you did that."

"Because he's a wheeler-dealer, a hatchet man who scares people. He's my point man and does all the heavy blocking for me. With him as the bad guy, I get to play the good guy. Melissa, I know where he's coming from. He's in it because he savors power. Also, he understands me and, more importantly, knows his limits." Pontowski squeezed her hand. "Go on back to work, Melissa. Keep sending me memos when you think it's necessary and let me worry about playing political games."

Melissa felt like crying for so badly underestimating the man. She smiled weakly at him and stood up.

"Melissa, who should I get to replace Bill on the NSC?"

"General Leo Cox," she answered.

"Please tell Tom to come on in." He watched her go. Oh, Melissa, he thought, if only you knew. I use Fraser like I use you. Without him, my campaign would have gone broke in the early days of the primaries. Without a bastard like him to dig the money out, launder it, and then pump it into the campaign, the opposition would have swamped me. You have no idea how hard it was to find him; a man not afraid to act on his own, not involve me, and smart enough not to get caught. But I'll burn him at the stake if I have to. What a popular sacrifice that would be and I can climb total innocence, the abused party betrayed by his friends now setting things right.

Matthew Zachary Pontowski, the President of the United States, could play hardball politics when he had to for he was a political animal, something his wife knew and understood.

Fraser stood in the doorway, waiting to be recognized. Pontowski heaved himself to his feet and walked over to his desk. "Who's first on the agenda?"

"A delegation from the Hill." He named two senators and three representatives.

"The Israeli lobby," Pontowski said. "I've been expecting them. Show 'em in."

The senior senator heading the small congressional delegation that looked after the interest of Israel in the U.S. Congress was satisfied by what he was learning. Now if he could just get the junior congressman to shut up, they could gracefully bow out of the Oval Office and get back to work.

"Mr. President," the young congressman said, "we appreciate that you have opened up the supply channels to Israel. But I'm telling you, it only amounts to tokenism and is not nearly enough to replace the losses in equipment the IDF has suffered."

Pontowski stared at the young man, willing him to silence. It worked. "I don't mind repeating myself. Like I said when we last met, I will not let Israel be destroyed or occupied by its enemies. Apparently, that promise isn't enough for you. But I urge you to remember that there are other problems—"

"Which you're using as a smokescreen to avoid committing the necessary support to save Israel," the congressman said, interrupting him.

"Mr. President, let me apologize for my colleague," the old senator said. He made a mental promise to teach the loudmouthed new kid a few political manners.

"John, it's not necessary," Pontowski smiled. "I was young once."

"Don't patronize me," the congressman said, slightly more in control.

"I must take the reaction of the oil-producing Arab states and the Soviets into account when I make any move in this war," Pontowski explained. "Unfortunately, no one is answering the telephone in the Kremlin now and we can't tell them what our intentions are. So our actions must speak louder than words or the Soviets might overreact. We do not want to give the hard-liners in the Kremlin the ammunition they need to come out on top. We must not embarrass the Soviets or, even now, we could find ourselves staring down each other's gun barrels."

"Mr. President, I don't give a damn what you say because I think you're more concerned with what the oil sheiks will do and are using the Soviets as an excuse to not intervene. The invasion of Kuwait and our reaction marked the turning point in our Middle Eastern policies. You're sacrificing our only worthwhile ally, the only truly democratic state in the Middle East on an oil barrel. And I'm going to prove it."

Pontowski's blue eyes turned crystal hard. "Ah yes, the question about illegal campaign funds. Please tell me what you find. I'd like to get to the bottom of it myself."

The old senator decided it was time to intervene. "Mr. President, thank you for your time." Within a few minutes, the delegation had been ushered out and were waiting for their limousines to take them back to their offices. The old senator invited the junior congressman to ride with him. It was not a request and inside the cocoon of his car, the old man pulled off his gloves. "Son, you're suffering a terminal case of the stupids. Zack Pontowski knows what he's doing. Now you get your act together or I'm going to rip your balls off."

"But . . ." the congressman stammered.

"There aren't any 'buts,' " the senator said. "Do you remember his saying actions must speak louder than words? Just why do you think Zack has left his only grandson in Israel? Learn to read the signs boy, or you're dead in this town."

The USAF colonel who headed the advance party setting up MAC's airlift command post at Ben Guiron Airport reminded

Matt of a hyperactive chimpanzee in rut he had once seen in a zoo. The man was all action and totally out of his element. While Matt piloted the embassy staff car through the organized chaos on the ramp at the airport, Furry sat beside him going through the charade of making notes as the colonel spewed orders from the backseat.

"I want that section of the ramp reserved for our aircraft," the colonel said, "and that hangar as a temporary warehouse where we can inventory all arriving cargo prior to signing it over to the Israelis."

A sardonic grin played across Furry's mouth that he took care to hide from the colonel. "I'll see what I can arrange, Colonel Walters."

"Don't see, do it," Walters barked. He leaned forward in the seat, trying to be conciliatory. "Look, I know you tactical fighter types aren't used to dealing with MAC, but we run the show based on accountability and flying safety. When that first C-Five lands, I'll show you how it's done. We'll get the cargo offloaded, debrief the crew, and if the plane is code one for maintenance, we'll get a fresh crew out of crew rest and fly her out of here. We'll do the whole turnaround in less than three hours. We'll process the cargo and have it ready for release by tomorrow. Colonel Gold at the embassy is an old MAC hand and that will impress the hell out of him."

Furry scribbled a note on his pad for Matt to see. The wizzo was of the opinion that the Israelis would not be impressed. But since this was the first assignment Gold had sent them on, neither said a word. The colonel had a lot to learn.

A dirty van drove up and a haggard-looking Israeli lieutenant colonel climbed out. He identified himself as the ramp marshal responsible for unloading cargo planes and clearing the ramp as quickly as possible for the next inbound aircraft. Colonel Walters bridled at his abrupt manner and tried to explain that he was responsible for all MAC aircraft on the ground. The Israeli logistics officer ignored him and acknowledged a call on the van's radio. Then he pointed to the west. Approaching the airport at four hundred feet and three hundred knots was a C-5.

"What the hell!" Walters shouted, his face bright red. "MAC doesn't allow approaches like that. I'll send that pilot's ass home in a—"

"Colonel," Matt interrupted. "Israeli air defenses are weapons-free . . ."

"Damn right they're free. The U.S. paid for 'em."

"Colonel," Matt explained, " 'weapons-free' means the Hawk batteries ringing this place will shoot at anything that is not positively identified as friendly. And Hawks don't miss. Your pilots have to fly that approach"—he gestured at the C-5 that was now almost over the field—"or the Hawks will hose it down. Believe it."

"I don't have to believe a goddamn thing, Captain." Walters fell silent as the huge cargo plane crossed the approach end of the runway, still at four hundred feet and three hundred knots. Walters gasped when the pilot reefed it into a climbing left turn to a thousand feet and circled to land, touching down at the same spot where he had initially popped.

The colonel was beet-red and huffing. Matt was certain he would hyperventilate and pass out. "Captain, what you just saw violates every safety regulation in MAC's book. I'm going to have some ass."

"Sir," Matt tried to calm the man, "that looked like pretty good airmanship to me. Why don't you talk to the pilot after he lands? He may not've had a choice." Walters shot Matt a look of contempt and stomped off to give orders to the cargo handlers.

Matt and Furry stood beside their car and watched the C-5 fast-taxi to the ramp. They heard another "Goddamn" as Walters exploded again. "That man's gonna bust a blood vessel," Furry allowed. The plane's engines remained at idle as it knelt down on its landing gear. Both the front and rear cargo doors swung open and ten Hummers with TOW anti-tank missiles mounted on top drove off both ends. Then an M2 Bradley armored fighting vehicle clanked down the front ramp. The plane raised up on its haunches and a low, flat-bedded cargo platform drove up. The driver nudged it against the cargo bay and pallet after pallet stacked with boxes were pushed off. "That puppy do carry a bit," Furry mumbled. "Most of those pallets are loaded with TOWs and Stingers," he added.

Walters bounced up to them. "Get on the ramp marshal's radio and order them to shut down engines," he barked. "The loadmaster says they're code two for maintenance. No way

I'm going to let them launch until it's fixed.'' The C-5's cargo doors closed and the engines spun up.

"Sir," Matt shouted over the engine noise, "is it flyable?" He knew the answer—code two simply meant the plane had minor problems.

"Damn it, I don't launch unsafe aircraft. Get on the radio and shut 'em down." Now the C-5 moved forward and taxied for the runway.

"Colonel Walters," Matt said, "this is a war zone and well within range of tactical missiles. The safest place for your aircraft is a hundred miles out over the Mediterranean."

"You're getting in the way, Captain. I need some action if I'm going to get things under control here." He spun to look at the departing C-5, which was now taking the active runway and rolling. It had been on the ground less than fifteen minutes. They could see the back of the ramp marshal's van as it followed the Bradley off the nearly deserted ramp. All the cargo had disappeared and only four men were left standing by a half-empty pallet with tool boxes and an F-15 radome. The colonel's head jerked back and forth as he tried to understand what had happened to his carefully planned and organized operation.

Finally, he found some words. "They can't fuckin' A do this to me!" he shouted.

Furry tried to explain but he doubted if the man would understand. "Colonel, the war over there"—he pointed to the north—"is seventy miles away and is eating up men and equipment like you wouldn't believe. Right now, the side that's going to win is the side that can resupply the fastest. The Israelis know that. They haven't got time to play paper-shuffling games."

"Amb," Matt said, looking at the four sergeants standing by the pallet, "I think those guys are the combat repair team that came in on the C-Five. Why don't you get 'em down to Ramon and get our jet fixed. I'll check in with the embassy."

"Love to." Furry grinned. "That'll give me a chance to pick a few more Israeli brains about the latest tactics they're using." Then the wizzo got very serious. "Matt, rule number four says 'Know when to get the hell out of Dodge' and I think it's time for us to cut and run." A rueful look crossed Matt's face. He gave Furry an abrupt nod and drove off, leaving Colonel Walters behind.

It took Matt over thirty minutes to find a phone and get through to Gold at the embassy in Jerusalem. The air attaché's reaction to Matt's report was a low-pitched belly laugh. "I know 'Bigshot' Walters," he said. "I'm not surprised they sent him here—he does look good on paper. I'll get him replaced. Don't worry, MAC's got plenty of colonels who have a clue and can move cargo.

"We've got an Army lieutenant colonel as an observer at Haifa," Gold continued, "and the Israelis have asked for him on the Golan. I want you to go up there and replace him. He'll brief you on what he's been up to." Matt copied down the detailed directions he needed to make contact, and when Gold told him to "Get going," he ran for his car.

The directions Gold had given Matt led him directly to the U.S. Army lieutenant colonel at the forward headquarters of Northern Command. He found the LC sitting in a mess tent, discouraged by his total lack of activity and usefulness. He explained how the Israelis kept him on a short leash and that he could probably learn more by reading press releases than by what he was seeing. "This is as far forward as they'll let you get," he warned Matt. Then he disappeared, hopeful that he would see more of the action on the Golan Heights.

Within minutes, Matt discovered that the staff officers had no time for him but were not going to let him go anywhere. Late that night, he stood outside the main command bunker and listened to the distant *whump* of artillery. Occasionally, he could see a red glow light the horizon. This is stupid, he thought and decided that if he couldn't go forward, he would go backward. "Or make an end run," he mumbled to himself. Fifteen minutes later, he was on the outskirts of Haifa, heading for Shoshana's apartment.

The Tamirs' large apartment was filled with children and four harried-looking grandmothers. One of the women spoke excellent English and explained how they had evacuated the children out of a kibbutz in the Huleh Valley at the base of the escarpment leading up to the Golan Heights. "They are not used to being cooped up like this," she said as she collared a four-year-old who seemed intent on turning the balcony's railing into a tightrope. Matt was able to piece together a connection between the kibbutz and Avi Tamir, but when he asked about Shoshana, he was greeted with absolute silence.

"The Israeli penchant for secrecy," he muttered. Finally, the women relented and told him to try the hospital. "Which hospital?" he asked. Again, he was greeted with silence.

After he had left, the woman made a phone call and identified herself as Lillian. "The young American just left," she reported. "Yes, he knows where to look." She paused, listening to the voice on the other end. "No, I'm not stupid. I didn't make it that easy for him." She slammed the phone down, hoping it split the Ganef's ear.

Tara Tyndle recognized the signs immediately. The secretaries were huddled in a corner and whispering to themselves, exchanging worried glances. B. J. Allison was throwing a rare temper tantrum and they were seeking cover until she cooled down. Tara smiled at the secretaries. The youngest one, his boyish face now calm, knocked at Allison's door and announced her. "Well," Tara said, "you've certainly livened things up around here." She gave her aunt a beautiful smile and sat down, crossing her long legs and making herself comfortable. "Would you like to hear about our mutual problem, Fraser?"

"Fraser," Allison snorted, "is not the problem. It's that dumb Polack, Pontowski. Do you know what he's done?" Tara knew better than to answer the question—Allison wanted to tell her. "Congress"—Allison was sputtering in her fury— "is going to give him the excess profits tax that he's asked for." The old woman paced her office while Tara waited. While Allison's temper tantrums were legendary among the staff, she usually regained control within minutes.

"You would think *we* were the enemy and not—" Allison had almost said "the Jews" but caught herself in time. She did not want Tara to think that she was a bigot, but she held deep-seated prejudices that had formed at an early age. "And if that's not enough, he's resupplying Israel, not that I'm surprised. Did you know his grandson is in Israel? If that's not giving aid and comfort to the—" Again, she bit her words off. She had almost said "enemy." "I can't tell you how much it disturbs me that the Israelis have a President of the United States in their pocket." Tara could sense that Allison was spinning down and would soon be rational. "If he's not going to be sensitive to the true concerns of our country, then I'm going to have to see him removed.''

A thoughtful look crossed Tara's face. ''I'm close to finding out how your money was funneled into Pontowski's campaign. There's a key middle man.''

''Hummm. How fortunate,'' Allison said. She sat down and ordered tea. ''The press is losing interest, what with all the news from the Middle East. We do need to provide them with a smoking gun.''

A secretary knocked at the door and stood there, waiting to be recognized. ''Yes?'' Allison asked. The young man told her that a certain congressman was on the phone and would like an appointment. Allison turned to Tara and smiled. ''Isn't he that nice Jewish boy who—''

''Yes, Auntie. He's the spokesman for the Israeli lobby. Fraser was telling me that he is very unhappy with Pontowski.''

Allison sensed an opportunity and she didn't care why the congressman was in opposition to Pontowski. Just the fact that he wanted to talk to her was ample indication that all was not well between the Israeli lobby and Pontowski. ''Oh dear, do you think he would like to know about illegal activities of our President?''

''Perhaps.''

''Of course I could never tell him myself. After all he is—''

''Aunt Barbara, please be careful. He probably suspects that you're feeding the press, maybe even the source of the money. How well are your tracks covered?''

Allison's soft southern accent never lost its charm and innocence. ''I don't make mistakes.'' Then she smiled. ''Dear, I don't care to meet the young man, but perhaps you'd like to, ah, establish a relationship?''

Tara Tyndle arched an eyebrow. ''Really, Auntie! He is—''

''Yes, I know but . . .''

''Well, I suppose if it's necessary.'' The two women exchanged smiles, understanding each other perfectly.

''He is rather handsome,'' Allison allowed.

The woman at the front desk of the first hospital Matt checked told him to talk with the ambulance drivers out back, next to the tents the army had set up. He tried to cut through the hospital, but the halls were jammed with wounded soldiers and civilians. One silent hall was filled with children engulfed in bandages and casts. He stood there trying to come to terms with what he saw. He had never thought of children being casualties of war. Then he realized that his rescue of the trapped girl in the basement had been the exception, not the rule.

A weary nurse told him to leave or start helping. "We've got more coming in. . . . A rocket attack on Ofra on the West Bank . . . the Syrians keep hitting the West Bank settlements . . . I don't know why. We're taking the overflow and the ambulances should be here any minute." There was no decision to be made and Matt went with the nurse.

The first ambulance backed up to the tent the hospital was using to receive incoming casualties and Matt pulled the door open. The first stretcher out carried a badly burnt child that he guessed to be five or six. He couldn't tell if it was a boy or girl. An overpowering stench of charred flesh and antiseptic washed over him. He froze. "Move!" the nurse barked. Stung into action, he helped a teenage girl carry the stretcher into the tent to a waiting doctor.

Matt lost count of the number of ambulances he helped unload and soon he found himself carrying the stretchers into nearby homes and office buildings as they ran out of space. Another ambulance pulled up and he stood there, wondering if the chain of shattered children would ever stop. This time, the last stretcher out held a body. Judging from the bandages, the child's chin and lower jaw had been blown away. "Carry her to the morgue," a voice commanded. "We need the stretcher here." It was Shoshana.

"What happened?" he asked, trying to come to terms with the carnage around him.

"A direct hit on a shelter at a school," she told him. "Probably a Scud rocket. The Patriots can't get them all." Shoshana looked at him and knew the inner turmoil that had to be ripping him apart. "Don't think about it," she said. "Just do something—anything." Shoshana had been through the hell he was experiencing and had given him the only advice she could.

Gently, Matt picked the small bundle up off the stretcher and cradled it in his arms. He looked up at her, fighting tears.

"Don't go. I'll be back in a minute." She watched him go and sank down on the rear edge of the ambulance and rested her head against the side panel. Four minutes later, Matt was back, still shaken. He sat down beside her and waited. "I was lucky to have found you," he finally said.

"I know," she replied. Silence. He turned and looked at her. She had fallen asleep, still leaning against the side panel. He searched inside the ambulance until he found a blanket. Then he eased her onto the floor and spread the blanket over her, willing to wait.

"Tamir!" a voice called. Matt realized he had been dozing and came alert. Shoshana had not stirred.

"Over here," he answered. A young woman in an unfamiliar uniform materialized out of the dark.

"She's needed. North this time."

"She's bushed," Matt protested.

"Wake her," the woman ordered.

"I'm awake," Shoshana said. "Where to?"

The woman jerked a map off her clipboard and brushed past Matt. The two compared maps. "The Syrians counterattacked and are pushing down the coast. Heavy casualties. Get going." Shoshana nodded and climbed into the passenger's seat. She had to wake her partner, a slender, dark-haired thirty-six-year-old schoolteacher from Haifa, to start the engine.

Matt shook his head, climbed into the back and closed the rear doors. Well, he thought, this is one way to see what's happening up front.

"We're getting close," Shoshana said. "I'm not going to wake Hanni yet. She drove most of the last run." Her partner had crawled into the back of the ambulance when Matt took over the driving and had fallen into an instant sleep. Shoshana, much more familiar with the road, was navigating. The first light of dawn was etching the eastern sky, punctuated by momentary flares of artillery. The dull *whumps* of the big guns would follow seconds later.

"There's something I don't understand," Matt said. "Why were all those kids still in Ofra? They should have been evacuated out like the ones I saw in your apartment."

Shoshana stared into the night. "The government tried. But the settlers at Ofra are hard-liners and wouldn't go.

They're afraid if they leave, the government won't defend their homes and will pull back to a better defensive position. By not evacuating, they force the government to defend their homes.''

"That's dumb," Matt said.

"Not to the settlers." She looked at him. "You don't understand, do you?" He shook his head. "The settlers moved in after we occupied the West Bank during the 1967 war. Every one of those settlements is illegal.''

"So why's that illegal?"

"We signed the Geneva Convention on Occupied Territories, which prohibits settlement.''

Matt was astounded. "But it's been going on for twenty-five years.''

"The government encouraged it.''

"That's dumb" was all Matt could think of to say.

"Not to many Israelis. They believe that all of Palestine belongs to them.''

"How do you feel about it?" he asked.

Shoshana stared into the night, too tired to discuss it further. "I just want the fighting to stop.''

A large shadow loomed up in front of them and Matt slammed his foot onto the brake pedal, skidding the ambulance to a halt. The hulk of a burned-out Merkava tank was blocking the road. "Christ," Matt mumbled. "I almost ran into it." He jammed the gearshift into reverse and backed up to maneuver around the tank. As he eased off the road to the right and rounded the tank, he stopped again. "There's someone next to the tank," he said. "We better check on him." He threw the door open and hopped out.

"Don't!" Shoshana shouted, jumping out after him. She knew what he would find and followed him. Matt was bent over the body of the Israeli tanker, not touching it. The scorched-black corpse was on its back, arms bent at the elbow, reaching up.

"My God," Matt whispered.

She reached down and checked the identity tags of the corpse. "A colonel." Then she looked inside the crew compartment at the rear of the tank. "Probably a brigade commander caught moving his command post.''

"What in the hell happened?"

"I don't know," she answered and pulled him back to the ambulance. "We've got to go. Our job is with the living."

Three kilometers down the road, they found five ambulances stopped in front of a low building. They pulled into line and Hanni got out and went inside. She was back within minutes. "We're at the aid station," she said, "but there's no one to transport. They're waiting for the medics to bring more in."

"Why don't you use helicopters for air evac?" Matt asked.

"We do when we can," Shoshana answered. "But we don't have enough helicopters to go around, so we still use a lot of ambulances."

Matt walked inside the temporary aid station and was surprised to see many wounded men, some lying on the floor, others sitting and resting against the wall. Anger flared when he realized they could be transporting many of them. He walked into the next room. It was filled with even more seriously wounded. "What the hell?" he growled.

A medic was giving a shot to one of the men and looked up. "Yank?" he asked, recognizing Matt's fatigues.

"Yeah," Matt answered. "I just got here with an ambulance. Someone said there's no one to transport. Why in hell aren't we moving these guys?"

The medic looked around. "Nothing anyone can do for them."

Matt's face turned rock-hard. It was his first experience with triage.

Matt pointed to the first room with the much less seriously wounded. "What about them?"

"They'll be going back in a few hours." The medic shrugged.

"Then why in hell can't we move them now?"

The medic looked at him for a moment before answering. "They're going back to their units, where they're needed."

Matt turned and walked out, determined to do something. Hanni was waiting for him. "You've got to go back. Shoshana found a stalled APC, one of your M One-thirteens that we use for an ambulance up front. She's got it started and we're going forward."

"Why doesn't she tell me to leave?"

Hanni shook her head. "She couldn't do that. Matt, you're tearing her apart. She wants to be with you but—"

"Come on, I'm going with you."

He and Hanni sat in the back of the M113 while Shoshana drove, working her way across a battlefield. Loud clangs echoed through the small compartment, deafening them when bullets ricocheted off the outer hull. "I thought vehicles with a red cross were protected under the Geneva Convention," he yelled at the woman, glad that he was wearing a flak jacket and a helmet.

"You think that makes a difference to the Syrians?"

The APC jerked to a halt. "Get out!" Shoshana yelled. "Syrian tanks!" Matt followed Hanni out, relieved to get out of the metal box and see what was going on around them. Shoshana had hidden them in a wadi, a dry streambed that had down-cut eight feet into the terrain. Matt could hear the distinctive clank of a tank coming from over the edge. It sounded like it was fifty meters away.

Ahead of them, a squad of Israelis had dismounted from their M113 and were also hunkered down in the wadi. One of them held a Dragon antitank missile. The squad leader motioned for them to deep down as the clanking grew louder. Then the squad leader pointed at his eyes with forked fingers, then to Matt, then back down the wadi. Matt understood immediately what he wanted and ran back down the dry streambed until he was well clear of the clanking sounds. He poked his head over the edge of the wadi. Much to his surprise, he saw only one tank moving toward them and it was at least five hundred meters away. He looked for supporting troops and counted nine on the other side of the tank, moving along in its shadow.

Since he didn't know the hand signals to flash what he had seen, he ran back to tell them. The squad leader nodded and deployed five men to the left and the Dragon team down the wadi to where Matt had been. When they were ready, he raised his fist and pulled it down hard. The men on the far left popped up and sent a rain of fire into the soldiers beside the tank. Matt stuck his head over the edge and saw the turret traverse toward the five men. A hand grabbed the back of his flak jacket and pulled him back down. "Keep down," the squad leader barked. At the same time, the Dragon team on the right swung the missile over the edge and fired. The boom of the missile hitting the tank washed over them. "That was our last one," the sergeant told him. "We'll be lucky to get him."

Matt fell down to the bottom of the arroyo and held on to his helmet as the tank continued to fire. Then a hand grabbed his flak jacket and jerked him to his feet. The squad leader pushed him in the direction of the Dragon team. Matt tired to find Shoshana but had lost both her and Hanni. Another soldier kept pushing him along until they were past the Dragon team and well away from the APCs. "Knocked off a track, but the bastard's still firing," the sergeant said.

Then Matt saw Shoshana and Hanni carrying a wounded man into their APC. "They had better get away from there," a voice said, "until we know who else is out there." The sharp realization hit Matt that it took a special type of situational awareness to survive ground combat and that he didn't have a clue.

"Your APC's got a gun mounted on top," Matt said. "Why don't you use it?"

"APCs don't engage tanks," the sergeant barked. Matt thought about that for a moment and then decided to look again. He could see that the Dragon antitank missile had blown off the tank's left track, but other than that, the tank was undamaged. The turret was swinging back and forth and the PKT machine gun mounted above the main gun was raking the ground in front of the wadi. They were trapped.

The tank crew was still buttoned up inside and Matt couldn't see any supporting infantry. Then he noticed the top of the turret; something didn't look right. He pointed it out to a corporal beside him who looked and only shook his head. "That's the hatch. It's got a dent in it."

Now the American was beginning to get a clue. Maybe the hatch could be pried open like a tin can and a grenade dropped inside. He ran back to the APC and grabbed a breaking bar he had seen inside. He ignored Shoshana and Hanni who were working on the injured man, trying to stop his bleeding. He ran back to the corporal. "Give me a grenade," he said. Again, he popped his head up, took a quick look and dropped back down. The tank was concentrating its fire in the direction of the APCs in the wadi, apparently aware of their position. Now he understood why the squad leader had moved away. APCs didn't engage tanks but tanks engaged

APCs. He looked again, screwing up his courage. He was going after the tank.

With a shove, Matt pushed himself over the edge of the wadi. But the corporal reached up and jerked him back. He lost his balance and collapsed in a heap in the bottom of the wadi. "Why were you going to do that?" the corporal asked.

"Because APCs don't take on tanks," Matt shot back. It was the best one-liner he had ever thought of.

"That was stupid," the corporal said, shaking his head. He pulled Matt to his feet and pointed behind him. Matt could see a Hummer with a TOW mounted on top coming toward them. "We had called for help."

There's many kinds of situational awareness, Matt decided.

"I swear I'll never even think of playing Rambo again," Matt said, trying to keep their spirits up with a little humor. The three of them were sitting beside the ambulance at the hospital in Haifa, eating after returning from their sixth run to the aid station to the north. Matt found it hard to believe he could be so tired and still keep moving. Shoshana only looked at him. "You know . . . attempt to do a John Wayne number on a tank." In quieter moments, he knew it had been rash to the point of stupidity. But he was also dealing with strong protective feelings that were wrapped around Shoshana.

"You would've been killed," Shoshana said, a concerned look on her face.

"Tamir!" Matt recognized the woman dispatcher's voice immediately. The young woman was standing there, slightly weaving, on the edge of a physical collapse. "There's a lull in the fighting," she said. "Only a few more to bring in—for now." While Shoshana and Hanni climbed into the ambulance, he asked the woman to call the American embassy and tell them where he was.

"How much longer can you two go on?" Matt asked, sliding into the driver's seat. He had been going for over thirty-six hours and knew they had been on duty much longer. Hanni was already dozing.

"As long as we have to," Shoshana said. "Let's go."

Matt joined the stream of traffic moving north. The road had been cleared and they moved along at a steady forty kilometers per hour, sandwiched between a supply truck and a freshly repaired M60A3 tank. He noticed that the tank commander standing in the hatch was a woman and realized how desperate the Israelis were if they were manning tanks with women. He mentioned it to Shoshana but she was also asleep. Occasionally, he would see a returning ambulance or a truck transporting wounded men with filthy bandages and still carrying their weapons. Those men were wounded, he thought, returned to combat and wounded again.

"Damn," he muttered to himself. Through the fog of his fatigue, he realized he had accomplished exactly what Gold had sent him north to do and he had to report it. He passed the spot where the destroyed Merkava tank had blocked the road. The tank had been pushed to one side and a team of mechanics were working on it. He counted six body bags piled off to one side. My God, he thought, they're retrieving tanks before taking care of their dead.

Overhead, two Israeli F-4 Phantoms crossed the road. He watched them weave back and forth. Flying a CAP over the road, he decided. He listened for artillery. Nothing. The fighting may have stopped for now, he calculated, but they were far from being secure and the Israelis were obviously rushing reinforcements and supplies forward. He looked at his watch—3:40 P.M. Probably another attack tonight, he decided. Which side will be on the offensive?

A soldier wearing the distinctive red brassard of the military police on her left arm waved them past the aid station and they continued north. He nudged Shoshana. "Wake up. Change in plans." She lifted her head, momentarily confused. Another military policewoman directed them to turn off the road toward a barbed-wire compound.

"POWs," Shoshana said as they came to a halt.

A lone MP was standing by a single stretcher, waiting for them. Shoshana and Hanni jumped out and loaded the stretcher. The MP climbed into the back and they closed the doors. Worry was written across Shoshana's face when they climbed back into the cab. "Don't like hauling wounded POWs?" Matt ventured.

"We've done it before," she said. He could hear the concern in her voice.

"Then what's wrong?"
"This one is wearing an Iraqi uniform."

19

Johar Adwan slipped quietly into the back of the squadron's ready room and found a seat in the back, next to a wall. Johar Adwan looked around, relieved to see only other pilots like himself—the nobodies. Every Iraqi air base like Johar's at Mosul had its fair share of nobodies—the little men, the pilots without family or connections.

The twenty-nine-year-old Iraqi pilot outwardly accepted his position at the bottom of the squadron's pecking order, trying to be content as a lieutenant, knowing that he would never be promoted beyond captain and that others, much less qualified than he, would rise far above him in the chain of command. But that was life in Iraq's air force. There were compensations. Johar Adwan flew Iraq's most modern fighter, the Soviet-built Sukhoi, the Su-27, that NATO called the Flanker. Johar preferred the other name the pilots had given the big jet fighter—Pugachev's Cobra—after Viktor Pugachev, one of its designers and chief test pilot.

Another pilot, Samir Hamshari, came into the room, saw Johar, and sat down beside him. Like Johar Adwan, Samir Hamshari was also a nobody. Samir glanced at the slightly balding Johar. "No practice today," he said. Samir was a year younger than Johar and had introduced him to a new form of air-to-air tactics. Most of the squadron tolerated the two lieutenants, amused by the way they pored over "Red Baron" reports and the issues of the *Fighter Weapons Review* magazine Russian agents had stolen from the U.S. Air Force and sent to the Iraqis. Because of their interest in American tactics, the other pilots had mockingly shortened the pilots' names to Joe and Sam.

What no one knew, and what Johar and Samir's privileged

and powerful superiors would not have tolerated, was that the two pilots practiced the tactics they read about whenever they had a chance. And in order to be unobserved by their own radar controllers, they did it below a thousand feet with their IFFs off.

"General Mana arrived from Baghdad ten minutes ago," Samir said. Hussan Mana was the commander of the base at Mosul and, according to his press releases, the number one fighter pilot in the Iraqi Air Force.

"I'm impressed," Johar mumbled. "You don't think he's going to fly tomorrow?" The two exchanged knowing glances. The joke around the squadron was that Mana flew once a month whether he needed to or not. "Did you hear the latest rumor?" Johar asked.

"That we're going to join Syria?"

"Not that one," Johar replied. "The one about Mana's younger brother being killed by an Israeli agent. Supposedly, she could stop traffic."

"A Mana interested in females?" Samir grinned. "I thought all Manas were alike."

A young and boyish-looking lieutenant colonel came through the door. "The commander will be here shortly," he announced. "Please take your places." The pilots shuffled into two lines on each side of the center aisle, making a corridor for the general to walk down. They lined up by rank, the lowest and least important near the door. Johar and Samir were the first in line. When the lieutenant colonel was satisfied that all was proper, he called them to attention. The two lines stood there, waiting for the general.

Five minutes later, General Hussan Mana entered, his immaculately tailored uniform resplendent with braid and medals. As he walked down the line, each pilot would click his heels and give a short bow. Mana didn't see the lieutenants, ignored the captains and majors, acknowledged the lieutenant colonels with a glance, and actually nodded at the four colonels whose uniforms matched his.

"Do you think they own flight suits?" Samir asked out of the side of his mouth, referring to the colonels and the general.

"It has been rumored," Johar whispered.

General Mana stared at the assembled pilots, all still standing at attention. "It is my honor," he began, his voice rigid and formal, "to tell you that we are now engaged in battle with our most hated enemy. Soon we will have the chance to show the world that their air force is nothing but a pitiful collection of half-assed Barbary apes who call themselves pilots." The general permitted a tight smile to cross his lips.

"Oh, I hope they are," Samir mumbled under his breath.

"I will lead you into battle," Mana continued, "and prove that our Sukhois are better than the American F-Fifteens and F-Sixteens that have allowed the enemy to dominate our Syrian allies. We will attack using a 'bearing of aircraft.' I will be in the lead and you will follow according to position."

A bearing of aircraft was a standard Soviet formation, a long line of aircraft that a radar ground controller directed into an engagement. It was a follow-the-leader formation in which each aircraft followed approximately two miles in trail and stacked slightly higher than the one in front of it. The arrangement allowed the radar ground controllers to maintain aircraft separation and tight control. By "position," Mana meant rank. Johar and Samir would be the last aircraft in the formation.

Now Mana's face hardened. "Victory is ours. *Itbach al-yahud!*" Kill the Jews! The general stomped out of the room.

On that late afternoon, Iraq had 604 men who could fly high-performance fighter-type aircraft. Two of them were fighter pilots nicknamed Joe and Sam.

The MP guarding the Iraqi POW directed Matt to drive to a headquarters compound near Acre where a doctor and translator were waiting for them. The doctor climbed into the back of the ambulance and examined the Iraqi while the translator relayed the doctor's questions. "He says his unit is the Hammurabi Division" the translator said. The Israelis exchanged worried glances. The Hammurabi Division was part of Iraq's Republican Guard.

"He can be interrogated," the doctor said and climbed out.

Time and the road blended together for Matt as he and the two women shuttled back and forth between the fighting and hospitals in the rear. From the wounded, he heard that the Israelis had mounted a counterattack and then had to fall back to their original positions. Matt was able to learn that fighting was the fiercest on the northern border and hinged on a low ridge that straddled the coastal plain. On one trip back to Haifa, a young wounded tanker described the battle to him. "If they push us off that ridge," he said, "the road to Haifa will be wide open."

The action ground to a halt as both sides ran out of tanks, fuel, and ammunition. Then Matt started hearing stories about how a small, ragtag collection of tanks and infantry called Levy Force had fought stubbornly for the ridge and had held on against repeated attacks.

Finally, they were headed for Haifa with their last load of wounded. It was early morning when they reached the hospital and Hanni collapsed from physical exhaustion while they were unloading. Matt carried her to an open place under a tree, amazed at how light and frail the dark-haired woman was under her bulky fatigues. She's been going on sheer willpower, he thought. He gently laid her down and covered her with a blanket.

When he returned to the ambulance, Colonel Gold, the air attaché, was waiting for him. "I got your message," he said. Matt sat down, too tired to answer or think. Shoshana appeared with a plastic jug of water and handed it to him. Matt took a long pull at the cool water and felt better. Slowly, he started telling Gold all he had learned and seen. The colonel listened quietly and made extensive notes. When Matt had finished, the colonel asked detailed questions, filling in the blanks.

"Matt, I was ordered to personally find you and get you out of Israel. The Israelis are taking a beating and this is the only place where they've stopped the Syrians. The Syrian Third Army has pushed them right to the edge of the Golan Heights and taken Mount Hermon. God, if they kick the Israelis off the Golan . . . It's much worse in Jordan and Jerusalem is being shelled."

"In the Sinai?" Matt asked. "The Egyptians?"

Gold shook his head. "No change. The Israelis still have most of Southern Command in the Sinai covering the Egyptians. If they can free those forces and move them north, the Israelis will have a fighting chance."

"The Iraqis are in it now and the Egyptians are going to attack," Matt predicted.

"I know," Gold said. Matt could hear pain in his voice.

"That's the reason you've got to get out of here. Furry says your jet will be fixed and ready to fly tomorrow. Be there and get the hell out of Israel.

"Matt, you gave me the first hard evidence that the Iraqis have come into the war. Look, I haven't got time to baby-sit you. I have got to get back and try to convince somebody in Washington just how critical things are here." He looked at the almost comatose young pilot. "You're in no condition to fly. Get some rest and get to Ramon on your own. If you have trouble, contact me here." He handed Matt a slip of paper. "I've moved to Ben Gurion Airport." The two men stood and shook hands. Then Gold was gone, running for his car.

Matt found Shoshana asleep in the ambulance and drove her home to her family's apartment. The woman Matt had talked to earlier answered his knock, took one look at Shoshana, and half carried her, half dragged her to the bathroom. "You," she said to Matt. "Go in the kitchen and get out of those clothes. Take a sponge bath."

In the bathroom, she lifted out the two small children who were sleeping in the tub and filled it with hot water. She sat Shoshana on the edge and pulled off her fatigues. As Shoshana slipped into the water, she came half awake. "Aunt Lillian," she mumbled. "That's him, Matt."

"I know, Shoshe, I know."

Shoshana let the hot water envelop her. "Aunt Lillian"— her voice was dreamlike and she was twelve years old again— "will I ever be pretty like you?"

"You're beautiful, Shoshe." She gently bathed her niece.

Lillian closed the bathroom door behind her when she was finished. "You need to soak for a week," she said to herself. In the kitchen, she found four giggly children standing over the American. He was half-dressed and passed out on the floor. She stripped him down to his shorts and ordered the children to wash him. The children fell over themselves with laughter and went to work while Lillian went to Shoshana's old bedroom and kicked the children sleeping there out into the hall. Then she went to the bathroom, retrieved Shoshana, and gently placed her in her own bed.

Back in the kitchen, she found the children scrubbing their victim with more enthusiasm than skill. "Now help me get him to bed," she said to the biggest girl. The two of them carried him to the bedroom and unceremoniously dumped him in bed beside Shoshana. "Not much of a wedding night," Lillian said to herself and closed the door. She leaned against the wall, closed her eyes and hugged herself, forcing the tears to go away. "I'll be damned if I'll call the Ganef."

The late-afternoon light filled the bedroom with soft warmth. Outside the door, the apartment was quiet. Shoshana lay there, trying to remember what had happened. The last thing she could remember was the warm water of the tub enveloping her. She touched the bare back beside her and felt a sudden warmth wash over her.

"Matt."

"I'm here."

"No, don't kiss me there. No, don't stop."

"Make up your mind."

"Quit laughing."

"Shoshana, I love you."

"I know. Oh, that's good. No, don't stop. Quit teasing me."

"I'm not."

"Oh. Yes. Help me, help me. Oohh, Matt, I do love you."

The apartment exploded with shouts and laughter when Lillian brought her small charges back. Shoshana and Matt were on the balcony and smiled at each other. "Have you ever thought of having children?" Matt asked.

Shoshana smiled gently at him. About some things, Matt was incredibly naive. "Every woman does."

"Let's get married," he said. "Now."

She reached out and touched his cheek, wanting to say yes, wanting to run away from the insanity that had engulfed her and all she loved. A basic need deep inside her wanted to hide inside the love he was offering her. But she couldn't. "Matt, if we could—"

"Good, let's do it."

"But it's not possible in Israel," she told him. He stared at her, not comprehending. "We don't have civil marriages. Only a rabbi can marry a Jew here and religious law forbids marrying a Jew and gentile. We'd have to go to another country and there's no time for that."

"Then that's what we'll do as soon as this war is over. It can't go on much longer."

For a few minutes, they said nothing, content to be with each other in the fading twilight. "Matt, you're going to have to go soon. Nighttime is probably the best time to travel and I've got to find Hanni."

Matt resigned himself to leaving. "I need to use your phone to check in with the air attaché. He probably knows if the roads are open. Who knows, maybe my orders have changed."

It took Matt over an hour to get through to Gold at Ben Gurion Airport. The colonel sounded relieved when he learned Matt was still in Haifa. "Furry says they're running into problems and it will be at least another twenty-four hours before the jet's fixed. I want you to go over to Ramat David Air Base. They'll be expecting you. Hurry."

"I'll be damned." Matt grinned when he hung up. "I was right. They're sending me over to Ramat David." He held her for a moment. "I'll be back."

A middle-aged woman was waiting to escort him at the first checkpoint blocking the road to the air base. She climbed into the car and eyed him suspiciously. "You must be some-one important," she grumbled. Ten minutes later, she led him through the concrete warrens of one of Israel's most closely guarded command posts. "You're the first foreigner who's ever been in here," she told him. "Ben David himself cleared you in." The tone of her voice told Matt what she thought of that decision. "They want you to observe a strike." She pushed through a door into a large, dimly lit room.

A strong odor of dried sweat and unwashed bodies as-saulted Matt's nose. A few heads looked up and took the newcomer in, every face tired and haggard. Three banks of consoles formed semicircles around a low stage where one man, the direction officer, sat behind a small console. From his position, he could direct the entire operation. Behind him, a massive Plexiglas sheet formed a wall. A map of Israel was etched into the Plexiglas and plotters worked behind it, post-ing new information. On a side wall to the left were three large computer-generated displays that had to do with air de-fense threats and Israeli force status. Large alcoves were set into the other two walls where he could see communications panels and radar screens.

Matt concentrated on making sense out of the three large computer displays. He sucked his breath in when he realized what the numbers meant. The Israelis had started the war with twenty-five front-line squadrons with 602 fighters and another 150 in storage; 436 of those aircraft had been destroyed or lost to battle damage. The remaining 316 aircraft had been reconstituted into twenty below-strength operational squadrons. He mentally calculated an attrition of 58 percent.

"We're facing over eight hundred fighters now that Iraq has come into the war," his escort told him. "Now, their flight to Iran pays off."

"Has my country flown in replacements?"

"Not that I know of," the woman said.

"This is what you really wanted me to see."

"Yes, I think so. And an attack on the new Iraqi nerve gas facility outside Kirkuk." With a few explanations from the woman, Matt was able to decipher the planned strike. The IAF was launching two attacks on the Syrian airfields at Shayrat and Tiyas as a cover for four F-16s that were going against the nerve gas plant near Kirkuk. It was a well-coordinated plan that had already started when Matt arrived. The four F-16s were holding in an orbit with a tanker over the Mediterranean between Cyprus and Syria waiting for a go.

RPV drones were penetrating deep into Syrian airspace, serving as bait to bring up Syrian radars and air defenses. Once the Syrians committed on the drones and the Israelis knew the exact location of the detection and tracking radars, they would attack the radar sites with antiradiation missiles from F-4s. At the same time, other aircraft would start wholesale jamming of Syrian radio communications and surviving radars. If the direction officer determined the Syrians were sufficiently blinded, he would clear in more F-4s, which already were airborne, to attack the two airfields.

The Israeli planners had calculated that the Iraqis would concentrate on the airfield attacks going on in Syria and be partially blinded by the jamming directed against the Syrians. Again, if the direction officer gauged the plan was working, he would order the four F-16s on the tanker against the primary target outside Kirkuk. The F-16s would then descend and head straight for the Syrian coast to make a four-hundred-nautical-mile, low-level dash across Syria and into Iraq. It was a long way in and out.

"Why don't you use Jericho missiles with conventional warheads to hit the target at Kirkuk?" Matt asked.

"Two reasons," the woman answered. "The Iraqis have not started to use their tactical missiles and we don't want to give them a reason. Also, we're 'withholding' our missiles." She didn't tell him that the Jericho lacked the throw weight necessary to send a heavy enough conventional warhead that could penetrate hardened bunkers at that range.

Matt stared at her. You did that deliberately, he thought. The word "withhold" had a specific meaning—the Israeli missiles were being withheld from conventional use and being reserved for nuclear employment. Pieces started to fit together. "Ma'am," he said, "may I ask you what your rank is?"

"*Aluf mishneh.*" A colonel.

"You want my opinion?" No answer. "Your F-Sixteens are looking at a fifty-minute low-level into Kirkuk. Too long. The Iraqis will have time after the airfield attacks are over to get their act together and figure out what's happening. They've got a squadron of MiG-Twenty-nines at Kirkuk and one of Su-Twenty-sevens at Mosul. Even though it's night, your F-Sixteen drivers are going to have to fight their way in and out. I'd say their chances are slim to none." He was thinking how his F-15E had been designed for this mission.

"You overestimate the Iraqis," the colonel said. "Besides, do we have a choice?"

Matt wanted to say something about the dangers of underestimating the opposition but contented himself with "Gutsy drivers. Who's leading the F-Sixteens?"

"Major Dave Harkabi."

A rock hit the bottom of his stomach. "It's a suicide run," he said.

On the center dais, the direction officer stood up and looked at a general sitting in the center of the front row of consoles. The general nodded his agreement and the direction officer keyed his mike. Matt heard him give the go.

"*Zanek!*"

* * *

The four F-16s were halfway to Kirkuk, hugging the ground at 420 knots. Dave Harkabi had deliberately planned to ingress at the slower speed to conserve fuel as long as they were still within the radar coverage of the E-2C Hawkeye supporting them. He was relying on the Hawkeye to give him early warnings of any hostile fighters that might be up and looking for them. With the Hawkeye keeping him aware of the situation, he could concentrate on sneaking through the hostile air defenses in front of him. Based on the total lack of radio transmissions from the Hawkeye, the covering attacks on the two airfields had deceived both the Syrians and the Iraqis.

Ahead of them, Harkabi could see the end of the low cloud deck they had been flying under and bright moonlight. The moonlight was both good and bad; it would allow them to more easily find and hit their target, but at the same time, they were easier to find. The weatherman had told them to expect cloud coverage almost into the target area. He checked his navigation computer for their position—they were outside the radar coverage of the Hawkeye. For the first time, Dave Harkabi was on a mission totally unsupported by other aircraft. He didn't like the feeling.

Still twenty minutes out, Harkabi calculated. He increased his airspeed to 480 knots as they moved out from under the cloud deck. The four fighters spread farther apart into a box formation in the bright moonlight.

Johar Adwan sprinted for his waiting Cobra, urged on by the sharp wail of a siren. A crew chief was waiting by the Su-27 and held the boarding ladder as he scrambled up the steps. As he sank into the seat, his hands flew over the switches and hit the start button, bringing the right AL-31F turbofan engine to life. The pilot tugged his parachute harness into place, glad that he had left it in the cockpit like the Americans did. Next to him, he could see that Samir already had his helmet on. He pulled on his helmet and started the left engine. Now both he and Samir were ready to taxi, but they had to hold and wait for General Mana to taxi out first. They were the first ready to go and the last to take off.

"Multiple hits on the nose, forty-five miles," Harkabi's wingman called over the radio, breaking radio silence. It was the first indication he had that interceptors were on to them. Fortunately, his wingman's pulse-Doppler radar was peaked and tweaked and had an early acquisition. Now they had to wait. Then his own radar got a paint at thirty miles. He checked the altitude of the bandit—six thousand feet—well above them.

He kept his radar in a 120-degree, four-bar scan, looking for other aircraft. Four more radar skin paints materialized, all directly in front of him, for a total of five bandits. He couldn't believe it at first; the Syrians were coming at them in a bearing of aircraft formation. He knew how to discourage that and called up one of his two Sidewinder missiles. Harkabi's radar detected a sixth aircraft. "Say bandits," he asked his wingman.

"Six." The brief transmission was followed by two clicks on a mike button and then two more clicks—his number three and four agreed. He glanced down into the cockpit and checked his Radar Warning Receiver. Numerous bat-wings, the symbol for the radar the Soviets used in their newest fighters, were at his twelve o'clock. It all made sense and he was certain of the threat. His four against six, either MiG-29 Fulcrums or Su-27 Flankers, both with a reported look-down/ shoot-down capability. But Harkabi was confident his ECM systems could jam the enemy aircraft's pulse-Doppler radar. It was the Doppler radar that eliminated ground clutter from a radar system by only detecting relative motion. Then a pilot could "look down" from a comfortable altitude above, find a low-flying aircraft, and then launch a missile to "shoot down" the intruder. Harkabi's ECM would make sure that no relative motion was detected by the Iraqi radar.

Harkabi keyed his radio. "Lead split." It was the command for a tactic they had practiced many times and used against the Syrians. Harkabi jerked his Falcon thirty degrees to the left as his wingman collapsed into a fighting wing position. The second element turned forty-five degrees to the right. At the same time, the four F-16s turned on the ECM jamming pods mounted under their centerline. The plan was for them to move apart and then turn back into the bandits, forming a pincers movement. The contract called for Harkabi to take a head-on missile shot with a Sidewinder and blow on through. The second element would do the same from the other side twenty seconds later.

The tactic had always created havoc among the Syrians and Harkabi was counting on it to work against the Iraqis. By the time the Iraqis got their act together and turned after them, he planned to have joined his flight up and be headed for the target. Since their ECM pods had been specifically configured to counter the pulse-Doppler radar in Fulcrums or Flankers, he was certain they would escape radar detection. The Iraqis would have to get a ''visual'' on them and come down into the weeds to engage. Common wisdom among Israeli pilots held that to be highly unlikely. At best, the Iraqis would end up in tail chase. The Israelis did not jettison their wing tanks that were still feeding fuel.

Harkabi turned back into the bandits and the harsh growl of his Sidewinder came through his headset. Now he had a visual on the first two bandits. He picked the number two man.

It would have worked perfectly except that there were eight bandits, not six. The last two were in trail but not in a bearing of aircraft. Instead, they were in a spread formation two thousand feet apart, down on the deck, and at a coaltitude with the Israelis.

The command radio exploded in a babble of orders and shouts in Arabic as the Israelis engaged. When Johar saw the flash of two aircraft exploding in front of him he keyed his mike. ''Go common,'' he ordered. It was a trick he had read about in a ''Red Baron'' report. Both he and Samir cycled their radios to an unused frequency. Now they could communicate. ''Check right, now,'' Johar said. The two Flankers turned twenty degrees to the right. ''Weave,'' Johar ordered. The two pilots flew back and forth, crossing each other's flight path. Johar was certain the Israelis would return to their original track and would be below three hundred feet.

Both Iraqis checked their own radar warning scopes and realized they were being jammed by highly sophisticated ECM pods. Rather than give away their own position, they both turned their radars to standby and strained for a visual contact. As agreed on, both had called up AA-11 missiles to engage with, not trusting the bigger and more complex radar-guided AA-10 missile. All that they had read and studied told them to expect a close-in, visual turning engagement, and for that they needed the R-60, a short-range, infrared-guided, dogfight missile that NATO called the AA-11 Archer.

Neither man believed they had much chance of finding the Israeli intruders unaided, at night, and down on the deck. But they were going to try. At least they were in the same patch of sky. Johar caught movement out of the side of his right eye. It had to be a bandit because Samir was on his left! Samir's voice came over the radio: "Two bandits, two o'clock, low, I'm engaged." As they had agreed on weeks before, the first pilot with a visual contact would lead the attack. Samir rolled in on the F-16s, which were now passing a kilometer in front of them. In the moonlight, the F-16 Falcons were little more than shadows.

Johar wrenched his big fighter into the vertical, rolled 135 degrees to keep sight of Samir, and then pulled down behind and stroked his afterburners. They were set up for a sequential attack. Then the nose of the lead F-16 came around, turning on Samir, while the Israeli wingman checked, turned, and extended away before pitching back into the fight. The Israelis had seen them. But Samir's reactions were lightning quick and he had been expecting it. He turned hard with the Israeli, matching his turn, fully expecting the second Israeli to come back and go for a sandwich. But Johar's job was to engage the second Israeli and prevent the developing sandwich on Samir, which he did.

The Israeli wingman was pitching back into the fight when Johar stuffed a missile up his exhaust nozzle. He had never seen Johar.

A United States Air Force AWACS orbited 150 miles north of the engagement, well inside Turkish airspace. The E-3A, the specially constructed version of the Boeing 707, had been on station for eighteen hours and had just come off its second in-flight refueling. The rotodome on top of the E-3A rotated slowly at six RPM, scanning an area out to 250 miles with its searchlightlike radar beam.

An operator at the center Surveillance console called the tactical director. "Sir, we've got one hell of an engagement going on at one-eight-oh degrees, one hundred fifty miles. Looks like those four Israelis we were monitoring have been bounced by eight Flankers out of Mosul."

"Keep on top of it," the tactical director said, following

the battle on the scope at his multipurpose console. He ran some quick checks, ensuring that they were getting it all on tapes and that another aircraft, an RC-135 communications recce bird, was still on station. Between the two aircraft, they would capture the entire engagement.

Dave Harkabi knew he was in deep trouble when he saw the second Flanker streak by after his wingman. He had turned 140 degrees and the first Flanker was still on his tail, turning with him. Russians! flashed through his mind as he hit the jettison button, shedding both fuel tanks and the pair of thousand-pound smart bombs he had been carrying under his wings.

Instinctively, he pulled into the vertical, trying to generate an overshoot. "I'm hit!" filled his headset. It was his wingman. "Ejecting!" The Flanker was still at his six and closing to a missile shot. Automatically, Harkabi ruddered his nose over, heading back down, turning his tail away from the threat. A missile flashed by. For a brief second, he wondered if the Flankers had a dogfight missile with a good infrared head-on capability.

Then he keyed the radio switch on the throttle. "Abort! Abort!" he transmitted. "I'm engaged, two bandits." He hoped his number three and four men could make it safely home. They had run into too many surprises on this mission and he was certain they couldn't take out the nerve gas plant with an air strike. Now they had to conserve their jets. He turned his full attention to disengaging, leveled off at two hundred feet, and turned hard into the Flanker.

"Joe," Samir radioed, "say position."

"Lagging at your eight o'clock." Johar was behind him, following the fight as the Israeli and Samir engaged in a flat scissors maneuver, barely five hundred feet above the ground. "Press and come off to the right." He was telling Samir to keep the pressure on the Israeli for a few more seconds as the two planes slowed, each trying to get behind the other. When it looked like Samir was going to reverse, he was to turn to the right and separate. Johar would be in a position to fall in behind the F-16 and take a missile shot. The two Iraqis were herding Harkabi around the sky, working him close so as not to lose him in the moonlight, and not letting him disengage, keeping him down on the deck.

"I'm off," Samir radioed.

"I'm in," Johar answered. As expected, when the Israeli saw Samir pull off to the right, he rolled out and stroked his afterburner, climbing straight ahead, trying to disengage. Johar fell in behind him and squeezed his trigger. The Archer he had ready leaped off the right outboard rail and tracked the F-16, its cooled seeker head ignoring the flares popping out behind the doomed aircraft. For good measure, Johar launched a second Archer, but there was no target for it to home on.

Matt sat on a small table against the back wall of the command post at Ramat David Air Base. His hands clutched at the edge, knuckles white. The command post was mostly silent as mission reports filtered in; two F-16s lost, two safely recovered. Then Ramon's operations report came in; Dave Harkabi last seen engaging two Flankers, his wingman reported hit and ejecting. "Damn," he muttered. Matt had liked the Israeli major.

"Have you seen enough?" the colonel asked.

He nodded and stood up, ready to leave. "Excuse me, ma'am," he said. "You never told me your name."

The woman looked at him. "Harkabi." Matt was stunned, not knowing what to say. But the woman was too young to be Dave's mother and too old to be his wife. "David is my nephew," she said. "I've got to tell his mother."

Outside, Matt took a breath of cool night air and looked up at the scattered cloud deck scudding across the sky. Damn, Dave, he thought, you were good. I know. I flew against you enough times and you should've been able to disengage from two ragheads. And the Flanker isn't any better than the F-16.

Then another thought hit him. Or was it?

His first stop after he left Ramat David was Shoshana's apartment in Haifa. He was disappointed but not surprised when she wasn't home. "Lillian, will you please see Shoshana gets this?" He handed Shoshana's aunt his Nomex flight suit. Lillian looked at him, not understanding. "It's fireproof," he explained, "like a tanker's jump suit. Her fatigues

aren't and this might protect her.'' He was thinking of the
burned-out tank and the charred body he had seen.

Lillian nodded and took the flight suit. "Matt, take care
and come back. She needs you.''

Matt gave her his lopsided grin. "I know. I'll be back.''
"Shalom.''

The road south to Tel Aviv was clogged with trucks and vans
of every description. Northbound traffic had priority and it
took Matt five hours to cover the sixty miles to Ben Gurion.
He used the time to take extensive notes, counting the number of trucks and types of equipment. He took pride in the
number of new tanks and Bradleys that were moving forward,
their United States insignias freshly painted over. MAC was
moving cargo. Then he noticed the troops. Many of them
were women, some still girls, wearing combat gear and carrying weapons.

He found Colonel Gold asleep in a makeshift office, his
head plunked down on a desk, and Matt was reluctant to
wake him. Gold's head snapped up at the sound of his name.
He grunted, shook his head to clear the cobwebs, and took a
drink from the cup of steaming coffee Matt handed him. "I'm
living on this stuff," he grumbled.

Matt handed Gold his notes on what he had seen at Ramat
David and on the road south. The air attaché scanned them,
shaking his head. "Right now, it's touch and go," he said.
"If the Egyptians come in . . .''

Matt nodded, filling in the colonel's thought. "It will be
over in hours.''

Gold's lips compressed into a grim line and his head shook
back and forth in tight little jerks. "No. It won't be over in
hours. The Israelis will go nuclear.''

"Oh my God," Matt whispered, stunned by the sureness
of Gold's prediction. In his preoccupation with the loss of
Dave Harkabi, he had forgotten about the Israelis' "withholding'' their Jericho missiles. He quickly filled the colonel in.

The air attaché picked up one of his phones. "I'm laying
on a helicopter to fly you to Ramon. Get out of Israel soonest.
I've got to get a message on the wires.''

The corridors of the command bunker were eerily quiet, as

if the inhabitants were holding their collective breath, waiting for something to happen. Avi Tamir followed the guard down to the third level, surprised that he was being escorted. "Two people cracked under the strain," the guard explained. "One of them got violent and attacked the prime minister." The people they were passing in the hall were not dirty or wounded but mental strain and emotional danger had made them haggard and gaunt-looking. The guard held a door open for the scientist and stepped back. Yair Ben David was waiting inside—alone.

"Do we have a thermonuclear weapon yet?" he rasped, coming directly to the reason for Tamir's summons to the bunker.

"No," Tamir answered, "not yet." In spite of his misgivings, the scientist had been working furiously on the weapon, driving his staff relentlessly.

"How long?" Ben David demanded.

"Two, maybe three weeks."

"You've been stalling!" Ben David shouted.

"Have I?" Tamir shouted back. "You have no idea. . . . Get someone else to finish it."

The prime minister sank into a chair. "I'm sorry, Avi. I didn't mean that. Please forgive me. But the situation is . . . critical. We're barely holding on in the north . . . Iraq is pouring three fresh armored divisions into Jordan, two into Lebanon . . . I'm pulling our last reserves out of the Sinai. . . . We might be able to hold them. But our latest intelligence reports say the Egyptians are moving more tanks into the Sinai. If the Egyptians attack, I will have to use our nuclear weapons."

"But why do we need a hydrogen bomb?" Tamir protested. "Surely, the nuclear weapons we have—"

"You don't understand Arabs," Ben David snorted. "A tactical nuclear weapon on a battlefield means nothing to them. But if the Egyptians attack, I will repay them for their treachery. One bomb, that's all, one bomb and Cairo no longer exists. Then the Arabs will listen to reason."

"Is that a step we want to take?" Tamir asked. He was thinking about the danger when a war leaps a firebreak, crossing the barrier that separates the use of conventional and nuclear weapons.

"Do we have a choice?"

* * *

Furry was waiting for the helicopter when it landed at Ramon Air Base. He motioned for Matt to hop in the mini pickup he was driving. "Got to hurry," he said. "We're coming under a Scud attack about every twenty minutes and we're out of Patriots." He gunned the engine and raced for the squadron's bunker. "They're trying to keep the base closed. Ain't working so far. The civil engineers here do miracles but I don't know how much longer they can do it." He slammed to a halt and the two men ran down the ramp to the safety of the underground bunker.

"How's the jet?" Matt asked.

"It's ready," Furry answered. "Our troops did some miracles too. It was damaged more than we thought."

"You got an extra flight suit handy?"

"Yeah," the wizzo said. "The captain wants to see us before we split."

They found the captain packing a mobility locker, getting ready to move. She was dressed in fatigues and moved with near exhaustion. Matt decided that in spite of the weariness that drew her face into a tight mask, she was still one of the most beautiful women he had ever met. "We're deploying to an emergency operating location," she said, "a highway strip in the Negev."

"That bad?" Matt asked.

She nodded and sat down. Slowly, she laid out the entire war. It matched what Gold had told him and painted the same grim picture Avi Tamir had just seen. But she left out all mention of nuclear weapons.

"Why are you telling us all this?" Matt asked.

"I was told to," she said. "You've got to make people understand."

"Meaning my grandfather?"

Again, she nodded, her brown eyes filling with tears.

"I doubt that I'll even see him," Matt said, being totally honest. "But we'll write an after-action report on what we saw here and I'll see that it gets to the right people." He turned to Furry. "Time to go."

Her soft voice stopped the two men before they left. *"Shalom."*

Matt turned to look at her. *"Shalom,"* he replied. Then they were gone.

* * *

The Ganef sat at his desk, fingering the glossy black-and-white photo. He dropped the photo and pushed his glasses back onto his forehead, rubbing the bridge of his nose, making himself think of other things.

So much, he thought, riding with one young man. Have I played it right? Will the message reach the elder Pontowski and convince him just how desperate we are? God, I hate this nether world of lies, deceit, and indirection I live in. Why can't we just say to the United States, "Look here, we need your help if we're going to survive"? No, we have to feed them information, let them discover for themselves what reality is. And for this, I play with people's lives.

Do I have Pontowski right? Do I understand the President of the United States? Few people do, he is so clever and complex. Was it pure luck that his grandson was here when the war broke out? And why did the President leave him here? He must know we are feeding information to him, letting him "discover" the reality of our position. Was using the Tamir girl wise? Was it too obvious? The way we held the young Pontowski here and let him see the war through her eyes? Is reality nothing but questions?

The old man pushed his reading glasses back into place and picked up the photo again—a reality frozen in black and white. He looked at the last picture of the only person he felt close to, the nearest thing he had to a family. He closed his eyes, the image now frozen in his mind—Gad Habish hanging by his neck from a rope in a public square in Cairo—swinging in the harsh wind of his memory.

20

The reputation of Brigadier General Leo Cox had preceded him into the White House's Situation Room, but not a single member of the National Security Council had been expecting the fierce intellect and mastery of facts that made his briefing on the current situation in the Middle East so convincing. Zack Pontowski was more than satisfied with Cox and made a mental note to move him permanently from the DIA to the NSC's staff and get him promoted. The President pulled into himself as Bobby Burke, the director of central intelligence, tried to poke holes in Cox's conclusions. The general was most tactful and respectful of Burke's position, but the result was the same—Cox was eating him alive. A polite form of cannibalism, Pontowski thought. Perhaps we need more of it around here. He made another mental note to thank Melissa for her recommendation.

"General," Burke sputtered, "I simply refuse to accept your conclusion that the Egyptians are going to enter the war."

"Mr. Burke," Cox said, his cadaverous face making his words more ominous, "I want to agree with you, but that contradicts what we're seeing and hearing." Cox then proceeded to swamp him with facts, all tied together and supporting his analysis. "The only response then available to the Israelis," he concluded, "will be to escalate—"

"Damn it, General"—Burke was losing his temper—"and just how will they do that if they're getting their butts kicked like you're saying?"

Cox bowed his head before he raised his eyes and drilled the DCI. "They'll go nuclear, sir." Burke sank back into his chair and a heavy silence came down. They all believed him.

"We must stop that from happening," Pontowski said, breaking the silence. "How do we do it?" For the next twenty minutes, the options open to the United States were examined.

Finally, Pontowski leaned forward and started giving orders. There was steel in his voice that most members of the NSC had never heard before. "I want immediate action on three fronts, diplomatic, logistical, and military. State"—he gave the secretary of state a hard look—"press for a cease-fire on all fronts. The Hot Line to the Kremlin is still down and their ambassador recalled. But there has got to be a channel open somewhere. Find it. I don't care who you have to talk to. Logistics, get whatever the Israelis need to them—now. Put the Rapid Deployment Force on alert. If I have to, I will unilaterally reinforce the peacekeeping troops in the

Sinai and force the Egyptians to attack through us. Call the Egyptian ambassador in.''

Pontowski stood. "When I say immediate action, I mean within the hour, not this afternoon.'' He moved toward the door. "General Cox, would you please join me?'' Outside, the two men walked slowly down the hall. "Leo, how good are your sources?''

Cox hesitated before answering. He knew the President was moving fast, based on the facts he had presented. "Sir, there is always 'noise' in intelligence: the information that doesn't fit, the deliberate misleads the opposition plugs into the system. Most of the time, the very mass of information we deal with is the 'noise' that masks the true picture. But the reports we're getting from our military attachés and observers inside both Israel and Egypt all support what satellite and aerial reconnaissance is telling us—the Israelis are losing and will go nuclear if Egypt comes into the war.''

"How reliable are the attachés and observers?''

"Very,'' Cox answered. "One of the reports was from Captain Pontowski.''

"Where's Matt now?''

"Out of Israel, sir. Back with his unit in England.''

"I'd like to see his report.'' The relief in Pontowski's voice was obvious.

"I'll get it to you within the hour.''

Pontowski stopped before entering his office. "What happened to Bill Carroll?''

Cox allowed a smile to crack his grim face. "We restored his security clearance, gave him a letter of reprimand for an unauthorized contact with a foreign government, and sent him to an operational unit. He asked to go back to his old wing, the Forty-fifth.''

"He's a good man,'' Pontowski said. "I'm glad you protected him.''

The general could only stare at his commander in chief. My God! he thought, he figured it out. He knows that I used Carroll to short-circuit the CIA and get the intelligence I thought was critical to him.

"Mr. President''—it was Fraser—"the Egyptian ambassador will be here in two hours.''

"Thanks, Tom. That's fine.'' Pontowski held open the door to his office and motioned Cox inside for privacy. "Leo, there's something I need you to do right now. Do you know Egypt's air attaché?''

The two pilots stood at attention in front of General Mana's desk. They were surprised that the general was wearing a flight suit, even though it had obviously been tailored for him. The general's aide minced in and handed him a folder. The general smiled at the twenty-year-old lieutenant colonel, thanking him. Johar and Samir kept their eyes rooted on a spot above the general's head.

Mana thumbed through the folder, throwing pictures of two crashed F-16s onto his desk, in front of the two pilots. ''By not following orders,'' Mana said, ''you two denied me the kills that were rightfully mine. Please explain yourselves.''

''Sir''—it was Johar—''I'm not sure we can. Everything happened so fast and—and we were just there.'' Samir nodded vigorously in agreement. ''The only way I can explain what happened is that''—he was thinking furiously, knowing Mana could be very dangerous and they were, after all, nobodies—''that your aggressive airmanship drove the F-Sixteens right into our faces. It was night, you knew that the Israelis would turn away from us, back towards you . . . But it was all very confused and we managed to get off two missiles. The shots were . . . pure luck.'' He had almost said ''The shots were golden BBs'' but that would have been too much of an Americanism and a mistake.

Mana rolled a letter opener between his thumb and forefinger, examining its blade. ''It is encouraging that you understand what happened. But it does not change the result.'' He drove the tip of the letter opener deep into his desk. ''Those were my kills.''

''Yes, sir,'' Johar said. ''We know that.'' Samir nodded vigorously.

''Then you will understand why I am receiving the credit for them. Please, this was not my idea. The other pilots who were there are insisting on it.''

''That is how it should be,'' Johar agreed with Samir, who was still nodding.

Mana smiled. ''There will be reporters and TV cameras on base today to report my victory to our people. I think it would be wise if you two were not here.''

"Thank you, sir," Johar said, "for your understanding."

"Dismissed."

The two pilots beat a hasty retreat. Outside the headquarters building, they glanced at each other, an unspoken comment that they had been lucky. But that was life in Iraq's air force.

The Egyptian ambassador was the model of diplomatic propriety. His distinguished reputation, polished appearance, carefully tailored dark suit, and expensive hand-tooled leather briefcase all marked him as a member in good standing of the Washington diplomatic corps. Pontowski stood and extended his hand when Matsom Hamoud al-Dasud was ushered into his office. "Mr. President," Dasud murmured. He was acutely aware that they were alone with no interpreters. Normal diplomatic protocol required translators even though his mastery of English was well known. It was his first danger signal.

"Mr. Ambassador," Pontowski said, his face dead serious. "Thank you for coming on such short notice, but a critical problem has arisen."

"We are aware of the situation and my government has told me to be at your service." For the next few minutes, the two men exchanged formal courtesies as they sparred.

When they had reached the appropriate moment, Pontowski came to the purpose of the hastily called meeting. "Mr. Ambassador, it is my intention to reinforce the UN peacekeeping forces in the Sinai while my ambassador to the United Nations pursues a cease-fire in the Israeli-Syrian war."

Dasud's right eyebrow arched. "That is not necessary. The intentions of my country remain as before, committed to peace and regional prosperity."

Pontowski deliberately glanced at his watch—another signal. "We are running out of time to stop this war before it escalates."

"The war is not of our making, Mr. President."

"Then why do you refuse to stand down your forces from your military exercise in the Sinai? Why are you moving up reinforcements as the Israelis withdraw their forces to meet the new threat from Iraq?"

"Mr. President, you must remember the troubled history of our two countries. While we remain committed to the peace treaty with Israel, there are many political factions in my country that demand we maintain a strong defensive posture at this time.''

Pontowski decided it was time to pull off the velvet gloves of diplomacy. ''Mr. Ambassador, my analysts tell me that Egypt is preparing to attack Israel.''

''Your analysts are mistaken.''

''I hope so, because if they are correct, I will consider our relationship with Egypt in a totally different light. I will embargo your country and close the Suez Canal. All foreign trade with your country will cease until the status quo is reestablished.''

Dasud's face paled. In diplomatic terms, Pontowski had told the ambassador that if Egypt entered the war, he would seal Egypt off from the outside world, forcing her to survive on her own resources until the fighting had stopped and Israel's borders were secure. In practical terms, he was saying that Egypt would not be able to import the food it needed. The ambassador immediately understood all that. It was his job to inform his government that the United States was playing hardball and start immediate damage control.

''Surely, Mr. President, you realize such action would mean an oil embargo and worldwide condemnation in the United Nations.'' No response from Pontowski. He tried another tack. ''If there were other options open to my government that the United States could support . . .'' Pontowski nodded and Dasud relaxed. There was room for accommodation.

''The role of Egypt as a peacemaker is well known,'' Pontowski said. Now they were back to polite diplomatic exchanges.

''It would be helpful if I had something positive to cable my superiors,'' Dasud ventured.

''Rather than see Egyptian military maneuvers in the Suez,'' Pontowski replied, ''I would like to see discussions on increased agricultural aid and more trade credits.'' No response from Dasud. Pontowski upped the ante. ''And if Egypt was to present a cease-fire initiative to the United Nations, my ambassador would back Egypt's claim to the Gaza Strip.''

The ambassador understood perfectly: Egypt gets its forces out of the Sinai, starts taking an active role in stopping the fighting, and in return gets the Gaza Strip and more foreign aid. It was doable. Besides, his air attaché had received an intelligence report from a source in the DIA on Israeli nuclear capabilities and intentions minutes before he had left his embassy. The source was, he knew, unimpeachable.

"Mr. President, please let me relay your comments to my government. I know they will be carefully studied."

Pontowski stood. The diplomatic formalities were over. "Matsom, again thanks for coming so quickly." He shook the man's hand warmly; they were old friends. "I need action quick. Otherwise all hell is going to break loose."

"I know, Zack. I'll do what I can."

As usual, Colonel "Mad" Mike Martin, the deputy for operations of the 45th Tactical Fighter Wing, felt an overpowering urge to get involved, get to the bottom of the problem, and crunch a few heads. But this particular dilemma did not call for such a violent reaction. Mike Martin was a contained and highly directed individual who controlled his natural combative urges and found acceptable channels for his energies. Martin shambled around his office at RAF Stonewood, his six-foot bulk shaking the floor, his round face brooding. His massive head of black hair and hairy arms made the man sitting in his office think of a gorilla or a Mafia hit man. But he knew what was beneath the surface—a consummate fighter pilot and brilliant combat leader, not happy in peacetime operations.

"Carroll," Martin growled, "you got your ass kicked off the National Security Council and you ask to be reassigned here. Why?"

"The Forty-fifth is my old unit, sir," Bill Carroll answered. "I thought I could do some good as your chief of intelligence."

The answer satisfied Martin. "Have you read Pontowski and Furry's report on how the Israelis are getting their heads kicked up their collective asshole?" Martin never spent much time on any one subject.

"Yes, sir. Other intelligence supports what they saw."

Martin grunted something unintelligible and jabbed at the buttons on his intercom with a stubby finger. "Get Furry and Pontowski in here," he barked. Seven minutes later, the two men were walking through the door of his office.

Furry ignored his DO and shook Carroll's hand. "Good to see you, Bill. Been a long time."

"Not since Operation Warlord." Carroll smiled.

Martin did not interrupt the reunion between the two old friends. He knew he had two of the veterans of the 45th under his command. Two men who went back to the legendary Muddy Waters. "You two done kissing?" he said, his voice warm and friendly. "Good. Let's get down to business. I want to kill some ragheads."

"Sir," Matt said, "that's not going to be easy."

"I know that, Fumble Nuts," Martin snapped, reverting to type. "That's why you three are in here. I want to know if there's any way, time, or place we might get involved in that pissing contest you got to play in?"

Matt's face turned hard. For the first time, he fully understood what it meant to have your "fangs out." "Kirkuk."

"Thanks for the clue, Meathead," Martin growled.

"Charming fellow," Carroll mumbled under his breath for Furry to hear.

"He calls everybody that," the wizzo said.

"Captain Pontowski, are you talking about the nerve gas plant and storage bunkers outside of Kirkuk?" Carroll asked. Matt nodded.

"Mind talking to me?" Martin barked.

"Sir," Carroll said, "the Iraqis have built a large new nerve gas plant and arsenal twenty miles west of Kirkuk replacing the one we destroyed during the Kuwait war. The Israelis tried to hit it but couldn't fight their way through Iraq's air defenses. Your 'ragheads' learned some valuable lessons in '91. It's a mission the F-Fifteen E was made for."

"That's a good starting place," Martin said. "Work up a target briefing for me in, say"—he looked at his watch—"an hour. I want to be impressed. Carroll, get with Plans and put together an ops plan for striking that target. Call it Operations Plan Trinity. I want it at headquarters in two days. Go. Kill." There was no doubt they were dismissed.

Out in the hall, Matt pulled Furry aside. "Is that the same Carroll you told me about?"

"Yeah," Furry answered. "Just the best damn intelligence puke in the Air Force."

21

The prime minister of Israel took his place in the command room of the bunker. He was freshly showered and wearing clean clothes, refreshed after a six-hour sleep. His eyes scanned the situation boards, and for the first time, a feeling of success warmed Yair Ben David's resolve. Don't get overly confident yet, he warned himself, we've got a long way to go.

A cup of hot tea appeared at his elbow and he took a sip. He glanced around the room. The men and women manning the bunker were weary to the point of exhaustion, the emotional strain telling, and the stale stench of unwashed bodies filled his nostrils. Still, he could sense a change—optimism had replaced the sense of foreboding doom that had hung there like a dark fog only twenty-four hours before.

A sergeant was working behind the Plexiglas map of the Sinai, posting new information. The room fell silent as every eye watched the sergeant mark up the latest disposition of Egypt's armed forces. Scattered applause greeted the sergeant when she was finished. The Egyptians had moved back into garrison and were standing down from their "exercise." Israel's southern flank was no longer threatened and they could use the full resources of Southern Command to defeat the Syrians and Iraqis in the north. With resupply from the United States going full bore, they could do it.

Ben David turned his attention to the other three fronts. The battle on the northern border with Lebanon had stalemated and was seesawing back and forth across the border. On the Golan Heights, the Israelis had been pushed back to the very edge but were stubbornly holding on. A commando assault force had retaken Mount Hermon but at a terrible price. Over 70 percent of the commandos had been killed or wounded. Only the last-minute insertion of reinforcements with Black Hawk helicopters fresh from the United States' arsenals in Germany had given the Israelis a much needed victory. But they had lost over half the helicopters.

The situation on the West Bank was the most ominous. The Syrians, reinforced with three Iraqi armored divisions, had pushed across the Jordan River and were within sixteen kilometers of Jerusalem. The Arabs were shelling the city around the clock but thanks to the fresh troops that had been rushed out of the Sinai and massive supplies now arriving from the United States, the line was holding.

More good news appeared on the boards; the first of ninety-five F-16s being ferried in from the United States had landed and were being turned for combat. But the major general in charge of Hel Avir, the Israeli Air Force, was worried. The air force was suffering from a severe shortage of pilots and every available body was in the cockpit. He had recently recalled to active duty retired pilots who were in their fifties and was rushing them through refresher training. They would soon be thrown into the battle.

Out of habit, Ben David scrutinized the "Status of Casualties" board last. His lips compressed as his eyes ran across the columns. He was caught up in the type of war he most dreaded, a long and protracted conflict, and the numbers told the story. His countrymen were in a war of attrition. How long could they hang on? he asked himself. But he knew the answer—as long as they had to.

An aide appeared at his side. "More good news, Yair," he said. "The Egyptian ambassador to the United Nations has placed a resolution in front of the General Assembly calling for an immediate cease-fire."

Ben David stood up and his presence filled the room. He knew they could do it! They could, without doubt, survive! The Egyptian call for a cease-fire was the first crack in the solid Arab front. Long experience had taught him how fast the Arabs could realign and seek an accommodation with Israel.

An old worry came back to haunt him, driving him back into his seat. Before a cease-fire was forced on him, he had to secure his borders and hold the best defensive position possible. He had to think ahead—to the next war. And punish them! he raged to himself. Those casualties, the cold numbers on the "Status of Casualties" board, had a personal meaning for him and every Israeli. In a country as small as his, every family had paid a price—a father, son, daughter, killed or wounded, maybe a POW. Please, not our daughters as POWs, he pleaded. An old wrath swept over him. So the Arabs would degrade his children in captivity, drive his people into the sea. I hope they are looking at the desert sands behind them, he told himself, for that is where I will send them.

"Get Avi Tamir," he ordered. Then he picked up the phone and made a brief call to Mossad. When the call was completed, he started issuing orders. Every person in the room responded to him, buoyed by his presence, feeling his resolve. They all could sense it—in spite of Iraq's entry, the war had been stabilized and now they were going on the attack.

Avi Tamir's face was worn and haggard, matching the way he felt, when he answered the summons to the command bunker. At least, he thought, I have some news that Ben David will like. He was surprised when the guard cleared him in without an escort. Inside, he sensed the change in the atmosphere. Loud discussions rang out and people were scurrying through the corridors. And then he caught it—the scent of victory. "Finally," he mumbled to himself. The door to Ben David's small office was open and he walked in.

The prime minister greeted him warmly and waved him to a seat next to the other man in the office. Tamir sank into the soft cushions and, for the first time in weeks, relaxed. All the signs were there. The tide of the war had turned and they would not have to use nuclear weapons. Ben David rose and closed the door himself while Tamir greeted the stranger. The wizened gnome uttered some perfunctory words but did not introduce himself. He rubbed at his bulbous nose with a handkerchief and focused his attention on Ben David, ignoring Tamir.

"Have you made progress?" Ben David asked.

Tamir nodded. "I've solved the boosting problem." For a moment, he considered telling them how he had devised a method of injecting lithium-6 deuteride directly into the core of an atomic bomb, making a thermonuclear reaction. He had even refined the process, and the yield of the weapon could be changed by throwing three switches in the warhead. "Five days and it will be ready."

"How big is it?" Ben David asked.

Tamir wasn't certain what the question was. "It will fit into the warhead of a Jericho Two missile," he answered.

"I meant how big . . ." the prime minister stammered, not knowing how to ask a question the scientist would understand.

"Yair wants to know the kiloton or megaton yield," the gnome said, still not looking at Tamir.

"Oh. It's selectable," Tamir answered. "Two point two, thirty, fifty, or one hundred twenty kilotons."

"I was hoping for a bigger bomb," Ben David said.

"There are problems . . ." Tamir protested. Then his anger flared. "My God! You have no idea how big a hundred twenty kilotons is."

"Please, Avi, I did not mean that as a criticism. You have done good work." Ben David put on his serious-but-relieved face. "We are stabilizing and I don't think we'll need to use our nuclear weapons. You know, I had always planned to use them only as a last resort to save our people from destruction."

A feeling of relief engulfed Avi Tamir and, for a moment, tears swelled in his eyes. His work would not give the world another Holocaust.

Ben David caught Tamir's obvious relief. "Still," he cautioned, "there are dangers ahead of us and we cannot afford to lose. When you say 'ready in five days' does that mean it can be mated to a missile?" Tamir told him yes. "Good." The prime minister stood up. "Please don't worry, Avi. The war is going our way and we won't need to use it. But I must take every precaution . . . our people have suffered too much ... . I must end this war quickly."

Tamir understood he was dismissed and left.

Ben David immediately punched at his intercom and ordered up a meeting of the Defense Council in ten minutes.

"Well?" the Ganef asked, blowing his nose again. "Why did you want me here for this?"

"Didn't you believe me when I said there were many dangers ahead of us?"

"That's obvious," the old man replied.

"I'm going to make sure the Arabs cannot start another

war like this one. It will be interesting to see how they react when we create more defensible borders and establish a security zone in depth.''

"That could prove difficult," the Ganef said. "Our success might force them to use chemical weapons.''

"I'm aware of that possibility and you're going to prevent it. I'm going to load Tamir's bomb on a Jericho missile and program it for one of two targets—Damascus or Baghdad. I will launch it against the first one foolish enough to use chemical weapons.''

"And you want me to—''

"Make sure the Arabs know we have the bomb and how we will use it if they use chemical weapons.''

It all made sense to the Ganef. "What size yield?" he asked.

"The biggest.''

"The war has taken an unfortunate turn,'' Sheik Mohammed al-Khatub said, watching for the old woman's reaction over his coffee cup. Khatub was one of the few people not impressed with B. J. Allison's mansion, her jewels, or power. He had more. Still, he felt comfortable in her palatial home in western Virginia and had enjoyed the private dinner. But he hated the discussion that came afterward.

For her part, B.J. was enjoying the evening and the chance to spar with the sheik, a man she liked and respected. Besides, she told herself, he is most handsome and only in his mid-thirties. He does remind me of a young Omar Sharif, she thought. A fleeting image of Tara and Khatub together flashed through her mind and she made a mental note to pursue the idea. How convenient that liaison might be, she decided, considering Khatub was OPEC's minister of finance. "Ah, the war. So, I've been told,'' she said, returning to the subject at hand.

"We cannot ignore what your government is allowing to happen,'' Khatub said, "and must consider our interests, perhaps a change in policies.''

"Surely, you are not thinking of another oil embargo?''

"It is foremost in our thinking at this time,'' the sheik replied.

"Is there anything I can do to, ah, persuade you to take other actions?''

The sheik smiled, skillfully masking his feelings for the woman. In his world, women were relegated to their proper position and he would never discuss such important matters with them. It was beneath his dignity to deal with Allison. "We were hopeful that the scandal about illegal campaign funds would preoccupy your President, perhaps limiting or moderating his actions in support of the Jews." He sighed. "But that all appears to be dying on the vine."

"If the press were to uncover new evidence," Allison said, "as we say, 'find the smoking gun,' would that convince you that other voices are speaking out for a more equitable solution to the war?"

Khatub leaned forward and asked for another cup of coffee, smiling. They understood each other perfectly.

Tara Tyndle had been waiting for the call and was fully dressed and ready when the phone rang at one in the morning. Three minutes later, she was on her way to the helipad to catch a hop to her aunt's home.

"You do spoil your aunt," Allison said, greeting Tara when she entered the elegant drawing room she used as an office. The handsome young secretary escorting Tara closed the door behind her, leaving them in privacy. Allison came right to the point. "I must limit Pontowski's support of Israel or we will be facing an oil embargo. Do you know what that means?" She didn't expect Tara to answer. "Government control of my industry, my company. Tara, I won't have it! I will destroy that man." She was pacing the room. "What else have you learned about his campaign financing?"

Tara related how Fraser had funneled money into a network of offshore corporations and secret bank accounts in the Bahamas and had linked them together with the electronic transfer of funds through Hong Kong. She still didn't know the details of how he moved the money back into the United States and the campaign. "He's very clever, Auntie, and does it all in his head, and he used a middle man to direct the money into political action committees and get-out-the-vote groups at the right moment. But Fraser orchestrated it all. Auntie, you weren't the only contributor. I think Fraser tapped some of the Mafia families and no income taxes were ever paid on much of the money."

B. J. Allison smiled. "There's the smoking gun. Imagine,

the President's campaign financed by the Mafia and being investigated by the IRS." Her mind wheeled with the implications. "We'll need proof. I'm positive that the middle man is the only link to Pontowski and everything hinges around him. Can you find him?"

"Oh, I think so," Tara promised.

"When are you seeing Fraser next?"

"Tonight. We're having dinner at his Watergate apartment."

"How appropriate," Allison said. "Can you have something for those nice reporters by tomorrow?" Tara reassured her that she would. "Have you met that young man we talked about the other day? The congressman who . . ." Tara told her that they had met and the congressman was nibbling at the bait.

"Drop him," Allison ordered. "After you finish with Fraser, there's a more interesting person I'd like you to meet. But it will have to be carefully arranged."

Mad Mike Martin was pacing back and forth in RAF Stonewood's Intelligence vault like a caged tiger, his limp more pronounced than normal. When he was worried, deep in thought, or the weather suddenly turned damp, his old war wound flared up and his hip would stiffen. All three conditions were affecting him as he listened to Matt cover the Iraqi defenses that they would have to penetrate in order to hit the nerve gas plant near Kirkuk.

Furry was dozing on a couch, worn out by the long hours he had spent with Carroll and Matt trying to put something together that would satisfy the colonel. But true to form, Martin was knocking their planning into the dirt—again. Carroll stared at his feet as he listened to Matt cover the fate of Dave Harkabi when he tried to lead a strike against the plant. When Matt was finished, Martin grunted an obscenity and turned to Carroll. "Okay, Roger Rabbit Redux, what've you got?"

Carroll caught the allusion, no, he corrected himself, a double allusion to fantasy and fiction. Why did Martin go to such lengths to cover a brilliant mind? "Colonel, the DIA sent us a videotape on that engagement Matt just briefed you on. Never seen anything like it." He shoved a cassette into a VCR. The videotape was a copy of the radar tapes from the orbiting AWACS that had monitored the engagement. The radar returns on the tape had been color-coded to separate the F-16s from the SU-27s and captions summarized the battle. The audio on the tape recaptured the radio transmissions between Juhar and Samir and had been synchronized with the action.

"That's really helpful," Martin grumbled, "I don't understand a fucking word of Arabic."

Carroll ran the tape again and translated as the engagement unfolded. Now the men were clustered around the TV set. "Run it again," Matt said. "Did you hear the one jock call the other one Joe?"

This time, both Matt and Furry made notes as the engagement replayed and Carroll interpreted. "Jesus H. Christ," Furry blurted when the short tape played out, "those two guys did that at night! They *are* good. And who the hell is Joe?"

"Brigadier General Hussan Mana," Carroll said, spreading out a Baghdad newspaper and a glossy magazine with Mana's picture on the cover. "According to these articles he got both kills. The tapes here prove that one pilot did shoot both F-Sixteens down. I think he's Joe." He translated the articles for the men.

When Carroll had finished, Martin sat down and studied his hands for a moment. "Gentlemen," he said, his voice changed, respectful, "you have just seen a professional aerial assassin at work who's as good as they get." He looked at them. "I think it's time to get serious here. Start taking notes." For the next twenty minutes, Martin laid out a plan that launched them out of Diyarbakir, a Turkish air base 240 nautical miles northwest of Kirkuk. He also integrated KC-135 tankers, an AWACS, and an RC-135 reconnaissance bird into the mission. The colonel gave the plan a polish and refinement that was the end result of twenty years spent in the Tactical Air Force. The lessons he had learned through Red Flag exercises and endless hours in the cockpit were now bearing fruit. No staff officer, a product of professional military staff schools and endless headquarters assignments, could approach his level of expertise when it came to doing what the Air Force was all about.

"Okay," he finally said, "this is a beginning. We still have the problem of Joe to solve."

"Colonel"—it was Matt—"Dave Harkabi told us how the Israelis deliberately go after a good pilot like Mana. It takes some coordination, but it can be done."

Martin jabbed a finger at the glossy magazine. "Sounds fair to me. Work on it. Mana is dead meat, Pontowski, and I'm gonna do the rendering.

"Next subject—training," Martin continued. "Program the flight simulator for an attack on Kirkuk. Every crew going on the mission runs the attack at least four times in the sim until they can do it in their sleep. I don't want this to be a first-look mission."

"Colonel," Furry said, "easier said than done. First, the low-level attack program in the sim is dedicated to nuclear strike lines. We'd need a waiver to the regulations from pretty high up to down load the computer."

"Is that regulation man-made or God-made?" Martin growled.

"Also," Furry continued, "reprogramming the sim's computer isn't that easy. It takes three, maybe four weeks to create a realistic data base."

Martin paced the floor, fully alive for the first time in months, eager to engage. His "fangs" were out. "You swingin' dicks know who the Gruesome Twosome are?" The three men exchanged puzzled looks. "Those are the two computer whiz kids who run McDonnell's simulator at St. Louis," Martin explained. "They can reprogram that damn thing to represent an entire low-level route, a target, and every air defense threat known to man whenever they get the urge."

"Colonel Martin," Furry protested, "our sim's nowhere as cosmic as McDonnell's. They got computer capability our pukes can't even spell."

"Yeah? Well, I want the Gruesome Twosome here to work on our simulator." A wicked look crossed his face. "The crews I choose for the mission have got to stomp the hell out of those two meatheads in the sim before they get to fly the real thing." Martin believed in competition. "They'll be here tomorrow," the colonel promised.

A nasty grin split Dennis Leander's elfin face as he rolled a hand controller on the console of McDonnell Aircraft Company's flight simulator. Inside the planetariumlike room, two young Air Force lieutenants were getting their first taste of air-to-air combat against a MiG-29 Fulcrum. Thanks to Leander, they were losing. His partner, Larry Stigler, was bored. They had defeated too many budding aces and needed a new challenge. Stigler stretched out his lanky frame that had at one time earned him the nickname Stork. Now he was known as the senior partner of the Gruesome Twosome.

"Give the kids a break," Stigler told Leander.

"Why? Better they learn some hard facts here than in real life." He was rolling the Fulcrum in for a "kill" on the crew inside. He was about to send an AA-11 missile up the crew's tailpipe when the door from the hall opened and the vice president in charge of F-15 production walked in. The two immediately became all business and froze the simulator. "Please stand by," Leander told the crew over the intercom. "We will resume in a few moments." Both he and Stigler assumed they were in trouble for something they had done. Their hijinks in the simulator were too many to catalog and both young men were certain that some Air Force colonel had lodged a complaint—again.

The vice president studied the frozen displays on the console. "Good move," he allowed. "By freezing the action, they may get a clue and sort it out." He kept a straight face. "What in the devil have you two been up to now?"

Stigler shot a worried look at Leander. "Sir, if it's about sandbagging that colonel who was in here yesterday with the good-looking captain, well, we figured he was only in here trying to impress her so we—"

"Right"—the vice president grinned, letting them off the hook—"you gave him a fuel transfer problem every time he approached to land so he would flame out and crash." The two young men hung their heads, trying to act ashamed. "She wasn't impressed," the vice president said. "Do either of you remember a Colonel Mike Martin who came through here about a year ago?"

The Gruesome Twosome nodded yes. Their experience with Martin had been a hard one to forget. Not only had the colonel soundly trounced them, but he had taken them out for a night on the town, hooked them up with three Tootie La Rues, drunk them all under the table, and then come back the next day for a repeat performance in the simulator.

"We got a phone call about ten minutes ago. Martin wants you two at RAF Stonewood in England ASAP for some special project. Want to go? When Martin says ASAP, he means yesterday.''

Leander spun in his chair and keyed his mike. "Gentlemen, you're free and flying," he told the crew inside the simulator. He rolled his hand controller and flew the MiG-29 Fulcrum out in front of the pilot and let him take a missile shot. When the image of the Fulcrum on the wall exploded in front of the crew, Leander and Stigler worked furiously, shutting the simulator down.

The two puzzled lieutenants crawled out of the mock-up of the cockpit and walked out of the dome. No one was at the console and the door to the hall was open.

The armored personnel carrier that had been configured as an ambulance clanked up to the makeshift aid station. The rear ramp flopped down and Shoshana and Hanni carried out a litter with a badly wounded soldier. "She was out there for three days," Shoshana told the waiting doctor. "We were lucky to have found her." Shoshana did not tell the doctor that it had taken her and Hanni almost six hours to carry the girl down a hill through heavy sniper fire to get her to the APC.

A private on the side of the tent was working a field telephone. "They're asking for transportation to bring in wounded POWs," the old man said. Shoshana got the details from the private, a reservist she estimated was pushing sixty years of age. We're reaching deep, she thought. "It's pretty quiet up front," the private told her, "so we're moving POWs. Probably want to interrogate them." Experience had taught the Israelis that a gentle questioning by a doctor while he was treating a wounded POW produced a wealth of intelligence. But it had to be a male doctor who spoke Arabic, otherwise the POW would clam up and not say a word.

The war that Shoshana was now caught up in amounted to endless short runs in an M113 APC between an aid station and the fighting. She would normally drive the twelve-ton tracked vehicle and take it right into the action to bring out wounded tankers and infantrymen. She and Hanni had turned into a well-rehearsed team and could quickly pick up a wounded man or woman. Shoshana would use the APC as a shield, and when she shouted "GO!" Hanni would drop the ramp while she darted back through the crew compartment to help. The two women could have a casualty back into the APC, buttoned up, and moving in less than a minute. They were a good team.

The run to the pickup point was quiet and they fell into a line of trucks and vehicles moving forward for resupply. Hanni had the top hatch open and watched the traffic for clues. They had become experts at judging the ebb and flow of the fighting by what was moving on the roads. Shoshana had no trouble finding the POW holding cage, which in itself was an indication that things were under control. While they waited for the MPs to bring the POWs out, they sat and ate in the shade of the APC. "I think we're building up for a major push," Hanni said.

"How soon?" Shoshana asked.

"At least forty-eight hours. They're still moving battle-damaged tanks to the rear and there's not much movement of fresh troops—yet."

"I could use some sleep and a shower," Shoshana said.

"And a chance to wash our clothes," Hanni added. They both smelled very ripe.

Shoshana pushed the sleeves of Matt's flight suit up above her elbows. "We got to get you one of these," she said. "It's much more comfortable than fatigues and dries a lot faster when you wash it."

"I don't think I'd look quite as good as you do in one," Hanni allowed.

An MP came up leading four Syrian POWs who were carrying two litter patients. "You get the bunch," he said. After the litters were strapped into their backs, he made the four POWs sit on the floor and chained them together. "Got a weapon?" he asked. Hanni showed him the Galil assault carbine they carried and cocked it, setting the safety. They had hauled POWs before and the guard couldn't be spared to escort them.

The trip back was uneventful and they deposited the POWs at a large barbed-wire compound. Then they drove the APC to a service point for fuel and maintenance. A technician inspected the APC and told them to clean it out while he checked the V-6 diesel engine. "Look at all that crap," he said. Hanni explained that the Syrian POWs had left the trash behind: mostly empty food containers and wrappers. The technician kicked a Syrian newspaper aside with his foot. "Why do they let them keep all this?"

"Well, those are personal belongings," Shoshana explained, "and they were just captured." She picked up the Syrian newspaper and glanced at it. The picture on the front page drove her to her knees. She knelt there, unable to move.

"Shoshana," Hanni said rushing over to her, "what's the matter?"

Shoshana handed her the paper. "I knew that man," she said. It was the same picture of Gad Habish that the Ganef had seen.

The grisly sight of the man hanging by his neck stunned Hanni as she translated. "It's a story about Egyptians hanging an Israeli spy in Cairo. They hung him in public."

"His name is Gad Habish," Shoshana said. "He worked for Mossad."

"A family member?" the technician asked. It was a common question.

She shook her head. "Somebody I used to know." Shoshana knelt there, trying to understand her feelings. She had driven Habish from her memory, refusing to think about the man who had been her control. If anything, she had always blamed Habish for the Mana affair and what she had become, a murderer and whore. But why didn't she feel relief at his death? There was no sense of justification, revenge, or even sympathy. Nothing. Had she become so hardened to death that she felt nothing?

Now the floodgate of memory opened and she could no longer control it. It washed over her, threatening to drown her. And kneeling in the crew compartment of that battle-scarred APC, surrounded by the quiet of a lull in a war that seemed to have no end, the tears came. Through her anguish, Habish's voice came to her out of the mist of memory. "You must put your personal feelings away. . . . Always remember where you hid them . . . that is the way you remain a human being. . . . There is no choice."

Slowly, the emotions wracking her quieted. "Do we ever have a choice?"

Hanni knelt beside her and wrapped her arms around her, comforting the woman. "No, child. We don't have a choice."

The technician looked away, not wanting to intrude. He kicked a small green round tube out of a corner. "Now what the hell is that?'' he asked, kicking it again, toward the two women.

Shoshana recognized it immediately and picked it up. ''I thought those were Syrian POWs,'' she said, her voice little more than a whisper.

''They were,'' Hanni answered.

''Then why did they have this?'' she asked, holding the combo pen, the antidote to Iraq's newest and most deadly nerve gas.

22

Thirty-five kilometers aren't very much, Shoshana thought, but they make all the difference. She was standing with Hanni in the shower room of a vocational school thirty-five kilometers south of the border, letting the warm water wash over her, filling her with pleasure. They had been pulled out of the front line fourteen hours before, loaded on a truck with twelve other women, and sent south for rest and recuperation. Shoshana could not believe what a hot meal, twelve hours of uninterrupted sleep, and now a shower could do for her morale. Or how the simple things could revive her and feel so good. She felt alive.

''Here, catch,'' Hanni said, throwing her a tube of shampoo. Shoshana quickly unbraided her heavy plait of hair and scrubbed vigorously, feeling it come clean.

''My hair's too long,'' she admitted. For the first time in weeks, she felt clean. She stepped out of the shower, wrapped her only towel around her hair, and found a spot at a large washbasin with three other women and scrubbed at her clothes. Matt's flight suit was easy to wash but she doubted that her underwear would ever come clean.

Hanni handed her a large towel that was still damp from its earlier user. Shoshana wrapped it around her and the two women went outside to a soccer field, spread their clothes out to dry and collapsed onto the grass. The warm sun lulled them to sleep.

A hand was shaking Shoshana. "We need to find some shade or we'll get sunburnt." It was Hanni. They gathered up their clothes and kit bags and moved under a lanai. All the chairs and sun lounges were occupied by other women so they sat on the cement deck. Shoshana found her hairbrush and ran it through her hair. "I need to do something with this," she said.

"Why don't you tie it back instead of braiding it," Hanni suggested, "at least for now."

Shoshana rummaged in her kit bag and pulled out a pair of scissors. "I know just the thing," she said. She grabbed Matt's flight suit and examined the long zipper that ran down the front. "The flap behind the zipper really chafes at my skin. I don't know why it's even there." She pointed to the red rash between her breasts and then went to work, snipping away at the flap. Finally, she had a long strip of cloth two inches wide and two and a half feet long. Hanni took the makeshift ribbon from her and pulled Shoshana's hair back, using the green strip to hold her hair in a loose plait.

When she was finished, the two women dressed. Shoshana felt the cool metal of the zipper against her skin and the chafing was gone. She laughed and played the model for Hanni. "Please note the color-coordinated head band and Nomex jumpsuit, the latest in fashion wear for your properly attired soldier." She stopped, sat down, and pulled on her boots, now serious. "How silly. I remember when clothes and how I looked was everything."

You are glowing, Hanni thought. It's more than just the rest and chance to shower. Something happened when you finally broke down and cried, perhaps a cleansing, I don't know. But you are beautiful. "Come on, let's get something to eat."

"Again?" Shoshana laughed. "We'll get fat as cows."

"I doubt it."

A loudspeaker squawked and rasped, announcing they would be picked up by a bus in ten minutes. A heavy silence came down over all the women.

Shoshana guided the APC under the camouflage netting, barely able to follow the man's directions in the dark. When he gave her the kill sign, she shut the engine off and stuck her head out the hatch, surprised how quiet it was. She glanced over at Hanni who was standing in the center hatch. "Where do you think we are?" Shoshana asked.

"Near the front, I'm sure," the older woman replied. "I know we crossed the border into Lebanon."

"It's awfully quiet."

A man materialized out of the dark and spoke in a low voice. "One of you come with me. And for God's sake, no lights or noise." Shoshana shrugged and followed him. The man picked his way through the darkness, collecting two company commanders and their platoon commanders on his way back to the battalion's command post. He led them down into a steep ravine and into the well-lit interior of a cave.

Shoshana blinked in the bright light, focusing on their guide. He was a small man who made her think of a weasel. It was Nazzi Halaby. "I got the rest of them, Moshe," he said. She followed his gaze to the man sitting on an upturned 105-millimeter shell crate. Every sense she possessed told her that there was something different about this man. He was as short as Halaby but stockily built. Judging from the uneven tan on his face, he had recently shaved off a full beard. It's his eyes, she decided, they reach out and capture everyone around him.

He stood and started talking in a low voice. "For you who don't know me, I'm Moshe Levy. They tell me I'm a lieutenant colonel now, but that doesn't matter."

The man standing next to Shoshana, like her a newcomer, stiffened. Then it hit her—this was Moshe Levy. The man had become a legend during the war and Northern Command had even given his battalion a special name—Levy Force. It was said that wherever the fighting was the hardest and most critical on the Lebanon front, Levy was there, holding on, counterattacking, refusing to give ground. NCOs had started asking if a new officer had "Levy's Luck" and their commanders often reported a successful engagement by saying they "had Levy's Luck."

Levy studied each person, drawing them to him. "What does matter is why we're here." He pointed to a map board propped up against the wall. "Brigade is expecting the Iraqi armored division facing us to launch an attack just before first light. We're dug in here"—he pointed to a high hill that blocked the southern end of a long narrow valley—"and they are expected to come right down the valley and bump up against us. Our job is to hold them while artillery and the Air Force chew 'em up. Depending on what condition we're in, we either lead the counterattack or let the rest of our brigade pass through." No one was shocked that a brigade was taking on a division.

A low wail came from the rear of the cave. "Shut up, Avner," Levy said, his voice normal. The wailing stopped. "My loader," Levy explained. "Obviously he doesn't think head-on counterattacks will help him live to be an old man. Personally, I agree with him. So we're not going to do it."

Levy used the map to lay out the way they would fight the battle. He planned to split his battalion, keeping one company with him at the end of the valley as the blocking force. The other two companies were to move up the western side of the valley under the cover of darkness, reinforce the teams holding the western slope, hide behind a ridge and wait for the order to counterattack. Instead of a head-on attack, they would sweep down onto the Iraqis' right flank, cut directly across them, and head for the hills on the eastern side of the valley. There they would regroup and reevaluate.

"When do we move out?" one of Levy's older company commanders asked.

"If the Iraqis follow their normal pattern," Levy explained, "they'll send three or four reconnaissance drones over us about two hours before they attack. We only let the first one get back and shoot down the others. That's when you move out. With some luck, the Iraqis won't know you've moved."

A second lieutenant fresh out of Armored Warfare School did not like what he was hearing. "Moshe, shouldn't we have a better plan than that? Follow-on objectives? You have only covered the opening phase. What comes next? I'd like to have a better idea of what my platoon should be trying to do other than cross the valley." His boyish face was serious and Levy knew that he was facing battle for the first time. They are so afraid they will run, Levy thought. One of the worst things that could be said of an Israeli officer was that he ran.

"Don't think in terms of what comes second, what comes third," Levy said, a deep sadness in his voice. "Think of three or four options you might use when you regroup on the eastern side of the valley.''

Shoshana could hear the beginning of a typical debate over orders. The average Israeli officer treated military like a point of discussion that often went on for an interminable length of time. "I know what you're thinking," Levy said, "a case of incompetent planning." The silence from the second lieutenant confirmed the young man agreed. "But look at the situation we are in. We are strained to our outer limits, men and tanks at half-strength, and we are counterattacking?''

"But we have to carry the battle to the enemy," the lieutenant parroted. He had learned his lessons well in Armored Warfare School.

"Because we have no room to retreat, right?" Levy replied. He had heard this argument before. It was always the same, the young ones, the fresh and eager, wanted to fight by the book. He only wanted to survive. "And all our wars should be short and decisive, right? And we can never permanently defeat our Arab enemy, right?" Levy was listing basic tenets that the IDF lived and died with. "Well, look at our situation. We have carried the battle to the enemy and are in an excellent defensive position in this sector. That's why we can take on a division with a brigade. If we hold them here while you cut across, what have we accomplished?''

The lieutenant studied the map. "Artillery and the Air Force will have cut the first echelon to pieces and we'll have done the same to the second echelon.''

"And," Levy demanded.

Light was starting to dawn for the lieutenant. "The valley has become a kill zone.''

"Earlier I said to consider your options when you regroup," Levy continued. "What happens if you regroup and then attack?''

"We engage the third echelon in the valley and could take heavy casualties as we will be at reduced strength from the first engagement and they will be expecting us.''

Reduced strength! Levy raged to himself. Does he know what that means? They don't teach them that in Armored Warfare School. Instead they make them into technicians, pump them up to be warriors, and teach them not to run.

Instead of berating the lieutenant, Levy only asked, "Is there a better option?"

The lieutenant was warming to it now. "Let the Iraqis' third echelon drive into the kill zone that we've created, soften them up with artillery and air strikes, and then either mount a frontal or flank attack."

"And how do we determine who is to attack?"

"By where the least resistance is."

"So what are you going to do when you reach the eastern side of the valley?" Levy asked. The discussion was almost ended and the lieutenant would know exactly what Levy expected of him and willingly do it.

"Dismount my infantry, secure our position, and since I'll probably have lost contact during the crossover, reestablish radio contact. Oh"—now he grinned—"depending on what's out in the valley, either lay doggo or pound the hell out of them."

"Keep your casualties to a minimum," Levy said, sending the men on their way. He turned to Shoshana and saw the worry on her face. "Is this your first time?" he asked.

"I've always been on the backside of the action, never in it from the very first."

Levy understood. "After the Iraqis' reconnaissance drones have flown over, we can expect an artillery barrage here. So we're going to pull back." He pointed to a rear area on the map where the rest of the brigade was dug in. "We'll leave a few observation and antitank teams in place until our counterbattery fire can discourage the Iraqis and convince them it's time to stop shooting and start scooting. That's when we move back into place. My tank is next to your APC. Just stay next to me until we need your Band-Aid."

"Band-Aid?" Shoshana asked.

Levy cracked a smile. "A Yankeeism for APC ambulances."

The radios at the rear of the cave came alive as reports of low-flying reconnaissance drones filtered in. "There's too many of them," Levy said. "Cruise missiles. Warn everybody to button up and get into their NBC gear," he ordered.

Shoshana ran from the command post and scrambled out of the ravine. She had left her gas mask and protective clothing in the APC. Why did Levy think they might be using nerve gas now? she thought. She prayed he was wrong.

* * *

"You are wicked," Tara breathed, her voice husky, exciting Fraser. They were lying on the bed in his Watergate apartment, their clothes heaped on the floor. She kissed his neck and ran her hand between his legs. A shudder coursed through the man's body.

"You made it so simple." She licked at his ear. Tara had coaxed him into revealing how he had orchestrated Pontowski's election by pumping money into the campaign at critical times. All that remained was to identify the middle man who would tie it all right back to Fraser and, therefore, Pontowski. "You're a genius," she said and rolled over on top of him.

Fraser was pleased with Tara's reaction and, for a moment, the thought of marriage crossed his mind but he quickly discarded it.

Tara decided to turn the heat up and learn the name she needed to complete the puzzle. She wanted to be finished with Fraser. She wiggled down his body and off the end of the bed. He watched her walk across the floor to the small refrigerator, mesmerized by the way she moved, the perfection of her body, her beauty. She bent over, pulled out a bottle of champagne, and disappeared into the bathroom. He could hear the sound of running water and the pop of a cork. She reappeared and stood in the doorway, steam curling from around her bare back. She beckoned to him with one finger and vanished back into the steam. He obediently followed, his breath coming in short, sharp pants.

She guided Fraser into the sunken tub, settled him on his back in the shallow but extremely hot water, and scrubbed him down with a rough washcloth until his skin glowed. Then she disappeared for a moment, only to come back holding a small black narrow case. She sat on the edge of the tub and arched her legs over him, opening the case. She gently removed an old-fashioned straightedge razor and a small sharpening stone. With short, practiced strokes she sharpened the razor, raising her eyes occasionally from her work to glance at Fraser. She tested the razor by drawing it along one of her legs, up to her crotch, satisfied that it was sharp.

Fraser gasped for air when Tara moved over him, straddling his big belly like she was riding a horse backward. She tossed her hair and looked back over her shoulder at him, wetting her lips.

"No way," he protested, giving a sharp little buck. But she ignored him and scooted her buttocks farther up onto his chest and tightened her legs, riding him. She bent forward, arching over his legs and drew the razor along the inside of his thigh, inching it toward his crotch. Then she grabbed the waiting bottle and splashed champagne over the freshly shaved leg. Fraser gave a little twitch as she licked at his thigh. "Don't," he moaned. She tightened her legs, wiggled her buttocks higher on his chest, and drew the razor over his scrotum.

Fraser was gasping for air and his heart pounding as she flicked the razor back and forth over his scrotum and wiggled higher. Then he felt the cold champagne and her warm tongue, quickly followed by the razor, only this time it was moving up his erection. "Please stop," he begged. A momentary pain shot across his chest as she poured champagne over him and her tongue went to work. Now he could feel the razor again, or was it her fingernails? her teeth? He gasped as the pain returned, coming down hard on his chest, clamping him in an unrelenting vise, crushing him. Just before he died, he knew what Tara wanted.

Tara felt her mount go limp and looked over her shoulder. Fraser's bulging eyes, gaping mouth, and frozen face shocked her. She had never seen a dead person before and bolted out of the bathroom, running for her clothes. Then she stopped, panting for breath, and forced herself to be calm. She sank to the floor, not moving for almost ten minutes. Back in control, she moved through the room, straightening, arranging, deliberately leaving traces to show that Fraser had shared his bed, but that his companion had dressed and left long before he had his heart attack.

She steeled herself and went into the bathroom. She drained the bath while she scrubbed the body and hosed it down. When she was satisfied that all traces of champagne and shaved hair were down the drain, she refilled the tub with hot water, hoping that the water would confuse a medical examiner about the time of death. Then Tara straightened up the bathroom, taking care to leave no traces that two people had shared the bath.

Carefully, she went over the entire apartment again, making sure it was right. She scribbled a note—"Call me in the morning"—and left it on his dresser in plain sight. Then she dressed, checked the apartment one last time, and left.

Shoshana and Hanni were in the APC when the first cruise missile hit. The low-order explosion drove both women to the periscopes as they tried to see what was going on. "Levy was right," Shoshana said, scanning the slope in front of them. "That wasn't a conventional warhead. It's got to be nerve gas." Panic was eating at her and she strained at the periscope in the driver's position. But the eyepiece on her gas mask kept getting in the way. Hanni was having better luck with hers.

"I count three, make that four, missiles hitting," Hanni reported. "I don't understand, they're hitting the area at random. There's five and six."

"Nerve gas is a wide-area ordnance," Shoshana explained, trying to beat down the panic that was threatening her sanity. Should she tell Hanni what she knew? She decided against it since there was nothing they could do if it was the new nerve gas the Iraqis had developed at Kirkuk. "They don't know our exact location so they saturate the area."

"What do we do now?" Hanni asked.

"Exactly what we had planned to do before, only we do it wearing our masks and NBC suits."

The radio crackled with reports of more inbound missiles. But these turned out to be the reconnaissance drones Levy had been expecting. Another report came in identifying the nerve gas vapor drifting over the area as VR55, an old Soviet-developed nerve agent. "We're going to be in these things for a while," Shoshana said.

"You sound relieved," Hanni said.

The harsh metallic rasp of the radio interrupted her with orders to pull back. "Moshe wants us to pull back until after the artillery barrage is over," Shoshana said and started the engine.

"What's he like?" Hanni asked.

"Not what you'd expect. He seems quiet and withdrawn, but when he talks to you . . . well . . . I can't explain it. You just want to follow."

"Is he married?"

"Oh Hanni, be serious."

"Not for you, child."

* * *

Yair Ben David's face was a rocklike mask when the first reports came in that the Iraqis were using nerve gas. Every face in the command room of the bunker was turned toward him, waiting for his reaction. "How much? Where? Type? Casualties?" he barked. "I want the answers." He slammed his fists onto the table in front of him. The prime minister forced his anger back into the cage where he contained it. This is not the time to overreact, he cautioned himself.

Then the answers filtered in. It was a limited attack in a tactical situation. Only six short-range cruise missiles had been used, the chemical weapons had been used in Lebanon, not inside Israel, and the IDF had been ready. More reports confirmed that it was the old type of nerve gas that the Israelis had an antidote for. "So," Ben David said to the general sitting beside him, "the Iraqis are testing the water, gauging our reaction. But why did they use cruise missiles? I'd always expected them to use artillery or aircraft when they employed nerve gas."

"Deception," the general answered. "They wanted us to mistake them for reconnaissance drones and be caught unmasked. It didn't work. Levy's Luck again."

"That man is charmed," Ben David agreed.

"Are you going to retaliate?" the general asked.

"What are our casualties?" Ben David replied.

"So far, none."

"Then we wait." His carefully masked anger raged in its cage.

The APC was moving again, this time forward, back into their original position. Shoshana was having a hard time seeing where she was going; the combination of gas mask and periscope didn't work well for her. Hanni seemed to be doing better so they switched places and Hanni drove while Shoshana rode in the crew compartment. Then they were back under the camouflage netting where they had started as the dark on the eastern horizon broke with the first light of dawn.

Shoshana could see movement in the valley below, moving toward them. The radio was silent.

* * *

Tara sat in her aunt's library next to the fireplace, feeling the warmth of the fire. B. J. Allison refilled her teacup and touched her arm. "There, there, dear," she cooed. "These things do happen. You did exactly what I would have." There were few higher compliments from the old woman. "But we must think about the future." She sat down in the wing-backed chair opposite Tara and sipped at her tea, deep in thought. Allison's strength was her ability to quickly reevaluate a situation and find new opportunities. Her thoughts did not follow a concrete, nicely ordered path from A to B to C, but rather she hovered over a problem and moved around it, darting in and out, looking at it from every viewpoint and finding a niche she could exploit.

At the same time, on another mental level, she was evaluating Tara. If she sensed the young woman had become a liability, she would dispose of her, taking whatever action was necessary. And she was very fond of Tara. Age had not diminished Allison's thought processes but sharpened them, making her a formidable power.

"Dear, when all this breaks in the papers, I think you're going to have to make a confidential phone call to a certain police lieutenant I know. Tell him you were the 'mystery woman' but that when you had left, Fraser was sleeping in bed. He'll be expecting your call. Don't be afraid to tell him your name but make him coax it out of you." Allison gave Tara a tight little smile. By the time Tara made her phone call, the lieutenant would already have "discovered" a witness who would swear that he saw Tara leave well before Fraser could have died.

Allison set the cup down and folded her hands primly in her lap. "We must change directions," she said. "I sank my money in a dry hole. Remember I had mentioned another person I thought you would like to meet? His name is Sheik Mohammed al-Khatub. Perhaps you know of him?" Tara's reaction indicated she did. "I will arrange for you to meet him tomorrow evening. Dear, it is very important that he take you into his confidence very quickly. I must know the timing of OPEC's next oil embargo."

Allison also knew how to make money out of that eventuality if she had a little warning. She gave an inward sigh. Exploiting an oil embargo was such a simple thing to do but she was only reacting to world events, not controlling them.

She made a mental promise that she would settle matters with Pontowski at another time, another place.

The radio came alive as the first Israeli artillery salvo walked through the tanks advancing toward Shoshana's position. She could hear the distinctive sound of Levy's voice respond to the eager requests of his company commanders to open fire. In every case, he ordered them to hold. He knew how long the artillery batteries could continue to shell the tanks before they had to stop shooting and start moving to avoid Iraqi counterbattery fire. Almost on cue, the artillery barrage stopped and Shoshana could hear the rumble of jets as they rolled in on the tanks.

Three sharp knocks on the rear ramp tore her attention away from the battle going on in front of her and she spun the periscope around to the rear. A fully NBC-suited soldier was hosing down the APC with a hose leading to a small tank trailer while two others were scrubbing it down with long brushes. It was a decontamination team at work in the midst of the fighting.

When they were finished, the team leader gave her the hand sign to drop the ramp. The team checked them and the interior of the APC for contamination. The leader put her mask next to Shoshana's and spoke in a normal voice. "You're clean," she said. "Keep wearing your suits, but you should be able to take your masks off in thirty minutes. Keep buttoned up until then. This stuff doesn't last as long as we thought." The team moved on to the next APC ambulance.

The radio crackled with urgent requests for support as the teams holding the northernmost sides of the valley came under heavy attack. Again, Levy did not respond. Now the closest tanks were less than two thousand meters away as the last F-4 pulled off. Two tanks exploded as the F-4s' Maverick antitank missiles found their targets.

Now Levy ordered his blocking force to commence fire and the hillside exploded as his tanks opened up. Shoshana's world narrowed as she watched, transfixed by three Iraqi tanks moving in a V formation coming straight toward her position. Levy's tank surged out of its deep rut and slammed to a halt when its turret was clear. It fired two quick rounds and reversed back into its hole. Two of the tanks exploded but the third pulled around its burning leader and came up the hill, directly toward their position, its main gun swinging onto her.

"Hanni!" Shoshana yelled. "Reverse out of here!"

She watched in horror as the tank, which she could clearly identify as a T-72, fired. "Hanni! Go!" she shouted. The APC jerked and then stopped, stalled. The shell impacted thirty meters in front of them as the tube of the T-72 raised for the automatic loader to eject the spent shell casing out of the breach. Hanni ground the starter and Shoshana knew she was going to die. She had heard tankers talk about how the tube on the main gun of a T-72 would first raise to eject the casing and then point downward with a fresh shell to slam into the breach. Then the gun's barrel would raise, retrain, and fire.

Levy's tank roared out of its hide as the T-72's tube was depressing to reload. With maddening slowness the turret of the M60 traversed toward the T-72. "Fire! Damn you, fire!" Shoshana shouted as the M60's 105-millimeter gun cracked. The muzzle of the T-72's gun had raised and was pointed directly at her when it disappeared in a flash. The APC's V-6 diesel came to life and now they were moving backward to safety.

The radio crackled. "Band-Aid, did you take a hit?" It was Levy.

Shoshana held the mike against her gas mask. "No damage," she reported. She could hear the trembling in her voice.

"Hold," Levy replied. "We're going to be needing you." Hanni slammed the APC to a halt. Levy did have that effect.

"Band-Aid," the radio spat, "a TOW team four hundred meters to your left and one hundred meters downslope needs a medic. Go." Hanni rolled the APC forward, past their last position and toward their first pickup. When they crested the ridge, Shoshana got her first clear look at the valley. Burning tanks and BMPs were sending up clouds of black smoke obscuring her view. Off to her right, she could see the Iraqis regrouping for another thrust up the slope. She swung the periscope to the rear to fix their escape route. A sickening feeling swept over her when she realized they had been well dug in and hidden in their old position. She had been looking at the battle through a raised periscope and had assumed that if she could see the tank, the tank could see her. Only Levy's sharp command at the right time had saved them from running away from where they were needed.

A sharp clanging deafened the two women as machine-gun fire raked their right side. The Toga armor the Israelis had covered the APC with had done its job and they were okay. The lightweight carbon sheets could stop a 14.5-millimeter shell before it hit the main hull. "Where's it coming from?" Hanni shouted, concentrating on driving and working her way across and down the slope toward the TOW team. Shoshana spun her periscope around until she found the machine gun. An Iraqi BMP on their right was racing them to the TOW team. The BMP had taken a hit on its turret disabling the 73-millimeter smooth-bore gun, but one of the troops inside was firing out of a gunport on the side, trying to take out the APC. Now Hanni could see the BMP.

"Don't they see our red cross?" Hanni shouted. A heavier burst of machine-gun fire beat against the Toga armor, across the freshly painted red cross.

The two vehicles were on a collision course and would collide at the spot where the wounded Israelis were dug in. Another gunport on the BMP swung open and Shoshana saw the snout of an RPG aim at them. Their Toga armor and 30-millimeter thick aluminum hull could not stop the Soviet-made rocket-propelled grenade. "Hard right!" Shoshana yelled. Hanni slued the APC to the right, directly toward the BMP just as the RPG fired. The rocket-propelled projectile flashed past behind them. "Ram the son of a bitch!" Shoshana screamed.

Hanni gunned the engine and roared down the hill, gaining momentum, headed directly for the BMP. Shoshana dropped to the floor and braced her back against the forward bulkhead. Gravity, inertia, and the slope of the hill worked in their favor as Hanni smashed the raked, heavily armored nose of their M113 into the left side of the BMP. The BMP lifted, slowly turned over onto its right side, and skidded down the hill. For a moment, neither woman moved, too stunned and bruised by the impact to react. Then Hanni restarted the engine and mashed the accelerator, ramming the bottom side of the BMP and turning it completely over. She backed away as flames licked out from underneath the BMP. They headed for the wounded Israelis.

Shoshana dropped the ramp when Hanni halted the APC

and jumped into the shallow ravine where the TOW team had hidden their Hummer. They had taken a hit from a single mortar round and only one man was left alive. She tried to pull his clothes away from the wound to stop the bleeding but her NBC gloves were too bulky. Then the eyepieces on her mask started to fog. Out of frustration, she ripped off the mask and heavy outer gloves, still wearing thin rubber surgical gloves. Unencumbered, she quickly stuffed a compress bandage into the gaping wound on the man's left side. Luckily his Kevlar flak jacket had taken most of the shrapnel from the mortar round. Hanni was beside her and the two women dragged the man out of the ravine and into the crew compartment of the APC where Shoshana could properly bandage him. Hanni headed for their next pickup.

After they had picked up six wounded, they headed back up the slope toward an aid station. The radio directed them to the rear area where the brigade was waiting for the order to counterattack. As they crested the top of the ridge, Shoshana stuck her head out the top hatch and looked back into the valley. Two kilometers away, she could see Israeli tanks coming down the western slope and cutting into the right flank of the second echelon of Iraqi tanks. They headed to the rear with their fragile cargo.

"Where is everybody?" Shoshana said to one of the medics who met them at the aid station in the brigade's holding area.

The woman gave her a frightened look. "They pulled out the rest of the brigade to reinforce the Golan. We've made a major breakthrough and want to push the Syrians back."

"My God, we're here all alone," Shoshana said. "Does Levy know?"

"He knows," the medic answered. "Go over there." She pointed to a decon area. "Scrub your APC down and change your suits. The nerve gas wasn't as effective as we thought. It's all gone."

Twenty minutes later, they were back at their original jump-off point. Two men and a woman were standing behind Levy's tank in the comparative safety of his hide, talking to him. All four had their gas masks off and NBC suits open, trying to cool off. Shoshana joined them and listened as the outgoing sounds of artillery punctuated the conversation. At least we've still got some support, she thought. Then what Levy was saying hit her—the Iraqis were pulling back.

Slowly, the pieces of the action filled in. They had stopped the Iraqi advance just as the order pulling the rest of the brigade out to reinforce the Golan Heights had come down. Then the two companies had counterattacked on the Iraqis' right flank to cut through the second echelon. But there it had all come apart and the Israeli tanks had taken heavy losses before they could cross through and regroup. Their counterattack had ground to a halt and only the withdrawal of the Iraqis had saved them. Levy's Luck, Shoshana decided.

"Casualties?" Levy asked. Shoshana was horrified as the tally mounted. The two men and woman with Levy were platoon commanders; their company commander had been killed. The exact status of the other two companies down in the valley was unknown. "Shoshana," Levy said, looking at her and then glancing down into the valley. She nodded and knew where she was needed.

The carnage among the tanks was the heaviest either of the women had ever seen. Two other Israeli APCs were picking up the wounded as medics worked furiously to save whom they could. A wave of a hand guided them to the eastern side of the valley where they could see numerous burning tanks and APCs. The first four tanks they came to were Iraqi. "Where are the Iraqi medics?" Hanni asked in frustration. Shoshana didn't have an answer but suspected the Iraqi high command was relying on the Israelis to take care of all the wounded.

The position of the destroyed tanks told the story. Three Israeli tanks supported by two APCs had taken on an Iraqi company of twelve tanks and twelve BMPs. The two women moved among the bodies, looking for the living. Shoshana found the lieutenant who had argued with Levy only to fall under his spell. His body was badly charred but he was still alive and conscious. She knew the man was near death and stopped to administer a heavy shot of morphine. It was all she could do.

The lieutenant looked at her. "Tell Levy," he whispered, "we never had a chance to regroup. But I didn't run."

"I will." Shoshana stood and moved on. The lieutenant understood.

* * *

The staff officer on night duty was standing in the communications room in the basement of the White House sorting the early-morning message traffic when the telephone call from the Washington, D.C., police came through. He took the call and listened, trying to mask his emotions. He knew that he should be serious, concerned, and properly subdued by the news. But why was he feeling so good? He broke the connection and punched a number on the telepanel. "I had better tell the President immediately," he said to the communications clerk.

"Without going through Fraser?" the shocked clerk blurted.

"I don't think Mr. Fraser is in a position to do anything about it," the staff officer said, giving up any attempt at burying his grin.

Pontowski listened to the report of Fraser's death and thanked the young staff officer. He returned the telephone to its cradle beside his wife's bed and pulled off his reading glasses. Although his wife was seriously ill, she was fully rational and the doctors were confident that her latest bout with lupus had stabilized and that she might improve. He knew it helped her spirits when he confided in her, a sure signal from him that she was on the mend. "Tom Fraser was just found dead in his apartment," he told her. "Heart attack."

Tosh looked at him, a deep concern in her eyes. "How unfortunate, the poor man." Her voice was barely audible. She was thinking how unfortunate for her husband to lose a key man in the midst of the current crisis. "This couldn't happen at a worse time."

"We'll survive," Pontowski said. "But I've got to find a replacement. Someone good at crisis management, with credibility." He paced the floor thinking. This should be the end of the illegal campaign funds affair, he decided. If I know Fraser, it died with him. But what message do I need to send now?

Then he remembered the report of the investigation on Bill Carroll that Fraser had ordered the head of the Secret Service, Stan Abbott, to carry out. The Secret Service's investigation had included Carroll's boss. "Tosh, what do you think of Brigadier General Leo Cox as Fraser's replacement?''

There was no answer for a moment as his wife mulled the name over. "I think that might be a very good choice. Why don't you have him checked out?"

"He has been—thanks to Fraser."

The APC jerked to a halt and Hanni dropped the rear ramp, kicking up a small cloud of dust. Two medics clambered on board and removed their last load of wounded Iraqi soldiers. Then the after-battle routine kicked in and Shoshana and Hanni went through the motions like robots, thankful they did not have to think. Shoshana drove to a service point and refueled the vehicle while mechanics checked the engine and tensioned the tracks. Hanni hosed out the crew compartment and the M113 smelled fresh and clean. Then they restocked their medical supplies and found a place to park.

They were eating their first hot meal in twenty-four hours and thinking about a long sleep when the radio squawked and ordered them to the command post. Shoshana drove the APC while Hanni finished stowing the gear. Levy was waiting for them when they pulled into line.

Shoshana introduced Hanni and noticed that she was the same height as Levy. "I saw you take out the BMP," he said. Hanni only nodded, too tired to think. "That was a brave thing to do." While they stood there, Shoshana told him about the lieutenant. The same sad look she had seen in his eyes before was back. "How much longer can I sacrifice them," he said, dropping his head and staring at his feet.

The major who served as Levy's second-in-command and had led the attack on the Iraqis' flank came up and handed him a message form. "A message from headquarters Northern Command," he grumbled. "They want an immediate reply."

Levy scanned the long message twice and Shoshana could see his jaw turn to marble. "Did you read it?" Levy asked. The major nodded an answer. "What do you think?"

"Not much," the major allowed.

"Those idiots want to know why we didn't counterattack and want us to renew operations immediately," Levy told the two women.

"What are you going to tell them?" the major asked.

"I'm going to ask them, 'What do you expect me to attack with?' before I tell them to go to hell. Then I'm going to dig in and hold this position. From now on, the war comes to me."

"That won't be long," the major said. "Intelligence says the Iraqis are moving more tanks and troops into position."

23

The two lieutenants were standing at attention in General Mana's office. Johar Adwan chanced a quick glance at his wingman, but Samir Hamshari's eyes were routed on a spot on the wall above the general's empty chair. Johar did the same. Thirty-four minutes later, they heard the sound of hard heels in the outer office and the shuffle of chairs as Mana's aides and secretaries came to attention. The two men could hear Mana's distinctive voice. "Are they here?"

"As you ordered, General," came the reply. The two lieutenants stiffened even more, if that were possible, as Mana entered. He walked around them and laid his swagger stick and ornate peaked hat on his desk. The general concentrated on pulling off his thin leather gloves, ignoring the lieutenants. He sat down and picked up the letter opener on his desk, finally raising his eyes to focus on the two pilots.

"You two were observed yesterday engaged in a dogfight with each other when you should have been on a routine patrol along the Turkish border." He rolled the handle of the letter opener between his fingers, studying the blade, finding it more interesting than Johar and Samir. "Apparently, you were doing this quite low." Now the general was staring at them, his eyes cold and hard. "What altitude were you at when you engaged in this reckless activity?"

Johar saw an opening. Whoever had seen them was not a flier, otherwise Mana would have known they were flying two hundred meters above the ground. "Sir, permission to speak?" he barked. Mana nodded, still twiddling the opener. "Lieutenant Samir and I were on patrol yesterday when a bright flash on the ground caught our attention. Our ground controller did not respond to our request to investigate." So far, so good, Johar thought. Once established on a patrol, the Iraqi radar ground controllers often ignored them since nothing had happened along the Turkish border since the war with Kuwait. Mana said nothing.

"Sir," Johar continued, "I took it on my own initiative to descend to six hundred meters above the area." Now he waited. Six hundred meters, just under two thousand feet, was still too low for the general but it explained why they were below radar coverage. "We then set up a weave pattern to perform a visual reconnaissance of the road." That explained what could have been mistaken for a dogfight. No sign from Mana.

Johar gave an inward shudder as he thought what Mana would do if he knew the truth. The two pilots had been practicing low-level engagements at five hundred feet, less than two hundred meters, above the ground. Johar had rolled in on Samir and closed to a guns tracking solution. Samir had then tried to jink out and reverse onto Johar.

"Weave pattern?" Mana finally said. It wasn't a question. "Visual reconnaissance? These are not authorized. Your sole function on patrol is to follow the directions from your ground controller. You are airborne only to shorten the response time from when the controller detects an intruder until when he can direct you into an engagement."

The two pilots looked straight ahead. "This," Mana continued, "is the second time you have acted irresponsibly and it will not be repeated." The general drove the tip of the letter opener into the desktop. "To make my point, you will be on standby alert until further notice. Dismissed." Johar and Samir clicked their heels, gave short bows from the waist, turned, and marched out of the room.

Outside the building, they breathed easier. "Standby alert," Johar said. "It could have been worse."

"So we sit in our rooms or in the squadron," Samir complained, "just in case they want someone to fly. When did anyone on standby alert ever fly?"

"Never."

"Why'd you tell him we had set up a weave at six hundred

meters?'' Samir groused. "He almost wet his pants. The only time Mana sees six hundred meters is during takeoffs and approaches.''

"I had to tell him something he'll believe," Johar explained.

"You got that from a CHECO report," Samir said.

The two pilots had recently discovered a complete set of United States Air Force Contemporary Historical Evaluation of Combat Operations (CHECO) reports an agent had stolen from a base in Germany years before. Johar and Samir had pored over the reports that U.S. Air Force historians had compiled during the course of the war in Vietnam. The reports had started out based on interviews with the pilots and aircrews who actually engaged in combat. The men had told it like it really was and the reports had been most revealing. After the first year, a pattern emerged in the reports: The targets and Rules of Engagement coming down from higher headquarters had little to do with the air war, what it took to survive over North Vietnam and, most important, to deliver effective ordnance on target. Like most sane men, the pilots did what was necessary to stay alive and generally kept their mouths shut. The CHECO reports got to the truth.

Unfortunately for history, certain generals in the Air Force read the reports, tried to have them burned, and, failing that, classified them secret. Then the same generals disciplined a few pilots and crunched at least one historian. The historians, also being sane and rational, took their cues from the pilots and started telling the generals what they'd believe.

The two Iraqi pilots walked slowly toward their squadron building. They had lots of time to kill. Then what started as a low chuckle in both men grew to a guffaw. Johar looked at Samir and roared with laughter. "It worked, didn't it?" That was life in an air force.

"Colonel Martin, what we're dealing with here is a classic case of 'you tell me what the threat is and I'll tell you what my tactics are,' '' Matt said. He and Furry were closeted with the DO, Bill Carroll, and the Gruesome Twosome going over their plans and training for an attack on Kirkuk. "We're going to have to take on the same defense array that Amb and I encountered when we hit the Syrian headquarters in Lebanon.''

"Gadflies and ZSUs?" Dennis Leander, the junior, very short, overfed elf half of the Twosome, asked.

"Right," Furry answered. "We were okay ingressing to the target," the wizzo explained, recalling the attack, "until we had to pop above a hundred feet to acquire the target while we were still outside the range of the ZSU-Twenty-threes that were surrounding the place. That's when the Gadflies became a problem. We popped to designate the target, dropped back down to get below the Gadflies, but then had to pop back up to get an upward vector so our smart bomb could get a release signal from the weapons computer. I want to tell you, things got hairier than hell."

"But," Matt interrupted, "we've got just the weapon and tactics to counter that threat."

Martin was way ahead of them. "So we use GBU-Twenty-fours and Israeli *B'nai* tactics."

"Sorry," Larry Stigler, the stork half of the Twosome said, "you've lost us."

"Explain it to the Meatheads," Martin grumbled, "and work out a low-level attack. Tell me when you've got the simulator ready and I'll fly the first mission profile." He heaved his bulk to a standing position and stomped out the door.

"He likes you," Furry told the Twosome.

Martin stuck his head back inside the room. "I want the sim ready by tomorrow morning, Meatheads." Then he was gone.

"He doesn't like us," Leander corrected. "No way we can do that. It'll take us five days to reprogram your simulator."

"You want to tell him that?" Carroll asked.

"We'll try to have something by tomorrow," Stigler moaned. "You better tell us about GBU-Twenty-fours and *B'nai* tactics."

Furry explained that the GBU-24 was a two-thousand-pound bomb with a guidance control unit on its nose and folding wings on its tail. The weapon could be released in level flight very low to the ground and "tossed" onto the target when the aircraft was still over five miles away. The wings on the GBU-24 would snap open and the guidance control unit would "fly" the bomb onto the target. The bomb would actually climb in-flight and the control unit would do trajectory shaping to optimize the impact angle. The bomb could penetrate fifteen feet of earth or three feet of concrete and, according to Furry, "not even scratch the paint."

But for pinpoint accuracy, the target had to be lased during the final seconds of the bomb's flight. The guidance control unit would sense the reflected energy and fly the bomb to within inches of the "usable laser spot." The GBU-24 was a very smart bomb with infinite courage.

Then Matt took over and covered *B'nai* tactics. In order to lase the target, two F-15Es would fly a coordinated attack in what could best be described as a pincers movement. The aircraft tossing the bomb would ingress slightly ahead of the other. It would toss the bomb while still well clear of the ZSU-23s used for close-in defense and under the minimum guidance altitude of the Gadfly SAM. The second jet would come in on the other arm of the pincers and would close to within eight thousand feet of the nearest ZSU-23, which was outside the ZSU's range but still close enough to see and lase the target without popping into the Gadfly's envelope.

Stigler stood up, ready to go to work. But something in him had changed; instead of looking like a stork, he resembled a lean and hungry hawk. "How soon," he said to Carroll, "can you get us the exact location of every SAM site and ZSU gun emplacement that's a player?"

"In thirty minutes," Carroll answered.

Leander's elfin grin changed to one of pure mean gremlin. "Martin's gonna find out who the meatheads are tomorrow morning."

The activity swirling around the Ganef in the command and control bunker was brisk and efficient. The officers were showered and rested as they hurried about their business directing the war effort, and the halls and command room had been recently cleaned. The chief of Mossad noted with grim satisfaction that the change in morale was driven by the status boards and that there was no doubt that Israel was now pushing the Syrians and Iraqis back on two of the three fronts. The Golan Heights had been cleared and Northern Command was massing for a push toward Damascus, eighty kilometers, or forty-three miles, away. On the front opposite Jerusalem, the Syrians and Iraqis had been pushed back across the Jordan River and Jerusalem was no longer being shelled by artillery. But the Israelis' last attack as they tried to force the Jordan River had stalled.

Only on the Lebanon front had all progress ground to a halt. The Iraqis had tried to push down a long valley just as Ben David had transferred forces from Lebanon to the Golan to exploit the breakthrough there. The battle in Lebanon had turned into a bloody slugfest and only the timely withdrawal of the Iraqis had saved the situation.

Now Ben David was pressing for a counterattack in Lebanon, claiming that the Iraqis had withdrawn because they were hurt. The Ganef shook his head because he would have to tell Ben David that he was wrong. All his latest intelligence said the Iraqis were re-forming for another attack.

The air attack warning lights on the panel above the main boards started to flash, capturing everyone's attention in the bunker. The sophisticated warning system had detected numerous incoming missiles and was analyzing their trajectories. Now the panel's readouts lit up, identifying the type of missiles and their targets. Sixteen Scud Bs and Scaleboards were headed for targets where Israel's Jericho missiles were bunkered. Then another warning flashed as twelve more missiles were detected headed for the same type of targets. The panel illuminated with a third warning as nineteen more missiles were detected. The Patriot batteries were saturated.

Ben David was on his feet, shouting. ''So they want to escalate!''

The Ganef studied Ben David, more concerned about the prime minister's reaction than the attack. A new worry claimed the Ganef's thoughts. Everything about Ben David pointed to a man on the edge of physical and mental exhaustion. The minister of defense, Benjamin Yuriden, was calming him, urging him to wait for the results of the attack before acting.

''If this is a chemical attack inside Israel . . .'' Ben David was shouting, clenching and relaxing his right fist, his face flushed.

''I don't think so,'' Yuriden counseled. ''We've told them if they use gas on our people, we'll use nuclear weapons. It's logical for them to strike at our nuclear delivery systems, our Jericho missiles.''

The damage reports started to filter in. The incoming missiles had all been armed with conventional warheads and the targets had been known Jericho missile sites. The Ganef was surprised at the accuracy of the Arabs' targeting and immediately wondered if the Soviets had used their satellite reconnaissance to help locate the Jerichos for the Arabs.

Ben David was settling down until the final results were tallied: The rocket attack had knocked out 28 percent of Israel's Jericho missiles. "Upload our warheads!" he shouted. Again, Yuriden calmed him, telling him that it was far too early to upload their nuclear warheads. Ben David smashed his fists down onto his console, hard, fighting for self-control. For a few moments he stared at his fists; then he jerked his head yes, agreeing with his minister of defense.

The Ganef decided it would be better if he waited a few minutes before he told Ben David about the Iraqi preparations for a new attack in Lebanon and slipped out of the room, into the corridor. His experience warned him not to overburden the prime minister and to be careful how he presented bad news. The man needed rest and was not in full command of his emotions. Besides, the ground commanders in Lebanon were aware of the impending attack.

A heavyset figure was lumbering down the passageway: Avi Tamir. The Ganef stopped him. "We need to talk," he said and motioned toward an empty part of the corridor. "Is it ready yet?" he asked.

Tamir's head snapped up. Of course, he had seen the old man with Ben David when they had last discussed the progress he was making, but he didn't know who the man was or what he did. "I'm the chief of Mossad," the Ganef told him, establishing his authority.

"We all need to talk," a voice behind them said. It was Benjamin Yuriden. He led the two men down the hall and into an office. He chased the occupants out and closed the door. "What's the status of the 'weapon'?" he asked.

"It's finished and is being moved right now," Tamir answered. "Once in place, it can be uploaded on a missile in about three hours."

"If the Arabs hit Israel with gas," Yuriden said, "he'll use it." The "he" was Yair Ben David.

"I thought the Iraqis had already used nerve gas," Tamir said, puzzled.

"That was in Lebanon," Yuriden explained, "not in Israel and in a limited tactical situation. Our intelligence from the field indicates it hurt them more than it did us. In fact, I think that's why they broke off the attack when they did. Levy's Luck again.''

Now Yuriden was pacing the floor. ''We're pushing the Arabs back and they're showing signs of aligning their political posture to support the Egyptian cease-fire proposal in the UN. But Ben David wants a military solution first. He wants territory to justify the sacrifices we've made. But I'm worried that the Arabs will resort to widespread chemical warfare if they think they are going to lose too much of their land.''

''They know we'd go nuclear if they did that,'' the Ganef said.

''Who said the actors in this war were rational?'' Yuriden snapped. ''Not only that, since the VR Fifty-five they used in Lebanon was ineffective, I'm certain the Iraqis will use their newest nerve gas now.'' Yuriden paused. ''And we don't have a defense against it. Thank God they haven't deployed it into the field yet.''

''Then why don't we destroy the nerve gas before they move it?'' the Ganef asked. ''Jericho missiles with conventional warheads should do the job.''

''Believe me, we thought about it,'' Yuriden said. ''The only warhead we have that can penetrate the arsenal's hardened walls at Kirkuk is too heavy and reduces the range of the Jericho. Kirkuk is simply out of range with a conventional warhead that can do the job.''

''Has somebody been working the problem?'' Tamir asked. ''Trying to develop a conventional warhead that matches throw weight with range?''

''Of course,'' Yuriden answered. ''Israeli Military Industries. But they haven't come up with . . .'' Tamir spun around, cutting him off, and ran out of the room, heading for his next challenge.

Yuriden studied the open door in the silence. ''I'm going to have to order another air strike against the arsenal,'' he said. ''It's suicide.'' The man drew himself up. He had been a fighter pilot, had flown Israel's first F-16s, and was still current in the aircraft. ''Damn, I'm going to lead the attack myself.''

''That would win an award for stupidity,'' the Ganef grunted, but he sympathized with Yuriden's yearning to take an active part in the war. "I think I know how to destroy the Iraqis' nerve gas before they deploy it."

"It's got to happen soon," Yuriden said. "I'm not sure how much longer we can contain this war."

The Ganef closed the door and stood close to Yuriden, his voice low and almost inaudible. . . .

Dennis Leander was sitting at the simulator's control console, working furiously, trying to nail Mad Mike Martin who was in the simulator. His partner, Larry Stigler, was asleep on the floor, totally exhausted from the forty-eight straight hours they had spent programming the sim's computer. They had missed their first deadline and drawn the full force of Martin's large and obscene vocabulary. Now the simulator was ready and Leander wanted revenge. "Oh, shit!" he roared when Martin skillfully avoided the latest combination of SA-6 and SA-11 SAMs Leander had engaged him with. "Damn it, Stig! Get your ass up here and help me."

Stigler staggered to his feet and scanned the color monitors that repeated the scene Martin was seeing inside the cockpit. Martin's wizzo had the nerve gas plant and arsenal on the Target FLIR and they were on a bomb run, doing their own lasing. "I thought they were using *B'nai* tactics and Martin's wingman was going to do the lasing," Stigler observed.

"I shot his wingman down," Leander said, his teeth grinding.

For a fraction of a moment, Stigler considered sandbagging the colonel inside the sim, but discarded the urge immediately. Too much was at stake here and this was not the time for games. "Don't cut him any slack, but make it realistic."

"How about him cutting me some slack?" Leander yelled. Then he relaxed and laughed. "This guy is tough." They watched the color monitor as Martin's first bomb exploded on target.

Thirty-five minutes later, Martin safely landed at Diyarbakir, Turkey, the launch and recovery base for the attack 240 miles away. The canopy that covered the cockpit swung up and Martin crawled out, his flight suit wringing wet and his face glistening with sweat. For a moment he stared at the Gruesome Twosome. "That was a neat twist, moving SA-Sixes in like that," he said. "Totally unexpected but realis-

tic. I liked it. Get every swingin' dick through here today."
The Gruesome Twosome exchanged tired looks as Martin
barreled out the door. The colonel stuck his massive head
back in. "You did good. Thanks." Then he was gone.

24

Brigadier General Leo Cox was sitting next to the President
on one of the sofas in the Oval Office, going over the agenda
for a meeting of the National Security Council that would
start in a few minutes. It was his first day on the job as Zack
Pontowski's chief of staff and he was impressed by the efficient organization Fraser had left behind. It had been easy
for him to step in and take over the position. But he would
have to make some changes. "This, Mr. President"—Cox
handed him a briefing book on the Arab-Israeli war—"is how
the CIA sees the current status of the war."

"I take it you don't agree," Pontowski said, surprising
Cox.

"Not entirely. But I usually disagree with the CIA's inter-
pretation of events in the Middle East."

"Why do you disagree with them?" The President was
interested.

Cox gave a little laugh. "Well, Mr. Burke will tell you that
I'm too pro-Israeli and spout their party line." Bobby Burke
as the director of central intelligence was the President's chief
adviser for all matters on intelligence and Cox knew he was
trespassing on his preserve, a sure way to earn enemies in
Washington, D.C.

"Are you?" Pontowski asked.

"Yes, sir, I am." He decided to be totally open with his
commander in chief. "It's because I have many personal contacts with Mossad and Israeli military intelligence and rely
on them."

"What are those contacts telling you now?"

Cox took a deep breath. "I was contacted this morning. The Israelis now have a thermonuclear weapon and one warhead is deployed. It has been targeted to hit one of two targets——"

"Either Damascus or Baghdad," Pontowski interrupted. Cox nodded, surprised at the President's ability to make instant connections. Cox had much to learn about the man. "No doubt," Pontowski continued, "they will use it if the Arabs employ chemical weapons against Israel's population." Again, Cox could only nod in agreement. "How's Ben David holding up?"

"Not well," the general answered, his mind racing to keep up with the conversation. "He wants a military solution that will guarantee Israel's security in the future. He's pressing the war as hard as he can, before a cease-fire is imposed on him."

"The Arabs won't accept a military solution like that," the President said. "They'll fight with everything they've got, including the new nerve gas the Iraqis have developed. Leo, in a few minutes, I'm going to have to make some hard decisions. I've got to know who your sources are." Pontowski knew the answer. It was Cox's first test.

Cox did not hesitate. "He's the chief of Mossad," the general explained. Pontowski stood up, ready for the meeting with the NSC. "Mr. President, why did you select me to be your chief of staff?"

"I think you can figure it out," Pontowski replied.

The briefing was finished and Shoshana walked out of the makeshift command post with most of the battalion's officers. Outside, she leaned against Levy's M60 tank and waited for Hanni to come out. Her partner seemed to be taking a very special interest in Moshe Levy lately. She watched Levy's driver and loader clean and reassemble the tank's air filter. Amos Avner, the loader, kept up a constant barrage of bickering and complaining as Nazzi Halaby, the driver, did most of the work. Finally, the gunner, Dave Bielski, climbed out of the turret and scampered down the tank's hull. "For God's sake, Avner, SHUT up!" he bellowed.

"They don't seem to get along at all," Shoshana observed.

"That's because Halaby is a Druze and Avner's Orthodox,'' Bielski explained. ''Orthodox Jews don't trust the Druze.''

''I knew a Druze once,'' Shoshana said, thinking of Zeev Avidar and the time she was in Iraq. Such a long time ago, she thought. Again, out of the mists of memory, Gad Habish's voice came to her. ''His loyalty spoke for itself,'' she said.

''So does Halaby's,'' Bielski said. ''But Avner is so thickheaded that he can't accept it.''

Hanni joined them. ''Levy thinks the attack will start soon,'' she said.

''He's usually right,'' Bielski said.

''What's it like being on his crew?'' Hanni asked.

''It's hard to describe,'' the gunner answered. ''One time he got so sick and fed up with Avner for the way he treated Halaby that he was going to replace him. Avner broke down and cried like a baby. He said he would do anything to stay on the crew. They cut a deal, Avner could stay as long as he shut up about Halaby being a Druze and cut out the Arab jokes. You know we never bad-mouth the Arabs in the tank.''

The three of them walked up the deep cut the tank was hidden in to the berm and looked over the long valley with its grisly reminders of death and destruction. The wreckage of tanks and APCs still littered the valley floor from the first battle. They crouched down, covered by the camouflage netting that covered the tank's hide, and Bielski swept the valley with binoculars. ''Looks like the retrieval crews have all pulled back.'' They all knew that was an indication the fighting would soon start.

The tank's radios squawked, warning of low-flying, inbound RPVs. ''Probably the reconnaissance drones they send over for a last look-see,'' Bielski said as he walked back to his tank.

Shoshana and Hanni headed for their nearby APC to wait for the orders to pull back after the drones had flown over and before the artillery barrage started. ''Levy says they are very predictable about the way they begin,'' Hanni said.

''I wish that was reassuring,'' Shoshana replied and climbed into her NBC suit, pulling it on over Matt's flight suit.

The secretary of state was looking at his notes as he talked while the rest of the National Security Council assembled in the Cabinet Room fidgeted and waited for their turn. "In short, Mr. President, the Arabs are now united in their support of a United Nations resolution calling for a immediate cease-fire. However, Israel is adamant in its opposition now that they are winning. Perhaps it is time to change our position and force them into a more rational stance."

"What are you suggesting?" National Security Adviser Cagliari asked.

"That we immediately curtail our resupply of arms and supplies to Israel," the secretary of state answered.

"That will have an effect down the line," Admiral Scovill, the Chairman of the Joint Chiefs of Staff, said. "But as of now, the Israelis have received enough logistical support to continue the current pace of the war for another week."

"What can the Israelis accomplish during that week?" Pontowski asked.

Now it was the turn of Bobby Burke, the DCI. "We calculate the Israelis will have pushed across the Litani River in Lebanon, be off the Golan and within ten miles of Damascus, and have encircled all the Syrians and Iraqis that have not retreated out of Jordan. It looks like the Arab front opposite Jerusalem is collapsing."

"And the Arab reaction?" Pontowski asked.

"They could use chemical weapons to stabilize the situation," the admiral speculated.

"That means the Israelis will retaliate with nuclear weapons," Cagliari said.

"We can't be sure of that," Burke protested.

"That's a firebreak I don't want to chance crossing," Pontowski said. "How do we keep it from happening?"

"I can pull out all the stops," the secretary of state said, "and launch a full-scale diplomatic offensive to get a cease-fire in place. It will take some doing, but if we halt all supplies to Israel . . ."

"Do it," Pontowski said.

"There's another option," Scovill said. "We can give the Israelis the missiles necessary to eliminate the worst of the threat. I'm referring to the Iraqis' nerve gas facility near Kirkuk. The Arabs' previous experience with using gas in Lebanon proved to be quite ineffective. Without the new nerve gas, they know it would be a one-sided exchange."

The secretary of state almost panicked. "Mr. President, we cannot, I repeat, we cannot use missiles of any sort at this point because of the situation in the Kremlin. We have indications that the hard-liners are prevailing under Marshal Stanilov. He's of the old guard and, to him, the use of missiles equates with a major escalation against Soviet allies and is a prelude to nuclear weapons. We cannot afford a misstep at this time. Using missiles of any sort against Kirkuk could well give him the excuse he needs to consolidate power in the Kremlin and maybe actively intervene in the war. He would like nothing more than an external threat to force an internal peace."

The consensus around the room supported the secretary of state.

The President looked around the table, capturing the attention of each person. "I firmly believe Yair Ben David will not use nuclear weapons unless the Arabs resort to the widespread use of chemical weapons against Israel's population. To keep that from happening, we will push on the diplomatic front for a cease-fire. But as a backup option, I want to be able to destroy the Iraqis' nerve gas arsenal without the use of missiles." He turned to Admiral Scovill. "How can we do that?"

The Chairman of the Joint Chiefs of Staff shuffled through his notes until he found the "talking paper" that had been prepared for him on that very subject. "The Air Force has been preparing for that contingency," he began, reading from the talking paper. "The Forty-fifth Tactical Fighter Wing at RAF Stonewood"—he glanced up at the President in time to see him stiffen; everyone in the room knew his grandson was assigned to the 45th—"ah, has prepared an operations plan called Trinity using F-Fifteen Es launched out of a Turkish air base, ah, Diyarbakir. Training for the mission is well advanced and the attack force can deploy and be in place within twelve hours. Only the permission of the Turkish government is required."

"Who directed the Forty-fifth to prepare that plan?" Pontowski asked, his voice low.

Scovill caught all the danger signs. "Sir, the deputy for operations at Stonewood, a Colonel Michael Martin, did it on his own. I am told he is a most unique individual and is like a firehorse. Any time he senses a fire, he gets ready to fight it.''

Pontowski's stomach twisted and knotted as he clenched his fists. "Get permission from the Turks. Order the Forty-fifth to deploy and await an order to execute.'' His voice was low and unemotional. But he knocked his chair back as he rose to leave.

''Sir, are there any special instructions for the Forty-fifth, personnel considerations . . . ?'' Admiral Scovill asked. He wanted to know if he was to specifically exclude Matt from participating in the mission.

''None,'' the President answered. ''Colonel Martin planned the mission and he will select the men he wants to execute it.'' He gestured for Cox to follow him.

Once inside the Oval Office, he stood looking out the windows at the President's Park. ''Leo, I want you to use your contacts with Mossad to get a message to Ben David. Tell him that we are going to take out the Iraqi nerve gas arsenal and that I expect him to absorb any minor chemical attacks as he has in the past without retaliating. Also tell him that if he employs a nuclear weapon on the battlefield without consulting with me first, I will break all relations with Israel. Further, if he uses a thermonuclear bomb on an Arab city, I will seriously consider active measures against Israel.''

Cox could only stare at Pontowski's back in shock. And suddenly he knew why the President had chosen him to be his new chief of staff.

The Iraqi artillery barrage was much heavier than expected and the APC rocked with a near miss and concussion of an exploding shell. Luckily, Levy had pulled most of the battalion well back from the valley and they were out of range of most of the Iraqi guns. Still, an occasional round reached their position. From the babble on the radio, Shoshana could tell that the Israeli counterbattery fire had not discouraged the Iraqi gunners and it was turning into a bloody artillery dual. Now calls for medics started coming in as the Iraqi shelling chewed up the battalion's forward positions. Shoshana started the M113's engine and jammed it into gear. ''Tell Levy,'' she shouted at Hanni, ''that this Band-Aid is going forward.''

She could hear Hanni's cool voice relay their intentions

over the radio to Levy in his command tank. "He wishes us luck," Hanni said.

We'll need it, Shoshana thought.

Matt and Furry were flying their second mission in Stonewood's simulator when it froze and Stigler's voice told them that they had an urgent phone call. Matt popped the canopy and scrambled over the side to take the call. Leander was asleep in a chair, his head resting on the console, and Stigler looked gaunt and worn. Matt listened, dropped the phone into its cradle, and shouted at his wizzo, "Amb, get your ass out of there. Martin wants us in Intel. Like five minutes ago." The two men ran from the simulator building, leaving both Leander and Stigler asleep at the console.

The big walk-in vault in Intelligence was jammed with bodies as Matt and Furry squeezed through the door. Martin was pacing in front of a map with their route of flight to Turkey. When he stopped, the room fell silent with anticipation. "For a change," he began, "someone in the Pentagon read their incoming mail instead of shoveling bullshit out the door. They bought Trinity." The room erupted in shouts, whistles, stomps, and applause.

"Okay, here's the lineup." Martin pointed to a chart on the wall that listed the twelve crews who would fly the mission. The call sign for the flight was Viper and it was organized in elements of two. As expected, Martin was in the lead ship as Viper 01. But what surprised everyone, except Matt, was that Sean Leary was his wingman, Viper 02. The young lieutenant had proven himself since he had almost killed Matt and was turning into an outstanding stick. Matt and Furry were Viper 03 and had been selected to lead the second element of two. "Start engines in an hour," Martin told the men. "Get moving."

The room rapidly emptied as Martin motioned for Matt and Carroll to join him. "Bill," Martin said, "I want you out on the first tanker. After they refuel us, it'll recover at Athens. The RC-One-thirty-five will be on the ground and waiting for you. Are you sure you can hack it?" The plan called for Carroll to be airborne in an RC-135 monitoring Iraqi communications when the F-15s flew the attack. He was to relay information to the orbiting E-3A AWACS controlling the mission. The problem was that Carroll would have to stay on board the RC-135 until the mission was launched. When the reconnaissance version of the Boeing 707 did land to switch crews and refuel, it would be immediately relaunched with Carroll on board. He might be airborne for days and Martin was worried that Carroll would become overly fatigued.

"Not to worry, boss," Carroll assured Martin. "I used to do this for a living and can sleep like a baby if I've got a sleeping bag. In fact, my first assignment was on an RC-One-thirty-five and Muddy Waters was my module commander."

"I'll be damned," Martin said, pulling a face. Of all men, Martin was not given to sentimentality, but it pleased him to be linked to one of the legends.

"Where's the Gruesome Twosome?" Martin asked Matt.

"Last I saw them, they were sleeping like babies," Matt replied.

"Let 'em sleep," Martin decided. "They did good. Thanks to them, we've got half a chance."

Matt and Carroll exchanged glances and an unspoken thought passed between them. The colonel, like them, knew just how tough it was going to be.

Twenty minutes later, a crew van pulled up in front of twelve waiting F-15s and the eight men flying the first four jets clambered out. Martin followed Matt down the steps, took one look at the jets, and roared out a deafening "Shit hot!" A stork and an elf dressed in civilian clothes were under Martin's F-15 hunched over one of the GBU-24s slung under the wing, stenciling in neat red letters, "Courtesy of the Meatheads."

The APC clanked to a halt outside the aid station and the rear ramp came down. Two medics were waiting and rushed on board, carrying out the sole casualty. The explosions of incoming artillery washed over them. "I've never seen a barrage last this long," one of the medics told Shoshana. "How bad is it up there?" The female medic looked in the direction of the valley.

"It's constant but not heavy," Shoshana answered. "Only a few casualties."

"Levy's Luck," the medic said.

Shoshana added a mental, I hope so.

The radio rasped with a hard metallic voice warning them of an air attack. Shoshana jumped into the driver's compartment and gunned the engine, heading for a nearby camouflaged cut a bulldozer had scraped out only hours before. She nosed the APC under the netting with only moments to spare as the first Syrian MiG-23 rolled in. A feeling of utter helplessness captured Shoshana as she watched the fast-moving jet sweep down on them. Two 550-kilogram bombs rippled off and bracketed the APC, stunning her. Then it was deathly silent. She shook her head and slowly sound returned; both she and Hanni had been momentarily deafened by the concussion.

The two women lay on the floor of the crew compartment as more bombs fell, holding on to the old-style tanker helmets they wore in the APC. Again, the radio came to life as warnings to don NBC gear were passed. Now the bombing stopped and they could hear artillery again. Urgent pleas for medics came in and Shoshana started the APC and headed back for the valley to pick up wounded. How much longer would this go on before they attacked? she wondered.

The Syrians and Iraqis were working together to soften up the Israelis and break Levy's Luck.

Melissa Courtney-Smith escorted the Navy captain into the Oval Office. "Mr. President, Dr. Smithson."

General Cox rose to leave and nodded at Melissa, his way of saying he approved her handling of the President's visitors. She turned to follow him out but Pontowski said, "Please stay, Melissa." Cox closed the door behind him, leaving the three in private.

"Mr. President," the doctor began, "I'm afraid your wife has suffered a relapse and is much worse."

Pontowski sat ashen-faced, trying to focus on what the doctor was saying. ". . . had hoped that she was recovering . . . very serious . . . strong-willed . . . she's a fighter . . . it could be hours or days now . . . need to take her to the hospital."

Melissa wanted to touch Pontowski, to find the right words to say. But she could only stand there, hating herself for not knowing what to do or say.

Slowly the President straightened. "I'll go with her to the hospital," he said. "Melissa, please come with me. Stay with

Tosh and call the family. I can't stay but if you need me, I'll be in the Situation Room." The three left the office as Zack Pontowski started on another long and difficult journey.

25

The RC-135 was on its second mission with Bill Carroll on board and had been established in its track along the southern Turkish border for six hours. The surveillance technicians had relaxed into a comfortable routine when they detected no unusual communications activity. The Syrians and Iraqis had not even reacted to the twelve F-15s that had flown in and landed at Diyarbakir, which was less than seventy-five nautical miles from their border.

At the time the F-15s had landed, one of the technicians had told Carroll that the Iraqis and Syrians were accustomed to seeing an RC-135 and the E-3A AWACS patrolling their border and tended to ignore any activity in Turkey. Complacency had given the Americans their first break.

Now a sergeant worked his way to the back of the aircraft, down the narrow aisle and past the crowded consoles and big equipment racks. He almost stumbled over the lump curled up in the sleeping bag. "Colonel," the sergeant said, "we picked up some radio traffic you should see." The lump stirred and Bill Carroll stuck his head out. The sergeant handed him a sheet of paper.

"Has this been sent out?" Carroll asked. The sergeant told him no. "Is the AWACS still monitoring heavy-vehicle traffic into the Kirkuk arsenal?" The sergeant said he would check on it and left. Carroll reread the transcript of the intercepted radio transmission. It was a request for a helicopter escort for a truck convoy and they were wanted at the Kirkuk arsenal in four hours.

The sergeant was back. "Colonel, I talked to the AWACS over the Have Quick." The Have Quick was a secure radio that used frequency hopping to prevent monitoring and jamming. The RC-135, the AWACS, and the F-15s were all equipped with the radio. "Their radar isn't picking up any road traffic now," the sergeant told him. The AWACS's APY-1 radar had a moving-target indicator that could be adjusted to pick up slow-moving vehicles on roads.

"We need to downlink," Carroll said. "The Iraqis are going to convoy their nerve gas in four hours."

Poor radio discipline had given them their second break.

The Situation Room in the basement of the White House is not big, perhaps fifteen by twenty feet in size, and is not impressive. What is impressive are the communications systems that feed into it. One of the transceivers was a highly secure system known to its operators simply as Apple Wave. A civilian with a security clearance so sensitive that only thirty-seven individuals held it was monitoring the Apple Wave when its high-speed printer came to life. He ripped the message off and scanned it for transmission errors. Since it was not garbled, he handed it to the duty officer who would take it into the Situation Room.

Because Apple Wave messages are concerned with intelligence, the duty officer delivered the message to Bobby Burke, the DCI, who was sitting next to the President.

"Mr. President," Burke said, "the RC-One-thirty-five supporting Trinity has monitored a request for a helicopter escort of a truck convoy leaving the Kirkuk arsenal in three and a half hours. That correlates with the earlier movement of road traffic into the arsenal." He handed the message to Pontowski.

"The logical assumption," Pontowski said, "is that they're moving their nerve gas." His advisers agreed with him to the man. "The question is, Will they use it?"

"I think that's a given, Mr. President," Michael Cagliari, the national security adviser said. "The Israelis are rolling the Arabs up on the Golan Heights and the fighting in Jordan has turned into a rout. Only in Lebanon have the Syrians and Iraqis halted the Israelis. And there's one hell of a battle going on there right now. Unless Ben David throws in reinforcements, it could go either way."

"And we can assume he'll start doing that as he frees up units in Jordan," Admiral Scovill added. "Unless we can get a cease-fire in place quickly, I belive the Arabs will resort to widespread chemical attacks.''

The discussion continued around the table for a few minutes. Burke was highly skeptical about the Arabs resorting to the use of chemical weapons. ''They aren't that suicidal,'' he claimed.

''Consider this,'' the secretary of state said. ''What if the Arabs believe the Israelis will not use nukes now, given the situation in the Kremlin and the fact they're winning? So if the Arabs show their resolve to escalate, a cease-fire may be in the offing.''

''Are you saying that the Arabs may think Ben David's response to a chemical attack will be to agree to a cease-fire?'' Cagliari asked. State did have a way of talking around things.

''It's a possibility,'' the secretary of state replied.

''Don't bet on it,'' Cagliari grumbled. ''I know Ben David.''

The duty officer slipped quietly through the door and handed Cox a note. He read the note and handed it to Pontowski.

''Please''—Pontowski held up his hand—''enough.'' He read the note. ''There are too many unknowns here and we are not sure if all the actors are rational. Our problem is simple: we've got to keep the Iraqis from using their nerve gas before a cease-fire is negotiated. And we've run out of time. There's only one option open now: we destroy the nerve gas before it is moved.''

He stood up, his face drawn and haggard, his seventy-four years weighing heavy on him. Then the inevitability of it all struck at him. Events had driven him down this road with an unrelenting sureness, as if the fates had conspired against him. For a moment he thought of a Greek drama. Is this the price to be paid in a quest for power? he thought. My family? ''We go with Trinity,'' he ordered. ''Transmit the order for an immediate launch and execute.'' He walked out of the room.

The men gaped at each other, surprised by his sudden disappearance. ''That was a note from Melissa,'' Cox explained. ''She asked if he could come to the hospital immediately.''

* * *

Shoshana had lost track of time and the number of runs they had made hauling out wounded. For the two women, the war was confined to a small piece of real estate on the southern end of the valley and they had watched the fighting ebb and flow as the Iraqis would attack, fall back, re-form, and then attack again. Shoshana was sure of only one thing, they were holding on. Time meant nothing and she wasn't sure if the battle had been going on for two or three days. Her world was made up of an APC stinking with diesel fuel, unwashed bodies, and the sickly warm smell of open wounds and antiseptic.

"Over to the left," Hanni said, using her periscope to guide Shoshana to another pickup. They were working their way down a hill, using what terrain masking they could find and hiding in the growing shadows of night. Shoshana mashed the accelerator and urged the APC out of the shallow wadi they were in and over the bank. The nose of the APC was coming back down when Shoshana heard Hanni scream, "Nooo!" The engine compartment next to her exploded. A wave of heat washed over Shoshana and knocked her out of the driver's seat and against the left wall. She was vaguely aware of hands pulling at her, dragging her back into the crew compartment. Then the rear ramp was down and Hanni was half dragging her, half carrying her back into the dry streambed where they had been a moment ago.

"Wha—?" Shoshana was still groggy from the concussion.

"An RPG got us," Hanni said. The rocket-propelled grenade's shape-charged warhead had struck them in the front right corner and the engine compartment had absorbed most of the blast. "I saw it at the last minute, but damn, I can't figure out where it came from." The APC erupted in a violent explosion and they could feel the heat. "We were lucky and took the hit in the engine compartment." Hanni was close to babbling, a way to ease the tension and fear that bound her. "Good thing you were wearing that Nomex jumpsuit underneath your NBC suit. I couldn't believe it, flames shot out of the firewall all over you. I thought for sure you were dead."

Shoshana felt the side of her tanker's helmet. It felt warm through her gloves. She tugged her helmet and gloves off and touched the right side of her neck. Hanni scrambled back down to her and examined her friend's neck. "It looks like a bad sunburn," she said. "Probably the only part of your skin that was exposed."

"I'm okay," Shoshana reassured her. She could feel the warm front zipper of the flight suit against her skin and realized why the flap that had chafed at her had been there. Shoshana wished she hadn't given in to a whim of vanity and cut it off to tie up her hair. She crawled up the low bank in front of her and looked over the edge. The heat from their burning APC made her duck her head. "Did you see one of our APCs down in the valley?" Shoshana asked.

Hanni crawled up beside her and looked over the edge. She could barely see the vehicle in the growing dark. She pulled her head back down. "There's five or six men out there," she whispered. "Arabs."

Now Shoshana looked again. Through the light of the burning APC, she could see four Iraqi soldiers leading two wounded Israeli soldiers. One of the Iraqis gave an order and the men pushed the Israelis to the ground and started shooting. It was over in a moment and Shoshana watched in horror as they bayoneted the bodies. The four men started moving toward the wadi. Shoshana held a finger to her lips and pointed downslope toward the APC they had seen. The two women crawled back down into the wadi and quickly disappeared into the shadows, leaving Shoshana's helmet and gloves behind.

The wadi they were following opened out into a flat area thirty meters from the APC the two women were headed for. Shoshana held her left hand out behind her and made a down motion, telling Hanni to stay back in the shadows. She crouched and ran across the open area, safely reaching the side of the APC. Up close in the dark, she could see that its left track had been blown off, probably by an RPG, she decided, judging from the lack of other damage. Under the scorch marks, she could make out a red cross on the Toga armor. It had been a Band-Aid like theirs. She motioned for Hanni to join her and the woman scampered across the open area, collapsing into the protective shadow of the APC.

Shoshana worked her way to the rear of the APC, again motioning Hanni to stay back. She poked her head around the rear and then pulled back in revulsion. A convulsive gasp wracked her body and she bet over, throwing up, choking. Hanni was beside her, trying to help. Shoshana gasped for air, ''Don't look.''

''What is it, child?'' the older woman murmured and then looked despite the warning. Stretched out in front of her on the ground were the bodies of two Israeli female medics. They had been stripped, staked to the ground, raped, then gutted. Their intestines were spread over their abdomens and flowed between their legs.

A ''My God!'' burst from Hanni followed by a retching sound.

Slowly, they brought their nausea and fears under control. Both had seen the horror, death, and destruction of modern warfare and had learned to live with it. But this was a vicious and senseless torture and mutilation that went far beyond war. For each of them it was a personal battle as they fought for their sanity.

The sounds of movement in the wadi drove them both into silence and they crawled under the APC. The same four soldiers Shoshana had seen murder the two wounded POWs emerged out of the dark and angled away from them, avoiding the APC. ''They know what's here,'' Shoshana whispered and waited until the four men were well out of sight. She crawled out from under the APC and worked her way into the crew compartment. Hanni followed her. ''Don't move them'' Shoshana said, pointing toward the bodies. ''As long as they're out there, the Iraqis will stay away.''

Hanni curled up in a knot on the floor, clasped her legs to her breast and rocked back and forth, still fighting her inner demons. She could hear Shoshana fumbling in the dark. Then the whine of the radio came on as Shoshana found the right switches. Now Hanni could hear the low crackle of the radio and Shoshana's voice. ''Mayday. This is Band-Aid with a Mayday.''

''Copy, Band-Aid.'' It was Levy's voice. ''Say position.'' Shoshana told him where they were. ''Stay where you are,'' he replied, his voice filling them with hope. ''We'll come and get you.'' Hanni stopped her rocking and tears streamed down her cheeks.

Shoshana knelt down and hugged her. ''Now we have to wait. It may be a while. But we've got all night.''

* * *

"The position of the United States is very clear," the minister of foreign affairs was saying. "They are pressing us on all diplomatic fronts to accept the cease-fire."

"I got the message," Ben David rumbled. "It's unacceptable. The interests of the United States are not ours." The prime minister was stalking back and forth in the command bunker's largest conference room. The meeting of the Israeli cabinet about the sudden cut-off of supplies was near its end and the whir of the air conditioner could be heard in the silence. Ben David turned to his cabinet. "How can we stop now, short of a victory that would give our people peace for generations? This may be our last chance to crush our enemies. How else can we justify the sacrifices my people have made?"

"The risks are too high," the minister counseled.

"I know about risks," Ben David snapped. He slapped his hands down on the table. "We continue the war for now." The meeting was over and the men filed out. Only the Ganef and Yuriden stayed behind.

"Then you think that Pontowski is bluffing," the Ganef said.

"I've heard it before," Ben David replied. "He thinks his air force can destroy Iraq's chemical arsenal when our air force has failed? What a fool. We have the best pilots in the world."

"You're believing our own propaganda," Yuriden said. "That's a mistake."

"I don't make mistakes!" Ben David shouted. "And what does he mean when he says, 'I will consider active measures against Israel'? Tell me, what does that mean?"

"Don't use nuclear weapons," the Ganef replied. "The consequences are too high."

"I will use everything in my power to protect my people. No man will take that away from me." Ben David fell silent and he paced the floor. "Two can play this game. We have friends in the United States Congress."

"Listen to yourself," the Ganef said. "Listen to your words. You are sounding like an egomaniac."

"I will protect my people."

"Perhaps," Yuriden said, trying to calm the man, "you can best do that by waiting. Waiting to see if the U.S. can destroy Iraq's chemical arsenal, waiting to see how much farther back we can push the Arabs, waiting to see if we can improve our position.''

The prime minister seemed to accept what Yuriden was saying.

"Sooner or later," the Ganef added, "we will have to accept a cease-fire and negotiate."

Now Ben David sat down, much calmer. "Yes, that's true. I can afford to wait a little longer." As long as the Arabs do not escalate, he thought.

Neither the Ganef nor Yuriden pressed him further on the subject of cease-fires. But both were thinking how desperately they needed one.

The pilots were lined up on both sides of the ready room's center aisle in their proper places when Brigadier General Hussan Mana arrived. He walked down the aisle ignoring the bows of the men and stepped onto the low dais in the front of the room. "Please take your seats," he said. The pilots were more worried than reassured by this kindness. Normally, Mana kept them standing at attention when he spoke to them.

"We have received a communication from Al Mukhabaret," Mana began, as every pilot stiffened at the name of Iraq's Department of General Intelligence, "that the Americans have secretly deployed twelve F-Fifteen Es here." He pointed to a map on the wall behind him and jabbed at the Turkish base at Diyarbakir. "The communication states that the American Eagles will be launched against a target here." He pointed to the nerve gas plant and arsenal outside of Kirkuk. "As you can see, we"—now he pointed to their base at Mosul located between Diyarbakir and Kirkuk—"are in a perfect position to intercept them. Further, Al Mukhabaret is certain that the Americans will launch within the hour and has placed two agents to report their exact takeoff time."

"I didn't know Al Mukhabaret used its spies in foreign countries," Johar Adwan mumbled loud enough for Samir Hamshari to hear.

"There's a first time for everything," Samir mumbled back.

"It is my intention to intercept and destroy them," Mana announced. He stepped aside and let the squadron's first officer go over the plan. It was the same "bearing of aircraft" formation they had flown in the past. Again, Mana would be in the lead. There was nothing in it for Johar and Samir and they were to continue to sit standby alert in the squadron.

The two pilots remained in the ready room while the remainder of their squadron rushed out to man their Su-27s and await the scramble order from ground control. "Can you believe it?" Johar grumbled. "A bearing of aircraft? Has Mana learned nothing?"

"I wouldn't want to take on an Eagle from that formation," Samir replied. "Our aircraft are every bit the equal to the F-Fifteen. Why don't we use them right?"

"I don't know," Johar sighed. "But I am certain about one item: Mana may be many things, but he's no coward."

The air base at Diyarbakir was little more than three hangars and a few low buildings off to one side of the commercial airport. The Turks used it for a forward operating location and to support the nearby American compound. No one knew what the Americans did there, but the massive arrays of antennas, satellite dishes, and radomes indicated it was a communications monitoring site. The only sign of any unusual activity were the twelve F-15Es that had recently landed with their support crews. Four of the dark gray jets were parked between the hangars, almost totally hidden in the heavy shadows, two were parked in the revetted shelter that was originally intended to house alert aircraft, and the other six were inside the hangars.

A sharp-eyed observer outside the perimeter fence scanned the F-15s with high-powered binoculars and noted that each of the jets was loaded with two GBU-24s, one on each wing pylon, four Sidewinder missiles on the shoulder stations above the GBUs, and four AMRAAMs slung under the conformal fuel tanks. The observer also noted that well-armed security teams were hidden in the shadows.

At 0215 hours local, one of the side doors of the middle hangar opened and twelve men walked out. They headed for the waiting jets. The hangar doors rolled back and at 0230 the distinctive, sirenlike wail of the F-15s' jet fuel starters echoed across the ramp as the twelve jets started engines. The first two jets taxied out of the alert revetments at 0235 followed by pairs at thirty-second intervals. The first two jets took the runway and a green light flashed from the tower, clearing them for takeoff. The two jets roared down the runway for a formation takeoff at exactly 0240 as the second set of two taxied into position and held, waiting for the green light that would come thirty seconds later.

The sequence repeated itself until all twelve F-15s had launched. By 0243 the base had reverted to its usual sleepy quiet. Colonel "Mad" Mike Martin, call sign Viper 01, had led the eleven other Vipers of the 45th Tactical Fighter Wing in a "com out" launch and was streaking toward Kirkuk at 540 knots, four hundred feet off the deck. ETA Kirkuk: 0310.

The observer who had been watching the air base started his car, drove to a nearby house, and made a phone call.

The shrill wail of the siren reached the small room in the officers' quarters where Johar was sleeping. He was fully awake when he heard the first bypass turbofan engine of a Su-27 crank, splitting the night air. Johar glanced at his watch: 0251 local time. He sighed, got out of bed, pulled on his flight suit, and walked over to the officers' mess for breakfast. Samir was already there, waiting for him.

The AWACS orbiting ninety nautical miles north of Mosul in the tri-border region of Turkey, Iraq, and Iran monitored the takeoff of eight Su-27s being led by Mana. The tactical controller punched the button that selected the Have Quick radio and tromped on his foot pedal to transmit, warning the ingressing F-15s that interceptors were airborne out of Mosul and moving into a formation. It worried him that the Iraqis had responded so quickly.

Matt's Tactical Electronic Warfare System came alive just as they copied the AWACS warning on the bandits coming at them from Mosul. "I'll be damned," Furry mumbled from the rear. "That's an SA-Three." The chirping on the TEWS audio shifted to a higher beat as the surface-to-air missile went into a launch mode. The SA-3 Goa was an old Soviet-built weapon with a range of eighteen miles. Its radar could track up to six aircraft and launch two missiles at a single target. Neither Matt nor Furry was overly worried about that missile since they were well below its minimum guidance altitude. But like Mad Mike had repeatedly yelled at them, "Always honor the fuckin' threat!"

Martin's voice came over the Have Quick radio. "Matt, nail that SA-Three. I hold him at your two o'clock, twelve miles." He should have used Matt's call sign, Viper 03, but the use of his name over the secure radio prevented confusion. In the heat of battle, it was easy to miss the numbers after a name.

"Roger, boss. Will do." By calling Martin "boss" instead of using his call sign of Viper 01, there was no doubt whom he was talking to. Now another threat popped up on the TEWS. Two SA-6 sites directly ahead of them had become active.

"Sean," Martin ordered his wingman, Leary, "get the one on the left. I'll get the right." As planned, the lead aircraft would engage whatever threat came up to open up a corridor for the ingressing F-15s. By taking out the surface-to-air missile sites, the following aircraft could concentrate on hitting the target and have a safe escape route. The operations plan named Trinity called for the Eagles to open up a corridor twenty miles wide and, for a very brief period, establish air superiority.

Matt pointed the nose of his jet directly at the SA-3 site, double-checked to be sure he had selected a GBU-24 and that the Master Arm switch was up, and looked through the HUD. The Navigation FLIR had penetrated the dark and was showing him a three-dimensional view of the world in eleven shades of gray. He saw the flare of a rocket plume directly in front of him—a SAM missile launch. The bright plume of the SA-3 captured Matt's attention as it corkscrewed off to the right. "Foxed 'em," Furry chuckled from the pit. The TEWS had done its magic and decoyed the missile's guidance system. "Designating," came from the rear. Furry had slued the Target FLIR onto the SAM site and locked it up. Matt mashed the pickle button and held it, waiting for the weapons delivery computer to reach a solution. The F-15 gave a slight shudder as the two-thousand-pound bomb under their left wing separated.

Now Furry concentrated on the Target FLIR and refined the placement of the cross hairs, laying them directly over the Low Blow fire control radar that was the heart of the SA-3. "Lasing," he said. Matt watched the second missile flash by well behind them. Then the target disappeared in a bright explosion. "That's wasting a perfectly good GBU," Furry allowed.

"Honor the threat," Matt grunted.

"I'll make it a rule," Furry answered. Two more explosions flared in front of them as Martin and his wingman worked over the SA-6 sites.

The voice of the tactical controller on the AWACS came over the Have Quick radio. "Viper Zero-One. Eight bandits zero-nine-zero degrees at forty nautical miles. Heading two-three-zero degrees, angels ten, cospeed." The tactical controller had told Martin that Mana's formation was forty nautical miles to the east of him at ten thousand feet and was on a heading that would intercept them. Matt ran the geometry through his head and calculated they would merge twenty-five miles downtrack.

But Martin had other ideas. "Aldo, have you identified the threat?" Aldo was the call sign of the AWACS.

"Checking with Duster now," the AWACS controller answered. Duster was the call sign for the RC-135 Bill Carroll was on. Carroll's job was to monitor the Iraqis' radio nets and try to learn if Mana was airborne. The Americans were going after him, the threat they thought was Joe. "Viper Zero-One," the AWACS controller was back within seconds. "Duster says the lead bandit is your target. KILL. Repeat KILL."

"Roger, Zero-One copies," Martin answered, confirming he was going after Mana. "Sean, go spread." He told his wingman to move into a line-abreast, combat spread position. The lieutenant was going to have his hands full just keeping his lead in sight, so Martin turned his formation and position lights to bright. Martin turned forty degrees to the left, onto a collision course with Mana. "Lead's engaged," he transmitted, telling Matt that he was now leading the attack onto Kirkuk, as planned.

"This is Aldo," the radio spat. "Multiple bandits now launching from Kirkuk." The tactical controller on board the AWACS had detected a second group of fighters launching. The warning had increased Matt's situational awareness and he knew he would have to fight his way into and off the target.

Now Martin and Leary were bearing down onto Mana, approaching from the Iraqi's front right quarter. On the ground, Martin had decided to open the engagement with head-on missile shots and then split to bracket their opponent, if he was still alive. The idea was to get Mana to commit on one of them, who would then become the engaged fighter. The other man would become the free fighter and protect the engaged fighter's back or, depending on circumstances, move in for a sequential attack. Like most things that sound simple, it was hard enough to do in daylight; at night it was almost impossible. But Martin never suffered from a lack of confidence.

Both attacking F-15s were down in the weeds, still four hundred feet off the deck, less than a thousand feet apart, with their radars in standby. They did not want the bandits' radar warning gear to detect them. Martin's wizzo concentrated on the picture he was getting from the Navigation FLIR. When he caught a glimmer of movement, he slued the Target FLIR onto that portion of the sky in front of him. The powerful sensing device broke out the heat signature and the image of a Flanker appeared on his screen. Since the FLIR was totally passive and the bandit would have no indication he was being tracked, the wizzo locked on. "Bandit on the Target FLIR," he told Martin.

Martin punched up the Target FLIR and was now looking at the world through a greenish soda straw. While he had a very narrow field of view, he could clearly make out the oncoming Flanker. His first thought was how much it resembled an F-15. Then he saw a second Flanker behind the first. He recognized a bearing of aircraft when he saw one and his combative instincts drooled with hunger. It was going to be a turkey shoot.

The colonel thumbed the weapons select switch aft; the radar came alive and locked on the nearest target, which was Mana. Martin shoved the switch full forward, which called up an AIM-120 AMRAAM, and hit the pickle button. A missile dropped out of its well underneath the fuselage and streaked toward Mana. Martin fully expected the target to reach and take evasive maneuvers when the pilot saw the missile's plume lighting the night. No reaction. Now Martin had closed to inside nine miles. He moved the weapons select switch to its middle detent and the reassuring growl of a Sidewinder filled his headset. He mashed the pickle button again and a Sidewinder leaped off the left inboard missile rail and homed on the Flanker.

Now Mana had two missiles coming at him and still no reaction. Martin's wingman, Sean Leary, wanted a piece of the action and when he saw Martin launch a Sidewinder, he locked up the second aircraft in line with his radar and repeated the performance, sending first an AMRAAM and then a Sidewinder at the second Su-27. But the lieutenant was overeager and had launched the Sidewinder too early. Unlike Mana, the pilot in the second Flanker had his head out of the cockpit and wasn't listening to the directions from the ground controller. He saw the two missiles coming at him and turned hard left just as Martin's AMRAAM flew under Mana's right wing. It would have been a near miss except that the proximity sensor worked perfectly and the warhead exploded, sending a hail of expanding metal core into the underside of the Flanker.

Mana fought briefly for control as the Flanker jerked to the left, its triple fly-by-wire systems able to handle most of the damage and keep the Flanker flying. But Mana panicked and jerked at his ejection seat handle. Fourteen hundred pounds of rocket thrust kicked Mana and the 450-pound K-36 ejection seat out of the aircraft just as Martin's Sidewinder flew up his Flanker's right tail pipe and exploded.

The pilot in the second Flanker honked back on the stick and climbed, not realizing that Mana was now between him and the missiles Leary had fired at him. Leary's AMRAAM was transitioning from semiactive guidance to full internal guidance when its radar detected the second Flanker climbing. It had no trouble homing on its target.

But Leary's Sidewinder was confused. It had lost the heat signature it was homing on and had gone into memory mode. Then its seeker head caught the heat signature from the rocket in Mana's ejection seat and homed on that. Mana never saw the missile that killed him.

As briefed, the two F-15s blew through the oncoming line of Flankers, shattering what was left of the formation's integrity as the colonel nailed his second Flanker with a Sidewinder. The Iraqi ground controller was screaming at the Flankers to maintain their bearing of aircraft so he could guide the remaining five Su-27s into an envelope where they could fire their weapons. But Martin and Leary had no intention of fighting that leisurely an engagement. What the Iraqis were doing worked well against unarmed airliners and possibly against bombers, but never against a fighter, especially one like the F-15E in the hands of a pilot who knew how to use it. It never dawned on the Iraqi radar controller that the Flanker pilots were scrambling for their lives.

Martin was surprised when his wizzo called out, "Bandit at seven o'clock, two miles, on us." He twisted his head around to the left and could barely make out the plan form of a Flanker converting to their six. He saw a missile fire and home on him. It had to be either an AA-11 or AA-8, the two short-range dogfight missiles with passive infrared guidance the Flanker could carry. "Flares and chaff," the wizzo said as he sent a stream of flares and chaff into their wake.

Instinctively, Martin pulled into a very tight oblique loop to reverse onto his attacker. All the time, he kept his eyes "padlocked" on the Flanker, evaluating the situation. By turning his tail pipes away from the missile, the guidance head lost its heat source and homed on the flares. But how had the Flanker found him when his TEWS had not warned them of a radar tracking them? He didn't consciously work the problem; the answer was just there. He had made a mistake. His left hand dropped off the throttles and, without looking, he turned his formation and position lights off, reached back for the throttles and selected guns.

The attacking Flanker pilot momentarily froze when the lights he had been following went out and the dark gray F-15 disappeared, blending with the night. For a fraction of a moment, he rolled out while he tried to reacquire the target. Then he hardened up his turn again, turning in the same direction as before, still looking for the fighter he knew was out there. In desperation, he turned on his radar. But his nose was not pointed within sixty degrees of Martin and he came up dry. Now his own radar warning gear was screaming at him, telling the Iraqi that he was being tracked by a fighter that was behind him. He twisted around to his left in time to see what looked like a solid line of tracers reaching for him. Martin had selected high rate of fire for his gatling gun and squeezed off a short burst. Only every seventh bullet was a tracer, but at six thousand rounds a minute rate of fire, it looked like an unbroken line of red. Nine rounds of 20-

millimeter high-explosive ammunition walked through the Flanker's cockpit.

There was no elation in Martin as he came off his third kill. He would celebrate later. His voice was all business when he called Leary for a fuel check and to join up on him. He headed for a low-level orbit point they had selected to wait for his next engagement. "Damn," he muttered to himself. "That was too easy." He knew that "Joe" was still out there.

Matt had copied the second bandit warning from the AWACS and decided that it was too early to react to that threat. They were still ninety nautical miles out and Furry was having a problem in the pit. The ring laser gyro that drove their inertial navigation system was advertised to be accurate within .8 of a mile per hour and normally was much better than that. But they had been airborne less than fifteen minutes, and when he visually fixed their position by map reading, he discovered they were over three miles from where the moving map on the Tactical Situation Display said they were. "Problems," he told Matt. "I need to make a map and update our position."

"Do it," Matt said. He worried that the Iraqis might detect their radar when it came out of standby, but he knew Furry. The wizzo wouldn't have even mentioned it unless it was absolutely necessary. Because the two men had flown together so long, they were a tightly welded team with an absolute trust in each other. Matt glanced at the radar video as it came active and waited for Furry to make a patch map. He kept his head up, looking through the HUD, using the Nav FLIR to penetrate the night. He heard Furry count down as the system froze the map to work on later. When Furry said "Done," Matt took control of the radar and swept the horizon for the second group of bandits. He came up dry and Furry returned them to silent running. "Where the hell are they?" he muttered.

"Ask Aldo," Furry grunted.

Matt keyed his radio and queried the AWACS. "Aldo, say position of bandits over Kirkuk."

"Aircraft calling Aldo," the AWACS replied, "say call sign."

"Viper Zero-Three," Matt answered, wondering who in the hell else they thought would be transmitting on a Have

Quick radio net. The Israelis would have never wasted time with call signs and would have recognized his voice.

"Roger, Viper Zero-Three. Be advised that bandits are still launching out of Kirkuk and being vectored to the west, well clear of you. Ah, stand by."

What the hell, Matt thought, I'm eight minutes out and they're telling me to stand by!

"Viper Zero-Three." The AWACS was back on frequency. The tactical controller had been receiving new information from Duster, the orbiting RC-135 that was monitoring Iraqi communications. "The bandits are being vectored to a holding orbit thirty-five miles southwest of target. Two bandits are now being vectored onto you, bearing one-six-zero, seventy nautical miles, heading zero-two-five."

Both Martin and Furry mentally ran the geometry of the developing intercept and where they would merge with the bandits. Thanks to the AWACS and RC-135, their situational awareness had increased a hundredfold. Now the TEWS started to light up with the first tickles of a search radar. Another symbol appeared on the video display—a Gadfly SAM. It was directly in front of them, next to their target.

"Holy shit!" Furry yelled. "They're going to jump us just before we get in range of the Gadflies around Kirkuk."

Time to find out how good the air defense pukes are at separating us from their scumbags, Matt thought. And time to change plans, he added. "Doc, Wedge," he transmitted, calling Viper 05 and 06. "Cleared in hot on the bandits." A cool "Roger" answered him and the two F-15Es behind him shoved their throttles into Mil power and turned toward the two bandits that Aldo had identified. "Boss," Matt radioed, "say position."

"Chasing Flankers to the north," Martin answered, his voice cool and matter-of-fact. "We'll keep them off your back." He and Leary had become separated and were jumping any stray Flanker they could find. The ground controllers directing the Iraqis couldn't keep up with the rapidly changing fight as the two F-15s effectively kept the Su-27s occupied.

Matt concentrated on his attack run. "Skid," he called his wingman, "take the lead, we'll lase. Ripple two." Matt had told his wingman to lead the attack and pickle both his bombs on the first pass. Matt would take spacing and follow on the opposite arm of the *B'nai* attack and do the lasing. ''Then get the hell out of Dodge,'' he ordered.

''Roger, copy all,'' Skid answered.

''Sounds good,'' Martin's voice said.

My God! Matt thought. How can he keep what he's doing sorted out and still pay attention to what's going on down here?

The two fighters started their run in. The TEWS scope was a mass of symbols and the audio was deafening him with chirps and wails. He turned the audio off and would rely on Furry to do his job. Now he could clearly see the compound housing the nerve gas plant and storage bunkers on the Nav FLIR. Furry worked the Target FLIR and told him, ''Target identified.'' It amazed Matt how familiar the target complex looked.

Sweat poured off him as he concentrated on the run. A string of tracers from a ZSU-23-4 arched across the sky in front of him. He heard himself breathing hard. ''Piece of cake,'' Furry said, his voice rapid and high-pitched. More tracers crisscrossed in front of him and he saw the bright flash of two Gadflies launching. Now Matt ''paddled'' off the autopilot and hand-flew the jet as they swung in on their side of the pincers.

Then: ''Bombs gone.'' It was Skid coolly announcing that he had gotten his bombs off onto their target, the main production plant. Matt had lost sight of him when they split up for the attack and it was reassuring to hear from him.

A Gadfly exploded, lighting the sky. In the bright flash, Matt could see Skid escaping underneath the fireball and more tracers reaching toward him. The second Gadfly exploded, but this time, there was no trace of his wingman.

''Lasing,'' Furry shouted. Matt was concentrating on the Nav FLIR, using it to fly around the target. It was a good run and all systems were working perfectly. A Gadfly streaked by less than a hundred feet above the canopy. For some reason, its proximity fuse didn't work and the missile went ballistic.

The plant erupted in an explosion as the first bomb hit within inches of where Furry had laid the laser. The bombs were fuse-delayed and the first one penetrated to the first basement before it exploded. The second bomb flew right through the explosion and burrowed through to the third basement, burying itself in four feet of concrete before it exploded. The labs and test chamber where the nerve gas had been developed disappeared in a fiery blast. But the scientists who had given Iraq the deadly weapon had been paid off long before and were safe in their homes in Europe and China. Only two technicians were on duty. A series of secondary explosions turned the plant into an inferno and flames belched and mushroomed over three hundred feet into the air.

Furry shouted, "GO!" as a wall of tracers mushroomed in front of the F-15. Matt broke hard left, still below a hundred feet. He flew around a radio tower and headed for safety as Viper 07 and 08 hit the first of the storage bunkers.

Then it was all behind them and Matt became aware of the chatter over the radios. He had effectively tuned it out. Still, he had been conscious of what was going on around him throughout the attack. It was called situational awareness. He reengaged the autopilot and coupled it to the TFR. He checked his fuel and ran a cockpit check, making sure they had not taken battle damage. Then it hit him, the simulator rides the Gruesome Twosome had put them through had been worse.

"Skid," Matt radioed, "say position."

"North of target," his wingman replied, his words staccato-quick. "Heading for home plate. Battle damage. Took a hit after we pickled. ZSU-Twenty-three."

"Need help?" Matt queried.

"Negative, I can handle it. This bird's a tank."

Matt hit the transmit button and called the AWACS. "Aldo, any trade?" He was asking if there was a bandit in the area he could engage.

"Negative Zero-Three," Aldo replied. "Are you continuing to your second target?"

"Affirmative," Matt answered. They headed to the northwest and Mosul.

Martin's voice came over the radio. "Sean, say position." There was no reply. "Aldo, do you have a paint on Viper Zero-Two?" Martin asked.

"Affirmative," the AWACS replied. "Viper Zero-Two is returning to base, com out." Martin relaxed—Leary was simply having radio problems and hightailing it back to Diyarbakir.

The second part of Trinity called for Matt to drop any

remaining GBU-24s on the air base at Mosul as he egressed. Other Vipers would do the same or hit the air base at Kirkuk. Since Mosul was a secondary target, they would use the great glide capability of the GBU-24, stand off from the base, toss the bomb, and lase as best they could. But they would not press in like they had on the nerve gas plant.

Furry took control of the radar and made another patch map to update their position. Then he checked his systems for battle damage. "Damn," he muttered, "I don't believe it." The TEWS had gone strangely quiet and was only detecting the periodic sweep of a search radar. "The SAMs, the triple A, have gone off the air," he explained.

"They're still out there," Matt answered. "Probably got their radars in standby and will bring them up when they get a visual. I don't like it." An inner alarm bell was going off, warning him that the Iraqis were using a new tactic. "Amb, radar delivery only on this one. Toss the damn bomb as far out as we can. It's time to get the hell out of Dodge while we still can."

"Roger," Furry answered. He went to work using the high-volume radar and computer. While he updated their position again, Matt set them up for an air-to-ground radar delivery. After he had updated their nav system, Furry placed the radar cursors over the base, which was now inside thirty nautical miles. "Going for the runway," he said. He refined the cursor placement. Then: "Designating." Matt stroked the throttles and pushed them up to just below the Mach. They were a well-trained team.

Matt's inner alarm bell was now gonging at him. He paddled off the autopilot when they closed to inside twenty nautical miles. "It doesn't feel right," he mumbled, primed to react at the first hint of trouble.

"Ready, ready," Furry said as they bore down on the release point where the system would automatically release the bomb. Matt mashed the pickle button and held it.

The TEWS erupted with symbols and its audio went wild just as they felt the bomb separate from the right pylon. The night exploded with tracers, engulfing them. "SAM three o'clock!" Furry yelled. But Matt had already seen it and jerked the big fighter into a tight turn barely a hundred feet above the ground, bringing the missile to his nose. Tracers were now passing directly in front of them. Matt brought the nose up and watched the SAM commit on his upward vector, hoping the tracers would pass underneath him. Then he wrenched the Eagle into a hard downward turn, leveling off at seventy-five feet. His heart pounded as he saw the missile follow him, and for a fraction of a moment, he knew he was dead. But the missile could not follow him through the turn at such a close range and broached sideways before it tumbled onto the ground. He concentrated on the HUD, relying on the Nav FLIR to give him the visual clues he needed to fly so close to the ground at night, and escape to safety. Only that strange sixth sense had kept them alive.

"Goddamn flak trap!" Furry shouted, venting the intense pressure of the short engagement. "No radar warning on that bastard. Probably an SA-Nine."

Great, Matt thought, they're backing up Gadflies and the ZSUs with SA-9s. The SA-9 was a short-range SAM that used passive infrared guidance and was reported to be effective below a hundred feet. He keyed his radio, "Viper flight, secondary targets are flak traps. RTB. Repeat, RTB."

"Border in nine minutes," Furry said, getting back to business.

When they crossed into Turkey, the tension from the mission started to shred. Both men could feel it wash off them as they climbed to twelve thousand feet for the last sixty miles to Diyarbakir. Matt jotted a few notes down on his knee pad as he thought of them. "Hey, Amb, what was all this shit over Kirkuk about it being a piece of cake?"

"I lied," Furry answered.

26

Johar and Samir were standing outside the entrance to the squadron watching the remnants of their squadron recover. "I can't believe it," Samir said, his eyes glued to the wall of flames and smoke on the runway. "One bomb did all that."

The lone GBU-24 had hit the runway at the halfway mark, blasting a deep crater thirty feet across. Frag from the bomb had reached out over a half mile, killing people and destroying trucks caught in the open. Two Flankers had also died in the blast. One was rolling out after touching down and its tail had been blown off before it exploded. The other Flanker had been on short final and had taken the full force of the blast head-on and had pitched into the ground, spreading wreckage and burning fuel along two thousand feet of runway.

The two Iraqi pilots were silent as a Flanker touched down on the unpaved surface that paralleled the main runway. They dissected the landing with a professional eye, appreciating the Soviets' near-fanatical obsession with designing aircraft that could take off and land from poor surfaces. "That's the last one," Johar said. "I didn't see Mana land. Think he bought it?" Samir shrugged. Neither felt any great sense of loss.

Samir couldn't take his eyes off the flaming runway and the wreckage of the two Flankers. "You think they've got some new type of smart bomb?"

"Maybe," Johar allowed. "Or it was a golden BB." A hard edge clipped his words. The two pilots incinerated on the runway had been his friends. "Only two made it back," he said. His eyes squinted and his jaw hardened as a burning desire for revenge consumed him. He wanted to even the score.

When the crews had finished debriefing intelligence, they straggled into the office at the back of the hangar at Diyarbakir that had been turned into a makeshift command post. Most of them sat on the floor against the wall and drank Cokes or coffee while Martin paced the floor like a caged tiger. One of the radio operators in the next room looked around the corner and told him that Duster, the RC-135, was coming in to land. "It must be important if it's landing here," the colonel mumbled. He ordered the security team that had deployed with them out of Stonewood to establish a perimeter guard around the highly classified aircraft when it parked.

"What the hell is going on?" Martin barked. "That was a fuckin' milk run." Matt shot Furry a look, wondering how the veteran wizzo would react to that pronouncement. Furry's face was impassive.

"If that was a milk run," one of the pilots mumbled, "I don't want to see the real thing." Matt agreed with him. The mission had been much tougher than the attack he and Furry had flown against the Syrian First Army in Lebanon. The Iraqis had learned much from the Kuwait war.

"Okay," Martin said, "let's get to it." For the next few minutes, they recaptured the mission, discussing results and what had gone wrong. It looked like they had hit and destroyed the nerve gas facility as planned. "Let's hope the recce pukes confirm the BDA you're claiming," Martin said. He knew how overenthusiastic crews could be in reporting bomb damage assessment. "Fumble Nuts"—he turned to Matt—"did you get a bomb on Mosul?" Matt told him yes, but that the results were unknown. Then he described the flak trap he and Furry had run into as they approached the base. Martin was nodding his head.

"Calling off the secondary attacks was a good decision," he said. "Obviously, they've got a damn good ground observer net around their air bases. SA-Nines are a perfect complement to the Gadfly—gives them low-altitude coverage. They've got their act together."

A very confident Sean Leary related how his Have Quick radio went "tits up" in the middle of an engagement at the exact moment he hosed down a Flanker. For a moment, he thought he had taken battle damage but it was a system malfunction. His crew chief had cannibalized a good black box out of Skid's badly damaged F-15 and Leary was ready to go again. Skid's F-15 wasn't going to be flying for a long time.

The major running the maintenance team came into the command post. He told them that two other jets had taken battle damage and would be out of commission for a few days. The remaining nine aircraft were turned and ready for the hop back to Stonewood. "Who told you we were finished here?" Martin barked. "Find out what type of ordnance is available here." The crews sat in shocked silence as the major beat a hasty retreat.

"Sir"—it was the command post controller—"Duster is landing now." Martin gestured at Matt and Furry to follow him and stomped out of the room.

"Shit-oh-dear," Furry said, sotto voce for the crews to hear, "his fangs are still out."

Bill Carroll was standing in the open crew entrance of the

RC-135 when the three officers reached the ramp. He yelled at one of the security guards who always flew on the aircraft to let them board. The guard checked their line badges and escorted them past the rope that had been strung around the recce bird. Carroll led them back through the maze of equipment racks and stations to a small open area near a buffet where meals could be heated. The mission commander, the colonel in charge of the technicians, joined them.

"Bad news," Carroll said. "A truck convoy escaped before you hit the arsenal."

"Why didn't the AWACS detect the traffic like they did when the trucks went into the arsenal?" Matt asked. "We could have gone after them."

The mission commander shook his head. "They had optimized their radar to detect aircraft and had turned the moving target indicator up to sixty miles an hour to reject any stationary or slow-moving returns. They're painting the traffic now." He produced a map that showed the convoy's location on a highway ninety miles southwest of Kirkuk. "At least twenty-five trucks, all westbound. Be sure they're hauling nerve gas." The colonel couldn't tell them that the RC-135 had monitored ground communications that reported the nerve gas was on the way.

The pieces started to fit for Matt. "So that's why the bandits out of Kirkuk were holding thirty-five miles southwest of Kirkuk—they were in a CAP to protect the convoy."

"That fits with the radio traffic we monitored," Carroll added.

Martin grabbed the mission commander's map and stared at it. "What's this?" He poked at a spot on the map sixty miles in front of the convoy.

"A ferry crossing over the Euphrates River," Carroll explained. "The convoy should reach there in about an hour and forty-five minutes."

Martin erupted with orders. "Matt, you and Furry work out an attack on that convoy, try to take out the ferry and back 'em up on the eastern side of the river. Make it look like we're going back after the arsenal. But that's a feint to open up the corridor. Use some of the jets strictly for air-to-air and nail any raghead that takes off from Mosul or Kirkuk. Colonel, you and Carroll are going to have to work wonders and convince the clueless wonders in the Puzzle Palace that we need a go for a reattack. We ain't got a hell of a lota time."

"I'll try, Mike, I'll try." Both colonels knew how slow the wheels of command could turn.

Martin stared at them for a moment. "Give it your best shot. We've got to be airborne in seventy-five minutes to catch 'em before they cross the river. I've got to find us some bombs and kick Maintenance's ass to get 'em uploaded." Then he was out of the aircraft, running.

"Time is of the essence," National Security Adviser Cagliari was saying, pointing out the obvious to the men in the White House's Situation Room. "We must destroy that convoy before it crosses the Euphrates River."

Only Bobby Burke, the DCI, was not convinced. "Mr. President, we've taken out the nerve gas facility. Now is the time to wait for Iraq's reaction. We may have well accomplished our objective. And we can't be sure that those trucks are transporting nerve gas."

Pontowski leaned back in his chair, thinking. Burke was always the cautious one. Time to listen to the other side. "General Cox, your views."

The general rose and walked to the map on the wall in front of the President. He pointed to the ferry crossing. "Once across the Euphrates, they are still four hundred miles away from the fighting. It doesn't make sense for them to convoy. They should be using airlift." Then the general's eyes fixed on Al Sahra Air Base located twenty miles south of where the Iraqis had established their CAP to protect the escaping trucks. "Oh my God," he whispered. "Sir, there's a damn good chance some of those trucks may have gone here," he jabbed at Al Sahra, "for airlift. Maybe the AWACS has monitored something. Let me get in contact with them."

"Go ahead," Pontowski said. Cox hurried into the communications room next door to talk directly to Aldo via satellite communications.

"Sir"—it was Burke—"we're starting to chase ghosts here. We need to wait for hard intelligence. Also, we must take the Soviets' reaction into account. I'm certain that the hardliners inside the Kremlin are going to come out on top. It's going to be the cold war all over again if Marshal Stenilov and his thugs win."

"Do you think so?" Pontowski said. "I wonder . . ."

The light on the telepanel in front of Cagliari blinked. He picked up the phone and listened before handing it to Pontowski. "Sir, it's Melissa, from the hospital . . ." The President took the phone and listened. He thanked the woman and handed the phone back to Cagliari as Cox returned.

"The AWACS has been monitoring a great deal of activity around Al Sahra," Cox told them. "Two aircraft landed a few minutes ago. Trucks are still on the highway headed for the ferry."

Pontowski stared at the wall map and then slowly pushed himself to his feet. "Order the Forty-fifth to attack the convoy and the air base. Please tell my helicopter to stand by, I'm returning to the hospital." He walked out of the room.

Bobby Burke slammed his fists on the table in frustration and glared at Cox. A week ago, Cox had been subordinate to him in the intelligence chain, and now the President was listening to Cox and not him. He didn't like the invasion of his bureaucratic turf.

The Turkish colonel in command of Diyarbakir was standing nose to nose with Martin outside the only weapons storage igloo on the base. "Colonel Martin," the Turkish colonel said, "I cannot release our weapons to you without an order from my general."

"Then wake him and get it," Martin said.

"But then he would have to call his general." The Turk smiled. Over his shoulder, Martin could see activity going on inside the igloo. Turkish soldiers were doing a quick inventory to make sure all the weapons were accounted for. "As I said before, I cannot help you." He barked some commands in Turkish and the lights went out in the igloo and the soldiers came out, locking the heavy double doors behind them. More shouting and orders and the Turks were gone in a cloud of dust.

"Damn," Martin raged to himself, "I should have thought to ferry in more weapons on the C-One-forty-ones." Martin's concept of operations had been to go in lean and mean and let the F-15s ferry in the weapons that they would use on the raid.

"Colonel," the major from Maintenance said, pointing to the side of the igloo, "in the shadows."

"I'll be damned." Martin grinned. Sitting beside the igloo were six weapons trailers, each holding four 500-pound bombs.

The major ran over to the trailers and examined the bombs with a flashlight. "Snakeyes," he announced. "Complete with fuses." He pointed to the small boxes sitting on each trailer. He spoke into his hand-held radio, calling for vehicles to come and tow the trailers to the flight line. "We can pull one ourselves," he yelled, jumping into his pickup truck and starting the engine.

"Snakeyes are better than nothing," Martin allowed, making a mental promise to return the favor if he could. The Turkish colonel had indeed helped them. But he had to do it the Turkish way.

Matt and Carroll were waiting for Martin when he pulled up in front of the hangar with his load of bombs. "We got a go," Matt said.

"Shit hot!" Martin shouted.

"There's more," Matt explained. "They want us to hit the airfield at Al Sahra." The colonel huddled with the two men while they explained the order that had been relayed to the RC-135.

Martin checked his watch. "Get everyone in here," he yelled. "We got to start launching in forty minutes." He paced up and down for a few moments. "Matt, figure out how to hit Al Sahra with two jets, one with six Snakeyes." The colonel paced back and forth. "Maintenance," he barked. "Upload the Snakeyes on four birds, six each, instantaneous fusing. I want the first two ready to launch in thirty minutes, the second two in forty."

"Colonel," Matt interrupted. "Three of our jets recovered with six GBU-Twenty-fours. Can I use them?"

"You got one bird with two GBUs," Martin answered. "Leary's on your wing." The crews were all assembled now. "Okay, Meatheads," Martin began. "We're going back in, so listen up . . ." For the next twenty minutes, he and Matt laid out the attack. No one asked questions, but they all understood exactly what was expected of them when they broke and ran for their jets. Martin checked his watch; it was 0509 hours. They were going to make it.

* * *

"Shoshana, wake up," Hanni whispered, shaking the sleeping woman. Shoshana shook her head and sat up, stiff from sleeping on the cold floor of the APC they were hiding in. A sickly-sweet odor assaulted her from the two bodies still lying outside on their grotesque deathbeds. "Shush," Hanni cautioned. "I hear movement."

The faint sounds of tracked vehicles moving in the valley drifted over the night air. "We're still okay," Shoshana said. "Time to check in." She worked her way forward to the driver's compartment and fumbled at the switches in the dark. The radio came to life with a faint hum. She listened for a few minutes, changing frequencies, not hearing a thing. "Must be maintaining radio silence," she said and selected an emergency frequency. "This is Band-Aid with a radio check," she transmitted. Two distinct clicks answered her. "Standing by for instructions," she radioed. Two more clicks. "They don't want to talk to us," she told Hanni. "Maybe it's time we try to make it back on our own." She checked her watch. "We've still got thirty more minutes of dark."

"Levy said he would come and get us," Hanni reminded her. They could now hear the clanking of tanks moving toward them, much closer. Hanni froze in terror, her mouth open.

The shrill whistle of friendly artillery passing overhead shattered the fear that bound Hanni and she threw herself onto the floor next to Shoshana, clasping her helmet to her head. The barrage increased its tempo and the APC shook as round after round reached over them, pounding at the advancing Iraqi tanks. "They must know we're here," Shoshana shouted.

The shelling halted as abruptly as it had started and they could hear the loud rumble of jets. Shoshana stood and looked out the periscope mounted in the top hatch. "They're ours," she announced. She scanned the valley and watched the second phase of a coordinated counterattack. Israeli jets were popping over the southern and eastern ridge for quick runs on the tanks. At the same time, TOW missiles were picking off the lead tanks. Still, the Iraqis came at them. The fires billowing from destroyed tanks and BMPs cast an eerie glow, illuminating the fresh carnage.

The distinctive crack-boom of Israel 105-millimeter tank-mounted guns echoed as the hills on the western side of the

valley flickered with muzzle flashes. Farther north, two Israeli F-4s were working over still more tanks and BMPs at
that end of the valley. Shoshana gasped, at last able to see
the size of the attack. The valley was filled with tanks and
BMPs, all moving southward, taking their losses, pressing
forward. More artillery rounds pounded at the tanks and they
could hear Iraqi counterbattery fire reaching over them, rang-
ing for the Israeli gun emplacements.

"We're going to have to run . . ." Shoshana's shout was
cut off by a loud explosion—a near miss from an Iraqi
122-millimeter howitzer. Two more rounds impacted, but
were walking away from their position.

"What's happening!" Hanni screamed, mind-paralyzing
terror capturing her again. Shoshana wouldn't tell her that it
was a major attack that Levy's small battalion could not possibly stop. Again she swept the area around her through the
periscope, trying to find the best direction to run. Now movement on the western side of the valley caught her attention
as Iraqi tanks swung away from the main line of advance and
turned toward the Israeli defenders on their right flank. The
APC's radio now came alive as Levy ordered his tanks to
sortie forward.

Shoshana counted three Merkava tanks that burst over the
western ridge and charged down the slope toward the advancing Iraqi tanks. Two APCs were in the protective shadow
of the V, moving with the tanks. An Iraqi tank burst into
flames, falling victim to the first shot from the lead Merkava.
Then more tanks broke from their hides, revealing a flank
attack in force. Shoshana knew that every tank Levy Force
had was engaged. Then it came to her why no one had answered her radio call—Levy was maintaining radio silence as
he repositioned the battalion under the cover of darkness and
before the attack started.

Two M60 tanks supported by a Hummer mounting a TOW
and an APC broke over the ridgeline and headed for them.
The Israeli tanks cut across the advancing Iraqis at an angle,
their main guns firing with deadly accuracy. The APC took
a hit and skidded to a halt. The second tank spun on its tracks
and went back to help. Shoshana watched in horror as a
T-72 seemed to fire almost point-blank into the lead M60 at
less than five hundred meters. The side of the M60 spewed
fire and sparks, but the tank didn't stop. The Israeli "Blazer"

reactive armor had blunted the Iraqi's round. The M60 turret traversed and fired a round. The Iraqi tank took a direct hit and slued to a halt. The T-72's commander's hatch flopped open and a figure bailed out. A burst of machine-gun fire from the M60 dropped the man.

The lead tank and the Hummer kept coming. The Hummer disappeared into a depression and stopped. Only its TOW missile was showing. Now the tank was almost to them. Hanni and Shoshana were out of the APC and running for it. The tank slowed but did not stop as its main gun fired again. Shoshana leaped on the front of the oncoming tank, her left hand grabbing the protective bracket that framed the right headlight and her feet scrambling against the front plate. Her left foot caught on a tow ring and she reached back with her right hand and grabbed Hanni to pull the much smaller woman aboard. The tank rocked with a recoil as the main gun fired again.

Hanni slipped and fell down in front of the still-moving tank. Shoshana tried to hold on but felt the woman slip from her grasp.

The tank jerked to the left and accelerated straight ahead, almost throwing Shoshana off, running over Hanni. Shoshana held on to the headlight bracket with both hands as her foot slipped off the tow ring. Her feet were dragging on the ground as the tank slued around to the right, both its main gun and machine gun firing. Shoshana saw an Iraqi tank flare. It was less than three hundred meters away. The M60 kept turning and now she would see Hanni lying on the ground. Shoshana's spirits soared when Hanni leaped up and ran for the tank. The driver had seen Hanni fall and centered up, driving the tank right over the woman. Now he was coming back for a pickup.

A burst of machine-gun fire from a BMP raked across Hanni as the M60's main gun fired, killing the BMP. Hanni was down again, this time not moving. The tank stopped momentarily and Shoshana leaped off, running for her. The tank was circling them, firing round after round.

Hanni was dead. Two rounds from the machine gun had struck her in the chest, ripping her apart. A third had glanced off the left side of her helmet, shattering the earpiece. Shoshana didn't want to believe she had lost her friend, the gentle woman who meant so much to her. Tenderly, she pulled her helmet off and held Hanni to her. Tears streamed down her cheeks.

She was vaguely aware that the tank had stopped. Its gun fired and the hatch on top of the cupola popped open. A man stuck his head out. "Come," was all he said, not loud, but commanding and urgent. It was Levy. In a daze, Shoshana gently laid Hanni down, and stumbled to the tank, not even aware she was still clutching her friend's helmet. "Hurry," Levy said. She moved faster and climbed up the side of the tank, over the tracks. The tank was moving as Levy dropped back into the turret. Shoshana followed him down the loader's hatch.

The colonel sat behind Mana's desk, enjoying the power and privileges that went with it. He hoped that his sudden elevation to command of the base at Mosul was not temporary. He picked up the ornate letter opener and fingered it, admiring the gold filigree on the handle. He stared at the two pilots standing in front of him. "Why should I countermand one of General Mana's last orders?" he asked. "He placed you on standby alert for good reasons. I only have five Cobras left and now you are asking for me to trust you." He jabbed the tip of the letter opener into the desk. "I'm not a fool!"

"Sir!" Johar barked. "Permission to speak." The colonel nodded. "Please remember that we were the two pilots fortunate enough to have downed the Israeli F-Sixteens." The colonel glared at them. He didn't want to deal with the truth of that matter. "As you know," Johar plunged on, "that was due to General Mana's superb leadership and airmanship. It was entirely proper that he received credit for the kills and it was Allah's will that Samir and I were the instruments of his wrath. Perhaps, with your leadership, Allah would so bless us again." Johar fell silent, waiting for the colonel's reaction.

The colonel considered what the lieutenant was offering. If he would allow them to fly, he would get the credit for any kills. And that might earn him permanent command of the base. But why were the two lieutenants so anxious to fly? The Americans had proven themselves to be most dangerous and he personally did not want to have to engage an F-15. What was in it for the lieutenants? After all, they were nobodies.

"Why are you so anxious to fly?" the colonel asked.

"Revenge," Johar said. The cold look on his face made the colonel believe him.

The phone rang and the colonel picked it up. He listened to the short message and slammed it down. "The Americans are reported taking off again. They are loaded with bombs." He stared at Johar and Samir, coming to a decision. "You will fly as number four and five."

The two lieutenants gave the colonel the bow normally reserved for generals and followed him out of the office.

27

The chain of people were passing 105-millimeter shells up the side of the tank while Halaby worked the hand pump of a refueling bladder, topping up the fuel cells. Shoshana was on top of the turret, handing the shells to Avner who would stuff them into the gray aluminum storage racks that lined the turret. "I wish we had more Imis," Avner grumbled.

"SHUT up, Avner," Bielski said. "We were lucky to have gotten these."

The remnants of the battalion were re-forming in a riverine valley that fed into the main valley where the Iraqis were attacking. Somehow, they had fought their way to safety and were redistributing ammunition while Levy tried to regroup his battalion.

Then they were finished and ready to move again. Shoshana sat on the fender and carved at the side of Hanni's helmet, cutting away the jagged edges of the earpiece so she could wear it inside the tank. She had banged her head numerous times during the last wild ride out of the valley and didn't want to repeat the experience. She tugged the helmet on but it was too small to fit over her heavy mass of hair. Disgusted with her vanity, she pulled a pair of surgical scissors she carried in the pencil pocket on her left arm and hacked at her hair. She felt better when she threw the last of her heavy tresses to the ground. "I should've done that years ago," she muttered, feeling better. So much of her past was cut away with her hair.

Levy was finished talking on the radio and motioned for the tank commanders from the seven remaining tanks to huddle up on him. "It's not good," he told them. "We're cut off here." He pointed to the spot on his map where they were hidden. "The Iraqis spearheaded a major attack right down the valley and overran our old position. Northern Command is bringing reinforcements up but the situation is extremely critical. We've been ordered to counterattack and slow them down."

"What the hell with?" one of the tank commanders grumbled. "We've got eight tanks and six APCs"—he waved his hand to the west—"and no artillery and no air."

"The Iraqis are hurting bad too," Levy said. "We don't have a choice. We've got to keep the pressure on until we can be reinforced."

"How do you plan to do that?" the same tank commander asked.

"By breaking out," Levy answered. "We cross the valley again and head for the coast. We make it a running battle." He sketched the axis of attack on his map and their objective. He deliberately folded the map.

"You must be feeling lucky today," the tank commander said. "Well, let's do it." There was resignation in his voice.

Shoshana tried on Hanni's helmet. It fit. Well, she thought, Matt's flight suit and now Hanni's helmet. My friends still help me. The thought reassured her. And there really was Levy's Luck.

Mad Mike Martin was in his element, doing what he had trained for his entire career—leading fighters into combat with a chance to take on a truly good adversary flying a plane equal to his own. He had elected to fly single-ship armed only with four AMRAAMs, four Sidewinders, and 940 rounds of 20-millimeter high-explosive ammunition. He would fly a one-man CAP so the eight F-15s following him in flights of two could go after the targets. The AWACS was feeding him information over the Have Quick radio and he was confident he could do a "hit-and-run" on any bandits that got in their way.

He didn't have to wait long. "Viper Zero-One," the AWACS transmitted, "five bandits airborne out of Mosul. Duster reports Kirkuk on a hold for launch. Bandits now zero-nine-zero degrees at sixty nautical miles from your position. Angels eighteen." Martin made a mental note to get on the tactical controller's case for being too wordy.

"Aldo," Martin replied, "say bandit's formation."

"Three are in a bearing of aircraft," the tactical controller answered. "Two are one mile in trail flying line abreast. Ah, stand by." A moment later, he was back. "Viper, those two trailers are below five hundred feet." His voice was full of disbelief.

Martin's jaw hardened—it was what he wanted to hear. The earlier kills had been too easy and whoever he and Leary had stuffed had not been "Joe." "Gotcha," Martin said for his backseater to hear. "Aldo," he transmitted, "the two trailers are the threat, don't lose 'em. I'm engaged." With that he put the five bandits on his nose. "Okay, Meatheads," he mumbled to himself, "do your thing while I do mine." He slammed the big jet down onto the deck, barely two hundred feet above the ground, and stroked the throttles as his airspeed touched 500 knots.

Martin had never been so alive. He concentrated on the HUD, focusing on the gray holographic images coming from the Nav FLIR that let him see into the night. He ignored the shadows that served as ground references and gave him a sense of ground rush. He was not even aware of the sweat streaking his face and soaking his back as ground turbulence jolted the Eagle and pounded at his body.

While Martin flew to the east, the other eight birds continued to the southeast, still in the old corridor they had opened up on the first attack. Martin had reasoned that any "raghead missiler who values his cajones won't be anxious to get our attention." Besides, they had learned the location of the SAM sites from the first attack and were flying around them.

Matt checked his TSD—they were across the border and approaching the split point. The jet banked hard to the right when they overflew the point and his wingman followed him through the turn. The horizon to the east was lighting with the first glow of sunrise and Matt had no trouble picking out his wingman two thousand feet to his left as they headed south for Al Sahra. The second element continued straight ahead for Mosul while the third and fourth elements headed south for the ferry.

"Damn, I hope this works," Matt muttered.

"Keep the faith, babes," Furry said.

"Bandits now zero-nine-zero at forty-five, angels eighteen," the tactical controller aboard the AWACS radioed Martin. "The threat is still in trail."

"Roger," Martin answered. His eyes narrowed as he considered his opening move. While Martin's fangs may have been out and his hair on fire, he was no fool nor did he have a death wish. Surprise was his number one tactic and he had every intention of sneaking up on the bandits unobserved. To accomplish that, he hid down in the weeds at two hundred feet and had his radar in standby. Martin had no illusions about what he was doing; it was the work of the assassin, not bold knights jousting in the lists of combat. "Aldo, say bandits' heading."

"Turning to the south," Aldo answered. It was what Martin wanted to hear. Now the Flankers' radar was pointed away from him and couldn't paint him. He doubted if the Iraqis' ground-based search radars could find him and with the AWACS serving as his eyes, he had the advantage of situational awareness over his opponents.

The colonel was almost in AMRAAM range. Should he turn on his radar and launch one of the highly sophisticated missiles or press for a close-in opening attack? He decided to keep his radar off and close. One of the Flankers would certainly detect his radar so why tell Joe he was out here? He uncaged the seeker head of a Sidewinder and let it search for a target. Almost immediately the comforting growl indicating a lock-on filled his headset. He pressed closer, now deciding to use his gun and do a hit-and-split followed by a reattack.

"Aldo, say position of trailing two aircraft," he radioed. He still didn't have a visual contact.

"Viper Zero-One, the bandits are now in a wheel on your nose at six miles, I cannot break trailers out."

"Are they still on the deck?" Martin asked, his voice still calm and measured.

"Unknown. Stand by," Aldo answered. The radar on the AWACS could differentiate altitudes but had to change its mode of operation and that took a few seconds, which Martin no longer had.

"Tallyho," the colonel called. He could see the bandits high in the sky, still in front of him, silhouetted against the reddening dawn. He pulled back on the stick and climbed, hooking into the six o'clock of the nearest Flanker. He had hidden, now it was time to be quick. The Flanker was still four thousand feet above him when he hit the weapons select switch, bringing his radar out of standby. The radar did as it was commanded and locked on the nearest target. The symbology on the HUD switched to air-to-air and he followed the steering dot. The pipper centered on the target and he squeezed the trigger, sending a short burst of 20-millimeter into the Flanker.

Now he skidded violently to the left and did a Split S, heading back for the deck. Joe had to know he was out here now. "Splashed the bastard," his wizzo told him, confirming that he had his fourth kill.

"Shit hot!" Martin shouted, not because he was one kill short of becoming an ace, but because his radar had just found two aircraft down on the deck below him. One of them had to be Joe. "One pass, haul ass," Martin promised his backseater.

Johar's head was twisted to the right as he scanned the sky above him, looking for the fighter that he knew was out there. He could see the falling dart of fire that had been a Flanker, the latest commander of Mosul. How many are out there? he wondered. Don't panic, take them one at a time. They've got to find me. Now his radar warning gear growled at him. He glanced inside the cockpit and saw a single symbol for a fighter at his six o'clock position. "Samir," he radioed, "bandit six o'clock, closing, no tally."

"No tally," Samir answered. They drove straight ahead and waited. Both men strained to see the fighter they knew was slashing down on them.

"Tallyho!" Johar shouted. He had finally seen the dark silhouette of Martin's F-15 against the morning glow. "Turn and hook . . . Now," Johar commanded. The "turn-and-hook" was a low-level tactic they had worked out while sitting standby alert. Since Johar had called for it, he would make a level turn to the right as low to the ground as possible. At the same time, Samir would reef into a hard climb, maintaining his airspeed. The goal was to make the attacker commit on one of them. It didn't matter which.

"He's on me," Johar called, watching for a missile, extending his speed break and slowing below 200 knots. As expected, a Sidewinder leaped off the F-15 and tracked on him. At the same time, Samir was ruddering his bird over to hook into the fight from above. Johar watched the missile close. His left hand dropped behind the throttles and bounced off a big button, laying a string of flares and chaff behind him to decoy the missile while he honked back on the stick. His airspeed was below 140 knots. Now his tail was turning away from the missile, presenting a reduced heat signature for the missile to home on. His angle of attack increased to above forty units as the nose came up and he slowed even more. The missile homed on a flare.

Johar watched the F-15 do exactly as he had planned. The American pilot had obviously seen Samir coming down from above and had to think about disengaging. The F-15 headed directly for Johar and accelerated for one last snap shot with his gun—something to keep Johar occupied while he ran for safety. It would have worked beautifully with an average pilot.

Now Johar honked back even farther on the stick and the Flanker mushroomed above a thousand feet, its nose high in the air. It resembled the head of a cobra rearing back to strike. Now the F-15 pilot had no chance for a snap shot and was in full afterburner as he flashed by underneath Johar's cobra, now disengaging, worried more about Samir. Johar had been counting on the American to see him as a sitting duck—a pilot who had let his airspeed decay and gotten himself into a stall while trying to avoid a missile.

But the Flanker was nowhere near a stall. Johar pushed the stick forward and retracted his speed brake. The nose of his Flanker dropped, the head of a cobra striking at its victim. Johar's timing was perfect and he sent an R-60 dogfight missile at the escaping jet. The F-15 pilot saw the missile and jinked to the left. Then he turned harder to the left, keeping the missile and the two Flankers in sight. Flares popped out behind the Eagle. But the missile NATO called Archer ignored the flares and followed the F-15 through the turn. It was still accelerating when it flew up Martin's left exhaust and exploded. The F-15 pitched into the ground.

"Samir, say position," Johar radioed. He was in a left turn, orbiting the burning wreckage.

"At your six, joining on your right." The two Flankers flew one 360-degree turn over the destroyed F-15. Johar tried to reconstruct the engagement from the dead pilot's point of view to analyze the effectiveness of the turn-and-hook tactic. The American had engaged using hit-and-run tactics and opted to "hit" on him when it looked like Samir had zoomed out of the fight. Johar's slow speed had tricked the American into closing for a guns solution after launching a Sidewinder. If the pilot had been less aggressive, not so sure of himself, and had turned away and disengaged immediately after launching the Sidewinder, he would still be alive. Would it work again? He didn't know.

The radio crackled with commands from their ground controller, demanding they report in. "Go common," Johar said, changing to a frequency where they would not be disturbed.

"What now?" Samir asked when they were established on the new frequency.

"Our controllers are worthless," Johar said. He checked his fuel, thinking. The Flanker carried more than twenty-two thousand pounds of fuel internally and could stay airborne for long periods of time. "We know the corridor the Americans use," Johar told his wingman. "Let's wait for them to come to us."

Michael Cagliari and General Cox were huddled over the Teletype operator in the small room that housed the Hot Line to the Kremlin. After being off-line for days, the machine was spitting out a message. Someone in the Kremlin wanted to talk to the Americans. The Teletype operator was fluent in Russian and read out the text a line at a time as it scrolled up. "Get another translator," he told his supervisor. The woman motioned for another Teletype operator to read the message. The two men conferred, wanting to be absolutely sure they had it right. An English language translation of the message started to type out. "The Russians want to be sure we don't botch the translation," the first operator said.

"Acknowledge receipt," Cagliari said. "Write your translation down and get it to me." He picked up the original copies and hurried into the Situation Room while Cox called the hospital to tell the President that the Hot Line was up and that the newest leader of the Kremlin wanted to talk to him. Then he followed Cagliari into the Situation Room.

The secretary of state was reading the message out loud to Bobby Burke. He carefully laid the message down when he was finished. "What do you think?" he asked Burke.

"Obviously, we don't know what's on his mind, but it's not going to be good. Count on it."

The message was from Marshal Grigori Fydor Stenilov, now general secretary of the Communist party and the leading hard-liner in the Soviet Union.

Levy was leading what was left of his tanks and APCs down a hollow that opened onto the main valley floor. When he saw movement in the gap in front of him, he ordered his tanks to disperse to both sides and hide, hoping whatever was out there had not seen them and would slip by. Levy didn't want to be trapped short of the jumping-off point for their breakout. Halaby guided the tank up a low ridge, heading for concealment on the other side. "GO!" Levy shouted. The movement had turned into three T-72s and the lead tank had seen them.

The V-12 diesel engine roared as Halaby buried his foot in the big gas pedal and the tank dropped over the crest with a jarring crunch as the torsion bar suspense absorbed the impact. The lead T-72 fired, but it was too late and the range too far. Now they were on the back side of the ridge heading for a deep wadi in front of them. Levy planned to take a hull-down position and drill any tank that came over the crest of the ridge after them. Halaby slowed as he nosed the tank down the slope, across some difficult terrain. Then the tank stopped.

"I threw a track," the driver shouted.

Amos Avner grabbed a long communications extension cord, popped the loader's hatch over his position, and scrambled out of the tank before anyone could say a thing. Shoshana was surprised at how fast the young man could move and plugged her com cord into the station Avner had been using. She could hear him talking.

"Nazzi, it's the right track. The top has driven off underneath the fender and is still on the rollers and the front idler.

It's partially on the sprocket." There was none of the harsh tones that usually accompanied exchanges between the driver and loader. "The right track is on the down side of the hill. You've done this one before." There was triumph in his voice. "Start backing up."

Shoshana stuck her head out the loader's hatch and saw Avner beside the tank, holding on to the com cord and guiding Halaby as he backed up. She felt him steer to the right, which stopped the right track. The nose of the tank inched slowly to the left.

"TANK ON THE RIDGE!" Levy shouted and the turret traversed to the left.

Shoshana dropped back into the turret but left the hatch open for Avner. Still the tank inched backward and she could hear Avner's voice directing Halaby. "Easy, easy, Nazzi. You've almost got it." The tank was turning back onto the track.

"GUNNER! IMI! TANK LEFT!" Levy ordered, going through the firing sequence.

"UP!" Avner shouted, still doing his job while on the outside of the tank. They had been battle-carrying the hyper-velocity armor-piercing round.

"IDENTIFIED!" (Bielski)—"FIRE" (Levy)—"ON THE WAY!" (Bielski).

The loud crack-boom of the main gun echoed through the open hatch and the tank rocked with the recoil. The round hit the underside of the T-72 as it came over the ridge.

"The track's on!" Avner shouted. "You did it, Nazzi!"

"GUNNER, IMI, TANK!" Levy had seen a second tank coming over the ridge at them, its nose still high in the air. But Avner was outside the tank. Shoshana had watched Avner load the main gun and knew where he stored the different types of rounds. She pulled an Imi out of its storage canister and shoved the fifty-pound round into the open breech with her fist. The breech automatically snapped closed, almost catching her hand. "UP!" she shouted.

Again, they went through the firing sequence and the spent shell casing automatically ejected out of the breech and rolled on the floor of the turret.

"Amos!" Levy shouted over the intercom. "Where are you?" No answer. The loader had been scrambling up the side of the tank when it fired and the recoil had thrown him off.

Again, Levy called out another tank and Shoshana went through the loading routine. But she lost her balance and dropped the fresh round. Rather than scramble for the round, she reached for another one. The delay was too long. The T-72 had crested the hill and got off the first shot. Bielski shouted "IDENTIFIED!" as the round hit the left side of the turret. It was a glancing blow and the reactive armor detonated, sending an explosion out, canceling the explosion coming in.

"FIRE!"

"ON THE WAY!"

The tank rocked and Shoshana could hardly believe they were okay. The turret traversed as they looked for other tanks. Only three burning hulks were on the ridgeline above them. Levy popped his hatch, looking for his loader. But Avner had taken the full force of both explosions and had simply disintegrated. There was nothing left that could be called a body. Levy keyed the radio and checked in with his small force.

In the silence, Shoshana could hear a low moan from Halaby. "Are you okay?" she asked. The driver turned and looked at her, grief, not pain, written across his face. He told her that he was not hurt.

Shoshana looked at Bielski, not understanding. "They were friends," the gunner told her. "They just didn't know it."

"We're moving out," Levy said. "We got them all."

Levy's Luck had held again, but this time at the price of Amos Avner.

Matt was talking to Sean Leary, his wingman, over the Have Quick radio, telling him how the flak trap at Mosul had been set up. "Al Sahra is probably the same so stand off as far as you can."

A cool "Roger" answered him.

"I hope he doesn't press it too hard," Matt told his wizzo.

"You know Sean," Furry answered. The attack sequence called for Leary to make a low-level run at Al Sahra and toss a GBU at max range, break off and move outside the range of the SAMs and AAA circling the field. Hopefully, the air defenders around Al Sahra would be concentrating on Leary while Matt ran in, right down the runway.

"I'm in," Sean radioed, starting his attack run.

"Don't press it," Matt mumbled to himself.

Leary's voice came over the radio: "Thirty seconds." He was thirty seconds away from pickle, the cue for Matt to start his run. He shoved the throttles into Mil power, touching 600 knots. Now the defenders started to react and the TEWS lit up with numerous threats.

"Bomb gone!" Leary yelled. "I'm outa here."

Matt could see numerous missile plumes, all on Leary. He concentrated on his run, sweat pouring down his face. Now he could see the runway. A hangar disappeared in a bright flash—Leary's bomb. "Come left," Furry said. He had their target on the Target FLIR—six Transport aircraft parked on the ramp.

"Tally," Matt replied. He could see the aircraft. One was starting to move.

Now they were over the edge of the ramp and Matt felt the six Snakeyes ripple off as the aircraft on the ramp disappeared under his nose. He shoved the throttles into full afterburner and went through the Mach. Furry hit the button that popped flares and chaff in their wake while he twisted around in his seat, checking on their bombs. "Got 'em!" he shouted. Now they were running for safety, overflying a gun pit and two SAM launchers. Then they were clear.

"Sean," Matt transmitted, "say position."

"North of target. Battle damage." Every word of the short transmission was strained.

Matt turned to the north and used his radar to find the F-15. He had a single, slow-moving target on his nose at thirty miles. "I'm coming," he told the stricken pilot. "Can you push your airspeed up?"

"Negative," came the reply.

"Say damage," Matt transmitted.

"Controllability problems. Smoke and fumes in cockpit, on emergency generator, MPDP out." The MPDP was the Multi-Purpose Display Processor that controlled the HUD and video screens in both cockpits.

"He's blind and flying on backup instruments," Furry said. "He must be hurt bad."

Matt felt a coppery taste in his mouth. Leary was in a world of hurt because of him. He had planned the attack. He had determined who would lead the attack. Now it was his responsibility to get Leary out. "Hold on," he radioed. "I'm on the way."

"Got him on the Target FLIR," Furry said. Matt looked down and saw the greenish image of an F-15 on the screen. They were still beyond visual range, but the FLIR was imaging the stricken plane. Most of the right rear vertical stabilizer was gone and smoke was streaming from under the right engine. Matt's resolve hardened.

"Aldo, Viper Zero-Three," Matt transmitted. The AWACS acknowledged the call and Matt explained the emergency and that he was escorting his wingman out. Then he asked for the mission results. Aldo told him that all aircraft were safely off target and that the convoy had been caught at the ferry and destroyed.

"Relay our status to Viper Zero-One," Matt requested.

There was a long pause. Then another voice came over the radio, the tactical director. "Be advised that contact with Viper Zero-One was lost during an engagement with two bandits. Suspect he was splashed."

The determination Matt had felt before turned to granite. Martin had led them in and now it was his job to get them out. "Roger, Aldo," he replied. "Copy all. Say bandits." He was asking if any hostile aircraft were in the area.

Aldo answered with "Two bandits on your nose at one hundred thirty nautical miles. Numerous aircraft launching out of Kirkuk at this time."

"Those two are right on the border between us and home plate," Furry told him. "They're going to sandwich us between those bastards launching out of Kirkuk." Then it came to him. "Jesus H. Christ, those are the two bastards that got Martin." After a long pause, he added, "That's 'Joe' out there."

"Fuck 'em!" Matt barked. "We got lots of fuel and Aldo." He keyed his mike and told the AWACS to vector the recovering F-15s around all bandits. "We did what we came for," he told Furry. "Now they got to find us down in the weeds. No way they can do that with Aldo vectoring us away from them."

They listened as the F-15s checked in and the AWACS called out headings to keep them well clear of the two orbiting bandits and the MiGs launching out of Kirkuk. Now Matt joined on his wingman. "Shit-oh-dear," Furry mumbled, "it's a wonder he's still flying." Matt moved in close to Leary and looked him over. The F-15 had taken numerous hits with AAA and at least one SAM. Not only was 50 percent of the right vertical stabilizer gone, but the right wing looked like Swiss cheese and fuel was streaming out of the fuselage.

"Sean, say fuel."

The answer was not good. "I might make it to the border."

"Aldo," Matt transmitted, "Have a tanker on station at the border."

"Roger," Aldo answered.

Matt checked their altitude and airspeed: eight hundred feet and two-eighty. Not good, but it was the best Leary could do.

"Viper Zero-Three"—the tactical controller's voice was rapid and tense—"the two bandits are now on your nose at eighty nautical miles, moving your way." Matt glanced down at the TEWS. The symbol for a Su-27's radar in search mode was on their nose and moving toward them.

"That's gotta be Joe," came from the backseat.

Smoke and dust rolled over the top of the low hill and engulfed the eight Israeli tanks and six APCs that were hiding in the rough terrain. What was left of Levy Force was careful to use terrain masking and maintain radio silence as they moved closer to their jumping-off point. A loud explosion echoed over them and Levy could see an F-4 pull off a bombing run. He turned in the open hatch and clasped his hands together, the signal to halt. "Can you get us behind those boulders?" he asked Halaby.

"I can do better than that," the driver replied. He inched the tank under a large outcropping, satisfied that the tank's sand-gray paint scheme would blend perfectly. Levy climbed out of the turret, dropped to the ground and scrambled through the boulders to the top of the hill. Shoshana watched him from the loader's hatch as he belly-crawled to the top of the hill. Then he was back, his face an expressionless mask.

"They don't know we're here. Tanks are still moving down the valley supported by BMPs. Some are passing right now, in battalion strength. We're going to cut across their rear. Halaby, take us over to that low area two hundred meters to the right."

Halaby moved the tank out while Levy stood in the hatch and extended his left arm to the side. Then he made an arching motion over his head, pointing in the direction he wanted to go. The tanks and APCs relayed the signal and followed him. As they moved out of the protective cover of the rough terrain, Levy extended both his arms in a downward V, the visual signal for a wedge formation. Halaby slowed as the tanks moved into position and the APCs moved inside the protective arms of the wedge. They were almost in the open and now arcing out into the main valley. Still the Iraqis had not seen them. Levy raised his right fist high above his head and brought it down with a hard jerk, the signal to charge.

Shoshana's head banged against the turret and she held on as Halaby gunned the engine. She concentrated on Levy's commands as they fired, loading the gun as fast as she could. Once the breech nicked her hand when it slammed closed, peeling off a layer of skin. She ignored it. The loud boom of a direct hit on the forward plate of their tank echoed through the turret and the concussion stunned her. She was vaguely aware of Levy shouting over the radio, telling one of the APCs to fire a TOW antitank missile at a target. Still they plunged on, her world focused on feeding the main gun.

Halaby jerked the tank to the right and hit the brakes, throwing her forward just as the main gun swung over the driver. She fell forward and landed on the battery pack right behind him. The tank rocked with a loud explosion and smoke. She heard Halaby shout, "Sagger!" They had taken a direct hit by a wire-guided antitank missile on the side of the turret where the reactive armor had already blown away and exposed an open patch of hull. Then another explosion rocked the tank. This time from an Iraqi tank round. A whitish mist filled the tank. "Fire extinguishers!" Halaby yelled.

Shoshana became aware that she was drenched in green hydraulic fluid. "I'LL BURN!" she screamed.

"DON'T PANIC!" Halaby shouted. "You're okay. It's got a high flash point." Slowly the mist cleared and she could see that he was also dripping with it. Now she could see into the turret. Dave Bielski was a pulpy mass of blood and flesh. Behind him, she could see Levy's legs dangling from the tank commander's seat. They twitched. He was alive. She grabbed a first aid kit and worked her way around the breech of the main gun to where she could work on him. Halaby followed her and popped the loader's hatch to look out. "Get ready to get out," he told her. Then he dropped back inside, closing the hatch. "We're not on fire. All I can see are T-Seventy-twos and BMPs. They must think we're dead. Maybe we can lie doggo."

The sounds of tracked vehicles moving by caught her attention. The image of the two medics who had been raped and mutilated flashed in front of her. She drove it away and worked on Levy. The lower part of his body had been cut to pieces with small bits of shrapnel, but his flak jacket had protected his upper body. Since he had been sitting in the commander's cupola, his head and shoulders were not injured and he was conscious.

"Halaby," he groaned. "Get us moving." Then he passed out.

While Shoshana worked on Levy, Halaby checked the tank. "We've lost hydraulics to the turret and can't traverse but we can still fire. If I can start the engine and the tracks are still on, we can move."

"We've got to get him to an aid station right away," Shoshana said. Again, she could hear tanks passing by.

"We'll have to fight our way out," Halaby mumbled. He moved forward to the driver's position where he could look out. "Two kilometers, maybe three to the hills. We might have a chance there. Can we wait to dark?" Shoshana told him that without immediate attention, Levy would be dead by then. "I need to be in his position to see better," Halaby told her. "Can we move him?"

The two worked gently to move Levy out of his seat. Halaby had to climb over them to get past in the cramped confines of the turret. He moved into the commander's seat and used a rag to wipe off the blood and gore that had splashed over the controls. He used the periscope and optical sight to see around him. "There's some BMPs moving past us but I don't see anything behind them. No, hold on, about two kilometers back, more tanks." He thought for a moment. "Can you aim and fire the gun?"

"No," she told him. "But if you can get the engine started, I can drive." Halaby grunted and squeezed back into the driver's compartment. The engine coughed and came to life. Halaby scurried out of the seat and Shoshana quickly jumped into the driver's position. She grabbed the T-bar and looked out of the vision blocks.

"Halaby, there's two tanks coming at us!" Directly in front of them she could see two T-72s moving out from behind a low hummock and headed straight toward them.

"GO!" Halaby shouted. "Head right for them!" Shoshana moved the shift from neutral to low and mashed the accelerator. The tank leaped forward. She saw a muzzle flash from one of the T-72s. She shifted into high.

In a bruising, headlong rush, she drove at the two tanks in front of her. A shell cracked off the front plate directly below her vision blocks and screamed away. She was momentarily blinded by the flash and was surprised that it had not penetrated into the tank. The reactive armor blocks had done their job, but now more patches of the tank's hull were fully exposed. "Right, go right," Halaby yelled at her. She shook her head, trying to clear her vision, and guided the tank to the right. "A little to the left," he shouted. She realized he was aiming the gun by moving the tank. "ON THE WAY!" he shouted and fired the main gun.

The Imi hit the lead tank in the frontal armor, the heaviest part of the armor, and penetrated with devastating results. Shoshana saw the tank pull sideways and smoke billow out. She knew the carnage that was going on inside.

"Head for the other tank," Halaby ordered. He scrambled out of his seat to reload. Again, Shoshana saw the muzzle flash and this time jerked the tank to the left. The round missed them by inches. She saw the tube of the T-72 raise for the autoloader to eject the shell. "Halaby, FIRE!" she shouted. No answer. He was still reloading. Now the tube was lowering to receive a fresh round. "HALABY!" The muzzle was raising. She slued the tank hard to the left, trying to break the gunner's aim.

"Come back to the right," Halaby yelled as the muzzle flashed.

The range between the two tanks was less than five hundred meters and the Iraqi's round hit the right side of the M60. The warhead of the 122-millimeter APDS projectile penetrated deep into the engine compartment and exploded. An internal explosion blew the turret off the tank and a tongue of flame licked at Shoshana's back when a fuel cell erupted. She reached for the lever that locked the driver's hatch with her left hand and felt a burning pain. She pulled and pushed until the hatch opened. Then she was lifting herself out of the burning tank. But her left hand wouldn't come free of the hatch handle. She jerked and a searing pain shot up her arm. Now she was out of the tank as her hydraulic-soaked outer clothes caught on fire. She threw herself onto the ground and rolled, snuffing out the flames.

Shoshana was vaguely aware that Hanni's helmet was still on fire and she ripped it off, throwing it away from her. She lay on her back and watched as the T-72 that had destroyed them clanked by, ignoring the burning hulk of Levy's tank.

Matt's mind raced as he tried to load the dice in his favor in the developing engagement with the two bandits. "Radar in standby, TEWS passive only," he told Furry. "Make 'em think we don't know they're out there." Then he hit his transmit switch. "Aldo, keep the BRA calls coming." BRA calls gave the bearing, range, and altitude of the bandits. As long as the AWACS could feed him that information, his own radar could remain in standby.

"Three-two-zero at forty-five, coaltitude," the AWACS answered. The bandits were still on his nose and closing.

"Damn," Furry muttered, "wish we had AMRAAMs." All they had were four Sidewinders and a full drum of ammunition.

Then it hit Matt, they did have AMRAAMs—on Leary's jet. "Sean, can you salvo your AMRAAMs on command?" he asked. The wingman thought he could do that. Matt collapsed into a tight formation with his wingman. "Amb, jam the shit out of them after Sean salvos."

Matt hit his weapons select switch and brought the radar to life and it automatically locked on the nearest target. Then he mashed the button forward as if he was going to fire a radar missile. The system did as it was commanded but no shoot cue was generated since there were no radar missiles on board. "Sean, fire four," he ordered.

The four AMRAAMs dropped out of their missile wells in quick succession. Their seeker heads picked up the reflected radar energy from Matt's radar and homed. Matt moved away from Leary, still keeping his nose on the two bandits so his radar could illuminate the targets until the AMRAAMs transitioned to their own terminal guidance. Matt watched in satisfaction as the four missiles reached for the bandits. He hadn't been sure if it would work. "Radar in standby," he told Furry and dove for the ground. "Now honor the fuckin' threat," he told the Flankers.

And honor the threat they did. Samir broke hard right when he saw the missiles and Johar pulled down and to the left. Samir wrenched his fighter back to the left so he could keep a visual contact on the missiles. If he could see a missile, he could defeat it. He brought the nose of his Flanker up and turned twenty degrees away. He watched the lead missile turn and climb with him. When the AMRAAM was committed to a collision course, Samir turned hard into the missile and down. The missile followed. He pulled up hard, loading the Flanker with nine g's, generating an overshoot. The proximity fuse on the AMRAAM detonated the warhead as it flashed by underneath, but Samir was outside its cone. He repeated the maneuver on the second missile but his airspeed was bleeding off and he generated an overshoot below 180 knots. The third and fourth missiles got him.

"It's you and me, asshole," Matt grumbled when he saw the Flanker hit the ground. He called up a Sidewinder and turned into Johar.

Johar saw the missiles take his friend out and felt a cold fury wash over him. He turned into the F-15 and called up an Archer. The two aircraft came at each other in a head-on pass, both jinking and skidding across the sky, both pilots intent on shooting the other one in the face.

At nine miles, they both launched missiles, almost simultaneously. Matt climbed into the sun that was just above the eastern horizon and watched the missile, then he broke hard for the ground and back into Johar as Furry sent more flares out the back. The missile lost the heat signature it was homing on and headed into the sun.

Johar turned away from Matt's Sidewinder and dropped to a hundred feet above the ground. Then he turned hard back into it and climbed. The Sidewinder tried to follow him, but hit the ground. Now Johar turned back into Matt. He barely had time to snap roll to the right as they passed canopy to canopy. Only the rattlesnake-quick reflexes of both pilots saved them from a head-on collision.

Both pilots pulled into the vertical, each reversing on his adversary. Now they were climbing almost straight up, still

canopy to canopy, when Johar pulled hard into Matt. Matt
did the same. Now they were in a scissors as they reversed
on each other and slowed, each trying to bring his cannon to
bear. Twice they passed, neither gaining an advantage, slowing down. It was a repeat of the fatal mission when Matt had
collided with Jack Locke in a midair.

Now they were going down and Matt unloaded and rolled,
reversing again onto Johar. He saw he would pass behind him
this time. Suddenly, the nose of the Flanker pitched up in a
high AOA, like a cobra rearing its head to strike. Matt
wrenched the F-15 to the left to avoid a collision. But they
were too close and Matt's right wingtip hit Johar's belly. It
looked like a gentle brush, but the forces generated were
shattering.

Matt found himself in a spin and buried his foot in the
rudder and held the stick all the way over against the spin.
The spin slowed and he brought the nose up and they were
climbing again. "No afterburners," Furry said. "We're
dumping fuel like mad over the right wing. Okay, it's slowing. The fuel-shutoff valves must be working."

"Check the right wing," Matt said, looking for Johar.
Then he saw a parachute.

"SHIT-OH-DEAR!" Furry roared. "WE AIN'T GOT NO
WING!"

The reports flooding into the command bunker told a story
of success and a victory. Ben David could not contain his
elation and had to move about, full of energy and resolve.
When the Ganef told him that the Americans had destroyed
the nerve gas arsenal at Kirkuk, he only jutted his jaw out
and said nothing. His eyes scanned the situation maps in the
front of the room and a new sense of justification and righ-
teousness swept over him. The Arabs were surrendering in
droves in both Jordan and on the Golan. Yes, he told himself,
a major victory.

Only in Lebanon was the victory clouded and the fighting
was still seesawing back and forth. Soon, he knew, he would
be able to reinforce the beleaguered Israelis there and secure
a total victory. Life was very sweet as he stared at the boards
and plotted the future.

The minister of foreign affairs caught his attention. "Yair,
I've received a communiqué from the United Nations. The

pressure for a cease-fire is overwhelming. We can't ignore it any longer."

"For twenty-four more hours we will," he replied, his voice hard and unyielding. Twenty-four more hours and he would have a victory in Lebanon, the elusive victory his predecessors had never found in 1982.

"Perhaps, Yair," his minister of defense, Benjamin Yuriden, ventured, "this would be the best time to negotiate—while the Arabs can still tell their people they were winning someplace and it was not a cease-fire forced on them by a total defeat."

"They won't win anywhere!" Ben David shouted. "I will drive them into the desert and—"

"Negotiate now!" the Ganef interrupted. He grabbed the prime minister's jaw and jerked his chin around, making him look at the "Status of Casualties" board on the side wall. "How much more can you ask of your people? How much more can they sacrifice?"

The numbers told a grim story and Ben David knew he was right—they had fought long enough. With a massive force of will, he drove his hatred back into its cage and became a politician again. "Arrange a cease-fire. Stabilize Lebanon but do not attack. Halt all actions in Syria and Jordan and withdraw to defensible positions." Then his eyes ran over the "Status of Casualties" board again. His people had indeed sacrificed more than enough and he did not have the right to ask for more.

"It seems to be stabilized around three hundred knots," Matt said, still feeling out the controllability of the F-15. "Below two-fifty or above three-fifty, it wants to roll."

"Right," Furry said. "Some landing at this speed."

"Want to eject?"

"No way. Not as long as it's flyable. What the hell do we get paid for?"

Good question, Matt thought. Definitely not for flying on one wing. He checked his fuel. Nothing. The gauge was dead. "How far to Diyarbakir?" he asked.

"Fifty-five miles," came the answer. "Eleven minutes. Think we got enough fuel?"

"Beats me," Matt answered.

"What the hell," Furry groused. "At least it's a straight-in approach and they got a barrier there."

"I wonder if our hook can take that kind of a shock," Matt said.

"Let's find out."

The tower cleared them for a straight-in approach and Matt lined up on the runway. He tried to bleed off airspeed, but the moment he slowed below 270 knots, he could feel the jet start to roll into the missing wing. He rooted the airspeed on 280 and extended the landing gear. The nose gear doors blew away in the slipstream. Then he lowered the hook and touched down. The hook snared the arresting cable and they felt a hard jerk when the cable had fully paid out. The hook tore out and the F-15 kept on going down the runway at 160 knots. Matt stomped on top of the rudder pedals, dragging the big fighter to a halt. They were barely moving when they ran off the end of the runway and the nose gear collapsed in the soft dirt. The canopy popped open and the two men scrambled out, worried about a fire.

They skirted the aircraft, amazed at what had happened. "How in the hell?" Furry wondered.

"The engineers are going to have some fun figuring this one out," Matt said. "My best guess is that the intakes give some lift and with the wing gone, that big horizontal stabilizer gets the full air flow and is very effective."

"Just maybe," Furry allowed, "this one wasn't built by the lowest bidder."

The blades of the helicopter were still slowly turning when the forward door opened and the steps dropped down. The President stepped down and automatically ducked his head, his long strides quickly covering the ground to the White House entrance. His face was worn and haggard, showing the strain of the last few days. The men following him were silent. Cox was waiting for him in the hall and also followed him down the stairs to the Hot Line. The general wanted to ask him about his wife but a mental warning kept him quiet.

Inside the room, the Teletype operator looked up. Pontowski put his hand on the young man's shoulder. "Tell Secretary Stenilov that I'm here, Larry," he said. The operator's fingers flew over the keys.

The room was silent as they waited. Then the Teletype started to rattle again, this time printing in English:

"Mr. President, let us work together and end this madness in the Middle East."

Shoshana lay on the ground in a state of deep shock. She wondered about the tanks that were now moving to the north. She held up her left hand and inspected the charred remains of her fingers. Two were missing but she didn't feel a thing. In the distance, she could see tanks moving toward her. But these were more angular than T-72s and the set-back turret made her think of Merkavas. Oh, she thought, Merkavas. Ours. But it didn't matter. Her war had finished when Levy's Luck had run its course and the fire had cleansed her, burning away all that was wrong in her past. She was content as the warm, welcome fog of unconsciousness claimed her.

EPILOGUE————————————————————

Pontowski sat beside his wife's bed, wading through the thick read file that waited for him each morning. But he couldn't concentrate and dropped the file into his lap. He looked at his sleeping wife and a slight smile cracked his tired face. Lupus, the disease they called the wolf, had released its hold on her and again she was in remission, but this time seriously weakened by the damage it had done to her heart. He saw an eyelid flutter. "Quit faking it, Tosh. I know you're awake."

Her eyes slowly opened, blinking against the soft light that filled the hospital room. Her hand reached out for his. "I do love you," she said. For a few moments they did not move or talk, sharing the moment of another morning. "You did it? Stopped the fighting?"

"For now. It was touch and go."

"And Matt?"

"He's alive and well. In Israel. Looking for a Shoshana Tamir. He says he's going to marry her."

She squeezed his hand. "Then we may have grandchildren yet."

Oh, love, he thought, if only you knew how close a thing it was. How I had to use Matt to get the Israeli lobby in Congress off my back so I could maneuver. It wasn't by pure chance he was sent to Israel. And then the way the Israelis fed him information thinking that would influence me. It would have been all right except that grandson of ours has a penchant for getting into trouble. And finding pretty girls.

"What's going on behind those steely blue eyes of yours?" Tosh asked.

"Thinking about Matt."

"And how you used him," she said.

Pontowski sighed. He couldn't hide anything from his wife. "Yes, but I hadn't planned on him getting involved with the raid on Kirkuk. That just happened because his unit was ready to do it.'' Pontowski shook his head. ''It seems that Matt's deputy for operations was a wild man who got ready for any fight he thought might come his way. Matt just happened to be there. I thought about getting involved, but I couldn't. You know Matt, he would've never forgiven me if I had sidelined him.''

''I suppose,'' Tosh said. ''That happens when you stand too close to a fire. They can burn uncontrolled and drag you in.''

''Then we need bigger firebreaks,'' the President decided.

The vice president for F-15 production at McDonnell Aircraft Company slipped into the flight simulator unobserved. He watched the two men at the console as they went through their well-practiced routine of teaching humility to some fighter pilot inside. ''What have you two been up to now?'' he asked, capturing their attention. Leander immediately froze the sim and told the crew inside that they would continue in a moment.

''Well?'' the vice president demanded, working to keep a straight face.

''Nothing, sir,'' Stigler answered.

''You two clowns are always up to something.''

''Meatheads, sir.'' Leander said. ''We're not clowns, we're Meatheads.'' He pointed to a prominent plaque above the console that announced MARTIN'S MEATHEADS.

''At least,'' the VP continued, ''can you cut the next congressman who comes through here some slack?''

The two young men hung their heads, trying to act ashamed.

The vice president relented. ''When you're finished here, the Old Man wants to see you. Says he wants to shake your hands. It beats me why . . .'' He grinned and left, leaving them to their work.

The battered jeep made its way down the dusty road, skirting the burned-out hulks of tanks, armored troop carriers and trucks that had been pushed to the side. Matt had to leave the road, detouring around a patch of uncleared mines. He almost drove through a collection of temporary graves—Syrians. All the scars of heavy fighting assaulted him, driving home the grisly reality of war's destruction and after-birth. In the distance, he could see the ruins of a destroyed kibbutz nestled against the western hills of the Huleh Valley.

Matt stopped to get his bearings. I flew up this valley, he thought, when Furry and I took out that command post. He checked his map and found the Huleh Valley. What had Avi Tamir called it, "the jewel of Israel"? He looked up the steep escarpment to the east. It was a cliff that rose fifteen hundred feet to a plateau—the Golan Heights. No wonder it is so vital to control the Golan, he decided.

Some hard fighting went on here, he thought. Maybe someone was at that kibbutz. . . .

In the confusion of the war's aftermath, the search for Shoshana had been, by turns, frustrating, confusing, and hopeless. It had taken a major effort just to wangle a hop aboard a U.S. Air Force C-5B hauling relief supplies into the devastated country. The harried Israeli officer who had met the airplane had ordered him not to deplane and to fly out on it. Rather than argue, Matt had simply walked off the cargo plane when no one was looking and started his search.

His first stop had been the Tamirs' apartment in Haifa. Instead of the woman called Lillian and her mob of children, he found the apartment occupied by two families of refugees from the West Bank, none of whom spoke English. He was about to give up when a well-meaning neighbor relayed a rumor that Avi Tamir was working at his old kibbutz in the Huleh Valley.

The jeep ground up the road to the fourth kibbutz he had found.

Surprisingly, he saw only one girl on guard duty as he approached. Since he didn't look like an Arab and was driving an Israeli jeep, the bored teenager waved him in. Children were playing in the yard of a freshly completed school building and their shouts and laughter offered a welcome change from the devastation on the road. Matt switched off the engine and leaned over the steering wheel. He was dirty, thirsty, and tired from his search. And I'm only fifty miles from Haifa, he told himself.

Fifty miles! he thought. Fifty miles of mute testimony to the death and destruction of war. And in the end, what had he accomplished? He had found three kibbutzim and no trace of Avi or Shoshana Tamir. This kibbutz had been the hardest hit of the lot. But the place swarmed with kibbutzniks and was full of life and purpose. They've got their priorities straight, he decided; rebuild the school first.

A young couple swung past holding hands. Both were tired and dirty from work and more engrossed in each other than where they were going. "Need help?" the boy asked. Matt told them whom he was looking for. The girl pointed to a new building under construction. The boy laughed. "Take a hammer. He needs help." Their laughter joined and they wandered off, still holding hands.

Matt found Avi on a ladder installing electrical wiring in the ceiling. "Mr. Tamir." It was almost a question, but not quite. He recognized the scientist but he had changed. He was lean, not pudgy, and his skin had been burned brown from the sun.

The man recognized him but said nothing and continued to work. Matt waited. Finally, Tamir climbed off the ladder. He held onto it for a few minutes, resting. Fatigue etched lines across his face. "Come, it's time for supper." He led Matt to a washhouse where they joined a line of men and women waiting for a turn at the wash basins. "Water is still a problem," Tamir told him. After washing, they entered the new schoolhouse that doubled as a mess hall and waited their turn in the serving line.

Lillian was serving food behind the counter. A look Matt did not recognize shot across the woman's face when she saw him. She methodically filled his tray and said nothing. They squeezed onto benches at a crowded table. Animated conversation in Hebrew went on around them as the diners talked about what work would go on after dinner. "Our discussions sound like arguments," Tamir explained. "Three Israelis equals four opinions." Thanks to the meal, his natural good humor was returning. "The lack of electrical lights and outlets is holding up work. I'm fixing that first." After eating, Matt joined Tamir and the two worked together, the scientist barraging Matt with a constant stream of instructions. It was after eleven o'clock when they quit.

Tamir found a bench in the schoolyard and sat down. He was obviously exhausted. "Why?" was all he asked, now ready to talk.

"I'm looking for Shoshana," Matt said, staring into the night.

"There's nothing here for you."

There, it was out. Now Matt knew. Shoshana was dead—the one thing he feared most but had half expected. The reality of her death drove a deep cold wedge into his emotions and he could feel tears well up in his eyes. "I want to visit her grave."

Tamir said nothing. Finally, he turned and looked at Matt. "What do you see here?"

Matt was surprised by the question. He could hear singing and music coming from the schoolhouse. "Life going on," he said. Silence. "It's amazing," he continued, "war is so impersonal and antiseptic from the air. You don't see the destruction and waste from up there." He was looking at the stars. "You know what's so wrong about war?" He answered his own question, not expecting an answer. "We forget the horrors and if it doesn't kill or maim you, it's the most exciting thing that can happen to a person. No wonder we can't get away from it."

"That's not the reason we kill each other here," Tamir said. "Too many differences, too many people want this small piece of the earth and are not willing to share it." He hung his head. "We haven't solved our problems. We'll fight again."

"Then why are you here in a kibbutz?" Matt asked. "There's so much you can do to help your country get ready if you're going to have to fight another war."

The scientist raised his head. Would the young man sitting beside him understand that this kibbutz was his home, the place where Shoshana had been born and his wife Miriam killed? "Here is Israel's moral compass, its conscience. If we lose this, we are nothing. And to think, I gave my country nuclear weapons, and almost created a Holocaust."

"That wouldn't have been your fault," Matt protested.

"Where does responsibility begin? Where does it end?" The pain in Tamir's words filled the night air. "Tell me, for I don't know."

Matthew Zachary Pontowski III, grandson to the President of the United States, didn't have the answer. "I think my grandfather knows," he said. Then: "You never answered the question, though. Why are you here?"

"This is my home and where I can help Israel the most." The crystalline hardness that had soured Tamir's life shattered as he sat in the clear night air next to the young American. "And where Shoshana can help."

For an instant, Matt would have sworn that his heart stopped. "But you said . . ."

"I said, 'There's nothing here for you.' She was badly wounded—burned. She won't marry you, not now."

"Let her tell me that."

Avi Tamir relented. "She's in a hospital outside Tel Aviv. I'll take you there tomorrow."

"Daddy, what are you reading?" Megan, one of Furry's twin five-year-old girls, crawled onto the couch beside her father, pulled the orders out of his hands, and pretended to read them.

"Those are orders assigning us to another base," Furry answered.

"Is it far away?"

"Yes, Meggie, it's in the United States. That's where you were born."

"Does that mean we all have to move?" The little girl could carry on the most serious conversations.

"Yep, it sure do." He threw her over his shoulder and carried her upstairs to the bedroom Megan shared with her twin, Naomi.

"Sleep tight," he said, tucking her in bed.

"And don't let the bedbugs bite," she giggled, completing their bedtime ritual. He checked on her sister who was already asleep. "Daddy," Megan's sleepy voice came from her bed, "why do we have to move so often?"

"Because it's what I do for a living."

"But I'll miss my friends. Can't you do something else?"

"Probably not," he told her. "It's what I am, Meggie. Go to sleep." He turned out the light and closed the door. Then he hesitated and cracked it open, so he could keep them safe.

The doctor was brisk efficiency and only took time from his busy schedule because his superior told him to. "Shoshana received third-degree burns over the left side of her face," he explained, leading the two men down a corridor. "A little of her scalp and a small part of her earlobe were burned away where her helmet had not protected her. But all that can be repaired with skin grafts." Matt could sense Avi stiffen.

"Luckily," the doctor continued, "the Nomex flight suit she was wearing protected most of her. She will have a zipper shaped burn scar down the front of her body. It runs from her crotch right up between her breasts." The doctor smiled. "For some reason, it amuses her. Her left hand was burned the worst when her tank was hit—two fingers burnt off—we can't fix that." He held the door to a large ward open. "This way, please."

Shoshana saw them coming and laid down the book she was reading beside her. Her eyes followed Matt as he made his way to her.

"I told you I'd be back," he said. His words were full and warm, unforced. He knew he loved this woman. Her right hand reached out for his and he didn't care about the heavy bandages that covered most of her head and face. She was alive.

"I wish . . . I wish," she began, her voice strained, "that you hadn't come."

"This doesn't matter"—he looked at her bandages—"reconstructive surgery . . . it doesn't matter."

"We do agree on that." He could hear a bitter amusement in her words.

"Captain Pontowski is right about the surgery," the doctor said. "We have you scheduled for a trip to Geneva. The Swiss have the best burn center in the world."

"I'm not going," Shoshana said.

"But you must," her father whispered.

"There's better things to do with the money," she said. "And with my time."

Matt smiled, for the surgery didn't matter to him. "When are you going to marry me?"

She squeezed his hand and looked at him. A slight shake of her head. She did love this man. "Not now. There's too much to do here."

The smile never left Matt's face. He knew she was telling him to go—at least for now. "I'll be back, you know."

She knew.

FURRY'S RULES FOR SURVIVAL

The collected sayings of Major Ambler Furry, USAF, are not the product of his wit and experience, but the distilled wisdom of men who have fought in combat since time immemorial. Without doubt, many of Major Furry's rules were in well-developed form when the Hittites first smote the ancient Egyptians. They were certainly around when Mr. Murphy discovered them and were alive and well in Southeast Asia and the Persian Gulf. It is important to remember that there is no priority to the importance of these rules. Whichever one is applicable immediately becomes number one.

1. Always remember your jet was made by the lowest bidder.
2. Train like you plan to fight.
3. If you're up to your eyeballs in Gomers, you're in combat.
4. When in doubt, use industrial strength deterrence.
5. Never fly in the same cockpit with someone who is braver than you.
6. Priorities are man-made, not God-made.
7. A plan never survives the first thirty seconds of combat.
8. If it's stupid but works, it ain't stupid.
9. Only turn to blow the opposition away; otherwise, run away and fight another guy.
10. Always honor a threat.
11. Know the opposition.
12. Know when it's time to get out of Dodge.
13. Always know how to get out of Dodge.
14. The important things are always simple.
15. The simple things are always hard.

Glossary

Throughout this novel, I have used many terms that may seem foreign to anyone who is not acquainted with military jargon. I hope the definitions below will help the reader understand the unique vocabulary of the Air Force. These definitions come from a variety of sources, such as the *Dictionary of Military and Associated Terms,* published by the Joint Chiefs of Staff, and the unclassified technical manuals associated with various weapons systems.

AAA: Antiaircraft artillery.

Active: Can mean when a weapons system is on-line and working or the runway that is currently in use.

AIM: An air intercept missile such as the AMRAAM or Sidewinder.

AMRAAM: AIM-120, the advanced, medium-range air-to-air missile.

APC: Armored personnel carrier.

APDS: Armor-piercing discarding sabot antitank round.

AWACS: Airborne Warning and Control System. Air surveillance and control provided by an airborne radar platform.

Backseater: Any person occupying the backseat of a fighter aircraft.

Bandit: An air contact positively identified as being hostile.

BDA: Bomb damage assessment. The determination of the effect of an air attack on a target.

BFM: Basic fighter maneuvers.

BMP: Soviet-built, tracked armored personnel carrier that weighs twelve tons. It sports a 73-millimeter gun, an antitank missile, and a 7.62-millimeter machine gun. Carries twelve people.

Bogie: An air contact that is unidentified but suspected to be hostile.

BOQ: Bachelor officers' quarters.

CAP: Combat air patrol. An aircraft patrol provided for the purpose of intercepting and destroying hostile aircraft.

CAS: Control Augmentation System. Senses pitch, roll, and yaw rates; vertical and lateral acceleration; angle of attack; g forces; and provides the proper electrical input into the control surfaces.

DCI: Director of central intelligence. An individual appointed by the President and approved by the Senate who is in charge of all United States intelligence agencies and functions.

DIA: Defense Intelligence Agency. The Department of Defense's intelligence branch.

DO: Deputy commander for operations. Normally, a colonel in a tactical fighter wing responsible for all flying operations.

Dragon: A medium-range, antitank missile that a single man can carry and fire. It is guided by commands transmitted through a very thin wire tailed out behind the missile and connected to the tracker.

ECM: Electronic countermeasures.

EMIS Limit: Emission Limit. A circuit that shuts down electronic emissions coming from an aircraft that might be detected by an enemy.

Flanker: NATO code name for the Su-27, a Soviet clone of the F-15.

FLIR: Forward Looking Infrared.

Flogger: The NATO code name given to the MiG-23.

Fox One: In an air intercept, a code meaning "A radar missile has been released from aircraft."

Fox Two: In an air intercept, a code meaning "An infrared missile has been released from aircraft."

Fox Three: In an air intercept, a code meaning "The aircraft's machine gun or cannon is being employed."

Fulcrum: NATO code name for the MiG-29. Looks like an F-15, but smaller, roughly the size of an F-16.

Gadfly: The NATO code name for the SA-11, the latest Soviet-built surface-to-air missile. By all reports, an awesome system.

GBU: Glide Bomb Unit. A guidance head and a steerable fin assembly attached to an ordinary bomb to make it "smart." The bomb then becomes highly accurate and possesses infinite courage to attack a target.

Have Quick: A radio that uses rapid frequency hopping to defeat jamming and monitoring.

HICAP: High-altitude combat air patrol.

HUD: Head-Up Display. A device that projects vital flight information in front of the pilot so he does not have to check his instruments inside the cockpit.

Hummer: The four-door, four-wheel-drive combat vehicle that is the follow-on to the jeep.

IDF: Israel Defense Forces.

IFF: Identification Friend or Foe. The discrete identification-friend-or-foe code assigned to a particular aircraft, ship, or other vehicle for identification by electronic means (usually by radar).

IG: Inspector General. A military organization that investigates complaints and conducts inspections.

IP: Initial point. A well-defined geographical point, easily distinguished visually or electronically, used for starting a bomb run to the target.

IR: Infrared. A device or film sensitive to the near infrared electromagnetic spectrum.

Jink: The constant movement by a fighter aircraft to avoid flying straight and level and to defeat enemy tracking. Absolutely vital to survival in an hostile environment.

Kiloton: The measurement of the energy of a nuclear explosion equivalent to 1,000 tons of TNT.

LANTIRN: Low-altitude navigation and targeting infrared for night system.

LAW: Light antitank weapon.

LOCAP: Low-altitude combat air patrol.

M113: U.S.-built, tracked armored personnel carrier. It weighs twelve tons and can carry a squad of infantry.

MAC: Military Airlift Command.

Mark-82: A five-hundred-pound bomb.

Maverick: An air-to-surface missile with launch and leave capability. It is designed for use against tanks, armored vehicles, and field fortifications.

Mossad: Israel's CIA: the Central Institute for Intelligence and Special Missions.

MPCD: Multi-Purpose Color Display. A video screen that presents information in color to the pilot or crew.

MPD: Multi-Purpose Display. A black-and-white video screen that presents information to the pilot or crew.

NBC: Nuclear, biological, and chemical.

NSA: National Security Agency. The U.S. intelligence agency responsible for monitoring communications and breaking codes.

NSC: National Security Council.

ORI: Operational readiness inspection. An evaluation of the operational capability and effectiveness of a unit conducted by a team from the IG. An ORI can be very realistic and a true measure of a unit's readiness or it can easily degenerate into a bureaucratic sham.

PI: Political influence. A term no longer used in the Air Force because those individuals with it can hurt any person foolish enough to so label them with it.

Puzzle Palace: The Pentagon. Lots of PI present.

Ramp: The parking area for aircraft.

Recce: Short for reconnaissance.

Red Flag: An extremely realistic ongoing exercise conducted at Nellis AFB, Nevada, that trains aircrews to survive the first ten days of combat when the casualty rate is the highest.

RM: Resource manager. One of a wing commander's deputy commanders. The RM is in charge of material and logistics.

ROE: Rules of Engagement. Normally, a collection of very good ideas designed to keep fighter jocks alive.

RPG: Rocket-propelled grenade. A Soviet-built antitank weapon similar to a LAW.

RTB: Return to base.

SA: A surface-to-air missile such as the SA-11. (By all reports, the SA-11 is a very dangerous Soviet-built antiaircraft missile that makes survival extremely difficult for fighter jocks.)

Sagger: Soviet-built, wire-guided, antitank missile.

SAM: Surface-to-air missile.

Sim: Abbreviation for a flight simulator.

SITREP: Situation report.

Snakeye: A Mark-82 500-pound high-explosive bomb that is selectable for either high- or low-drag delivery. Currently being phased out of the inventory.

Stand Eval: Standardization and evaluation. A section of officers responsible for conducting proficiency flight checks and insuring aircrews obey standard rules and procedures.

Tallyho: A code meaning "Target visually sighted."

TEWS: Tactical Electronic Warfare System. The system of "black boxes" in the F-15 that can detect and counter an electronic threat.

TFR: Terrain-following radar. A radar system that provides the pilot or autopilot with climb or dive signals such that the aircraft will maintain a selected height above the ground. Preferably the "selected height" will be in the near vicinity of rocks and weeds.

TSD: Tactical Situation Display. An electronically generated map that scrolls with the position of the aircraft at the center. Navigation and tactical information is superimposed over the map.

UFC: Up Front Controller. Controls many systems in an F-15E through a keyboard.

UHF: A radio transmitter that is limited to line of sight in range and transmits in the ultrahigh frequency band.

USAFE: United States Air Force in Europe.

Vee: A verbal abbreviation of "versus," as in "one vee many."

Weapon systems officer: The second crew member in a fighter who performs many functions such as copilot, radar operator, etc., from the backseat. A WSO dies six feet behind his pilot.

Wizzo: A nickname given to weapon systems officers.

ZSU-23: A 23-millimeter antiaircraft artillery cannon with either two or four barrels built by the Soviets. In its radar-guided configuration, it is very effective and feared by pilots.

Enter the World of Richard Herman

After serving in the United States Air Force for twenty-one years, Richard Herman has a story to tell.

On the face of it, Herman's novels are techno-thrillers and he writes about the aircraft he loves. But there is much more. His stories are really about the men and women who would fight in defense of their country—and Herman knows them well. His characters chronicle the way of leadership and the obligation for service that was formed in the distant past. Yet they are all too human, replete with frustrations and frailties, the wants and weaknesses we experience every day. They struggle and fail and triumph. And they die.

Herman writes about things his characters would never admit to openly: duty, honor, trust, and the best reward of all, homecoming. They are as true to life as your next door neighbor and, occasionally, they mirror the best in this strange tribe of people called Americans.

But, like his characters, Herman would never admit it.

AGAINST ALL ENEMIES

At the end of the millennium, the United States of America is a country on the edge. As tempers ignite over racial differences, the court-martial of a traitor fuels the madness sweeping the country. It is a firestorm only Jonathan Meredith, a ruthless and charismatic manipulator of crowds, can exploit for his own ends.

At the heart of the battle is Hank Sutherland, a principled prosecutor determined that justice be done. It is Sutherland who must unravel the conspiracy that is threatening the very fabric of American life and, in the end, he must stand alone Against All Enemies.

5:50 P.M., THURSDAY, MARCH 4, THE WHITE HOUSE, WASHINGTON, D.C.

Three men clustered around the TV in the President's private office in the west wing. The sound was turned low and the voice of the reporter at the scene was only a murmur. The grisly image on the screen said more than any words could describe. The President hit the remote control and turned off the sound. The silence was complete as the men continued to stare at the screen. "Do they have a casualty count yet?" the President finally asked.

Kyle Broderick, the chief of staff, picked up the phone and asked the same question. He didn't like the answer. Broderick was a young man, hard and street savvy, who delighted in using the power that went with being the President's chief of staff. "I want a hard number in the next five minutes or you're history." He punched off the connection and turned to the President. "Sorry, sir. Everyone seems asleep at the wheel." Almost immediately, the phone rang. Broderick picked it up and listened. He hung up without saying a word. "The initial count is over two hundred and rising fast," he told the President.

"You'll have to go there," the Vice President said to the President. He was a handsome man who had his eye on the presidency in five years. But first, they had to survive the upcoming election. He looked at his watch. "Time your arrival for early in the morning while it's still dark. Make it look like you've been up all night. We'll work the networks at this end and have you lead the morning news."

The President nodded in agreement. Again, they stared at the TV. The silence was broken by the distinctive beat of a helicopter's rotor as the aircraft settled to earth on the South Lawn. "That must be Nelson," the President said. A few minutes later, the door opened and a stocky man with thinning brown hair was ushered in. Nelson Durant was fifty-four, and his rumpled clothes gave no clue about who, or what, he was. He was average looking in the extreme and could disappear into a crowd with ease. His image shouted "wimp" but his blue eyes carried a far different message. "Thanks for coming so quickly," the President said. The Vice President moved over so Nelson Durant could sit next to the President.

"Have you seen the TV coverage on the bombing?" Broderick asked.

The answer was obvious and Nelson Durant ignored the question. Besides, Broderick wasn't worth his time. "What can I do for you, Mr. President?" Durant asked.

"We need quick answers on this one," the President replied. "Can you help?"

Durant ran a hand through his thinning hair. For those who knew him, it was a warning gesture that he was wasting his time and had better things to do. "If you're referring to the Project, we're still a month away from startup and then we're looking at another year before coming on-line."

The President looked disappointed. The Project was a highly advanced intelligence-gathering computer system that one of Durant's many companies was developing for the National Security Agency. If the Project lived up to

Durant's promises, it could find and track any foreign or terrorist threat targeting the United States.

"But I'll have my people check into it," Durant said. The President looked pleased. Durant's worldwide business contacts gave him an intelligence database that rivaled the CIA's. A discreet knock stopped him from saying more. Broderick opened the door and Stephan Serick, the national security advisor, stomped in.

"You need to see this," Serick said, holding up a videocassette. Stephan Serick's childhood Latvian accent was still strong, and the basset hound jowls, heavy limp, and twisted cane were famous trademarks of the man who had served under two presidents of different political parties. "Communications took it off a satellite feed." He collapsed into a chair while Broderick fed the cassette into the TV. "A tourist filmed it. Damned videos."

At first, the scene was a repeat of what they had seen before; the huge crater in Market Street, the mangled cars and the gaping hole that once was the façade of the San Francisco Shopping Emporium. Serick shuddered. "They even got BART." BART was the Bay Area Rapid Transit subway that ran under Market Street. Then the scene on the TV changed as the tourist ran through the debris following a fireman. The camera jolted to a stop and focused on a man emerging from a cloud of dust and debris, his clothes smoking. He was carrying an unconscious girl in his arms.

"That's Meredith," Serick muttered. They watched as Meredith handed the woman to the fireman, his face racked with anguish.

"Just like Oklahoma City," Durant said in a low voice. On the screen, Meredith collapsed to his knees, panting hard. A blanket was thrown over his shoulders.

A voice from off screen said, "My God, the man's a real hero."

Meredith looked up, his lean, handsome face ravaged. He pointed to four firemen wearing respirators descending into the smoke billowing from the underground BART station. "There's your real heroes." He struggled to his feet. "I had to do something. . . . I was there." The tape ended.

"Son of a bitch!" Broderick roared. Then more calmly, "Would you care to guess when this will hit the air?"

"About the time the President lands in San Francisco," the Vice President replied. Meredith was going to preempt the President's arrival on the morning news.

Broderick looked at Durant. "Can you stop it?"

"I don't see how," Durant replied.

"Well," Broderick said, "Meredith is your boy."

Durant's face turned to granite. Kyle Broderick, arguably the second most powerful man in the United States government, had overstepped his bounds. Durant's next words were spoken quietly. "Nothing could be further from the truth." Durant was seething at the suggestion he would have anything to do with Meredith. He stood up to leave.

"Ah, Kyle," the President said, frowning at his chief of staff, "why don't you check with the communications section for foreign reaction?" Broderick nodded and hurriedly left the room. Durant sat back down. "Sometimes I think that boy is suicidal," the President said soothingly. "But seriously, we are concerned about Meredith and there have been rumors. . . ." He deliberately let his words trail off.

Durant looked at the Vice President and Serick. "I need to speak to the President in private."

The two men stood and Serick led the way out, his limp more pronounced. The President's personal assistant took the opportunity to stick her head through the open door. "Mr. President, the British Ambassador and Secretary of State are waiting in the Oval Office." She looked at her watch, a sign they were far behind schedule.

"Ask the ambassador if she'd like another cup of tea," the President said. He waved a hand and his personal assistant closed the door. "What's bothering you, Nelson? If it's Kyle, he's gone."

Durant shook his head. Kyle Broderick had only given words to what the President was thinking. Chasing the chief of staff out of the room had been enough to set things right. He looked at his hands. "I'm not in contact with Meredith. We have no common interests." The President was stunned. It was a tacit admission that Jonathan

Meredith was beyond Durant's influence. "And Meredith is running for President," Durant added.

"You're not telling me anything I don't already know," the President replied.

"Jim, Meredith fancies himself an American Caesar, and he's about to cross the Rubicon." Durant's analogy to Caesar taking the fateful step and ordering his army to cross the Rubicon in his quest to become Rome's emperor hit home. Nelson Durant stared at his President. "All of Rome couldn't stop Caesar. Can you?"

1:00 A.M. FRIDAY, MARCH 5,
SAN FRANCISCO

"It was Oklahoma City all over again," Marcy said. She was sitting beside Sutherland in the hospital's waiting room, which had been turned into a makeshift emergency ward. The room was filled with walking wounded from the explosion. "The doctor said you've got a bad concussion," she told him. "They want to hold you awhile for observation."

Sutherland reached for her hand, needing human contact. She responded, her hands clasping his. "The other people on the roof?" he asked.

She shook her head, and he could feel her tremble. "We were the only ones. Hank, you saved me. I was going over the side, you grabbed me . . ." She lost her voice.

"The waitress?"

"She's going to be okay." Then, stronger, "Thanks to you. I could've never gotten her off the roof or gone down that stairwell by myself. If you hadn't been there . . ."

The enormity of it all came crashing down on him. "Oh, shit," he moaned as a new emotion swept over him, driving him into deep despair. "The hostess, she jumped me to the head of the line, if she had sat us at any other table . . ." That was all he could say as guilt claimed him, demanding a penance for being alive.

"It was just one of those things," Marcy said, understanding what he was going through. "It was just coincidence."

Sutherland lay his head back. *Just coincidence,* he

thought. *We're alive and they're all dead because of coincidence.* He tried not to think about it and focused on the TV in the corner.

"The FBI is now certain," the commentator said, "that this was a calculated act of terrorism gone wrong. The bomb exploded prematurely while being moved down Market Street. So far, the death toll has reached four hundred twenty-two and is expected to go higher. We're awaiting the arrival of the President, who is due to land at any moment."

"Screw the President," Marcy grumbled.

As if on cue, the commentator held his hand to his ear to be sure he heard right. "The video coverage we are about to show was taken by a tourist moments after the explosion." The screen flickered and the back of a fireman appeared as he ran toward the collapsing building. The camera came to a stop and Meredith appeared running out of the building with an unconscious girl in his arms. Sutherland pulled himself into a half-sitting position. The movement made his head hurt. "That's the waitress," he said. "Holy shit, it's Meredith!"

Marcy waved a hand at him, commanding him to be quiet as the scene played out. Meredith's face filled the screen as he uttered, "I had to do something. . . . I was there." The scene cut back to live coverage. Meredith was being interviewed by Liz Gordon, CNC-TV's premier reporter. In the background, floodlights lit the façade of the Shopping Emporium. Sutherland had to concentrate as his mind reeled.

Meredith was forty-six, handsome, six feet tall, with dark hair that was lightly streaked with gray. His lean body was taut and conditioned, the result of countless hours of exercise. But it was his voice, full of warmth and honesty, that captured the moment and came through the glass. "We could have prevented this," Meredith said. His face filled the screen. "We need to go after these cowards and stop them dead in their tracks. We've been too concerned with *their* constitutional rights. Where are the rights of the victims? We need to send a message to our leaders, our judges, that this must stop. Give the FBI, our police, the power they need to root out this evil before they kill again.''

"He's right,'' Marcy whispered. Then, louder, "So right.'' Sutherland turned away from the screen and studied Marcy, taking the measure of her reaction. She stood up. "My editor wants a follow-up. I've got to go.''

Sutherland sat up but almost passed out. "Marcy, take some time to get over this.''

She stood and touched his hand. "Do we ever have enough time?'' She bent over and kissed his cheek. "See you around.''

He watched her walk away. "See you around,'' he repeated as the guilt came crashing back.

In The Warbirds, *Richard Herman's first edge-of-your-seat Air Force thriller, all Colonel Anthony "Muddy" Waters ever wanted was to command a tactical fighter wing. When the call comes, he will discover what true leadership and sacrifice means in the face of real danger, real bullets, and real death. But first, the call must come.*

The crew chief marshaling the F-4 into its parking spot on the ramp at Luke AFB crossed his wrists above his head, signaling for Waters to stop, then made a slashing motion across his throat, the sign to cut engines.

Waters' hands went over the switches, shutting the big fighter down. He unstrapped and threw his helmet and then the small canvas bag carrying his flight publications to the crew chief, who motioned toward the edge of the ramp, pointing out the waiting staff car. Waters scrambled down the boarding ladder and quickly walked around the Phantom during a post-flight inspection, before heading for the car. The wing commander, Boots McClure, crawled out from behind the wheel and stood by the car, a slight smile on his face.

"Congratulations, Muddy. You've got yourself a wing—the 45th at Stonewood. The word came down about thirty minutes ago." McClure grabbed Waters' right hand and pumped it.

Waters just stood there, unable to speak.

A command . . .

A wing . . .

The fulfillment of his dream. The years of hard work, loneliness and frustration suddenly evaporated . . . A wide smile came across his face. A warmth that he had only experienced at the birth of his daughter captured him. It was a high few men ever realized.

"It's going to be different from anything you imagined," McClure said softly, doubting that Waters could catch his meaning. "Why don't you tell your bride and get her away from the O' Club pool." McClure laughed and pushed Waters towards the car. "She's driving some of my young jocks bonkers . . ."

Later, Anthony was ragging Sara a bit about Boots McClure's randy comments, and acting—well, partially acting—a little teed-off. She picked it up fast, and fed him a few more anxiety moments before playing it straight.

"I met Mrs. McClure the other day at a luncheon and liked her," she said. "She doesn't wear her husband's rank like some of the other wives do. God, what a sad crowd they can be. You'd think in this day and age they'd get out and do *something* besides eat lunch and sit around the pool and gossip, gossip, gossip. For some reason I think the lieutenant colonels' wives are the worst— do you suppose it's because they're bucking with their spouses for the big eagle and letting off *his* frustrations? Oh, never mind—now what about the big news? Where are we off to in the wild blue yonder and so forth?"

"No way, lady. You got to pay for your intelligence. Ante up . . ."

And she did, and afterward, his head against her bare breasts, as she checked carefully for more signs of gray— "I love a mature man, stop worrying"—he told her it was England, and she told him that that was too easy, that she had paid too much for such available info.

"You've just begun," he said, and proceeded to make love in a way he never thought he could again, the inhibitions from the tragedy of the past finally giving up the ghost.

FORCE OF EAGLES

The legacy of Muddy Waters is safe with Jack Locke, a superb and dedicated fighter pilot. In Force of Eagles, *282 men and one woman from Muddy's 45th Tactical Fighter Wing are POWs in a terrifying hostage situation in Iran. In mounting their rescue, Jack proves he is that rarest of individuals, a true combat leader, when he defends a lone C-130 against a sky full of hostile aircraft, including U.S. built F-4s, an aircraft he loves.*

The two F-4s had a late tallyho on Jack and barely had time to split, one going high and to the left, the other diving to the right. Jack chose the high man and went for a head-on pass. He selected guns, snap-rolled to the right, squeezed the trigger for a long burst of cannon fire and brought the F-4 aboard, passing almost canopy to canopy. He saw smoke puff from behind the F-4 as he turned his attention to the other bandit. "Watch him," he told Byers, "don't lose sight."

Byers turned to look at the rapidly disappearing F-4 behind them just as Jack wrenched the fighter after the other jet. The sergeant's head snapped to the left and his helmet banged off the canopy, but he did keep his eyes on the first Iranian . . .

The second Iranian, for his part, was concentrating on the C-130, trying to get behind the slow-moving cargo plane. Actually Kowalski's low altitude and slow speed were causing problems for the Iranian pilot . . .

Jack selected a Sidewinder and sweetened the shot, taking his time to get well inside the launch parameters of the missile. The reassuring growl of a lock-on grew louder and louder. He pressed the pickle button and watched the missile streak home. The rear of the Iranian jet flared into a long plume of flame as the plane spun into the ground.

"My guy ran away," Byers told him. "What happened?"

"We got one," Jack said as he flew past Kowalski. "You did good, Byers. Rule number one is always check six. You did that. That guy died because he forgot rule number two."

"What's that?"

"Never forget rule number one—"

"Bandits," Kowalski called over the UFH, "ten o'clock high."

A welcome voice came over the radio. "Snake and Jake on the way." Snake Houserman and his wingman were now off the refueling tanker and headed into Iran.

"Hurry, Snake," Jack answered. "Multi-bogies on us." He checked his armament-control set. Two AIM-9 missiles and 450 rounds of 20mm showing on the rounds-counter were left. In a hurry, Jack missed that he still had one Maverick left hanging under the right wing and creating drag. He turned toward the four Floggers that had their noses on him . . .

FIREBREAK

First Lieutenant Matt Pontowski is a wild playboy, a pilot whose career in the Air Force owes more to his grandfather's position as President than to his own undoubted, but unreliable, talents. As Matt parties and drives his commander, Jack Locke, crazy, Iraq's leader, infuriated by the loss of the Gulf War, directs an arsenal of devastating chemical weapons against Israel. But the Israelis are prepared to respond with nuclear warfare. It's a desperate gamble when Matt's wing of F-15E Strike Eagles is sent to the Gulf. In the heat of battle, Matt Pontowski will be forged from a reckless boy into a determined and dangerous man.

Matt concentrated on his attack run. "Skid," he called his wingman, "take the lead, we'll lase. Ripple two." Matt had told his wingman to lead the attack and pickle both his bombs on the first pass. Matt would take spacing and follow on the opposite arm of the *B'nai* attack and do the lasing. "Then get the hell out of Dodge," he ordered.

"Roger, copy all," Skid answered.

"Sounds good," Martin's voice said.

My God! Matt thought. How can he keep what he's doing sorted out and still pay attention to what's going on down here?

The two fighters started their run in. The TEWS scope was a mass of symbols and the audio was deafening him with chirps and wails. He turned the audio off and would rely on Furry to do his job. Now he could clearly see the compound housing the nerve gas plant and storage bunkers on the Nav FLIR. Furry worked the Target FLIR and told him, "Target identified." It amazed Matt how familiar the target complex looked.

Sweat poured off him as he concentrated on the run. A string of tracers from a ZSU-23-4 arched across the sky in front of him. He heard himself breathing hard. "Piece of cake," Furry said, his voice rapid and high-pitched. More tracers crisscrossed in front of him and he saw the bright flash of two Gadflies launching. Now Matt "paddled" off the autopilot and hand-flew the jet as they swung in on their side of the pincers.

Then: "Bombs gone." It was Skid coolly announcing that he had gotten his bombs off onto their target, the main production plant. Matt had lost sight of him when they split up for the attack and it was reassuring to hear from him.

A Gadfly exploded, lighting the sky. In the bright flash, Matt could see Skid escaping underneath the fireball and more tracers reaching toward him. The second Gadfly exploded, but this time, there was no trace of his wingman.

"Lasing," Furry shouted. Matt was concentrating on the Nav FLIR, using it to fly around the target. It was a good run and all systems were working perfectly. A Gadfly streaked by less than a hundred feet above the canopy. For some reason, its proximity fuse didn't work and the missile went ballistic.

The plant erupted in an explosion as the first bomb hit within inches of where Furry had laid the laser. The bombs were fuse-delayed and the first one penetrated to the first basement before it exploded. The second bomb flew right through the explosion and burrowed through to the third basement, burying itself in four feet of concrete before it exploded. The labs and test chamber where the nerve gas had been developed disappeared in a fiery blast. But the scientists who had given Iraq the deadly weapon had been paid off long before and were safe in their homes in Europe and China. Only two technicians were on duty. A series of secondary explosions turned the plant into an inferno and flames belched and mushroomed over three hundred feet into the air.

Furry shouted, "GO!" as a wall of tracers mushroomed in front of the F-15. Matt broke hard left, still below a hundred feet. He flew around a radio tower and headed for safety as Viper 07 and 08 hit the first of the storage bunkers.

Then it was all behind them and Matt became aware of the chatter over the radios. He had effectively tuned it out. Still, he had been conscious of what was going on around him throughout the attack. It was called situational awareness. He reengaged the autopilot and coupled it to the TFR. He checked his fuel and ran a cockpit check, making sure they had not taken battle damage. Then it hit him; the simulator rides the Gruesome Twosome had put them through had been worse.

CALL TO DUTY

Matthew Zachary Pontowski had the loneliest job in the world: the presidency of the United States. As a young man he answered the Call to Duty and flew Mosquito fighter bombers with the Royal Air Force in the air war against Nazi Germany. Now he must order young men to risk their lives against a different enemy in Burma's golden triangle, where drugs are the common denominator. But the past will not let them go and he is the link between two missions separated by fifty years and two continents.

"The press conference has been set up for two o'clock this afternoon," Leo Cox told Pontowski. The two men were sitting in the Oval Office going over the day's revised schedule with the press secretary.

"We expect most of the questions will be about the kidnapping," Henry Gilman, the press secretary said.

"Any feel of the mood of the press corps?" Cox asked.

"Still digging for angles," Gilman said. "Right now they are neutral and waiting to see what develops."

"Good," Pontowski said. "Leo, have the Vice President cover the luncheon with the delegates from the American Bankers Association for me. I'll have lunch with Tosh and join you both in the Oval Office for a final review before the press conference. Have all the players there." The two men rose and left the room.

Outside, Press Secretary Gilman said, "He always talks to Tosh before a press conference."

"She's still his best adviser," Cox told him.

Pontowski walked upstairs to his wife's bedroom. He knocked gently at her door and waited until the nurse answered. It was one of the small things he did to keep his wife's morale up; she always wanted him to find her looking her best. The way the nurse smiled at him as she held the door open signaled that Tosh Pontowski was having a good day. A smile spread across his face when he saw her sitting at the small table near the windows. He walked across the room and joined her.

Tosh Pontowski smiled at him. "The wolf is losing today," she said. As always, her lilting accent captivated him and touched the love he held for her, a love made stronger by her courage in coming to terms with and fighting the disease that ravaged her—systemic lupus erythematosus (lupus—the wolf). The disease was well named for the way it came and went unexpectedly, suddenly leaping out to rip and tear at human flesh and then sneaking away, only to return without warning to attack another part of the body. At first, it had only been a mild skin rash and Tosh had not been overly worried by the flare-ups that continued for a number of years. But then lupus had attacked her joints, and then had returned as kidney paralysis. But that had disappeared and then the wolf had returned again, this time attacking her heart.

He reached across the table and took her hand, hoping that she was in remission again. But his inner alarm warned him otherwise. How much longer? he wondered. He knew he could go on without her but life would lose most of its luster.

As usual, Tosh Pontowski refused to give in to her disease. "Press conference today?" He nodded a yes. "L'affaire Courtland no doubt."

"Can't hide much from you, can we?" Pontowski observed. Charles, his valet, entered with a tray holding his lunch.

"Courtland will turn this against you," she said, watching him eat. "He knows he must discredit you if he is to defeat the candidate you endorse in the next presidential election."

"I know," he answered. "No matter what we do, he'll claim it isn't enough. He'll work the sympathy angle for all it's worth."

"Then you must defuse it," she counseled. "Recall your own escape."

"But I was never in captivity."

"No, but you were wounded, frightened, and pursued. It was a near thing. Build on that."

Matthew Zachary Pontowski leaned back in his chair and recalled when he had indeed been a terrified, desperately wounded fugitive.

Edgar Award Winner
STUART WOODS

New York Times Bestselling Author of
Dead in the Water

GRASS ROOTS   71169-/ $6.99 US/ $8.99 Can

WHITE CARGO   70783-7/ $6.99 US/ $8.99 Can

DEEP LIE   70266-5/ $6.50 US/ $8.50 Can

UNDER THE LAKE
70519-2/ $6.50 US/ $8.50 Can

CHIEFS   70347-5/ $6.99 US/ $8.99 Can

RUN BEFORE THE WIND
70507-9/ $6.50 US/ $8.50 Can